The Mighty Goblin

Denis Messier

ISBN
978-1-77097-802-7 (Hardcover)
978-1-77097-803-4 (Paperback)
978-1-77097-804-1 (eBook)

Produced by:

FriesenPress

Suite 300 – 852 Fort Street
Victoria, BC, Canada V8W 1H8

www.friesenpress.com

Distributed to the trade by The Ingram Book Company

"Nothing to lose becomes a great strength."

Life is a succession of incidents; some pleasant most others dreadful. Like a brush stroke on a canvas, purposeless if isolated and out of context, these incidents depict life during a single instant. The sum of these episodes adds up to one's karma.

The life story of Johannes Barcelo differs from that of most other migrants of the 1930's. Youngest of a Portuguese family, Johnny was raised by his sister, both parents working in order to make ends meet. America was the Promised Land where they could play with a new deck, hoping for a better hand and maybe cheat their destiny.

Johannes' sister Henrietta had a large influence in wiring his brain together. Naive and candid, however principled and conscientious Henrietta was to pass on an above average intellectual heritage to her younger brother. Henrietta's early demise yanked Barcelo's karma out of its *"proper place"*, setting him free of the social trap and at liberty to break away in search of a better future.

Intuitively Henrietta had prepared him for this constant struggle against inbred poverty. Johannes was always in hot pursuit of anything beyond his reach, recklessly daring, insatiably looking for more: he was one of the first to turn scrap into millions; later, looking for new challenges he diversified into the lucrative business of bootlegging and very private club. In both ventures he had to deal with the rapacity and greed of organized crime and the social elite.

Early on he was made aware of the injustice and oppression imposed by a closed society. Quick to see the collusion between religion, politics and big money he openly rebelled; never a docile player.

Worn out by this constant struggle, several years of his life were wasted in a drunken stupor, squandering the not so small fortune he had accumulated. When hospitalized during what he thought to be his last stand, a chance encounter with a disenchanted priest, kindles his innate need for a good fight and diverts the path of his life from a futile finale to an honorable last page.

This last caper rattles the complacency and snugness of pedophiles. It is probable that the repetitive incestuous rapes of his sister Henrietta by his brothers had prepared the ground for his crusade. This last act of rebellion, illegal yet just and honorable contributed to save a family from one of these warped criminals.

—— CHAPTER 1 ——————————————

Stepping awkwardly between pop cans and a variety of other rubbish, Gelda sighed, exhaling deeply in preparation for the next puff on this last cigarette. Without knowing the meaning of the word she was a true hedonist; in her constant quest for pleasure, breathing like drinking, was considered wasteful if not linked to some addictive gratifications. Anything to improve her drab existence, anything to fill in the vacuity, the emptiness of her reality: smoke, alcohol, drugs, sex, even maternity. Annoyed, she jerked off one of her stiletto shoes and with the tip of a dark-red painted big toe, scratched her calf where a mosquito had left a ruddy blotch. She knocked again on the weather beaten door, surprised that her first rap had not prompted the usual raspy: - Come in if you're honest, it's not locked. -.

Three years ago, she must have been a cute kid. Now going on twenty three, Gelda was still not a bad looking woman, though the remnants of good looks were being rapidly smothered by her continuous search for cheap pleasures. From morning to night she would tend to her numerous addictions, making this occupation a full time vocation.

Fourth in a family of six, she was the typical product of ingrained poverty. Like old money, old poverty has its label. Alcoholic parents, raised by older sisters who didn't give a damn too busy surviving themselves; Gelda had always been sawing the bars of her cage.

When she turned sixteen, sixty one year old John Barcelo came along on his white stallion and offered evasion. As it turned out, this new freedom was only another dungeon, not much better than the first one. Now, six years later, she was still sawing away at her prison bars, looking for a flight out of her bleak reality. Flight out for two passengers by then, Todd her five year old son was excess baggage. Without his consent he had been dropped in the river of life and like his parents, would have to swim counter current all the way to hell.

Chance had decreed that rather than being a church going mother or some princess, Gelda had been earmarked to be a drug addict, a drunk, an occasional whore and the mother of future losers. Her solemn vocation: the perpetuation of despair, poverty and misery.

She thought it queer that Johnny wouldn't come to the door. He couldn't be far as the banged-up 89 caddy was rusting away in the drive way.

-Todd honey, take a look out back, see if your father is there. - She always felt like saying grandfather.

Todd, five year old, Johnny's 27th consecutive left handed male off-spring, soon came back reporting that there was no one in the back of the dilapidated house trailer. Almost burning her lips, Gelda managed to coax one last puff before expertly catapulting the lipstick smeared butt. The little guy ran over and stepped on it. She smiled, baring perfect teeth.

Gelda was upset. More than upset, pissed off was more like it, having relied on her old husband to baby sit Todd for the night. A heavy date was waiting for her in a motel east of Lewiston. This guy was known to have the chemical arsenal she craved for. Of course she would have to perform, but sex was not important, just a way to satisfy her other cravings. She couldn't count the number of time she had submitted to dull intercourses, several before her thirteenth birth date; one more didn't matter.

-Do you think you could wait for your father, he shouldn't be long, his car is in the yard? Where could he have gone on foot? He never walks anywhere.-

She was gentle with her son, always using polite almost deferential language when speaking to him; making up for her poor performance as a mother. Realizing too late that the little guy would have been better off staying out of life, she often felt like apologizing for the nasty joke she had played on him. Gelda became pregnant on the first week of her marriage; like kittens, Todd had been conceived unconsciously, not a second thought given to the long time liability. Only when she could feel life inside her did she grasp the far reaching consequences of being a mother, or worse, of no longer being a child.

Her own mother had been rough and tyrannous: -Do this, do that-, never asking, always ordering and slapping: her wicked left hand ejecting out of the gray apron pocket like the striking head of a cobra. Always landing perfectly on her right cheek; so often that by the time she turned twelve, the skin on that side felt like leather.

-I can wait for daddy. I'll play outside. - Said the little guy, used to being left alone.

After kissing him gently on the forehead, she choreographed her way back. Half way she stopped, having second thoughts; Johnny would have cigarettes stashed in the house. Could also have partly been that her maternal instinct was not yet completely atrophied. Whatever it was, she turned and zigzagged back between the pop cans and boxes. This time she tried the door; it was not locked and she walked in followed by Todd.

-Anybody home-. She called out in her falsetto voice.

Like iron filings on a magnet, her voice seemed to stay close to her mouth, the sound waves unable to find a suitable path in this Capernaum of wall to wall dusty furniture, carpets, dirty clothing and stale air. To better listen, she stopped breathing for a moment; nothing but the deep regular tic-tac of the clock breaking the heavy silence.

No sound but if odors made noise, the decibel level would have been deafening. A mixture of urine and rotting vegetable was slowly overpowering her cheap perfume. Todd, who had preceded her into the main bedroom, came out mumbling something Gelda did not understand.

-What did you say?-

-Daddy's on the floor... He's making a funny noise. -Repeated the little guy who turned to go back.

Following Todd in this bedroom where she had so often faked orgasm for her Viagra primed husband, she almost tripped on part of him, lying on his back on the floor, the other half of his nearly naked body in the bathroom. Like Todd had said, Johnny was making a whistling and gurgling sound when he inhaled. His bluish penis and one enlarged testicle were hanging out of his shorts, Johnny's thighs being so scrawny that the smallest man size boxer shorts were way too large but could not hold the disproportionate genital package. Barefoot below two hairless chicken legs, his head tilted back to the left, mouth gaping showing a row of nicotine stained teeth, his toupee lying near his left ear, completed a scene Jerome Bosch would have loved to paint.

-Jesus Christ, there goes my date. - Was her first reaction.

Gelda was and would remain a very primitive creature; never evolved beyond Freud's pleasure principle. Looking at her 67 year old, almost, by the look of it, ex husband, she understood that this could be curtain time. The son of a bitch was really sick and could be on his way to making her a young and poor widow.

Courage not being her strongest quality, she quickly retreated without touching the still breathing body. After following the wire under a pile of dirty linen she found the telephone and dialed 911. In the mean time Todd had thrown a blanket over his father's puny carcass and was standing guard, trying to swat the numerous flies away from his helpless genitor.

Gelda had just enough time to search the house for cigarettes and money; found and pocketed eighty three dollars and half a pack of Lucky Strike. She also snatched a cheque book lying on the kitchen table, her husband would not need it for a while by the look of it and she could do wonders with somebody else's cheques. If he died, she could clean out the bank account, although she did not anticipate much of a surprise.

The State Trooper who answered her 911 call was Mark, a young stud she knew from school. Like most of the boys in her class, he had been intimate with her. Next to the school urinal Gelda was what most boys in the school had in common.

-We don't need the police Mark we need an ambulance. He's in the bedroom and looks as if he's dying.-

Johnny had not stirred, was still on his back wheezing, paler than death; Mark did not hesitate and called the paramedics.

-Too bad your son is here we could do it for old time's sake. - Ventured Mark.

-You're crazy.-Was all she said, while thinking it could have been kinky to be that wicked.

Two days later, in a hospital bed, needles and tubes in both arms, a Foley catheter in his penis and another one up his nose, Johnny came out of his coma. By his side, a doctor was scratching his erudite head, trying to determine where to start.

-It would be shorter to write a list of what he doesn't have. - Mumbled the doctor to a nurse looking on.

There were several obvious impediments affecting the body he was examining: diabetes, cardiopathy, urinary tract infection, high blood pressure, and chronic bronchitis bordering on emphysema, possible cancerous growths here and there, ulcers and maybe more. His priority was to treat the double pneumonia which was suffocating the patient, and he had already started pumping penicillin into this incredibly broken animal.

-Amazing. The human body is a master piece of survival. It beats most other creatures for the abuses it can sustain. The camel might be better than most men, but no camel could stand up to a comparison with this specimen. - Said the doctor to no one in particular.

Barcelo was dying and it was touch and go for several days. He remained semi comatose for more than a week during which he relived his entire life.

──── CHAPTER 2 ────────────────

A man can do as he wills but not will what he wills.

Year 1939

His earliest memories were not of his mother but of Henrietta, his older sister. She had taken up most of the space in Johnny's childhood, becoming the center of his universe; then she died. A great trauma, not only had Henrietta been a mother and a friend, she had also been his private tutor in most matters. The relationship with Henrietta had been gentle, affectionate and sensual in the animal sense. Henrietta had given him all the love and attention she craved for and was deprived of, playing the role of the devoted mother she knew every child was entitled to.

Henrietta had been abused sexually ever since she could remember. Retreating into her imagination, living beyond her reality, was how she had endured. Reading, learning, excelling intellectually, she developed a cerebral life as a way out of her grim bodily existence. This way she could shield enough of her self esteem from the constant abuses of her two older brothers, Claudio and Balthazar. They had started their sexual explorations even before she could walk. Andres, her unmarried weird uncle would join in whenever he could.

One day, as they once again were manifesting their intents, she suddenly stopped in mid flight; and freezing into a trance-like posture let out a high-pitched shriek.

-Jesus, Jesus is here... right there. .... He's telling me that I'm under his protection .... Can't you hear him... listen, he says that if you don't stop he'll open your belly and spill your guts. –

Not moving an inch, she was looking intensely at a point on the wall behind them.

The previous Sunday, when Angus the priest had said that Jesus was always there for his friends and could see everything everywhere, the thought of playing this little game had sprouted in her mind. Claudio and Balthazar were dumb, having been too busy playing with their penis to bother much about their brains. Both were confirmed idiots, their only interest centered between their legs.

-Jesus talks to you? I don't believe you. You're lying. - Said Claudio the older of the two morons, nevertheless releasing her arm as if burned.

He could not be absolutely certain. In the 1940's, any divine intervention received loud press: Fatima, Lourdes and so many others. Miracles were habitual godly manifestations; even the pope had paid a visit to Lourdes. Closer to home, the Holy Virgin Mary appearing to some shepherds in Fatima Portugal contributed to give enough credibility to Henrietta's declaration. From the pulpit, the priest had described the incident in great length. Later that day it had been the subject of the Sunday dinner conversation; weirdo Andres even said that it was perfectly reasonable. – God can do everything. - Portugal was their country of origin and they could not help but relate and feel some pride. Now fear moved in.

Like Lot's wife, Henrietta stood there, transfixed, her eyes locked on a spot over the dining room dresser. As if on cue, a ray of sunshine reflecting on an ashtray was playing the color game on a crack over the decrepit wall. With some imagination it could be construed as a bearded face. Even Henrietta was taken aback. Could her little game be supported by the real object?

For these simpletons the vision was real. The two brothers looked at each other and pulled back; their fear overcoming their libido. Out of sight behind a full length drape, spying as he had done often, little Johnny became a true believer in his sister's super power.

From that day on, without admitting that they believed her story, the dumb brothers left her alone. Henrietta had used this stratagem with little hope of success; realizing that it worked, regularly, from that day on, she continued her conversation with Jesus. After a while she came to believe in her metaphysical endowment.

In need of an audience, Henrietta had been performing for her kid brother. For as long as Johnny could remember and probably before the onset of his memory, Henrietta had educated him, teaching him to think, to read and to question. She compensated for her own desolation by inundating her kid brother with love and affection. In her need to be generous Johnny had become her goal in life. Maybe she could sense that in the 1940's a woman in her condition could only be successful by proxy and was preparing her kid brother as best she could to represent her. When his sister died, Johnny lost the only good thing he ever had.

Looking at her cold and bluish face emerging from the white silken marshmallow like garniture of the cheap coffin, trying to pry open these glued eyelids, touching the dry, cracked lips also fastened closed by the undertaker, he understood that Henrietta would never awaken from this sleep. One last time, he touched the plastic like skin with the tip of his fingers and ran out of the room screaming. Meeting his brother Claudio in the hallway, he stopped long enough in front of him to almost break his tibia with as hard a kick as he could summon. He continued his flight while Claudio was bawling. Hidden in his favorite closet Johnny cried himself to sleep.

Until that time, death had been hardly more than a word; a friend of the family had passed away and Johnny vaguely remembered visiting the funeral parlor with Henrietta. She had taken the time to slowly and carefully explain that death was the only way to enter heaven.

-We all die one day....... to go to heaven and be with Jesus. No one lives forever and dying is why we're born.... I know, because Jesus told me.- Ending her explanation with a knowledgeable look upward, her arms spread apart like the Virgin Mary's statue.

Except for the Jesus part, Johnny was not impressed with this explanation. Why be born if it is for the sole purpose of dying; fine story as long as the dead people remained strangers. Seeing and touching Henrietta's cold face, framed as it was in white satin, her body jammed into this tiny pine box, made the full meaning of death sink deep into his brain. But comprehension comes in short bursts and only several years later would he grasp the full meaning of death. Henrietta would have been a teacher to the end.

That fatal night, after several attempts to confront this mysterious Jesus and inquire about his sister's fate, he finally fell asleep, cursing the son of God, swearing at him with every wicked words he knew.

- If that's the way you love your friends, piss off and fuck you. - He was afraid and angry.

Being left alone was the worst of injustice. He wished that he also was dead, sharing Henrietta's coffin on this long trip to heaven, somewhere behind the moon and the sun. Henrietta had told him that it was far away. The trip would be long and she would be lonely he thought. How does a kid know that one needs to be dead to travel beyond the sun? Suicide never came to his mind; the subject had never been discussed. The thought of taking his life was not an issue. Only later was he to learn that the only real freedom is that of deciding of the moment to exit life.

He turned nine a few weeks after Henrietta's death. Contrary to kids this age who have a need to brag, he had never told anyone about this special relationship with his sister. Both she and he had been a victim of this extreme violence poverty brings on. Rather than being born in a family where incest and abuse were transmitted as surely as the shape of the nose, they could have been brother and sister in a plush and comfortable family, where discipline and rigor would have protected them from maltreatment.

Hidden and powerless, he had often been a witness to these scenes where one of his brothers would lay on Henrietta's half naked body, while the other would hold her. Every time she would cry and plead but they seemed to take a sadistic pleasure in tormenting her. Once, as Claudio had finished his wiggling on Henrietta, he had pounced on the bastard and landed a solid blow with a stick brought into the house for that very purpose. But Claudio was six years older and had given Johnny a severe beating. This useless act of bravery had cemented the bond between Henrietta and Johnny: someone cared enough to risk a beating for her.

-Luck... good or bad...that's all there is to life. You're born into shit or money.... Luck could have made you the son of MacFarlane. You would have plenty of toys, good food, nice clothing, a room of your own and a maid .... Why not us... I asked Jesus why he was so much nicer to them than to us. He would not answer. He might have a boss.-

Henrietta could listen and understand the meaning of words. Most of her ideas had been acquired by paying attention when older people spoke. Miss Whitehead, the librarian, still a maiden at fifty one had been the beacon guiding Henrietta. Donna Whitehead had been quick to spot the precocity of this ugly duckling and would take pleasure in sharing her thoughts with Henrietta; the fallout would often be very daring and unorthodox explications of life's iniquities. The librarian would be in perfect harmony with Henrietta's intuitive insight; intuition, one of misery's by products. Life had been harsh and prematurely threatening, for both Henrietta and Miss Whitehead.

Even though not overwhelmed with the little guy's efficiency as a problem solver, Johnny was always impressed when Henrietta would allude to her unusual alliance with Jesus: good at dancing around the issues but not much of a closer, thought Johnny.

Their mother being the MacFarlane's maid, allowed Henrietta a daily comparison between the disparity of the two worlds. Their own mother would spend more time pampering the MacFarlane's single tyke than she would her own. Henrietta felt abandoned by her mother.

-Poor or rich, good or bad luck, just like bingo. - She kept repeating over and over Donna Whitehead's theory.

Johnny did not know the meaning of the word Bingo but one day, felt he had to butt in and ventured the opinion that he thought this "to be unfair".

-Yes I suppose it's unfair, but Jesus wants to see who the strong people are. - She had said in defense of Jesus' obvious management downfall. This thought had been proposed by Angus the priest. How else could he defend the fascism religion and God were practicing.

While she was admitting that pure luck was the master of their destiny she also proposed a way out. According to Donna Whitehead, all was not brick-walled; somewhere, somehow there had to be a place for hope during this life.

-You don't have much of a choice in choosing your parents but if you're strong enough in your head, you can go places. – For a nine year old, this kind of language was Sanskrit but he could vaguely see where it was leading; seeds were dropped here and there in his fertile mind. Like some frogs spending years under ground until the right weather conditions occurred, the urchin would keep the seeds alive until thoughts sprouted.

In 1939, the -proper place- of a poor émigré was to remain a poor émigré and be happy as such. Henrietta's readings were opening secret doors. She had learned that a few recent immigrants had been successful in rising above their proper place. As a matter of fact had pointed out Donna Whitehead, all USA citizens were immigrants. –We stole the land from the Indians when our ancestors emigrated from England.-

-Work hard and become a rich man. It's possible, others have done it-. And she would cite their names.

Between Dale Carnegie and Jesus, with the help of Miss Whitehead the librarian, Henrietta was beginning to be aware of treasures within her puny carcass.

-You know too much for your own good. - Would comment her mother while bursting with pride.

The combination of Henrietta's premature death, her cultural influence and Johnny's diminutive body size contributed to concoct an explosive mixture.

More than a month passed before Johnny came out of his daze. Depressed and as dysfunctional as a newborn, he hardly ate or slept, experiencing emptiness, loneliness and engrossed in a constant state of panic; he went from top of the class to the very last rung: day dreaming, unable to focus, tired and frightened when not angry. While he had been attentive and alert, Johnny was now living on a cloud where no one could touch him. Unusual noises reached him from time to time, but never loud enough to jolt him out of his stupor.

As in nature, where weak and injured animals are easy prey for predators, in schools throughout the world, frail and sick kids will be picked upon by their class mates. Not unlike games played by kittens or young wolves, when not abusive, this process is nothing but the evolutionary preparation for life's struggle, toughening up or culling the weaklings.

Barcelo had become a perfect prey. Smallest of the class, ugly, weak and lonely, it was a propitious time for the school bully to make a move. Stealing lunch boxes, clothing and even money from most kids in his class, Dudley had not yet gotten around to Barcelo; too easy and maybe ill at ease with the difference in size, or too poor..., who knows.

-Hey Parcelo, -Dudley couldn't pronounce the B's, - what do you have for me?- This was the usual opening summon to a raid.

Barcelo's puny carcass was standing there, with his mind in neutral, not a spark firing, in a state of total oblivion to the outside world. From far away, ensconced in this cocoon he had retreated into since Henrietta's death, he vaguely felt that he should be concerned; but only when Dudley touched his arm did a red flag appear in his dormant head.

There was no doubt in Dudley's mind that he could raid this pygmy's lunch box with the habitual impunity. It started this way. The other kids quickly gathered around to enjoy the almost daily show offered by Dudley.

Without uttering a word, following a ploy often tested with his brothers, Barcelo collapsed to the ground. His body continued the motion and rolled over on his back where he laid, eyes closed, seemingly unconscious. Dudley backed away, surprised by so much collaboration. He then bent over to snatch the lunch box which had fallen close to the head of the now inert creature on the ground.

-I'd bet you don't have much…, you know what happens if … - He didn't have time to finish his threat. As he was grabbing the lunch box, the seemingly cataleptic heap of bones came to life; then all hell broke loose. Acting purely on instinct stemming from a glorious madness generated by gross injustice, driven by impulsive courage springing from a hopeless situation, the runt's little hand shot out. Fuelled by a mixture of fear, despair, hatred and rancor, Barcelo had grabbed Dudley by the hair, while his other puny arm was repeatedly ramming a dirty and sharp thumbnail into the bully's eyes. Having had to fend off his dumb brothers ever since he could walk Barcelo was deceivably strong and quick for a pip his size.

Coming from a weird angle, the first blow caught Dudley by surprise, eye lids wide open, his eyes exposed. The thumb kept pounding, like a piston, going methodically from one eye to the other; the hard and dirty nail digging into the fragile eye membrane, causing excruciating pain.

The surprise should have allowed the little guy a prudent retreat but no; this mini pit-bull rolled over from under the large mass and nimbly got back on his feet. His head released by the now standing goblin, Dudley had also been able to stand. Clumsily standing on the curb, momentarily blinded, this Goliath couldn't see more than a vague shadow moving quickly from one side to the other; like a fly buzzing around rotting meat, later described one of the onlookers.

Then Dudley made his second mistake. Not used to being attacked, certain that the little guy was now running for his life, he began wiping his eyes with the bottom half of his T shirt while anticipating the sweet taste of revenge: -was he ever going to beat the shit out of this mouse - ….., as soon as he could see him.

He was still trying to recover his ability to see when, coming from nowhere: - Bang- , a first blow squarely on the nose left him dizzy and bloodied; - Bang- again, a real wallop, then another and again. The goblin's fists were striking from all directions.

Such a small guy shouldn't have hit so hard, what a punch. Vision still blurred, unable to grab the little shadow moving around him like Casper the ghost, Dudley buckled on his knees after the sixth or seventh blow. In this position, he was shorter than Barcelo and the next blow sent him on his side.

The now demented Barcelo should have decamped, having clearly won this bout; he almost did. But no, he was driven to finish the job; either by the crowd of cheering kids assembled around them and rhythmically crying out his name, or was it the intuition that nothing short of killing the bastard would save his ass from severe retaliation.

Kneeling behind his opponent's head, away from the powerful arms, now flailing harmlessly like windmill blades, he continued to pummel the bigger guy, focusing on the nose and mouth. The bully was slowly losing consciousness, not feeling the blows any more just hearing the thuds, blood oozing from his nose and entering his gaping mouth.

Only later did he learn that Barcelo had picked up two rocks the size of his fist and was using them as our Cro Magnon ancestors had done forty thousand years ago. As it did for them it worked so efficiently that Dudley could have been maimed, or worse.

Fortunately for Dudley, the gallery of kids, ecstatically rooting for the winning underdog, most having been trounced by Dudley, yelled out that one of the teachers was coming up the road. It will never be known if this teacher saved Dudley's life. Subconsciously, Johnny had identified Dudley as the source of all his tribulations. As such he felt that he had the sacred right to exact revenge for Henrietta; revenge from his brothers, from life, even from Jesus. Now that he knew the ugly face of death, making Dudley as lifeless as Henrietta was in the back of his mind.

This episode contributed to rescue Barcelo from his torpor and also from the drab existence he was destined to. It sparked him back to a full recovery from the loss stemming from Henrietta's demise. In another unexpected way, it saved Dudley from a gloomy and dull life most of it earmarked to be spent behind bars.

Three days later Dudley was well enough to shyly sneak back to school. That morning he had spent several minutes in front of a mirror, feeling sorry over his disfigured face, glowing in black, blue and green with reddish area around the still bloody nose and cracked lips. His brother had hinted that it was not unlike the genital organs of a female baboon in estrus. –Right below the ass hole. - Had he smirked.

Like St Paul being thrown from his horse by the ire of God or hypoglycemia, Dudley became a full convert to the cause of civility; or was it reciprocity. He had seen the light, acquiring a more Christian attitude towards his classmates in general and Barcelo in particular. While not the greatest mind in the city, Dudley was able to recognize real anger against which nothing but death works; he was not ready to kill while Johnny had demonstrated that he was and could. "Reversibility of violence" was now a reality principle well understood by Dudley.

Interrogated by the principal of the school and his mum, Dudley never ratted. Jim Donegan, the teacher who had accidentally intervened, had recognized Johnny, this modern David as he called him; when asked he maintained that he had not been close enough to identify the protagonists. For the rest of his life he would redundantly describe this memorable brawl.

-Poetic justice, - he had told one of his colleagues. – I've often been at the mercy of such bullies in my time. This goblin was half the weight of the big slob but was possessed with more guts and fury than Jesus chasing the merchants from the temple. David had a lucky throw when he felled Goliath; this fight was close combat all the way; vicious and almost professional. I would have paid a hundred dollars to be there at the beginning. -

As this incident occurred in front of several other kids, Barcelo's reputation was recognized in the entire school; he never again had to yield passage, being given a wide berth by everyone.

A month later, a new kid tried to push him around only to feel Dudley's large paw on his shoulder. -Leave him alone if you know what's good for you. –

The new kid perceived Dudley as Johnny's body guard. While that was not the message intended it served the purpose. Dudley had chosen his camp and would remain close to Barcelo for most of his life, in time becoming his only friend.

The lesson retained by Barcelo was that determination, which can sometimes be mistaken for or is a product of desperation, is a more dangerous weapon than size or fire power. Several times during the following years, he would work up to the same suicidal frame of mind, each time it would work out just as it had the first time. -Not fearing death makes one invincible-.

He was sure that Henrietta, most probably enjoying retirement in paradise, would have been..., was..., proud of her tiny brother. This belief mattered and made everything right again.

CHAPTER 3

"New potential often stems from difficulty"

For the next several years, life continued uneventfully, as boring and imma-terial as a rainy October Sunday morning. Johnny was getting an education, while further mastering the subtle art of surviving against all odds.

Jim Donegan, the teacher who had saved Dudley's ass, was the only free thinker of the school and most probably of the entire city. In the 1940's thinking outside the habitual paths was considered unpatriotic; socialism and worse, communism, was dreaded more than the plague.

Most of his colleagues were teachers either because the job carried security and long summer vacations or did not qualify to be something else yielding a better pay. Donegan was different; he had always wanted to become a teacher, mostly because of the influence of one when he was thirteen. Father Joe kept drilling into his pupils' heads that: –Teaching is the most important profession in the world. Our leaders are only as good as their teachers were.-

Contrary to most of his colleagues, Jim knew that in order to be any good at teaching he had to keep his mind in top shape. Reading was as much a must for him as physical training for a boxer. So he read voraciously: from Faulkner to Marx, from Spinoza to Voltaire to Oriental and Western phi-losophers, Shakespeare, Byron, Browning, the Greeks, the Romans, history, novels, even newspapers; in fact he spent more time reading than teaching.

Often, after having swiftly covered dull academic subjects, he could not help but comment on some of the new ideas he had gleaned, or to think out loud some of his most profound, sometimes disturbing and indeed downright subversive thoughts. Barcelo's mind had been tilled by Henrietta and he could follow, even enjoy some of these extra curriculum essays.

Rather than being conventional, evasive and fickle, Donegan preferred hitting the class with what could prepare his students' intellects for their adult lives. He had pet subjects and would repeatedly hammer away that as adults, they had to be prepared to face several handicaps:

-The pariah like stigma of poverty is the worse handicap most of you will face. Almost impossible to shake-.

-Racism is a close second. Not being of the same color, race, creed, social status, size or, guilty of whatever other differences, is perceived as a danger that society will deal with by force if necessary.-

-The last one of these handicaps is the lack of a higher education. Education is the great equalizer. It cancels out racism, reduces fertility and eradicates poverty. - He would continue:

-Poverty is usually an insurmountable drawback and clips the wings of those contaminated by it. - And he would stress the word contaminated. - Infected because it's a disease transmitted sexually as well as genetically. – And he would repeat the word disease, before continuing:

-Unless they have special aptitudes, are unusually gifted in some discipline, -usually sports-, success is rarely available to the poor.-

-The - haves not- are de facto excluded from expensive higher education, therefore shut out of good jobs.- And then he would really get emotional:

-To add insult to injury, the poor's are often pegged social leeches by the affluents. Mistake, because in the final analysis, the rich elite is the real parasite. Keeping the poor's uneducated and in conditions of hardship provides the fat cats with cheap labor. Slavery was never different. - He would pause to look at these future zombies as he would describe them. After a little jig to wake the class up he would keep on:

-And this is unfair because the poor's have more health problems and die ten years earlier because they are more susceptible to become obese and diabetic. They also smoke and drink more than the affluents which can only make matters worse. -

Then to again jolt the class awake, he would jump up from his chair and ask.

-Who profits from the sale of tobacco and booze? - And always Barcelo would answer to the satisfaction of Donovan.

-The rich bastards and the government.-

Donegan would then walk to the door of the class and look in the hallway to make certain no one was close by before continuing.

-Guess who, between the rich and the poor, have more kids? – Looking around at the day dreaming students he would carry on.

-Procreating abundantly is a survival reflex the poor's have. Fine but this careless fertility creates greater obstacles to surmount, perpetuating the state of destitution. From generation to generation the vast majority of the poor's offspring's are as poor as or poorer than the parents. The girls suffer most. Life is meaner to a poor girl than to a poor boy. Marriage only precipitates the poor woman into a deeper and faster whirlwind of degradation and servitude.-

Then quoting Marx and Engel almost verbatim he would rise from his seat and dig in.

-What is society doing to help those in need? - He would answer his own question.

-Nothing, not a thing other than charity which comes with a high price tag. Maybe someday there will be a social system allowing the poor's to have access to higher education and climb out of their predicament. But don't count on it before several centuries. The question is:

-Is having two classes of citizens a goal pursued by the wealthy and governing class to procure cheap labor and front line soldiers.? The answer is yes.

-Could the Egyptian nobility have built the pyramids and flourished without the masses of serf-like peasants kept in a state of poverty by religion and laws: again cheap labor and front line soldiers? Could the cotton growers of the United States have thrived without the slaves from Africa? Could the carpet makers of India sell their goods without the contingent of kids they enslave? Marx was not off the mark when accusing the ruling classes of practicing economic slavery. Imposed poverty, or eternal scarcity as someone had named it, is one of the main building blocks of social control and capitalism; not all bad though, it has promoted civilization by allowing a few to think ahead. –

And he would laugh, looking at a point above the sea of heads. -Some of you may understand what I'm saying. -

For the Barcelo family living in Lewiston Maine, a poor city providing cheap labor and front line soldiers, the class difference was tangible enough to be felt by even a nine year old. Johnny's mother was a six day a week, twelve hours a day maid, working her ass off for a rich neighbor. Once in a while, the only kid in this family was allowed to play with the maid's son, this ugly duckling -Johnny- as Ms Mac Farlane would name him pinching her thin lips in a show of loathing for those others.

Auburn Maine, the city just across the Androscoggin River was home to the affluent class. There lived the "bosses", directors and managers of the mills, while Lewiston was home to the poor textile and leather industry worker. The social stratification was discernible to even children.

Because of the doors and avenues opened to Henrietta by Miss Whitehead; because of Donegan's crusade and also because of the almost weekly comparison of his way of living with that of nine year old Tim Mac Farlane, whom he was sometimes forced to play with, young Barcelo was conscious of the social cliff. Unusual conditions generate unusual individuals; Johnny was fertile soil, prepared to grasp the meaning of Donegan's social theories.

-Barcelo, you be the Indian, I'll be the cowboy. - Tim the brat would always say.

-My turn this time.- Would reply Johnny.-

-No, always my turn. –

And Tim would argue that he owned the toy guns as well as all the other toys they were playing with. Scarcity had been stingy to the Mac Farlane family.

Swimming in the societal tank with the oligarchistic consortium made out of religions, politics, and big bucks, was a multitude of smaller fish exploited as food stuff by these ravenous predators. Seeking their advantages, religions are courting and enrolling the poor's to increase their holy might. Religions may help the poor's, contributing to avert mass suicide by promising equality and justice after death; while promoting inequality, suffering and misery as entrance ticket to paradise. -Everyone will be equal when the second coming assembles the souls of the deceased. - Would claim the parish priest. Donegan applauded this accomplishment as the greatest marketing ploy ever.

And yet he professed that religions could have made the world a better place, could have helped humanity to evolve from the suicidal pleasure state to a disciplined reality. But no: Rather than implementing the doctrines imposed by the founders, these sublime philanthropic guidelines have been sidetracked from their initial paths to suit the less altruistic motivation of the subsequent power monger high priests.

Preaching acceptance of hell on earth as a way to earn eternal divine gratitude was an easy and only answer to most of the human problems. If you suffer it's for the good cause and there should be a just reward after death. If you don't suffer, don't worry about it, you will eventually. Politics follow the same approach and both, religions and politics are essentially people-control instruments.

Donegan was wise to the real motives behind this consortium created by religions, politics and money. Barcelo often feared that Donegan's anger would choke him. He would use carefully thought out sentences, well honed, the fruit of long hours of reflection and discussion over gallons of beer. Hope, he would repeat, was the bait, hope, this elusive abstraction, this far off possibility never attained but always flashed and promised if... certain conditions were met. Of course no one has ever come back.

-Hope is precluding happiness because it is in its constant pursuit. Can one be satisfied with this eternal chase, only catching the occasional glimpse of what happiness could be, never connecting; like foreplay without coitus?- The class would laugh at the coitus word. Donegan would turn and mutter. - Stupid peasants, maybe you deserve this fate. - Then louder, -you're like the parasites living in the bellies of termites, never seeing the light of day, dying with your hosts. - And he would dismiss the class.

After these sorties against the system, Barcelo would needle young Mac Farlane, tricking him into admitting the gross class disparity.

-Why do you have everything and I don't.?-

-Because my father has money and yours doesn't. - Tim would reply.

-What has he done to deserve it? - What have you done to deserve it, other than be born in the right family? - That would close the argument. Tim would chase him away and refuse to play with him for a few days.

A few years after her death, Johnny remembered that Henrietta, back from another Sunday Grand Mass, had asked him in her own inimitable technique:

-Why do you think Father Angus likes poor people.-

Johnny did not have a clue and did not think the surly priest liked people anyway. This did not make much difference as she was not expecting an answer only wanting to make a point.

-Because they'll go to mass on Sunday and pay his salary. The same for Mister Macfarlane; he wouldn't have anyone to clean his big house if Mama wasn't poor. I don't know exactly how but I'm sure he also makes money out of the poor. -

Like Donegan, Henrietta was a true rebel; and she had fashioned Johnny to her image. Spurred by the abuses she had endured, her mind had been looking for ways to take control rather than submit to injustice. Courage is indeed the only asset poverty allows its vassals. Intuitively, she could see that her situation at home was similar to the larger social model: weakness is always abused. After her death, Donegan took the relay and confirmed Henrietta's intuition. By hitting some of the same notes, he imbedded the tune deeply into Barcelo's hard disk.

The seed was planted in Johnny's mind. As he got older and more cynical he understood that despair and misery could be alleviated by the expectation of a brighter future; even if it meant conning one's brain by *"concealing the truth under veils of lying lore. "*. Hope, happiness and paradise after death were the rewards promised by this wise and cunning man who invented "the fear of gods", as Plato's uncle, Critias wrote more than two thousand years ago.

"Then came, it seems, that wise and cunning man, the inventor of the fear of gods. He framed a tale, a most alluring doctrine, Concealing truth by veils of lying lore."

Donegan's contribution to the formation of Barcelo's character was a complement as crucial as Henrietta's. The "knowable" is accessible only to the educated. Ideas are like water on a sand bed, creating their own paths and pursuing their own objectives. Isolated neurons are as useless as micro chips on the shelf; but as soon as they are linked together and organized, their power is incommensurable. Linking neurons takes time and repetition, often a second and a third imprint are necessary for the idea to become alive and activated; causes and effects following a mechanical course.

In the end, Donegan and Henrietta had created an unusually cynical thinker. He had learned by heart Donegan's favorite tirades and would pepper Dudley with them:

-"On religions: Happiness is bad for religions; man will suck up to god when in trouble, weak, old and near death; or when buried under his debts, or when hit by a tragedy. The mysterious is appealing to man; a good fable is preferred over the naked truth, truth being so inconvenient. Don't give people facts; give them a good story laced with miracles."

-" On fertility: Multiple births are a good and proven way to create and perpetuate poverty and misery; "grow as numerous as the lilies in the field "is a winning formula, as amply demonstrated in economically depressed countries, where families of six are small, while religions are flourishing amidst hunger, illiteracy and misery. Religion and poverty are compatible bed fellows, one providing metaphysical relief and hope to compensate for the inescapable tragedy of the other. "

Coming home every night rubbed Johnny's nose in some hard facts which concurred with Donovan's theories: his father was working like a sheep dog but was sucked into the black hole of hopelessness and despair, always hitting a wall, being exploited by a system depending on low wages and poverty to thrive. As Jim Donegan was professing loudly, -Keeping the neo slaves hungry with barely enough to eat was better than the whip. If one is kept hungry and too tired to think he'll perform and won't cause any trouble. Add inexpensive and unrestricted accessibility to alcohol and you have complete power over your population.

Maria his mother was working even harder and longer hours for less money than his father. At the end of the week, between the two of them, they would have toiled sufficiently to barely make ends meet. Balthazar and Claudio, Johnny's two brothers, abandoned ship soon after Henrietta's death. They married and created their own microcosms of misery and hardship, dragging under two poor girls who would fulfill their brood mares' destinies.

CHAPTER 4

"Something good always comes out of something bad."

Now that his brothers had flown the coop life should have been more comfortable; but by then, Adriano had found relief in alcohol and his mother Maria became ill, tired of chasing the next meal, crushed by a life of servitude and empty promises. The mind can only keep the body in working condition so long; there comes a time when the will yields to the subconscious acceptance of the perceived destiny. The realization that success is an out of reach target extinguishes the fire.

Tuberculosis dragged Maria Barcelo to eternal rest. Like an ant or a bee, Maria had scrubbed the Macfarlane's floors until the very end. Johnny hoped that she would not reincarnate, once around should have sufficed to absolve her of all these crimes she would have loved to commit. Jim Donegan had explained how Hinduism justified the cast system by the theory of reincarnation; perpetuating the merry go round to completely expiate sins and other misdeeds, so the cycle would end and nirvana be attained; always these virtual promises; a Ponzi scheme of sort.

-May God receive his servant in paradise. Maria has earned eternal reward, having been a good Christian, a good wife and a good mother. - Said Angus, the parish priest.

All dressed up in white and black, Angus continued to do his number and recited other empty words in Latin. Johnny had stopped listening and was spinning somber thoughts in his mind:

-If suffering during most of your life, then dying spitting blood is a prerequisite to achieving immortality and eternal happiness on God's lap, I'd rather not have any part of it.- Then he thought that his mother and Henrietta could be sitting on the same cloud, holding hands and smiling. That made it right.

He must have been speaking out loud. His brother Claudio looked at him and asked what he had been mumbling about. During the rest of the ceremony Johnny kept wondering if one could also go to heaven after a life of happiness or was it a prerequisite to pay for the ticket with misery and hardship; like his mother and Henrietta.

Paradise, death, hell, purgatory were question marks in Johnny's mind. That his mother was faring better in death than she had been in life made him wish that she had died earlier, much earlier, even before he was born. All of a sudden he became aware that he had grown up; six years ago, Henrietta and now his mother.

Dudley attended the funeral and had agreed to be one of the pall bearers along with Johnny, his brothers and Uncle Andres, the same who had abused Henrietta. Andres said a few words at the cemetery and cried a little. Johnny and his brothers also cried when the coffin was lowered in the hole which had cost ten dollars to dig.

Henrietta and now his mother; he had less sorrow for the loss of his mother and felt bad about this. He was now old enough to regret this very special attachment for Henrietta. Discreetly probing without revealing his secret, he had not been able to find any such relationships among his friends; except Abe who was bragging about his experience with an older cousin. Probably wasn't true, just bragging.

He had come to the conclusion that it was better for Henrietta to have died; he could not imagine the awkwardness between the two of them as grownups. He was to learn later that the Pharaoh's and generally the Egyptians during an epoch of their history, didn't have second thoughts about incestuous relations; Cleopatra had been the incestuous spouse to her pharaonic brothers, Ptolemy XIV and XV, before she was wed to Caesar and then to Marc Anthony. Also two thirds of the population of a small city in Egypt married their siblings. In Egyptian poetic language, brother and sister are the same words as lover and mistress. History was a great buffer; that made him feel less of an odd ball even if these events occurred three thousand years ago.

While the priest was babbling away, Johnny was absentmindedly passing in review those in attendance: he couldn't miss the elaborate hat Mathilda Macfarlane was wearing. Did she really care for Maria -the person-, or was she sorry for herself, now deprived of a perfect maid she would find impossible to replace. Her son was fidgety and could not stay in place more than a minute, either picking his nose or scratching his groin. The others, more than a hundred, mostly from the Portuguese community, had donned their best apparels and presented a sea of gaunt faces emerging from somber clothing, mostly black but here and there a flash of red or blue. Someone was missing, he looked again; Adriano was missing, he could not find his father.

-Where's Adriano.?-

-He's home, couldn't get him up this morning. He's sleeping off the booze he drank last night. Got so pissed that he passed out cold. I thought he would also die. - Whispered Claudio before Balthazar could answer.

Stunned, Johnny didn't say a word for a while trying to find excuses for his father not attending his wife's funeral.... looking hard for justification. Then he tried to brush it out of his mind but ... it kept coming back like a migraine headache. Finally, not able to neither find a good enough alibi nor ignore the fact that his father was home sleeping off a binge while his wife was being buried, slowly, like a hurricane building up in the south seas, Johnny became very angry; so furious that rage soon replaced his grief.

During the interment, while the coffin was being lowered into the grave, his anger continued to build up. He kept looking over his shoulders hoping that Adriano would show up; he did not. After the burial, not waiting in line to shake all the hands extended by friends and distant relatives, he hurried home. There he found Adriano hunched over a beer, sitting abjectly at the kitchen table, both elbows on the table, a cigarette burning between his yellowed fingers, feeling sorry for himself.

He stood a long moment at the door, looking at this despicable, contemptible excuse for a human being: his father. Without uttering a word, he grabbed him by the throat, squeezing the protruding wind pipe to the point of rupturing it, yanked him up on his feet and proceeded to thrash his old man.

-You son of a bitch... how could you not be at the funeral..., she was a good woman and didn't deserve to be left alone at her funeral. .... she was our mother, your wife for twenty two fucking years she was your wife.... Even Uncle Andres was there. He paid the priest, the coffin, the grave diggers ..... Adriano, you had no business to be so fucking drunk. I'm beating you for her sake and for the times when you were bad and mean to her and for letting my brothers and uncle Andres screw Henrietta when she was just a kid....-

For the first time he had called his father by his first name. He had not planned it but spontaneously Henrietta's plight came up. Through the tears of rage he could see the pathetic face of his father grimacing behind his raised hands.

-You're right... I'm a bum, lower than a snake but don't hit too hard, you'll hurt me and the police will come if I have to go to the hospital. - After a few seconds which seemed like an hour, Adriano fell down on his knees, crying like a baby, vomiting a repulsive mixture of blood tinted beer and bile.

Johnny didn't hit too hard. The poor critter would not remember much of what happened except for a black and blue rib cage. Claudio and Balthazar came in at the end of the bout and remained paralyzed, mouths opened like when they had been introduced to Jesus protecting Henrietta. Since the Dudley incident, they had come to fear their younger brother's wrath.

The following morning, on his way to school:

-Where will you live? - Asked Dudley who had heard about the altercation. - You may not be welcome to live with your old man -.

-I'll live at home, it's my home and I'm still a minor for a few years. My old man was wrong and he knows it. ... The funny thing is that I feel closer to him now that we have had this ....understanding. You know ... maybe the same thing as for us.-

-If you need to almost kill someone before becoming friends with him, the list will be short. - Quipped Dudley with a wink. He understood what Johnny meant.

Father-son relationship is never easy even when there is no conflict; the scuffle had changed that. Johnny was thinking that he should help Adriano stop drinking or the next grave dug in the old cemetery would be his. Not that he cared that much; but blood is thicker than water and the old bastard was his father. As it turned out, their relationship improved considerably, from almost nothing to a good average. Adriano had seen the light. His younger son was a revelation to him as he had been to his school mates six years ago. Adriano was proud of the character displayed by his son.

-My younger son loved me enough to have almost killed me. - As he explained the situation to his friends.

Weaklings will find comfort in any event chastising their shortcomings; is it a death wish, a proof of affection or a desire to reform and get back in the rank? For Adriano, the gesture of his youngest son was an act of love. And it was; why else would a fifteen year old have taken the trouble to administer such correction to his drunken father? Most would have written off the derelict. But immigrants stick together; their survival as a group depends on it.

Whatever had motivated Johnny, the ultimate result of this incident was that it reprieved the death sentence hovering over Adriano's head; momentarily saving his life. From that day, he stopped drinking. There is always something good out of something bad.

CHAPTER 5

"One man's garbage can be another's fortune."

Like the water molecule falling from a cloud, finding its way to the ocean and then back to the cloud, life in Lewiston Maine continued its futile merry go round. Initially, because of the accumulated doctors' bills, it turned out to be more difficult for only one bread winner to bring enough money home. But after a few months, the debts were paid and a miracle was happening: Adriano was bringing home more money than was needed; first time ever; before always short, never a penny in excess. Adriano had found a gold mine. The nuggets were tires, used tires; the collection, disposal and-or sale of used tires was his new business.

After the First World War motorized vehicles replaced horses. In the short span of ten years, horses were almost totally replaced by trucks and cars. Four tires, designed to be indestructible, were part of this new system of locomotion. Accumulation of used tires soon started to become a problem; small at first but with the potential of a major catastrophe. By the year 2000, the American people would dispose of and accumulate three hundred million tires per year, each one of these tires having a potential life span of more than five hundred years before nature degrades them back into carbon. The numbers are formidable: three hundred million tires by three hundred years.

As always, politicians waited for the problem to get out of hands before proposing a solution. Let's bear in mind that in the 50's, most people were still disposing of their garbage as the American Indians had: in rivers, lakes or buried in abandoned camp sites. There was a garbage dump at the outskirt of Lewiston as everywhere else in the USA.

It took until 1975 and a couple of huge scrap tire fires for the government to wake up and react. Then some smarter technocrat learned how to use the multiplication table and got scared by the result. In the mean time Adriano had, as he was saying, hit the mother lode. Initially, after his day job, but soon full time, he was calling on service stations, garages and other tire points of sale. For a tipping fee he would agree to collect the used tires left behind by customers who had bought new ones. As some of these tires still had mileage left, he would hoard and sell these to his former co-workers and other -haves not-, for a fraction of the price they would have had to pay for new ones. Having been paid to collect the tires which he would then sell or dispose of at no cost, was indeed a tremendous business opportunity.

Very soon Adriano was no longer able to cope with the demand. The time had come to put an end to Johnny's formal education. Late one Saturday night, coming home tired with a pocket full of dollars, he went to his bunk:

-I need help; it's getting too big for just one old man. You'll be seventeen. How about coming in with me. -

With some pride, Johnny had been following his father's resurrection from the dead and had helped him from time to time. This was September of 49, as good a time as any to put an end to his academic career. He could count well enough and had the rudiments of knowledge that would allow him to think for himself; that would suffice. He knew that another ten years of learning was out of reach for guys like him. He had the brain but not the doe. The decision was easy and quick.

-Deal, he said, what do I get? -

They agreed on a salary and a work schedule. That Saturday night, the biggest pile of scrap tires on the east cost of the USA got started. For very different reasons, this date was to become a historical moment for Johnny and for the Department of Environmental Protection of the State of Maine.

It did not take long for the Barcelo's, father and son, to need another truck and another driver. Dudley, never far away, was enrolled in the emerging and already financially successful family business.

CHAPTER 6

"Finis rerum."
"All things end."

Not that it mattered, but like an old and tired horse teamed up with a vigorous stallion, Adriano was lagging behind, not pulling his share of the load. Years of smoking, drinking and other abuses to his body were demanding repayment. Reimbursement of health debts is exacted around age fifty; Adriano was fifty one and owed a lot.

For a few years now, he had stopped drinking but had kept on smoking, even though he knew intuitively that smoking was draining his very last health capital. Contrary to what the tobacco companies were advertising, he was addicted to nicotine and even though he gave it his best shot, he could not quit.

-I should be able to order my body to stop smoking, I know it is bad; but this habit is stronger than my will. My mind is weak. - His friend agreed that he too was unable to control his smoking habits as well as so many other desires.

Came the time, when fully aware that it was too late, short of breath, coughing almost constantly and becoming weaker by the day, Adriano decided to consult a doctor; a first in his life. It was a significant decision for him to make and only sheer terror bordering on panic could force him to go to such an extreme. In his youth old men died at home without the doctors' help.

Dr Talbot was fresh out of medical school. New at this game, it was however easy for him to place a name on these text-book symptoms. The growling and ratchety noises emerging from Adriano's rib cage were not indi-cations of good health. He ordered x Rays at the General Hospital of Lewiston, a good hospital managed by nuns. The x Rays were taken and in two days an unambiguous diagnostic of lung cancer was confirmed; the craters in the left lobe left no doubt.

When Adriano came back the following week, the young doctor took out the x ray films and pretended to look at them while working up his courage. He had already studied them carefully and knew every dark spots eating away at Adriano's lungs.

-Mister Barcelo, you have a lung cancer.... We might have been able to operate if you had come to us six months ago. As it is, there is not much we can do. – He was using the – imperial we—in an effort to dilute his responsibility for being the bearer of such awful news; the medical profession was backing Talbot's verdict of this death sentence.

Taken aback, Adriano repeated every word in his mind, looking for a hidden meaning. After a few minutes of silence, he seemed to come to.

-If you can't operate, does that mean that I'm going to die? - Asked Adriano, not fully understanding the extent of what he was hearing and saying.

Being still a young man, at fifty one, he had taken for granted that he could at least have lived until sixty, maybe sixty five. Was he being told that his time would come sooner? Now that money was pouring in, he would have liked to enjoy life, maybe travel back to Portugal, brag a little to those cousins who had predicted, maybe wished his failure. Dying would not have been a problem during the hard times of his life but now that he could pay the bills and have money left over, living was a better option. The ultimate revenge of the poor is that they don't fear dying, leaving nothing behind but gloom and pain.

-I'm sorry sir, but I don't think you'll see Easter. –

Bang, like a rifle shot, these words echoed for a long moment in the cold sparsely furnished doctor's office. It was the first time doctor Talbot had to predict an early departure. He would have to do it often in his chosen profession. Saving lives was the nice side of doctoring, admitting defeat was the dark side, an old professor had told him.

Doctor Talbot felt the content of his stomach turn to lead. He would vomit after Adriano's departure. In a few months he would take all this in stride and no longer feel this beautiful compassion.

What he did not tell his patient was that he would be dead before Christmas, not Easter. But who knows, life is fragile but yet so tenacious, remissions had been seen. Looking at the X Rays once more he had to admit that only a miracle could work in this instance.

-You should put your affairs in order and come back to see me every week. I'll try to make you as comfortable as possible.-

Without a word, Adriano lit a Lucky Strike cigarette and walked out of the office, angry at this young doctor who obviously did not know his business. What did he mean by "making me comfortable"?

-He's full of crap,-. Said Adriano loudly. A passerby turned his head angrily, thinking the insult intended for him.

The young doctor knew his business. He helped Adriano slide into a comfortable coma before he was buried in a plot near his wife and Henrietta.

Having experienced a few years of relative contentment, the last three weeks were not the happiest of his otherwise miserable and drab life. The young doctor tried to make the transition as painless as possible. While he would have euthanized his dog suffering of the same terminal ailment, he was restricted to giving strong painkillers and, during the last few days, morphine. Adriano refused to go to the hospital and died at home in Johnny's arms; who was a helpless witness to the pain a person could endure when in the process of slowly running out of air to breath.

-I come from nothing and I'm going back to nothing. - Would repeat Adriano.

He believed that God would be lenient and have him in paradise; maybe a few years in purgatory for his past sins. Old Angus the parish priest was summoned. He heard Adriano's confession and performed the Last Rite. That appeased the moribund and removed some of the stress; deliverance was coming.

During the last two days, Johnny had kept Adriano on a steady liquid diet of Four Roses bourbon and milk. With the morphine-whisky cocktail, panic and pain were alleviated even though the lung function deteriorated further. Adriano suffocated in his bed but never felt it.

-I'm proud of you Johnny and I'm happy to have been able to start this business. I now have something to leave behind. Maybe you'll remember me kindly. Make it go well, I'll be looking on, make me proud. We can talk about it when we meet again at the last judgment. - Were his last coherent words.

Again, Dudley, Claudio, Balthazar and Uncle Andres were the pall bearers. Andres pronounced a timid but much improved eulogy and Johnny paid the funeral expenses. His father had given him the tire business and the two trucks. The other two sons were not very happy about being left out of the deal but Adriano had realized that an emerging business cannot be divided in two or three. Furthermore, they were lazy, spending more time bemoaning their fate than working, having accepted to be permanent victims. Johnny was a rebel and would make the new venture thrive.

But he did not want to be accused of cheating his two brothers and their families out of their inheritance; he made them a reasonable offer.

-There's enough work for all of us in this business. Why don't you two come in tomorrow morning at five o'clock. We'll split the work load and increase the volume.-

He had said two words which had a profoundly repulsive effect on his two brothers: work and five in the morning. The following morning he and Dudley were on their own and never heard another word from Balthazar and Claudio. On the third day, Johnny made a deal with his siblings.

The business was not worth much at the time of Adriano's death. Johnny gave them each one hundred dollars on the spot and promised to pay one thousand dollars each in a year or two. Six months later he settled in cash. They had not believed that their younger brother could come up with the money ever; who had ever heard of making money out of scrap tires.

—— CHAPTER 7 ————————————————

"Man truly loves only once, the first time."

From convenient sheds and barns, the place of business was finally anchored to a derelict garage of large proportion, situated in the middle of an otherwise vacant lot. A small office was part of the complex. In the office, Emilie, a pretty brunette answered a phone and shuffled whatever paper work had to be dealt with.

Emilie Roy, the oldest of a family of twelve, had had to forgo higher education in order to help her family. Vivacious and dependable she could be trusted, a quality that was foremost in Johnny's employment criterion.

It was only a question of time for Johnny to notice that she was a girl, and an attractive one at that. True enough that he was of the right age; but while his exposure to sex had been early and inappropriate, and while he was as bold as any Harvard educated MBA in day to day business dealings, he was timid and shy with girls. Since Henrietta he had not ever been promiscuous and had put off this moment until now. Why was not clear, maybe a sense of loyalty or, devotion or fear, most likely the latter.

But the time had come. At the ripe old age of nineteen his pals were beginning to look sideways at him for not having a girl friend. Could he be gay? His looks, not being that of a Hollywood stud could perhaps explain his shyness with girls. Whatever the reason, it had to come to an end and Emilie would be the test.

-Emilie, I was thinking that if you don't have anything better to do on Saturday night we could go out for dinner .- He wanted to add – and dance after dinner- but he did not know the first thing about dancing.

He had been rehearsing his proposal to Emilie. That latest edition was declared perfect and Johnny would use it that Friday morning to casually ask her out. Repeating in front of a mirror, using low and high pitches he was not yet comfortable with the overall quality. Cowardly, for the second week, he decided to postpone the moment until next Friday.

But fate had decided otherwise. Dudley came in that morning. He too had been ogling Emilie ever since she started working. He coughed and made his little speech not knowing that Johnny was in the adjacent bathroom, zipping up in a hurry.

-Emilie, I was thinking that we could go out for supper and go dancing this Saturday night ... if you don't have anything better to do. - said Dudley.

In the bathroom, Johnny bolted to attention. In his haste to come out of the can, he almost caught a piece of foreskin zipping up his fly.

- The son of a bitch is using my line, could he have overheard? - Not thinking a second and before Emilie could answer, like a muraena eel he was out of the toilet and cut in.

-Dudley, if I had known you wanted to go out with Emilie this Saturday, I wouldn't have asked her. As it is I just did before you came in-. ...Then after a second...-But maybe Emilie has a friend who would be free this Saturday?-

Blushing like a twelve year old in front of a naked starlet but looking squarely in Emilie's eyes, Johnny was silently praying that his bluff would work. It did.

With a sly smile Emilie said that she had a friend who would be very happy to join the party. Looking at the two contenders, one a perfect specimen of masculinity, the other an ugly runt of a man, she had chosen boldness over beauty. Why, she did not and would never know, intuition maybe. The rest of the day went by quickly. Johnny was happy and never even bothered to justify his fib to Emilie. She did not bring it up either; leaving well enough alone being a sound policy.

Between the two of them, Johnny and Dudley owned two pairs of not so clean jeans and four shirts that repeated washing could never bring back to the original color. Most of two hours were spent buying proper garments.

Another problem was transportation. Trucks are not very romantic or practical to court girls. Even more so with Barcelo's trucks, sporting hand painted signs on both sides reading: JOHNNY's SCRAP TIRE DISPOSAL

In a panic he decided to rent, borrow, steal or buy a car for the occasion. He had the cash and decided to buy. One of his customers, a Dodge-Plymouth dealer had been trying to sell him a car for more than a month;

he bought a brand new black De Sotto "fluid drive", the only one in stock that could be prepared and readied in time. Driving it back to the office, he felt for the first time in his life that he could achieve any goal he would dare aim for. Boldness, a date and a new car: he was superman, indestructible and powerful.

They picked up the girls and the evening went great guns until Dudley became drunk, so drunk that they had to drag his big hulk to the car. After making sure that he was emptied of all food and beverage, they sat him in the back seat and drove him home. Emilie's friend was sorry and a bit disturbed, but understood. Drinking was not uncommon in her family. Johnny took her home first and then went dancing with Emilie. Dudley's little mishap could not have been more –à propos- if planned.

Like boldness and courage, money and power are strong erotic enhancers; something like the flamboyant feathers, birds flash to advertise a receptive mood and find a mate. For a while after our ancestors descended from the trees, we continued to secrete sex appealing substance, sending aerial invitations to copulate. After a while the human sense of smell became atrophied and we had to depend on other attributes like brute strength, money, good looks, even superior intellect could work as an aphrodisiac. Barcelo was lacking most if not all of these attributes. Never would he be good looking but he was smart and looked as if he might be rich one day. Like an option on a stock, some sort of initial public offering where it is advantageous to own a ticket and board before the train picks up speed.

The evening ended better than it had begun. Alone with Emilie, Johnny was able to fully appreciate the company of a female for the first time since Henrietta had died. He could not help but compare and, in the final analysis, Emilie won against the absent Henrietta. Closing his eyes, during the last dance, the odor, the delicate skin texture, the warmth exulting from the body he was holding in his arms, reminded him of his abused, misguided defunct sister. Would he ever forget or was it necessary to forget; regarding this episode in his life as an accident of nature was a more judicious and pragmatic choice. Opening his eyes he looked at Emilie and whispered into her ear:

-I spent a wonderful evening. The best ever, thank you. I'm tired and would like to take you home.-

She pushed him gently away from her to better see his face while continuing to dance. Her eyebrows arched, there was a surprise in her eyes; she had not thought that Barcelo could be a thoughtful and gentle person. She had expected him to be ruthless and tough, without feelings or rules, like his business.

-I'm glad you asked me out. - She managed to whisper before exploding in a cascade of giggle.

Trying to stop giggling and regain some composure, she hugged Johnny tightly, half choking him. Knowing very well why she was hysterical he also let out what he had been able to contain all evening. They stood still, standing and laughing in the middle of the dance floor like two idiots and loving the feeling.

Elated, he escorted her back to the table and admitted how he had acted on the spur of the moment, having had the intention to ask her out frightened to death that she would refuse.

-You know that you're the first girl I've taken out. - He was going to add. - Since my sister died-. He continued:

-And I enjoyed the experience so much that I would like to do that again soon, like..... maybe tomorrow night.-

Wow, she thought, this one is fast and keen; realizing that her chances of dying a spinster had been reduced considerably.

-I'd love it- She whispered.

Suddenly bashful because vaguely aware of the long term implications of what he had just done, Johnny got up and was almost out of the dance hall when the waiter caught up with him. He had forgotten to pay the bill. A large tip got him back in good standing. They slowly walked out to the beautiful new car, his first car and his first date. Hopefully, the car would not turn into a pumpkin.

Emilie was in for another surprise. Contrary to what she had been apprehensive of, he did not try to kiss her good night. Awkwardly, he almost ran away, as if guilty of a crime not yet committed, culpable of an intention. Relieved, yet puzzled and annoyed, Emilie stood alone on the porch long after the black car had silently glided away. What a bizarre young man. Not good looking by any standard but nevertheless handsome, projecting a presence that none of the people she knew had. Charisma she thought it was called, although not entirely sure that it was the right word. Whatever it was, he had it. And his eyes could drill into hers like hot rays of June sunshine or cold wisps of arctic air.

She spent the next day cleaning the house; so much and with such energy that her mother became alerted and stopped preparing dinner to stare at her. Reminiscence of her own youth, already only a vague souvenir, helped her understand that her little girl was getting infatuated. She smiled, one of these impenetrable and knowledgeable smiles that mothers turn on when they have divined a secret.

Five o'clock on the dot and Johnny was parking his shiny car. The kids in this neighborhood were not used to seeing flashy new cars parked on their street. Only cops called in to settle a family feud, bailiffs to repossess some equipment, doctors delivering babies; those were the only visitors who drove new automobiles in this part of town. Coming out of nowhere, a bunch of barefoot kids suddenly materialized, swarming around the new De Soto like bees around their queen.

-You can look but don't touch. - Johnny growled before slowly climbing the three steps leading to the front door.

Not wanting to be seen wearing the same attire as the previous night, he had bought a new pair of tan colored pants which had been called trousers by the salesman, and had let the clerk convince him that very narrow leg hems were "in" this year. A black belt with a flashy buckle, a new pair of shoes and one of these Hawaiian shirt with red and yellow motif, the whole harmonized with a greenish velour blazer, completed Johnny's new look. Dressing with taste is not a question of money. His enthusiasm filled in the voids.

Semi conscious of the odd spectacle he presented but unable to determine whether it was good or bad, Johnny had avoided driving through the usual streets, evading his rowdy friends.

The front door opened and he was formerly introduced to the mama and to some of the kids. Emilie's father was away until later, probably drinking beer with some friends or, maybe and most probably avoiding meeting this young hoodlum his daughter was going out with.

The immaculate interior smelled of clean poverty: a mixture of food, wax and Clorox. A mute witness to countless drama; it had kept new babies warm and been the cold stage for final departures, most premature, a few timely and welcomed.

To his surprise the mother was still comely; having had so many children left a trace but Johnny was amazed at not finding the usual disfigurement associated with multiple consecutive pregnancies. She looked tired but alert, her dress was old but well cared for; she had obviously put it on a few moments before his arrival.

Ill at ease, flashing one of his often rehearsed artificial smiles, Johnny felt like a prize goat at the country fair. That this woman was also a potential mother in law did not improve his self awareness. From the corner of his eye, he caught Emilie looking at his tapered pantaloons and decided that he would not wear them again.

-I've made reservations for six o'clock and Portland is a good forty five minutes from here, if you're ready we should leave soon -.

-Be careful, vacation time, people drive so dangerously. We hear about accidents every morning on the radio. - Some things never change, a mama is always a mama and worrying is part of the mama game.

-Don't worry I'll take good care of your little girl-. Said Johnny as he edged toward the front door, almost tripping over one of the younger kids.

The drive to the coast took less than forty five minutes as Johnny wanted to try out his new car. Emilie was scared when he pushed it faster than sixty miles per hour but soon found it exciting. At eighty five Johnny lifted his foot and grunted in admiration.

-It could go a hundred. Emilie you drive, you don't have to change gears, it's automatic.-

-Oh no, I've never driven. Maybe some other time but not now. You know something, I enjoyed going fast... after the fright.-

Leaving home and for as long as they were in Lewiston, Emilie had kept to her side of the car. Immediately out of the city limits, as if on cue, she edged slowly nearer and nearer to Johnny's side of the car, until he could feel her warmth on his thigh.

He became voiceless for a while, could have been this heat on his thigh. After an eternity he rattled his brains in search of something to talk about. Blank, no thought came to mind. After a while he capitulated and left it to Emilie to come up with some small talk. She surprised him with a question she had had stewing for the last two weeks:

-Already two weeks since I started working for you? This business of collecting used tires is an odd one, nobody I've talked to has heard of another business like it. Tell me more?- Here was something he could talk about for hours.

Johnny was off on a subject he knew well. He gave a lecture to Emilie who had asked the question more or less to fill in the conversation but was soon very interested. So much in fact that she interrupted often to make sure she understood. Emilie's education about the scrap tire business continued during the excellent dinner in one of the good restaurants in Portland and during the return trip until they reached Old Orchard Beach.

From Portland, Johnny had gone south a few miles on the scenic "route one" following the sea coast. At ten o'clock, the moon was slowly rising in the June sky and the mild wind was massaging the water as if it was a curtain made of fine silk. After finding a place to park the car, they took their shoes off and started walking on the still warm sand; the day had been a scorcher. Johnny was happy; happy because he had been talking all evening about his favorite subject, happy because he had removed his shoes that were new and had been torturing his feet and, most of all happy because she was there, beside him, holding his hand for the first time.

Holding a girl's hand for the first time can be gauche; maybe even trickier than to dare the first kiss. There is always the fear that the contact will be refused, that the hand will be removed as if it had touched something wet and cold or hot and greasy.

It was dry and warm, comfortable with just the right amount of strength and tonus. Emilie's hand was just a little smaller than Johnny's but fitted exactly. It was the very first time he held a girl's hand in his.

Hand in hand they walked, admiring the surf pushing a silver mane, the moon tinting the ocean and the beach. The smallest rocks were taking on fantastic proportions, the sand under their feet made of millions of bluish diamond chips, immortalizing their passage for a moment until the next wave erased it. Like life, Emilie was thinking, walking backward to observe the destruction of their footprints by the water. –Like time, erasing every second fades away to make room for the next one.- She muttered.

Meandering in and out of the advancing sea, they were soon wet to their knees. Except for a few couples, also taken in by the immensity of the ocean, the calmness of the night, the charm of the moon, they were alone in this paradise, savoring their first intimacy in a celestial setting.

Emilie was surprised that Johnny had not made a move to kiss her. Not that she was unhappy about this, having always thought that the first move should be at the initiative of the girl. He sure was thinking about it but did not dare, having never before been in a position to have to make such a decision. He could not remember a more uncomfortable moment. The whole process of courtship was making him very tense. They had been talking all evening about scrap tires; why not talk about that new emotion he was experimenting.

-I am not a romantic type of a guy and to tell you the truth I have never been out with a girl before you. A kind of .... Virgin if you want. Just holding your hand like this is wonderful-.

He was saying this as if he had rehearsed it; as if he was the lead actor in a movie; as if he was a professional of the -*right thing to say*- to a girl.

Surprised and bothered by the moon, the whispering of the sea and mostly by this strange candor, Emilie twisted around and planting her feet in the wet sand, grabbed his head with both hands and slowly lowered it to her lips.

-If you want to kiss me that's how it's done. -. She murmured.

CHAPTER 8

"Compos Sui"
"Be your own boss"

Answering Emilie's question about the scrap tire business, while enjoying that wonderful « Portland dinner » as they remembered it, a strategic business plan had been created. As it turned out the business plan for the next ten years had been drafted during that evening.

One of the first steps was to buy a large piece of land where the tires could be stockpiled. Getting rid of the scrap tires by dumping them in lakes, rivers or wooded area was not a long term solution; the law would soon be on their tail. Johnny started looking for the proper piece of land and finally found one in West Bowdoin.

West Bowdoin is a marvelously refreshing hick town, truly the back of beyond, and a wide place in the road some ten miles east of Lewiston. Rolling hills after rolling hills, stone fences of all shapes and sizes crisscrossing one another, shadowed by large mature trees. Essentially a farming community with little other activity, West Bowdoin was perfect for his business. The site for sale was a twenty two acre former gravel pit. A deep ravine cut the property in half, making it unattractive for farming. For Johnny's purpose, a ravine as deep as this one was a godsend.

After walking the periphery of the property, he knocked on the door of the owner who lived on the adjoining lot. He had to knock repeatedly before a man, fiftyish, not likely to blow the candles of his sixtieth birthday, limped his way to the front of the house, squinted through the window and opened the door. A gray cat crashed out between his legs.

-What the fuck do you want from me on a Sunday morning? I hope for your sake that you're not peddling bible stories or insurance. - The foul mouth was in line with the ill shaven, stub teeth, jaundiced and balding individual.

Johnny reckoned that this weirdo out of Dickens was the perfect neighbor for his kind of business.

-Not selling, buying is my business this morning. I'd like to buy this piece of property next door. I hear that you're the owner.-

After craning his neck to check the vehicle this tender foot was driving, Ed concluded that he could be talking to a real buyer. His puffy and grouchy face became softer at the idea of making a few bucks out of this piece of land he had been trying to dump ever since he had lost his gravel contract.

-Come on in and have a cup of coffee or something stronger if you fancy. -

The place was a cesspool such as Johnny had never seen. Cats all over the place and the stench of cat's urine was so strong that he started sneezing. A quick glance around told him that this Ed was a champion juggler; nobody else could have stacked so many dirty dishes in one single sink.

Common knowledge has it that driving a bargain with an ebriated seller is advantageous. Also the drink might offset the cats' urine and the other unidentified odors.

-Ok I'll have a short one.-

Johnny did not usually drink alcohol, let alone on Sunday mornings. He accepted, hoping that the glass would be cleaner than the surroundings. In any case he had heard that alcohol was a strong disinfectant and could kill all beasts even the two legged variety.

Ed preceded him into the living room kitchen combination and opened an antique wooden cupboard which may have had some value under the filth that had accumulated, undisturbed for more than fifty years by the look of it. Out came a half empty bottle of Four Roses whisky; two shot glasses followed which were soon filled with the amber colored liquid.

-To your good health. - Said Ed.

Johnny drank in one gulp and almost choked. This potion was a very distant cousin of the Four Roses it was impersonating.

-I make it myself, several distillations, pretty near 80 proof. - Boasted Ed as he sipped his ration with prudence knowing the effect it could have on an empty stomach.

Slowly regaining his composure, his voice temporarily out of commission because of the severe injury to his vocal cords, Johnny nodded his approval wiping a tear from his eyes.

-I'm looking for land. I want to build a house and I like my privacy. At least 20 acres. - He managed to mumble.

This could be a live one indeed thought Ed as he poured himself and Johnny another shot, suddenly excited by the prospect of finding a sucker for this piece of land.

-That's the perfect spot for a house. A nice little creek in the back, the trees all around the property and quiet neighbors. Not much good for farming but for a house it's just about perfect.-

And he was right, even the ravine became a plus in this context. Not everyone could boast of a hundred foot deep ravine in his back yard.

-How many acres. - Asked Johnny his voice still altered. Ed knew the cause of the voice alteration and smiled coyly.

-Another shot before we continue? Obviously Johnny was not the only one thinking that a couple of shots could improve a deal.

He refused, acknowledging that he was out of his league.

-I only close deals when I'm able to sign my name. Another shot and I may disqualify myself.-

Ed had another just the same and told him there were approximately twenty two acres.

-Let's walk the property line. You'll see what a good deal this is.-

As they completed the tour an hour later, Johnny agreed that it was a perfect fit. Thickly wooded on the periphery so as to make an almost curtained area; a former gravel pit in the middle with still plenty of gravel to build roads and do other things like land filling over the scrap tires and, finally the ravine. This was the piece de resistance; it would gobble up several tens of thousands of tires and other scrap. The ravine was about one hundred feet at the deepest point, four hundred and fifty feet in length and an average width of fifty yards.

-How much per acre- Asked Johnny.

-I was thinking of $100.00. - Replied Ed.

Johnny opened his wallet and let Ed see a fairly thick wad.

-My thoughts are more around $ 50.00 per acre.... That's my price and I'd close the deal now with $500.00 on account. The rest when we know the exact surface from the surveyor.-

After years of trying to sell this property Ed knew that he would not get a better offer soon.

-I'm tired, sick and getting on in life. Deal. - He said, celebrating the sale with the last of his drink.

Johnny proceeded to draw a simple offer to purchase and fifteen minutes later gave Ed $500.00 in cash. Tom, his lawyer friend, would come up with the proper paper work.

It was twelve o'clock and what had started as a leisurely Sunday morning ride in the country ended up with a very important step in the realization of his plan; a plan leading to create the first millionaire in the Barcelo lineage.

Keyed up, still reeling from the wallop of the home made drink, he phoned Emilie. After telling her the good news he took her to lunch. After lunch they walked the property line together; John felt that Emilie was becoming a part of his future. He enjoyed having Emilie admire his audacity. Narcissism on his part, but aren't most entrepreneurs looking to please the gallery?

While waiting for Johnny to pick her up, Emilie had told the good news to her father, trying to repeal the unfavorable opinion he had of her boy friend. Buying a piece of property that size was remarkable for a boy Johnny's age.

-I suppose this business is not as bad as it looks. - Said Paul Roy reluctantly. He had never seen a thousand dollars and would never hold that amount in his hands. He had been wired to accept life as it was dished out: at work before he was thirteen, underpaid and over worked, he had been slaving in one of the mills for over twenty years. After feeding the family, paying the rent, heating the place, there was nothing left. Emilie was now helping out with her salary but soon she would be married; that was the unwritten law; marry your girls as soon as possible. Paul Roy was an active member of the union and was beginning to realize that he had been duped by greedy individuals under covers of paternalism.

In this neck of the woods, everybody knew their neighbor's past. It turned out that Paul Roy knew Ed and proceeded to tell Emilie a very unusual story:

" Ed's father was made a widow when his wife gave birth to his first son. He never fully recovered from the loss of his wife of less than a year. Brokenhearted he sought refuge in the bottle and soon became a drunk.

From birth, Ed was raised by his mother's sister Suzanne, who treated him like her own.

When Ed turned ten, the still grieving and still drinking inconsolable widower, by now a full time spineless victim, decided that he wanted to have his son back. At ten a boy can help on the farm. Ed was broken hearted about this decision. He tried to convince his biological father to let him stay with Suzanne and continue going to school where he was doing very well; to no avail. Even the parish priest tried to intervene. That didn't help either. Ed's father was blaming heaven and the whole world for the loss of his bride.

Ed moved in with his father, and for the next six years was badly treated by this man he hardly knew; an authentic brute when drunk. Because he was drunk most of the time, Ed's life changed from being comfortable and homey to a continuous series of beatings and hardships.

When he was fourteen, Ed was given two German shepherd puppies by his aunt Suzanne; he raised them in one of the barns. His father ignored the dogs and let Ed keep them as there was more and more pilfering in the neighborhood; dogs were good deterrents against thieves.

Like most tormented kids, Ed became attached to his pets and spent all of his spare time with the puppies, training them to do just about anything he wanted. In the mean time the dogs were growing to impressive size.

One night, George, Ed's father, came home drunker than usual. Not finding his son in the house, he went out to the barn looking for him. There was a light filtering from under the closed door; peeping through a crack in the wall he saw Ed playing with the dogs and enjoying himself.

Without reasons, out of pure wickedness and in reprisal for the miseries in his own life, he could not tolerate that his son could have any kind of pleasure. His pickled neurons gave the order: The dogs had to be destroyed, immediately, that very moment. Hurrying back to the house he came back with his double barreled shot gun loaded with buck shot.

Kicking the door opened he came in reeling and screaming. Ed was used to these outbursts and without looking at his father ordered the dogs to sit. Nothing unusual about this scene, until he turned around and saw the shot gun leveled at the dogs and realized what his sick father was about to do. Without hesitation he stepped in the line of fire to protect his friends, still sitting as ordered, but by now, sensing the danger, emitting a deep threatening growl.

These dogs meant more than life to Ed. He was not going to see them killed by this madman. George had already started to squeeze the trigger as Ed was moving and the shot went off, some of the large pellets tearing Ed's shoulder. Ed was pushed backward by the impact.

Realizing that their master was in trouble, the dogs attacked before the sound of the deflagration had stopped vibrating the old planks of the barn. Without a sound, as was described by Ed during the inquest, they both jumped at George's throat and killed him almost instantly.

As was later graphically depicted by the coroner in his report with ghastly pictures to support: *"the throat was torn by long and sharp canine teeth. The victim bled to death in a few seconds, the carotid arteries and the jugular veins ripped out of his neck. The head was almost severed when the two dogs bit and pulled simultaneously on each sides of the emaciated neck. I refer to exhibits 1; 2; 3 and 4".*

During the few seconds it took for this tragedy to begin and end, Ed looked on, bleeding and numbed by the impact of the 12 gauge gunshot but content to have saved his friends' lives. He'll never know if he would have killed his old man. As it turned out the animals did the world a favor; Ed did not have to plead self defense for killing his father.

Bleeding profusely, the teen ager was able to walk to the nearest neighbor before losing consciousness. He had however taken the time to hide the dogs in a cave he had found by accident while hunting grouse the previous fall. A small opening sprouting about ten feet from the bottom of the ravine, expanded into a large gallery of about twenty by thirty feet with a height of ten feet. No one knew of this place and the entrance was well hidden by under growth. He brought enough food and water for a few days. Aunt Suzanne would take over feeding the animals until he came back if he was away longer than two days. –Don't tell anyone; they'll kill them.-

The judge ruled that a gunshot wound of the magnitude Ed had sustained prevented him from reacting quickly enough to save his father's life. No one really cared as Ed's predicament was known to the entire community. His father had become the kind of mad dog you dispose of before it bites and kills.

But, the judge decreed:

-The dogs have to be destroyed; that's the law. –

Ed was distressed, he would have done all this for nothing; the dogs would have been killed anyway. However, the story goes that the sheriff, after reassuring himself that the animals were not vicious, had destroyed two stray dogs instead of the two German shepherds, reasoning that man's best friends should not be punished for doing their duties. Nobody ever knew for sure about this ending because Ed maintained his version that he had been given two other dogs by his aunt Suzanne. "

-What a story, I feel sorry for the poor guy. No one deserves that kind of life. That's probably why he never married and started making his own booze. - Replied Johnny when told this tale.

They continued the visit of the property Emilie sharing Johnny's enthusiasm. On the way back to the car they stopped at the house. The cats came looking through the windows but no sign of Ed. The gray cat who had exited in a hurry through Johnny's legs that morning, was waiting for someone to open the door; it was not locked, the cat walked in.

-If he kept on drinking that stuff no wonder he's in no shape to come to the door.-

It was early afternoon and they drove randomly until they reached Ogunquit. The end of June, one of those superb days one uses as standard; sunny but not burning, breezy but not windy, warm but not hot.

They parked the car and Emilie removed her dress, emerging as a mermaid. Johnny had never noticed that she had a near perfect body. Ogling for a moment until she threw a handful of sand at him, he proceeded to take his jeans off. He also had his swimsuit under.

Less than perfect, Johnny's body was at its best when fully clad: skinny as a one inch nail, on the short side and balding at twenty, slightly humping back, chicken legs, bones sticking out where muscles should have been, all this covered with skin as white as milk, except for a farmer's tan.

Once over the initial shock, the most noticeable and striking body part was hanging between his scrawny thighs. Emilie was amazed and a little aroused at the sight of the bulge showing through his loose swim trunk. She had once read about a French painter, the degenerated son of a bourgeois family. Toulouse d'Autrec was deformed, hairy, had a large head, a large upper body, was short, skinny and bowlegged, but was endowed with such large reproductive organs that he was nicknamed « petit Priape » by the prostitutes and dancers he used as models. Emilie had looked up the description of the word Priape in a good dictionary owned by her teacher and found that Priape, son of Dionysus and Aphrodite was the god of fertility. The phallus was his symbol. It sure could apply to her guy who did not have much of anything else.

-I'll race you to the water my little Priape. - She said giggling, already ten feet away and digging her bare feet into the hot sand.

This little Priape was already a heavy smoker and his initial outburst lapsed into an agonizing finish fifty yards later. He slowed to a halt, puffing like ninety year old emphysematous Donna Hasting. Walking the rest of the way he continued to admire Emilie's athletic rear end until she entered the water with glorious splashing, yelling her pleasure at the feel of this invigorating cold water, typical of the coast of Maine. Except for a few bathers they were alone and soon were clinging to each other.

-I'm hooked and I hereby ask you to marry me Miss Emilie Roy.-

This was unexpected; they had known each other only three months and while the courting had been intense it was not customary to proceed so quickly. Johnny was physically the opposite of her dream husband. Emilie was conscious of her better than average good looks; some said she was beautiful, intelligent and lively.

She was astonished to hear her answer.

-Okay my man, but not before September. I've always wanted a fall wedding.-

She had agreed to enter into wed lock at nineteen years old. Her mother had beaten her by one year and like a good animal, early mornings to late nights, had served the cause of reproduction: kids to conceive, kids to dress, feed, clean. At night, dead tired she would have to spread her legs for her man, as directed by the Holy Church. Paul her husband did not know anything about the forty sixth verse of the Conjugal Catechism as prescribed by Balzac: *Each night must have its menu.* In all her years with this man the menu had always been equally bland.

Not because of anything she had done, one year she missed giving birth and the parish priest refused to let her have communion. She repented and soon became pregnant for the eleventh time in 14 years. Emilie was thirteen when this incident occurred and stopped believing that a god could be as stupid and misguided as to allow himself to be represented on earth by such vicious creature. Had he not been overly affectionate when she was last in line to go to confession; pawing at her budding breasts, his intentions as clear and evident as those of Uncle Adolph the previous year.

Running is often a girl's best defense. She ran out of the rectory leaving the frustrated priest with a far from abstinent organ in these same hands handing out god's corpus every morning. Still crying when she got home, her mother had silently sat with her until she told the story. After a few moments of heavy silence, she had taken her daughter in her arms and whispered:

-Nobody will or will want to believe you ....but I do, it happened to me when I was your age. You have to stay away from men in general, otherwise they will try to touch you.-

She had not been as nimble as Emilie and had been caught by a horny man of the cloth. May the devil burn this Pope for having decreed celibacy.

CHAPTER 9

"Greatness hovers close to failure."

The tire recycling site had been officially open for a few weeks and already there was a significant accumulation of scrap tires in the ravine. To the neighbors inquiring about his long term plans, Johnny had answered that after filling the ravine with various materials, he would build a large house. A large house would increase the value of all other properties on this road. But one of the neighbors was curious and having nothing better to do was mounting guard becoming suspicious about the quality of the filling material.

Smashing a mosquito as he raised his left arm to look at his watch, Johnny muttered his favorite four letter word. Almost ten and no sign of the very first truck load of scrap tires Isaac Weinstein was bringing in. Nine o'clock he had said. Coming from Milton Mass., south of Boston, Isaac thought that he would show up in West Bowdoin around nine on Monday night. It was Monday night and a little before ten. Johnny had phoned Isaac's home only to be told by Mrs. Weinstein that he had left the house at five o'clock and was on the way.

-I'll wait for him. Tell him if he phones. -

Mrs. Weinstein said that Isaac had to complete the load on the way and felt this was the cause of the delay. No sense travelling that distance with half a load. For a hundred dollars, Johnny would wait all night if he had to. Isaac's semi would contain twelve hundred tires if stacked correctly. Ten minutes later he heard the distinct sound of a large truck shifting gears. He stood in the middle of the entrance and waited for Isaac. –

-What took you so long, did you stop for a beer?-

Johnny had met Isaac some time ago, when caught red handed in the act of trying to snatch one of his customers, a large garage scrapping more than two hundred tires per week and paying good money for the service. Even though Johnny had offered to cut prices, the customer remained faithful to Isaac.

Realizing that he could not poach this customer he tried to sell Isaac instead by proposing to dispose of the scrap tires he collected. They had agreed on a price of one hundred dollars per truck load. Isaac was charging his customers twenty cents per tire. About twenty five percent of these used tires could be culled and sold at two dollars each. The deal was good all around.

Johnny had parked his pickup truck across the only entrance of the property. He knew, having often done it himself, that there is nothing easier than to enter a site, dump and leave without paying the tipping fee to the owner. His rule was payment up front.

Holding his opened hand to Isaac, Johnny stood firm in front of the over-heating truck.

-Cash up front as we agreed. - Said Johnny.

-I thought we'd unload first, have a beer and talk. - Isaac answered not unexpectedly.

-I wouldn't want you to think that I'm one of those trusting green horns easy to pluck. - Answered Johnny not budging an inch.

With a loud sigh, designed to draw tears, Isaac pulled out an envelope and handed it to Johnny.

-I had it prepared; you can trust me one hundred percent. - Isaac whined.

Up yours thought Johnny, I don't trust anyone any more than I expect to be trusted; even less if I'm told to be trusting. He pocketed the envelope without further verification, as Isaac intended. Locking eyes with the man, he understood the purpose of the whining. One hundred to one the amount in the envelope didn't come up to one hundred dollars. Taking the envelope out of his pocket and still looking at Isaac, he proceeded to open it. Hell the amount was right, five twenty dollar bills. Losing a bit of his composure Johnny began to apologize for being so careful when he detected a very faint glimmer of excitement in Isaacs's eyes. Something was not right, he could feel it.

Removing the five twenty dollar bills from the envelope a second time and feeling them between his thumb and index finger, he perceived a slight irregularity in the texture of the paper. A closer inspection over the truck's head light established that three of the bills were counterfeited: same serial number and a difference in the paper texture as compared to the other two.

During this inspection Isaac had played the offended virgin, telling Herb, a very large African American working for him, that this was the first time he had been treated so badly. The big guy was looking down, attempting to hide a grin.

-I don't think we want to do business with this man, - Isaac said. - we'll go back home with the load.-

Johnny knew the load would be dumped somewhere on the way back and that he would be blamed by the local cops. This time unjustly.

Isaac reached out and yanked the enveloped from Johnny's hands. The envelop was lighter; after his inspection, Johnny had replaced only the bogus bills, furtively appropriating the good ones.

Offering Isaac a way out, he said:

-You must have been fooled by one of your customers. You should be careful about counterfeit money. I hear that this sort of thing is current in the Boston and New York area. Just last week my banker educated me when I tried to deposit a false twenty with the same serial number as these. It was confiscated. I can't accept your load unless you pay the tipping fee as agreed. That's what you'd do.-

-No, I would trust you but never mind. Come on Herb we're leaving.-

Jack Madden, the snoop who lived in the cozy little house directly across the road was straining his eyes to see what was going on. His dog, a black Labrador was pulling at its leash, trying to get to his favorite pee stop. Seeing the intruder, Herb had gone back to the truck, signaling Madden's presence to Isaac. After a short conference, they left, gunning the motor in frustration and swearing at Barcelo.

On the way home Johnny phoned the state Troopers and reported that a white truck, bearing Mass plates was about to dump a large quantity of scrap tires in the Lewiston area. He also gave the probable routing. The morning after, he learned that the polluters had been caught with a smoking gun and jailed for the night. Isaac had to pay a fine of two hundred dollars and return with his full load.

While ratting was unusual for Barcelo, he felt perfectly justified in this case. He would have been blamed for the illegal dumping and Isaac knew it. A lesson had to be given to establish the rules early in the game. This bastard would know better than to try something like that again and, better still would tell everyone in the industry that Barcelo was a mean hombre. Odds were good that he would hear from Isaac again soon, if only to recuperate his two good twenty dollar bills. He would be expecting him this time even though he had not fared too badly for a first time.

CHAPTER 10

"Poverty to the poor, riches to the rich: that's the ultimate human justice."

Year 2000

In his hospital bed, more than fifty years after this incident, the now older, sicker but none the wiser Barcelo, was thinking that he had played poker with his life on that June evening. He had learned later that Isaac was part of the organized crime scene and Herb, the large African American riding shotgun, was his enforcer. He owed his salvation to Jack Madden walking his dog; this had saved him from sudden death.

Ratting and the substitution of the two good twenty dollar bills was an act of incongruous bravado that would brand him as a fearless entrepreneur, one to be reckoned with. But to drive this point home he had made a mortal enemy.

Recapping this incident, Johnny was rather proud of the manner he had conducted himself during the first act. His memory kept flashing back details of the second act which took place the next day: the sudden hot flush over his skin when Isaac pointed his nasty little revolver and the rest of the events which had sealed his destiny. All these images flashed through his mind with the speed of light and the perfection of a motion picture; more than fifty years ago and yet so vivid.

At this very moment a nurse came to inspect a catheter sticking out of his penis like a defective wire. She seemed happy that he had produced a small quantity of urine and congratulated him as a mother would a child having used the potty for the first time.

Dialysis would not be necessary at this time but the nephrologist had asked for a complete evaluation of Barcelo's residual kidney function. Johnny knew about dialysis, a friend of his had been treated: three times per week, five hour procedure, a severe diet, no energy, no fun and not worth it.

-No- he had thought, -dialysis will not be my contribution to the medical profession but who knows, let's keep all options opened for now.

The nurse replaced the blanket over the skeletal body. Some of the cadavers released from Auswich were in better condition. Retreating in a merciful slumber, John had a dream of scrap tires burning for weeks and spewing black acrid smoke all over the Lewiston-Auburn area, polluting the coast for several miles with dirty black ash. He kept trying to escape his mobile home but the door was jammed closed by Jim Barker, the Department of Environmental Protection agent who had contributed the most to his tribulations with the State of Maine.

The flames were getting closer to the methane tank. In a state of panic, unable to breath, he woke up in a sweat, yelling and screaming obscenities at Barker and at the judge who had put him in that jail for three months. Alerted, the nurse rushed in and injected a yellowish fluid into the intravenous line connected to his arm.

-You'll sleep now -. And she walked out of the room casually swinging her well proportioned lower back as if life was wonderful. Just a job for her, completely detached, efficient and cool.

Slowly, Barcelo sank back into his past. His last image of the nurse walking away, brought back the memory of Emilie, his first wife, the only one he had really loved; as much as he had been capable of this emotion. The other six were nothing but incidents in his troubled existence.

In September 1953 they were married. Emilie had opted for the 15th of September. During the previous month, she had had a sumptuous, almost regal gown made by the best dressmaker in town. She had carefully picked the material and whatever else needed to match. Johnny had offered to pay but she had refused, almost insulted by the offer. Never would he have a better assistant, she could be trusted and possessed a sort of survival intuition, not taught in business schools. In fact, so intuitive that the day before the marriage she had told Johnny:

-We'll give it a shot but frankly I doubt if you'll be able to remain satisfied with only one wife. You should join a polygamous sect. - And she had left him to mull this thought over.

Almost fifty years later he could see in detail the cozy little house she had rented. A well manicured lawn and a garden fenced in with cedar posts setting the stage for a rustic but handsome cottage. Made of squared pine timbers, the outside texture was weather tinted several shades of gray and green, the slate roof, showing signs of wear and tear was in need of repair but the perfect complement. On the east side, the Mac Namees, an older couple, whittling the last years away by covering each square inch of their property with flowers and shrubs; the autumn flowers were in full bloom and the spectacle presented was out of a Manet painting.

A gurgling brook formed the western boundary. Trout could be seen jumping at flies during the summer months; the creek giving the property a soul of its own. Barcelo could still hear the babbling of the water bouncing around stones and rocks on its way to the Ocean, barely thirty miles away.

The interior was spacious enough for two, maybe three persons: a large living room kitchen area with a bay window opening on the brook and featuring one of the largest fire place Johnny had ever seen. The fire place was the only vestige of a larger house which had burned several years ago. The actual cottage had been built around this magnificent, one hundred and twenty year old walk-in fire place; the surface of the entire first floor also made with the original boards salvaged from the old structure. The ceiling, unusually high, was supported by a cubic foot cedar beam. The walls made of thick maple planks and polished with bee wax were worthy of a place in a good museum.

Emilie had heard about this gem from one of her old aunts, a friend of the owners, an old couple getting on in age and choosing to move closer to medical and church services; the Maine winters could be severe for older people. They had refused to sell the place being emotionally attached to it but had promised to give Emilie a right of first refusal should they change their mind.

The second floor was accessed by a wooden stairway opening on a passage leading to three doors: the bathroom and two bedrooms. Spacious enough, the main bedroom featured two large windows overlooking the meandering brook and the edge of the forest with its large mature white pine trees. A canopied bed polarized the attention, and was matched by a weathered oak dresser, both authentic antiques dating back two hundred years. He remembered not being enthusiastic about old stuff, but if Emilie liked it that was good enough for him.

The other room was smaller and more the size of a baby's room; unfurnished for the moment Johnny could not help but feel moved when he entered it for the first time. Hell, he John Barcelo might have kids; unbelievable, he felt sorry that neither one of his parents would be around to play grandparents and spoil the brat. He had wondered what Henrietta would have thought about becoming an aunt. After the tough and exacting lives his parents had endured, he would have enjoyed playing Santa Claus during their old age.

To complete the picture there was a large dog house attached to the cottage; the dog house was a smaller version of the entire cottage, minus the fire place and the baldachin bed. Neither Johnny nor Emilie knew the first thing about dogs, their parents having had enough trouble to feed the kids, let alone feeding a dog. He knew exactly who could best advise him about dogs. His neighbor Ed had been a perfect dog trainer.

There was a glitch in his dream; a sad event in his life, one more and as always, of his doing. He could see the determination on Emilie's face when she had asked him to leave.

-I give up, you'll never be able to subdue this restlessness, and it will always consume you. I'm not willing to endure and suffer until you become old enough to understand some basic facts.-

Brokenhearted, yet relieved, he had packed his stuff and left Emilie and his dog Paw. He had been the happiest he would ever be. If the nurse had been passing by she would have seen tears gushing out of his eyes. Emilie would later buy the –*cottage on the brook*- and remarry. She was now a widow.

Maybe the tears and sweat covering his emaciated cheeks prompted him to think about this first marriage. It was raining cats and dogs; that part was the only unpredictable element and the ever optimistic Emilie decided that it might be a good omen for the life of the marriage. – can't trust these omens.- Her beautiful gown got all wet, while Johnny splashed mud on his shiny shoes and gray woolen trousers; but all in all everyone, including Isaac and his wife Rebecca, had had a hell of a time until early Sunday morning, dancing, eating and drinking on Johnny's tab.

The honeymoon, which had been planned to last two weeks, lasted less than one. The Poconos were silent witness to Johnny's restlessness; being away from his business for so long was a cause of great concern. He had drilled Dudley who was by now an old trooper. However, like most entrepreneurs, Johnny had difficulty delegating. He had confidence that Dudley would deal perfectly with routine business; anything out of the ordinary would be a problem. After five days Émilie said:

-Hey, let's get back home. Your head is already there, we may as well get your ass to join it.-

Gratefully he agreed and they left that afternoon arriving home early the next morning. Honeymoons are fine if you don't have anything better to do and can learn to relax. Emilie was perfect and he was great, but all in all, having never been idle for more than a fortnight, neither one of them felt comfortable about getting up to enjoy each other and looking at mountains all day until they went to bed, bloated with too much food.

Then he felt the freshness of the first snow, early that fall and with it, the volume of scrap tires doubled, car owners replacing summer tires with snow tires. Business had never been so good and his married life was as smooth as Emilie's inner thighs. Ed, their recluse neighbor, who had been grateful but had nevertheless refused the invitation to the wedding, offered, as a wedding gift, a four month old German shepherd with paws as large as Johnny's wrist. According to Ed, this was a sign that the dog would be large.

Most mornings, sleeping the profound slumber of a hard working man, he would be smothered by the large dog jumping on the baldachin bed to wake his masters. This little wolf became their constant companion, coming to work with them every morning. The Barcelo BRE Inc became his territory, his property, his private play ground. This is where he peed on his first tire and where he became acquainted with the deer's and other animals criss crossing the property. As Dudley did not have time to hunt let alone poach, the twenty two acres had become a refuge for wild life. Paw would not allow any other male dogs to visit; females were welcome.

Then Johnny's mind went fuzzy, nothing but pink fog wrapped around him like a shroud while the old maple tree was flaunting its thick branches at him. He could hear Madden calling his dog.

—— CHAPTER 11 ——————————

"Ungibus et rostro."
"By hook or by crook."

Back in 1950

An opportunistic predator, Isaac Weinstein had always been able to devour any prey caught in his web. The name of his game was money; making money dealing with scrap of any kind. Recognizing Barcelo's business full potential did not require him to be an economist graduated from Oxford.

In 1950, the state of Maine provided the right environment for this offbeat, soon to become illegal, project of amassing large quantities of scrap tires under the pretext of disposing of them. He could see where the legislators would be busy fixing other more politically-in projects and would be lenient and complacent about finding a solution for a problem being merely potential. -If it ain't broke don't fix it - sort of attitude.

Like a cuckoo, Isaac had taken over his present scrap business when Bruce, the then owner, could not repay his gambling debts; once a cuckoo bird always a cuckoo. He wanted Barcelo's dump site and would get it, by hooks or by crooks.

As soon as he arrived home on that Tuesday afternoon after spending the night in jail, he phoned Johnny and, admitting his defeat to better win the second round, congratulated him for his brilliant performance. Isaac was a smart operator, smarter than would appear after this first confrontation; he had underrated Barcelo and would not do that again. Who could expect this runt, furthermore a Portuguese and a Mainer, to be so astute. His strategy would have fooled most people he knew: dump before paying, then argue about the price, and finally pay with two good bills and three bad ones in a sealed envelope. The really dreadful finale of this caper, was that not only he had, the smart ass Bostonian, been skinned of two good bills but had also been taken by the state troopers, undoubtedly alerted by Barcelo. The fine of two hundred dollars was the cherry on the Sundae. But that he had had to re-load the truck, because the hidden troopers had sadistically waited for the last tires to be thrown out of the truck to make the arrest, was the last straw.

Hats off to the little bastard Portuguese; revenge would only be sweeter, but in the mean time he had to be smart. Should it be known, his associates would laugh him out of town; Herb was the only witness to this incident and would keep quiet if the tables were turned on Barcelo. Even though Herb was not known for his sense of humor, he had been exhibiting a smug smile ever since.

Never be proud when you have a job to do; so he would crawl back and start again. Staying close to the target is the best way to hit it. Biting his tongue and with tears of anger blurring his vision, he picked up the phone and dialed Barcelo's number:

-Johnny my friend –, the word friend didn't have any meaning or value for him, - you're the winner of the first round. I have learned my lesson and you pass the exam with high marks. Now -, he continued not waiting for a reply – as you know, I still have to get rid of that load and would like to start fresh, - after a moment of hesitation waiting for an answer from Barcelo who kept quiet, he continued, - tonight at the same time. Everything will be kosher-.

Sooner than I thought, reflected Johnny, but why not, this abscess will have to be lanced. The thought of not doing business with this crook occurred to Johnny, but he needed the business and Isaac could deliver. Sooner or later he would have to mix it up with the big boys. Nothing ventured nothing gained; furthermore, and this was the real motivation, there was this need to continually exceed his limit, to go over the edge, to play with danger.

-OK, you know the rules. You can send business my way and I'm not against giving you a commission on referrals. We can talk about this tonight. There won't be any one here to help you unload. This big guy should come as well.-

Isaac had intended to take Herb along but for a different purpose. Dudley was sitting across from Johnny who had just finished amusing him with the details of the previous night's caper. Dudley was slapping his big thighs, still laughing so hard that Isaac heard him.

-Hope you're not doing anything important tonight, Dud. You'll need to be with me for most of the night. -said John. -Bring your Marlin, one never knows with these city slickers. The Negro is as mean and as large as you; he'll be in the ring.-

The Barcelo Recycling Enterprise, (BRE Inc) as he now called his dump site, was protected from intruders and inquisitive neighbors by an eight foot fence. It had cost an arm and a leg but did a great job in preventing jobbers from dumping tires at night without paying the tipping fee.

That night, after a light meal, Johnny and Dudley drove into the yard of the BRE Inc at about eight. The weather was acting up. The July sky which should have been the stage for a great sunset was as dark as the soul of Genghis Kan. Lightning was crisscrossing this dark canvass as ominous clouds charged in blindly, accompanied by the rumbling of thunder too close for comfort and getting closer. The mosquitoes sensing the presence of warm bodies, were lining up for the last supper.

A little shack which Johnny called his head quarter, had been built close to the entrance. Painted a light green with white trim, it gave the scene an innocent ecological look. From its single window, one could watch the front gate which was the only access to the property. This is where Johnny planned to have a private discussion with Isaac.

On the opposite side, about fifty yards away, an old poacher's blind was sitting in a two hundred year old maple tree. Some fifteen feet from the ground, it allowed a commanding view of the entire area including the BRE's head quarters. Branches and new leaves had grown back, concealing it perfectly while not preventing the person sitting comfortably in it from overseeing the scene.

-Do you think you can hide in the old blind; I climbed up yesterday and found the platform still very sound. Once up there keep me in your sight at all times. – he stopped for a moment to make sure Dud had understood the importance of the words -at all times- and repeated it, - I don' t trust this guy farther than old man Gus' prostate will allow him to pee, and I wouldn't be surprised if he tried something other than passing bogus bills. He would have done me in last night, if Jack Madden had not walked his dog. My friend Joe the state trooper, told me to be careful with these people. Isaac is a dangerous animal, never been caught but never far away from the murder scene. The big colored guy is a known criminal and was jailed for aggravated assaults and other niceties.-

-If you can manage to always stay clear of the big guy and keep the place lighted, I can pluck both bastards as easily as I would a deer. But what if it rains and you guys go inside the shack?- Remarked Dudley.

-If we move into the shack, follow us and hide behind the cabin, the walls are so thin that you'll be able to follow the action from there. If at any time I mention the words - For god's sake-, move in, ready to fire that rifle of yours.-

This is why that evening, Dudley was carrying his lever action Marlin, a .35 caliber rifle. Loaded with 200 g soft point bullets, it would explode the brain of a black bear at three hundred yards. Hunting and poaching since early youth, Dudley was able to hit any target from a reasonable distance. With six bullets, five in the magazine and one in the chamber, the fire power should suffice for most emergencies.

Reaching behind the seat of the truck, Johnny removed his sawed-off double barreled shotgun loaded with buck shots. He decided to hang it from a branch sprouting behind another smaller maple tree, mid way between the gate and the shack. Moving out of sight and yanking the gun loose would take a second. Better to be prepared than sorry.

The adrenaline already flowing, they both had the premonition that this July evening would bring excitement other than that of being eaten alive by hungry mosquitoes. The storm settling in would provide a perfect background for the stage; might even cover some of the noise.

Ten minutes later, between the rumbles of two thunder claps, they heard Isaac's truck reluctantly climbing Post office hill about two miles away. Dudley scrambled up the ladder and settled in the blind. He introduced a cartridge into the chamber and released the safety before training his rifle at the gate. Johnny continued to quietly smoke his cigarette realizing that contrary to popular belief, the mosquitoes were not bothered in the least by the smoke. Enjoying it was more like it.

Nine o'clock, low ceiling helping, it was almost dark, lightning's momentarily illuminating the scene from time to time. The old white truck squeaked to a stop at the gate and both Isaac and Herb stepped out of the cabin as it started to rain.

-Great weather for mosquitoes -. Sang Isaac with his Bostonian accent, as he slapped the back of his neck with a vengeance. Pulling up his shirt collar he strode in Johnny's direction.

Herb the wrestler, stayed behind having a private fight with several of the little winged cannibals, favorably impressed by the size of the dinner offered.

-Let's get going before the sky opens up.- Said Isaac as he counted five crisp twenty dollar bills in Johnny's open palm who in turn pocketed them without any further verification; these would be legit.

Johnny pointed out the direction and Isaac crawled back into the cab while Herb continued on foot; backing the trailer carefully as close to the edge as possible, they both started heaving the tires out in the ravine.

Maybe Johnny had done too much about nothing. Smoking another cigarette, he could see the blind from where he stood and while he would normally have volunteered to help out he stood there enjoying the feeling of earning one hundred dollars while others were working.

He yelled at Isaac:

-Let's have a chat when you're done with this.-

Walking towards the venerable maple tree he looked up but could barely make out the poachers' stand. The rain had stopped and he stood at a forty five degree angle from Dudley's perch. The twilight had been replaced by complete darkness and the flood lights at the entrance were diffusing a yellowish light on the scene, giving an appropriate theatrical color to the stage. Act one had been played, let's see if the second one would be as easy.

The truck coughed up and started pulling the now empty trailer. It stopped at the gate and Isaac came out.

-You want to talk. ..Good...I also have something to tell you. –

Except for the dark rings under his eyes, his face, gleaming with sweat, was almost incandescent under the yellow light; a wide grin was baring yellowish teeth. His hands in his pockets, he strolled towards Johnny. As he got nearer, he nonchalantly pulled out a small revolver, keeping it pointed to the ground.

-Are you going to kill me.? Asked Johnny.

-Depends on your response to my offer. - Answered Isaac, moving awkwardly from one leg to the other.

-And what is your offer. One that I can't refuse I suppose. - Quipped Johnny, enjoying the situation, having outguessed this snobbish and arrogant Bostonian.

-I won't beat around the bush. My associates and I want to take your business over. We're prepared to pay you very good money for this little piece of land.-

-Holding a gun to my head is hardly a civilized way to negotiate a business deal .... I have grown very attached to this little piece of land as you put it and I don't think you're going to offer enough,.... but go ahead.-

-Over and above the forty dollars you stole from me last night, you will receive a five thousand dollar dumping credit...And you get to stay alive as a bonus. - Replied Isaac as he leveled his gun.

Out of the corner of his eyes, Johnny had seen Herb sliding out of the truck, also holding a gun in his right hand.

Barcelo's shotgun was just a few yards away but he couldn't get to it unless Isaac got distracted; very little time to make a decision. He moved closer to the tree and as if talking to Isaac:

-No matter what I say or accept, you'll kill me anyway. Your body guard doesn't trust you to do the job correctly and is coming out to help .....I'm sure that only one of you is sufficient to kill a little fart like me. - And raising his voice one full key, as if to be heard by God, he continued:

-I'll ask God to take that big ape out of the picture.... Now. -

God was attentive to the supplication of his beloved Johnny because not a second after the last syllable had been pronounced there was a deafening detonation just above their heads. Big Herb was hurled back against the truck before falling to the ground clutching his right shoulder.

« Clic clac » the sharp metallic cranking sound, broke the silence which followed the ear shattering bang; Dudley was reloading, ejecting the spent cartridge, replacing it with a brand new one.

Taking advantage of the surprise, Johnny had sidestepped behind the tree, reached up and pulled hard at the shotgun dangling from a string just strong enough to hold it. He came around the other side of the tree crouching on one knee aiming at Isaac's mid section.

-You're dumber than I thought, you must be used to dealing with lobotomized monkeys. Just in case you're thinking of using that pea shooter, let me tell you that a rifle is pointed at your head and I would only be too happy to have to defend my life by gutting you out with this toy called a Lupa...., it's loaded with buck shots.... What will it be, you have one second before we both start dismembering your carcass.-

Out of his mind with fright, Isaac could see Herb struggling to get up, bleeding profusely from his right shoulder, grimacing with pain; there would be no help from him. Not even certain that he could retrain his side arm at Johnny before being hit by both shooters. Knowing he was beaten, he let his gun fall to the ground before raising his shaking hands.

Barcelo stepped up to Weinstein and kicked the revolver away from him.

-Now let's talk while Dudley finishes the job and gets rid of the corpse..... Maybe you would like to watch. Yes... I think you should see what we do to smart asses like you.-

-But, muttered Isaac, Herb is not dead. He needs a doctor....-

During this interlude Dudley had climbed down from the blind and was moving quickly towards Herb. The big guy was in a bad shape: blood gushing out, a major artery severed by the mushrooming impact of the 35 soft hollow point bullet; his right shoulder was completely shattered, his arm dangling like a silk scarf.

-You're right, he's not dead yet but we'll fix that. – Then to Dudley - As we planned Dud. Bring him behind and do what you have to do.-

Isaac was dumbfounded and could not utter another word, his brain turned to mush. He had peed in his pants and was shaking like a drunk in need of a drink.

Some toughie thought Johnny, a very thin coating of varnish, no guts. He was starting to feel the whiplash of the adrenaline in his body. Several more times in his life would he experience this harsh metallic taste in his mouth; the first time had been when he had realized that Henrietta would never breath again, the second when he had taken on Dudley. Several deep breaths calmed his nerves and he could again speak normally.

-We've acted in self defense. We could call the cops, with the records you both have...., but why bother. We'll save the state the expense of pros-ecution..., but we'll make sure justice is served. - Looking carefully at Herb he continued. - Herb is beyond saving and wouldn't have made it more than another five minutes anyway.-

The blood was now spurting in diminishing jets as the big heart was performing its last routine. Dudley got behind the big black man and grabbing him by the belt, pushed him a few feet behind the maple tree where there was a large drum half full with used motor oil. When he was within a few feet of the gaping container, he suddenly released the belt and with the palm of his hand landed a hard blow to the back of the head. Stunned, the big guy fell forward and had to support himself on top of the drum with his left hand, the right arm trailing and useless. Dudley had retrieved the Smith and Wesson 44 caliber Herbert had planned to waste Johnny with; raising it he squeezed the trigger, exploding the massive cranium.

As Herbert was falling head first into the drum, Dudley tilted the legs upward and stuffed the large body into it. Throwing the gun after its owner he replaced the lid and secured the closing ring. Looking up for the first time, Dudley was not overly surprised to see Isaac vomiting his last meal: spaghetti by the looks of it.

Johnny had held Isaac's head so that he would not miss a second of the third act. He released him when he feared being splashed with vomit. Dudley was now rolling the drum towards the ravine and soon they heard a muffled thud as it rolled and bounced on the tires at the bottom of the ravine, some hundred feet below.

-We have another one; it's now up to you. Let's go to the shack and have a conversation about your immediate future. - Said Johnny.

Pushing Isaac ahead of him, they reached the shack where Johnny ordered his prisoner to sit down. Dudley arrived soon after.

-The drum didn't burst open did it? - Asked Johnny more to break the silence than to reassure himself.

He could tell by the sound, that the lid had held and that no odor would percolate from the oil. Herb would be well preserved for generations to come, and some day a paleontologists would unearth a perfectly pre-served specimen.

-No, the lid held. There were enough tires at the bottom to cushion the fall. Hey, I have another one if you want to use it for this little one. –

Even though they had not rehearsed, that last piece of information did wonders to facilitate the outcome of act four.

-We'll see. – Replied Johnny. Then to Isaac,

-Sit down and don't try anything funny. Dudley will be behind you during this conversation and you know what he's capable of. Empty your pockets.-

Isaac did as he was told. The inventory showed a wad of bogus bills, and another one, smaller, of real ones, a switch blade, driving permit, truck registration, some pictures of his family and finally a little black address book which Johnny grabbed and started to read with attention.

-I'll keep this until we see each other again...... if you live. - He pocketed the address book.

He gave Isaac all his other possessions including the cash and the switch blade. Dudley made a sound when the real bills were handed over.

-We don't want to rob this guy Dud. We want to do business with him. You'll be well paid for the over time you're putting in tonight.-

Looking at Isaac, who by now had understood that he could survive his failed coup, Johnny lit a cigarette and threw the pack to his guest.

-Here's the deal, and I may as well tell you now, you don't have any more choice than I had.... First, nobody should ever try to fuck with me again. The next time I have the faintest inkling that you or someone else from your group is preparing to pull a fast one, you're dead. I know where you live and now, -taking the little black address book out of his pocket-, I think I know where your partners live. Secondly, you'll bring all your scrap tire business to this site. I'll give you a 20% discount on yours and a 10% commission on all others you'll bring in. - He paused to make sure Isaac understood.

-Do you understand or do I need to repeat? – Isaac nodded that he understood and Johnny kept on.

-You'll sign a confession where you admit having killed Herb with his own gun. I'll keep this confession and use it only if you are dishonest and stupid with me again.-

Looking at a picture retrieved from the wallet, he continued.

-I have no intention of hurting your daughter or any member of your family, but I swear that if you double cross me, you'll be tortured for several days before you die. Herb's death was strictly business, he'd have died anyway and taking him to the hospital would only have been embarrassing and useless. Yours, however, would be to drive a point home. You're free to leave after you write the confession. -

Johnny had never spoken so much. Reaching in the only drawer of the little table separating him from Isaac, he pulled out a bottle of Southern Comfort and three glasses; he poured generously and raised his glass in a toast to Isaac.

-To your health or to your death. Your choice.-

Isaac, who needed that drink more than oxygen, grabbed his and gulped down the content. Dudley refused his and placed it in front of Isaac.

Killing Isaac would have been a useless act of revenge, very unlike the business approach Johnny wanted to favor. Isaac controlled a large portion of the Boston area scrap tire collection and while he would continue to be dangerous, he would no longer be unpredictable. Better to work with a devil you know.

The clincher would be the commissions paid on business brought by Isaac; he could easily make an income of six figures; much more than he would have been able to keep for himself in the first scenario, his partners undoubtedly would have taken the lion's share.

Pouring another glass for Isaac he proceeded to illustrate to him the potential revenue of their new association. Coming from the dead into paradise was about the feeling experienced by the little fellow. Two hours later, fairly drunk, the bottle empty, Isaac had written the confession as dictated by Johnny and was on his way back home; the passenger seat empty.

Herb would not be missed by anyone other than his mother. Having a nasty temper, he had managed to fight with all the members of his family and his friends; they had nicknamed him -the Tasmanian devil- and the name was well suited. However, the following morning Johnny went down the ravine and tying a strong rope around the steel drum, loaded it into his pickup truck and drove to the far end of the site, where he buried it in a very deep grave. Playing safe is always better for peace of mind, less stress.

When retrieving the drum he had seen the entrance of the cave where Ed, the former owner, had hidden his dogs during the inquest following the death of his father. Later on that day he came back for a closer look. Who has not dreamed of owning his own private and secret cavern?

As it turned out the very speculative business deal struck with Isaac started paying dividends a few days later; from that moment on a steady procession of trucks and trailers filled the ravine and Johnny's pocket. Of course Isaac got paid handsomely upon delivery; he too felt that the deal had been advantageous for him even though not of the kind one boasts about to his friends or associates.

CHAPTER 12

As reliable as sunrise, the daily routine was getting to a sloppy start in the Lewiston General Hospital. So far Barcelo had been successful in postponing the inevitable and was regaining enough of his dwindling health to resume his futile existence. The will to live was gone, no real interest other than this animal instinct men have to fight off and postpone the ugly end.

A nurse craned her neck around the half closed door of his room.

-Mister Barcelo, a lieutenant Paterson came last evening while you were sleeping. He said he'd be back today. - Said the cute nurse. She continued.- Would you like to see a priest Mister Barcelo? - Her name tag read Jennifer King, a psychiatric nurse.

The top nun of this very Christian hospital was of the opinion that the patient in room 512 was not really on the ball and might need some counseling. Nurse King had been trying to make sense out of Barcelo's ramblings. She had enlarged her portfolio of experience but could not help her patient very much. Her report read: -"patient intelligent but amoral".-

-A priest...?. I don't want to see a priest unless I'm going to die. Do you know something I don't? And even then....what good would it do. - Was patient 512's reply.

-Every one dies one day Mister Barcelo and you might want to go to confession. I heard that you have not always been a good Christian. - Was the reply.

Cute but a pain and a busy body as a bonus, thought patient 512. On second thought, why not see a priest; it could help pass the time of day. Hospitals were so boring during the day, at night it was another story, there was always someone to wake you up for this or that and interfere with the greatest healer: sleep.

-Rest, I need rest, not another fucking tube up my penis or a needle in my veins. - He had told the pre-dawn Nightingale.

Nothing doing, she had done her thing and been unnecessarily brutal to punish him for his bad choice of words. Ogling Jennifer's glorious shape, partly hidden but discernible to the trained eye, he said in his best imitation of Perry Mason:

-Confidence for confidence, I heard that you have also been a rather wild female. You have a reputation in this hospital. – Joshed Johnny, going fishing with the assumption that such a pretty nurse must indeed have had a glorious past and a turbulent present.

The nurse blushed; the old fart had hit a nerve. Noticing the sudden rosy tint flooding her cheeks, he smiled and continued.

-Okay, I'll see this priest friend of yours, but only to chat a little, none of the last rites or confession, I'm allergic to anything that's holy or oily. The last time I ran into a priest was in jail and only because that was the only way I could smoke.-

Conscious that she had blushed like a school girl, nurse King was debating whether she should retaliate or brush it off as the rambling of an old fox fishing and fencing.

-You're a wicked man; the kind I love. Too bad you're so old and tired. - She returned the ogling, slowly inspecting the puny shape hardly showing under the white blanket.

The morning after, around ten, a tall, portly man of about fifty five, waltzed into room 512 and cheerfully shook his hand as if trying to break it.

-Easy on the hand father, I'm a sick man.-

-My name is Father Donnelly, Tim to you. I've known of you since 1951. I was one of the choir boys at your wedding. I still remember that day as if it were yesterday; the tip of one whole dollar you had given us was the largest we had ever received from any one. Even the Mac Farlane son had not been as generous.-

Johnny looked at him carefully to make sure he was not edging to extract a confession; there must be brownie points as a bonus for salvaging a lost soul of his caliber. This priest looked genuine enough and his age jived with the year of his first wedding. To shock him a little he mentioned the fact that he had married six more times since and had sired 27 male heirs.

-I know about this too. I'll admit being envious of guys like you. Celibacy has not always been the easiest part of my job. Why some fruity pope decided that we should masturbate rather than copulate is still an unanswered question. The tragedy is that several of my colleagues are finding sexual gratification fondling young adults and even kids. -

What do you do when someone admits that his adult life has been a nightmare? At least Johnny's had been mostly fun, certainly hectic and different. True, some of it, and he could hardly remember the details … had been hellish as well. If the good father had wanted to break the ice he had succeeded.

-Ok you pass the test, - said Johnny, - have a seat, we can smoke a cigarette or two, I have the time it seems, nothing but time. -

Donnelly sat down and peeled off his jacket, revealing all the signs of a person addicted to good living. Probably as incarcerated in his chosen profession as Johnny was in this room; most likely convinced, several years ago that he had the -vocation-, chosen by God himself. Once in, he had courageously, even stoically accepted to bend to his sacred destiny against all his natural instincts: no sex, no money no future and generally no fun. Some of his friends and colleagues could enter into some trance-like state of spirituality and really believe in their faith or was it fate; he had tried, to no avail.

Thirty years or so later, finally realizing that Shakespeare had hit it on the head when he said: -"Conscience makes cowards of us all. "-, he felt cheated and sorry for his wasted life. The worst was that this ordeal would not end any time soon, his health had never been better. Now that he was fully aware of his misguided decision, would he have the courage to put an end to this simulation?

Tim Donnelly could have been a doctor, a lawyer or a sturdy farmer, a factory worker, a cab driver or a cook in a greasy spoon; he could have been a husband to a lovely wife and the father to a bunch of kids. Questions, doubts had been permeating his universe. Close scrutiny and an erudite skepticism had destroyed his faith. He no longer believed that there was a god or a paradise or an afterlife. He could not identify any valid reason for having spoiled the only life he would ever have. As it was, he spent it listening to the confessions of pseudo sins, committed against dogmas as unbelievable as the decision he had made and stuck to against his better judgment.

On several occasions, the first one barely a few months after entering the seminary, he had doubted and come to realize that he was making a monumental blunder. But he had stuck tenaciously, or was it cowardly to his vocation, not listening to reason, frightened by the ostracism which would have tracked and haunted him throughout his life had he dared to bail out. Now he realized, had realized for some time that he had squandered his destiny on an illusion, totally devoid of substance.

His bright eyes squarely on Johnny's, he pulled out a pack of cigarettes and offered one. Then out of nowhere he produced a small vial which was not filled with holy water. Reaching over, he snatched one of the plastic cups on the table, poured a measure of an amber colored liquid into it and offered it to Barcelo.

-Not what the doctor would prescribe but guaranteed to cheer you up better than the word of God would.-

He then proceeded to pull at the vial and probably emptied it by the nostalgic sound it made.

-Here's looking at you father; I don't know why this cute nurse waited so long to bring you over. - And he drained his plastic cup. Scotch, and a good one; too bad the vial was empty.

-If you're not here to read the bible ... why are you spending time with me rather than with some more deserving souls. - Teased Johnny.

Getting rid of his roman neck tie, Tim Donnelly breathed in slowly as if to start a long speech.

-Lewiston is a small village and it has been easy to follow your life since your first wedding. Don't ever forget that priests are people watchers. I have found your life to be most interesting. Of course some of it was dramatic even pathetic: like your bout with alcoholism, your stay in prison and also the porno movie caper with your last wife but, all in all it was an interesting life for a guy emerging from the ass hole of this earth. You had as much chance of being a success in life as a ring worm inside the gut of a dying dog ... Yet, you turned this shitty- potential into..., not a saintly but interesting life; as interesting as any life I can think of. Congratulations. -

Johnny had been told exactly the contrary by the judge. It took him a while to reply but there was no hurry; in a hospital room, one on one, you don't have to reply before you are ready, not fearing that someone will cut you off and change the subject before you are finished thinking out your answer.

This time, Barcelo could not come up with smart remarks or answers. He was programmed to attack and defend; could always take criticism but was not used to being congratulated; did not know how to react; was not sure this smart ass was not joking.

Yes he thought, this is one of the few episodes in my life where I am thunderstruck. Should he give this man of God the benefit of the doubt? Funny thing happens when you try to concoct a smart answer, after a while your mind goes blank. To break the silence he said the first thing that came up. Priests made him think of death, his mother, his sister, his father. Death, this real purpose of life, was a topic he had been mulling over and reading about a lot during his life and more so lately.

-If I was a believer I'd say that you're sent by God. I've been looking for a person like you. Maybe you can answer some of the questions I have. We met just a few minutes ago, but I feel that I have known you since my childhood. Who knows we may be ring worm brothers feasting away at the same dying dog's gut. - Johnny had appreciated the analogy.

-My childhood was pretty much like yours, a good Irish catholic father, drinking his way to an early grave and a devoted mother, who toiled and worked to get my ass educated. Not much difference except that my mother had decided that I would be educated. - Answered Tim.

He was an only child; the father had died early and had preferred drinking to fornicating. His mother joked about his father's pickled testicles. Something good out of something bad...

-Well, - continued Johnny, -this question of mine is not very original. You must have had, and maybe still have the same one. When you're young and strong, superman is your brother, dying being far down the list of your worries. As one gets older, Kryptonium becomes scarce and running out of the stuff a real danger.... I lost my superman cape father Tim. –

A ``code blue`` alarm sounded and they heard hurried footsteps. Someone was missing a heart beat or two thought Barcelo. He continued.

-Also had more time to read and think, more time to separate facts from fiction. Finally, I arrived at a stage where I need to make some sense out of God, death, paradise, hell. Where do religions fit into this riddle? -

Tim was annoyed by the question; visiting Barcelo had been motivated by sadistic curiosity: how would a dare devil like Barcelo die. For priests, people are fish in a bowl and he wanted to see how this fish would play out its last chapter. Would he be brave or frightened? As the Padre of the hospital he had access to the patients' medical chart. He had read Barcelo's and was impressed with the number of ailments this man had accumulated. He decided to give a convoluted answer, one of his specialties.

-Man has been trying to find an answer to this question ever since he descended from the trees: knowledge...you're looking for knowledge and the wisdom to understand it. You know what they say about knowledge: the smarter one gets, the unhappy he'll be and those who increase their knowledge also increase this melancholic gloom that the French call -mal de vivre-. Why do you think man has always preferred poesy to facts; anything but the bare truth. Sometimes it's better to leave these questions unanswered. ....you know, - to leave well enough alone- sort of thing. Believe me John Barcelo, if knowledge increases your freedom or the perception you may have of the word, it doesn't foster happiness or peace of mind. Knowledge only provides more choices, more reason behind your choice. Then you have to deal with the consequences. - Sighed the good father who had been addressing this very same question for the last forty years.

Tim had reviewed his faith and restored religion in a context more suited to his state of mind. He kept thinking about this verse in the bible when Jesus said that: -*Blessed is the innocent because he will have access to my kingdom*-. Jesus was shrewd; He established the rules of the game: no questions asked. He posed as postulate that the Prophesies would be accomplished; no questions asked. Skeptical minds like Thomas or Zachary would be scolded. Blind faith or no faith. That's where Tim was at: no faith.

Before the nineteenth century, faith and science were in synch; religions adjusting science to biblical wisdom. The scientific state of the art was compatible with blind faith for the vast majority. It became increasingly more difficulty for the erudite-believers to accept the dogmas, the Bible and to not even question the existence of a benevolent God presiding over the miseries of our world. Even the historical birth of Christ was questioned as early as the seventeenth century; to this date, absolute historical proof has not been made that Jesus Christ existed.

Historical scrutiny can sometimes open closets we should have left closed: Mohammed had several wives, the last one having been given him when she was still a child, the marriage consummated when she was nine. What kind of sexual creature Jesus was will never be known, and who cares; he started something so impressive that it survived two thousand years, as did Mohammed.

Whoever and if he ever was, Jesus improved on the Judaism of his time, responding to the needs of all, not just of a few; to the needs of the poor, the sick, the slaves, all nations, men and women, and He introduced a new aspect into the equation: compassion.

But religion is not compatible with science. For the last two thousand years, like a cancer, the mass of knowledge has been proliferating and spreading. The conservatism of most religions, which were in tune with the culture of our ancestors, is now so preposterous for a large portion of the world population, that far reaching doubts are being sown. Knowledge seems incompatible with most organized religions, at least in their present states, the existence of God being questioned more and more. Fortunately Tim was cut short in his reflection by John.

-Ya, that's what I'm finding out. Not always smart to ask too many questions, but now that I've started on this path, I have to finish the trip. Almost like eating peanuts. - Johnny took another sip, working on his question.

-You see father, I've come to realize that religions, contrary to what their founders are saying, are nothing but human inventions. - He paused, organizing his thoughts before continuing. -The sole initial purpose is to provide answers, although without scientific proof, to some basic questions we have and for which we need to be reassured. Otherwise life becomes even more frightening. – He continued. – It is disturbing that religions seem to have evolved in ...political and marketing organizations. The more members the more power. I can't help but feel abused, manipulated and lied to: you know, not much different than fortune-tellers, crystal ball-gazers and all other sorcerers; but much better organized. I suppose that Jesus didn't have this scenario in mind.-

Donnelly nodded. He too had realized that the world was not a better place because of religions, maybe worse. Yet religions could have made the world a better place. He had researched the subject and was not surprised to find that even several thousand years ago, the Egyptians, the Indians, the

Romans and the Jews, had used religion to support their rulers; the priests, often abusing the naiveté of the people, to get rich, govern and enslave.

Today, refusing to adapt, religions continue to force archaic dictates down the throats of their adherents, no longer bringing responses and remedies to humanity; often the contrary. Worldwide communication now allows immediate awareness of cultural changes. One can see that in third world countries where poverty and illiteracy are rampant, religions are still viscerally needed and popular, in tune with the metaphysical needs of the people. As soon as the standard of living becomes higher, faith in religions vanishes in a proportion which is directly related to the increase. Tim had been an advocate of keeping in tune with the times rather than forcing the times to be in tune with religions. A losing battle, it was going against the interest of those in the drivers' seats.

The most flagrant example of this abusive utilization of religion is seen in several countries of the Middle East where a few merchants and soldiers became Princes and Kings early in the twentieth century. Controlling the oil, this new wealth coming out of the ground, they kept their population under religious rule, abusing for their own gratification, the rights of every one, in particular those of their women. Could this be extortion? Like is it pedophilia to marry and consume this marriage with a nine year old bride?

Barcelo could see that Tim was lost in his thoughts. A fly hanging from the ceiling caught his eyes. This very distant relative was not keeping its -proper place-; Johnny could relate to that. He decided to rescue Tim from his inner turmoil.

-Over the years, ever since my sister Henrietta died, when I was only nine, I've been trying to make sense out of the organization of life. You know justice, equality, happiness, life after death, heaven, hell, and creation and so on, these nice words we hear all the time. Yet, you and I know that life is a bitch and that justice, equality and happiness are so far reserved for the wealthy few, the rest of us have to do without. –

Taking a pause to reorganize his thoughts, he continued.

-The rich and powerful are always the cruelest and the most efficient predators. We all know that most of the largest fortunes were the fruits of unchristian dealings. -

Not aware of the influence his sister and Jim Donegan had had on his intellect, Donnelly was surprised about the extent of Barcelo's anger. He obviously had given the subject a lot of attention.

-I'm not convinced that religions are better than the ailments they're supposed to cure. You're Irish and I don't have to point out that religions are a major cause of dissention in your country of origin. Religions, like Santa Claus, may be dangerous illusions without any real meat to them. Scams serving political objectives.-

Continuing to be amazed, Tim meekly cut in :

-If I'd known that I was going to be questioned by an expert....However - he continued in the same breath – you have to understand that if you're looking for reassurance I won't be able to help. - He looked at Barcelo for a long moment before continuing.

-I'm no longer convinced about the goodness of religions. Most religions started as social codes of ethic, "-do unto others as you would like them to do unto you", a retro version of the "reversibility of violence" realization. Religions were all filling a void and providing plausible answers; like evolution, trial and error within a given cultural context. Man has always been seduced by miracles and mysteries, so to make religions more exotic, dogmas, miracles and even God dictated scripts have been produced by imaginative and foxy prophets. These metaphysical considerations no longer stand their ground to the close scrutiny of modern man. Clifford's law has replaced the gullibility of our fore fathers: "Don't believe anything, anytime, anywhere unless you have absolute proof." Physic has dethroned metaphysics.-

Not missing a word of what the priest was saying, John was focusing on the busy fly buzzing around his bed, wondering how long it would take for flies to be conscious and create religions.

Relentlessly Tim was continuing:

-I have a hard time in believing blindly as I was programmed. I qualify as what Huxley called an "agnostic", which is a position where one believes only what can be proven scientifically, until then, "nada". Dogmas based on blind acceptance of the scriptures, the infallibility of popes or the sayings of some Imam or Ayatollah, or whatever by whoever, are discarded as fairy-tales. Too bad someone does not stand up and rewrites the script. -

Still admiring the aerobatics of his winged roommate, Johnny realized that he had been holding his breath, he exhaled slowly. This priest was having as hard a time as he, even harder because of the commitment he had made. Harder because he was further than he on this road, having received better thinking tools and having started the trip earlier. It must have been hell to admit that one's lifelong commitment was a hoax.

-What you're telling me father, is that you're keeping your options open by being an Agnostic. But, - he continued without waiting for a reply, to the greater satisfaction of the good Father, -assuming that religions may or may not have anything to do with God, if there is such a being, what happens after death?.-

There it was, the question of a man getting older and seizing the sense of the word death, realizing that finality is the name of the game.

-Where do I go after I no longer live? - Asked Barcelo, point blank.

Thinking a moment, Tim opted to be candidly honest about his answer. This was not his usual answer, but with this brother, lying would be detected immediately, you don't spend a lifetime fibbing without developing a nose to spot deceit.

-I'll tell you what I think. I may be as far out as right on. After thousands of hours of cogitation, my best bet is that you simply disappear from the screen. Your blip disappears from the radar screen, the body rots and is recycled, atom by atom forever and ever. This ability to think and formulate questions is an electrical function that will stop to exist when your generator no longer provides the bio electricity required. My dear Johnny I believe we're programmed like a computer and that we go where old computers go after they are no longer functional. –

He waited a while and continued.

-Christians, like most others, have a need to believe in heaven and hell, punishment and reward, justice, whether now or after death. Some other religions like, Hinduism or other transcendental and abstract philosophies such as Buddhism, support an unjust social system by claiming that it may take several lives to attain perfection and merit Nirvana where the reincarnation cycle is broken; that's when their blip is disappearing forever. To put it simply, in their context, a perfect life means having succeeded in taming your needs and desires as well as having been good to your fellow man but essentially to accept your karma. Sounds pretty sensible to me and not much different than the basics of most religions. The "Do unto others what you would want others to do unto you" encompasses the essence of a realistic path to happiness.-

-Ya, I read about that reincarnation jig. I think it's a lot of bull. It was also very useful to make the cast system tolerable; the pariah phase being a sort of purgatory: more adversity being dispensed to those in need of more expiation. Sounds like expert manipulation to me. Blaming one's misery on his own past lives is.... a smart way to explain elitism and disparity.

Hypothetical heaven or hell is not a choice I feel comfortable with. It means the presence of a god managing our lives, and when looking at the world with its genocide, wars, inequalities, cruelties, hunger and misery I have second thoughts about a superior being overseeing this mess. –

Johnny continued on the disappearing Blip theory after coaxing the last drop of alcohol from his plastic cup.

-So, you think that a dark hole of nothingness and complete destruction is where we end up.... for eternity...at least that part would be true. That makes more sense than the other alternatives. But- he continued relentlessly, - who created life, and why is there a need for man to exist? Is it a fluke, a mistake... who's pulling the fucking strings,... if any one. Darwin's theory of evolution places chaos, survival and chance as the real architects of the universe. The errors unfavorable to life being naturally scrapped, only the beneficial changes improving the genes, like the ability to speak for instance. ?-

Tim had taken the relay baton from John and was keeping track of the busy fly, now licking something out of the edge of a paper cup. He looked around to make sure they were alone and candidly admitted.

-I wish I knew where we've come from and why we're here. You know as much as I. Scientifically speaking we know pretty well how the known universe came about. Probably as a continuous process, a big thermo nuclear explosion some fifteen billion years ago dispersed various components which were chaotically subjected to various laws of physics. These elements aggregated to become planets, stars and eventually, by pure luck, life emerged and flourished, at least on one of the planets. The whole universe is in continuous motion from the initial push of the explosion, expanding forever until the parts are too far from each other's and until the stars become extinct. The mass of the universe will then become an eternal frozen system....Until, maybe, it reaches a pre existing contracting phase and there's another explosion. The big bang would then become the outcome of something rather than the cause of everything....If you ask me, this is where physics dissolves into metaphysics.

Isn't it poetic justice, a full circle: from metaphysics to physics and back to metaphysics, like continuous Big Bangs since always for eternity. –

-I can see that you're as confused as I am.... Even more because you know more, or think you do... until a new theory surfaces. But I'll be damned if I can even start to understand or even dream about what happened before the first Big Bang. ...if there was a first one...?- Replied Johnny before he burst out laughing so much that the cute nurse rushed in, fearing that the inevitable was happening; Barcelo's laugh sounding more like a death rattle.

Looking at the sudden apparition of the cute nurse, her dark eyes opened wide in anticipation of a catastrophe Barcelo managed to say without choking.

-Tim, if you think nurse King is looking at us right now, it's only a product of your imagination, a mirage. Could these great brown eyes not be tangible, could this great body be a product of our imagination. - Said Johnny between hiccups like sounds of catching his breath.

Tim was used to being with clients trying to get their next and sometimes final breaths. He was in no fear about Barcelo, knowing that he would not die without a hell of a fight, would hang on for years, looking for answers and making the system pay for not adapting fast enough to his reality.

-Looks real to me; the kind that makes celibacy impossible. ...-Then taking his eyes away from this work of art, he continued: - Barcelo, you're good and I'm surprised at this erudition. To answer your question, nobody knows anything about the second preceding the Big Bang or if there ever was a first one, assuming a succession of these events..... Some theories have been formulated, you can expect one every month for the next hundred years or more. My feeling is that one of these days in the not too distant future, we'll have a theory that will stay a while. Don't ask me what it will be. Here again we're bordering on dogmas; the metaphysic dethroning the physic...The proof for most of that stuff is theoretical and will remain educated guesses for a long time; maybe this is where eternity resides: in the question.- Said Tim thinking about bringing quantum physics into the portrait but changing his mind.

There was a heavy silence. Nurse King had retreated just outside the door, eavesdropping and amazed that there could be such an exchange between Barcelo and Father Donnelly. But then, she had once read a small book written by a stevedore, something Hoffer was the name and if a stevedore could write about "mass movements" why couldn't a dying scrap tire recycler talk about astrophysics. Fascinated she got nearer the door in order to not to miss a word.

-Are there other man-like and conscious beings elsewhere in the universe? - Asked John.

-Probably. In the billions of galaxies, the laws of probability support the claim that there are other freaks like us, asking the same questions and not finding the answers. Maybe, like this fly that we've been observing, these other creatures are not yet conscious and are spared this existential enigma? - Replied Tim.

-Pretty frightening when you think about it. Frankly I prefer the belief that my blip will fade away or evaporate from the screen rather than having to live several lives. You and I know that even for the very rich, life is not kind. Once around is good enough. - Said John.

-Amen to that my new friend.– Said Tim opening his little brief case where Johnny thought the priest kept his chalice and other trade tools. He came out with a half full bottle of Glenfiddisch.

-Let's drink to this. Then I'll have to leave but, if you're still here tomorrow I'll drop by. – Said Tim refilling the cups.

- I'll be here, they're checking my kidney function. A few more days. It might be interesting to talk about man himself and why man is different from other animals. This guy Darwin thinks that we all come from little microbe like creatures and that we're cousins to plants, birds and all other animals. That's gross but, except for the people believing strictly in the Bible version of creation, where God, out of his goodness, created man with a magic wand, everybody else seem to agree with him.-

Still tuned in, nurse King almost said that she did. She was out of tune with her evangelist Husband.

-I don't know what I could tell you that you don't already know. But yes why not, it beats gossiping and confession. –

They emptied the bottle and Tim Donnelly left Johnny Barcelo to his somber thoughts, surprised to almost run nurse King over on his way out. The fly had settled down in a corner of the ceiling digesting its meal or taking notes.

—— CHAPTER 13 ——

"Ennui is the daughter of routine."

Year 1952

It did not take long for Émilie to get involved as an owner in what she was now referring to as the " family business". Still flat bellied and giving no signs of getting pregnant; not a surprise since she had decided to avoid pregnancy for at least two years, time to accumulate a little cash of her own and enjoy her new freedom. The question of whether she could domesticate this wild animal she was married to continued to be a sound rationale for delaying pregnancy.

-The world will do just fine without another baby. - She told her husband.

Her mind was set. She would not yield to social pressure. Her mother and friends kept glancing sideways at her, disapproving openly of her slim waist. This decision to delay pregnancy was not a whim but a lucid option.

-Pregnancy and motherhood are to be treated with the greatest respect. Raising kids is a major achievement if done properly. It lasts twenty years and doing a good job is the difference between throwing a baby in the Androscoggin river in January or giving this innocent a fighting chance.-

Privately her mother agreed but her aunts and both grandmothers thought she was being selfish and not fulfilling her sacred duty. The bottom line was that they were jealous and could not tolerate that one of them had enough common sense, and was strong enough to live her life.

-They're all fucking jealous. – Johnny would swear when one of them would say something nasty to his Emilie.

Her life with Johnny was easy as long as she did what he ordered at work, where he was a dictator; at home he was unconcerned and performed like a trained animal. During the rare moments spent at home, Saturday afternoons and Sunday's, he would play with Paw or try to seduce Emilie. Making love was a revelation and enough was seldom enough.

He enjoyed the little house and furnished it with the best money could buy. Someone took care of the grounds and cut the lawn whenever the grass grew long enough for Emilie to notice. However his real pleasure was to spend long moments, sucking on a cigarette while sitting on the old bench near the water, fascinated by the silvery cascading water, amazed by the curves and forms it etched on the rocks lying at the bottom. From time to time a bold and hungry trout would jolt him out of his reverie.

That winter he enjoyed the roaring fires in the old time fireplace. So large that he could enter the hearth and sit on one of the two juxtaposed stone benches, his feet almost into the glowing embers. After spending long hours supervising trailers dumping scrap tires into the now almost full ravine, his body would be energized by the warmth generated by the red hot cinders. From early fall to late spring, Emilie would have a fire going every day. She had never felt the warmth of a fire place until they moved in their home. It gave her a sense of ecstasy that remained unsurpassed during her entire life. The dog shared her contemplative admiration for the flames; stretched out to his full length by the fire side, his black fur absorbing the heat until he had to move back slightly, almost purring with contentment.

For the first time in his life, everything was running smoothly; but as to be expected Johnny was getting bored with this trouble free existence. His mind was forever searching for a mountain to climb. Like hanging over a cliff or running a marathon, some people create their own mess so they can struggle out of it and be proud of their achievement once they have succeeded. While getting to be financially well off was great he could not find fulfillment in the contented monotony of achievement.

Worse still, he could not be satisfied with the monotony of having but one wife and was unconsciously gawking at other girls, none half as pretty or smart as his Emilie. To conquer seems to be the life blood of guys like Barcelo. Man is a predator, a beast of prey; taking what is there to be taken is how man survived when other creatures became extinct. Ever since his ascent into consciousness, man has taken, dominated and exterminated everything during his drive to conquer the world. When in doubt, destroy and kill. Is it survival or escape borne out of fear?

In Barcelo's subconscious mind, his sister's imprint was still, and would always be predominant. Nobody can fight against a dream or a memory embedded in your mind at the dawn of your consciousness when your programs for learning are so acutely efficient. Emilie and all his other spouses would be compared to and categorized according to Johnny's first emotional incestuous experience.

He felt jilted and betrayed by this early situation. He never was a virgin and had his first sexual experience before knowing about sex; never had a choice nor felt remorse, ignoring the difference between good and bad. Like talking and walking, he automatically learned about sexual matters rather than having been lead to sex by increased hormonal levels when at the right and proper age.

The previous week he had run across one of his school day hero. Three years older than Johnny, Thomas had it all: good looks, athletic, football and baseball star. Auber was also in the tire business, had started with not more than the skin of his teeth, selling tires from his home, installing them on the street. A few years later he had three tire stores in the Lewiston Auburn area, and in 1999 when the business was sold, had owned more than fifty stores in New England.

-Sure you can collect my scrap tires. Your price is fair, I'd pay anything to get rid of them. - Answered Auber to Johnny's request. - And he continued. -I've been looking for a place where a hard working man could relax and have a good time. Nothing like that in this area. I have to travel to the coast. Do you know of any fun place around here?-

-I don't – answered Johnny. - Why don't you get one going-?

-Never. You'd need to know my wife to understand what you're proposing. It would take her less than a week to know about it. She would cut off my balls and boil them in acid.-

In Lewiston Maine, after the war, veterans came home looking for jobs. Not satisfied with the barely -bread and butter salaries- offered by the textile industry, several started their own businesses. The largely French speaking population was poor; some of the early immigrants who had come seeking work and a place to call home in early 1900 were slowly coming out of poverty: like the Roy brothers trucking business, the Gendron's construction business, Vallée's restaurant. Most of the others were still living from hand to mouth and would continue for generations to come, unable to escape the gravitational pull of poverty and misery.

In such a social climate, taking advantage of the people already weakened by life's blows is as easy as stealing candy from babies. Several bootleggers were in business and prostitution was thriving. Johnny was well aware of this underworld. These people were his former school mates or neighbors.

One Friday night after a most profitable week, Johnny and his employee but nevertheless friend Dudley decided to visit one such place of ill repute, a private club which was only private in terms of not letting the cops in. The Red Baron offered liquor, music and women. The poor girls from the area were looking forward to making a few extra dollars; easy work, the only requirements, being to be nice to paying customers and not to get drunk or pregnant.

After several toasts to the business of scrap tire collection, Dudley went to get rid of some of the fluid and came back with two pretty looking girls not yet eighteen they later found out. They all had several other libations and after some timid negotiations the party moved to the brand new Chalet motel.

Renting the largest and most sumptuous suite, they congregated in apartment 302 and continued drinking while getting comfortable. The girls were of the giggling type and swayed by too much gin and tonic, were more than willing to oblige these gentlemen who had money enough to arouse them.

More negotiations and the male toads selected their female toads as fornicating partners. Just as the dance was about to start, a loud bang on the door cooled the ardor of the gentlemen to the rigidity of a silken flag by a windless day.

Not bothering to dress his two hundred and twenty pounds of muscle, Dudley decided that he would open the door and promptly teach better manners to whoever might be standing there. Surprise surprise, the intruders were the fathers of the girls flanked by a police officer. It turned out that the girls were not yet eighteen.

But not all bad news: the cop was Frank, Barcelo's state trooper friend. With difficulty Frank succeeded in pacifying the two irate fathers, who after calling Johnny and Dudley an assortment of descriptive names, were about to take their daughters home where they would undoubtedly receive a hell of a beating. The girls guessed as much and one of them, sobering up, but still intoxicated enough to be vindictive and gabby, slurred with much difficulty, addressing her father.

-It's ok for you to fuck me but not for strangers. – She was mumbling while her father was desperately trying to make enough noise to drown her statement. When she repeated it once more the state trooper was able to make out what she was trying to say.

-Everybody back into the room. - He stopped everyone at the door, closed it and slowly produced a note book out of his pocket.

-I heard what your daughter said. You've been having inappropriate relations with your under age daughter. Incest is a felony and you'll be prosecuted. –

Looking sternly at the alleged incestuous father, he waited for a reply. Mumbling meaningless words, to the effect that the girl was drunk and didn't know what she was saying, the pervert's skin had suddenly turned ashen.

Realizing the implications of what she had said, the young girl miraculously sobered up and came up with a solution.

-My father doesn't remember that I turned eighteen yesterday.... I was joking about him fucking me.-

Eyes closed, head tilted forward and to the left, it was obvious that she had told the truth about her father fucking her. The officer replaced the note book in his pocket.

-I heard what I heard and these two gentlemen as well. If I get wind that you've molested your daughter again I swear that I'll personally go after you. What will it be?-

Neither of the fathers wanted publicity over this incident. Any scandal could have ruined the chances of marrying their daughters. Who wants to marry an incestuous whore? In the fifties, virginal was the only way to be for a girl, and while these two would have a hard time producing a hymen on their wedding nights, their mothers would show them a few tricks they might have used themselves. A drop of chicken blood mixed with aspirin to prevent clotting, surreptitiously sprinkled on the bed sheet would be all the assurance the groom would need to thump his chest, proud of having performed his manly duty of defloration. The male of the species is slave to his pride and will believe anything as long as it serves his narcissistic requirements.

The lesson Johnny came home with that Saturday morning was that the bar owner should have been more careful about the girls he allowed in his establishment. He had risked causing his customers to spend time in jail, which is where Johnny and Dudley would have ended up had an officer other than Frank been on the spot.

As Auber had mentioned, there was a niche for a well kept and well organized …. Watering hole or Meeting place. He would look into this, not later than Monday. In the mean time, after spending several minutes in reflection, contemplating the turbulent water moving as fast and as deranged as his thoughts, he quietly opened the front door of his cottage where Emilie was waiting. She looked at him for a while before speaking. With tears in her eyes, she told him.

-Is it too much for you to be faithful one full year? Don't do that again if you want me to continue to be your wife.-

She was flushed and beautiful. What is the matter with me thought Johnny, why screw up something that is working so well.

-I won't insult you with a lie. We got drunk and stupid. That's what men do sometimes. Sorry.-

Lifting her head, she sadly nodded.

-I don't want to be a jealous wife and keep you tied to the kitchen stove. Your life is your life...-she hesitated knowing that what she was about to say was sincere, - but so is mine and if you abuse it I'll leave you, I have seen so many wives destroyed by accepting being continually humiliated that …-

She let the rest hang in the air like a dark cloud ready to burst and unload tons of rain and thunder. Then she continued.

-This incident is water under the bridge and I won't nag you about it anymore.-

Quickly she stepped outside to hide the tears her eyes could no longer retain. Listening to the babbling of the brook, she was able to regain her composure and some serenity. The brook would always provide a faithful and loyal presence, assisting her through many other unpleasant episodes in her life. The coolness and purity of the water tumbling around the stones soothed her wounds and pacified her angry soul. The brook was there for her long after John had departed.

Johnny was surprised, expecting to be yelled and screamed at; further proof that his Emilie was a gem. He also knew that he should smarten up and count some of his blessings. -She's pearls to this swine-, he thought.

Deep inside he knew that while he had intended to be a loyal husband, his flighty nature would not allow serenity, his libidinal instinct taking over his life. He felt sad about his inevitable destiny, his moira as the Irish would say. His mind was forever searching for something new, new challenges, new faces, creating new needs that he would then have to cater to. Was it a disease; he had heard of people never being satisfied with their own lives, always looking for pseudo improvements, creating new needs quickly replaced by others.

Eating a great meal or living any unusual experiences always had its anticlimax. He would experience depressive moods for several days following a special event, like after Christmas when he was a kid. The higher he would get the lower his spirit would sag; forever looking for the next best and more powerful thrill. His desire for new experiments was unbridled and this craving for enjoyment was undermining his stability. Maybe he should consult a psychiatrist and become crazier; or at least have a good reason to be nuts and be documented as such.

Whatever was affecting him, the seed to create the coolest and plushest pleasure dispensing establishment, was germinating in his mind. This hedonistic heaven would be safe and private; one that would allow any kind of extravagances for those vicious but otherwise saintly pillars of the community.

In the nineteen fifties USA, a prudish and puritanical culture still prevailed and dictated the social code of ethics. Carnal pleasure seekers, those libidinous and impure citizens, would marry to some straight laced, sanctimonious girls and dutifully accept a life of frustration. For the female, even the pronunciation of the word sex would be a sin and could produce an orgasm, which was a terrible sin. Under these conditions, the pursuit of unallowable penchants for these natural needs was only permitted in a strictly prissy and fastidious fashion. Those too horny to exercise control over their libido would become sexual predators in milieus where they could impose secrecy.

Auber was right: if humanity is to be driven by sex and money, the organization of sexual activities should be as well managed and part of our culture as doing business. Nothing new here, sexuality has been central to social amusement throughout recorded history. It seems that the importance of this commodity was enhanced by the numerous restrictions and taboos imposed by most religions: "tax salt and water and you'll make them precious, restrict sexual activity and you'll turn sex into a business".

Contrary to the general belief, prudish individuals are not deprived of hormonal discharges and sexual wants. They deal with these natural needs any way they can, mostly and preferably in secret. They feign total lack of interest, pretending to be immune, vaccinated against pleasures of the flesh. False, nobody, man or woman, laborer or priest, rich or poor, between the ages of twelve and eighty five, is immune; all are subject to nature's reproductive mechanism. Notwithstanding vows of chastity or cultural taboos, the hard facts remain that from age twelve, boys and girls masturbate, fornicate and have orgasms any way they can. Man has a way of denying the obvious. The great Saint Augustin, renowned to have had an unbridled sexual life, would recite this prayer:

-God, he would say, help me become chaste and continent, but please take your time as I'm in no rush.-

This son of Sainte Monique, must have been like Barcelo, who had since long recognized that narcissism was his motivator; a craving to shine at all costs. Johnny's diminutive size had exacerbated this trait and might have had something to do with his deeply rooted desire to dominate. Having been born "à propos" he could have been Hitler or Alexander or Napoleon or Saint Augustin; right place right man, right size. He was also as immoral and unethical as the great political or religious leaders, past and present; as a matter of fact he may have been as demented as any of the above and, given the right political climate, would have developed fully his potential for paranoia and megalomania, a pre requisite to greatness.

This new venture was in line with Barcelo's passion to innovate and change things around.

-Booze and sex can't be bad and if someone wants to have a good time that's his business. As it is for the collection of scrap tires, there's a need. We'll fill this need, assist humanity in its constant fight to prevent the atrophy of its collective libido and, make big bucks doing so. – Dudley couldn't believe his ears.

A perfect associate, Dudley was a late bloomer, now ready to face other responsibility. An excellent sergeant, Dudley was honest, meticulous and did not have any difficulty to work with people. Working in tandem with a good and honest accountant overseeing financial management while giving the place this aura of respectability that professional accounting never fails to convey to even the shabbiest of companies, "The Saint Augustine" was bound to become an overnight success.

He couldn't resist naming this high class bordello " The Saint Augustine". Looking around as he had for the BRE Inc location, Barcelo soon found the perfect spot for his private Club. A few months later they were in business; proposing to their select customers: a sauna, a plush bar, a fine cuisine restaurant, a dim lit dance floor, a billiard room and twenty luxurious apartments.

Far enough but within easy driving distance from Portland, Lewiston and Auburn, this new age bordello soon became a renowned lupanar, a name, which according to Dudley, sounded better than "whore house'. Only the affluents were courted, exorbitant prices discouraging the paupers.

Dudley and a few others kept the place "orderly". The very best booze and food were offered, served by hostesses of the right blood line. Like the ancient vestals serving Dionysius, after a two week in house course, new personnel could cater to most needs and desires of the members. Yes, the price tag was scary and could cause fibrillation to the faint hearted members. Most did not notice as the claims and promises put forward by the establishment materialized into realities. As one of the girl would sing: - The Saint Augustin Club is a place for the horny not the miser.-

As was to be expected, Johnny had been his usual weird visionary. He had a secret: two of the twenty lavish apartments had been conceived with a purpose and lacked the privacy heralded by the establishment. Those rooms had two way mirrors allowing cameras with wide angle lenses to immortalize some very private moments. A small cubicle, camouflaged between the two suites, allowed special equipment to noiselessly capture special moments. The price paid to the specialist imported from New York to build the cubicle and the purchase of the equipment had been significant. The work was done during a week end and no one but Johnny knew about it. This new project became the most interesting and fascinating gamble in Barcelo's life, his little secret; looking on during the most private moment of a person's life and having a high quality film to preserve it for posterity was giving Johnny a weapon of such potentiality that he spent several nights debating as to whether he would ever use it. The debate was futile and more academic than conscientious. Knowing that there was a market for what was dubbed "dirty movies" he reasoned that the two rooms would be used essentially to film professionals and make movies that would be sold for stag parties. Other opportunities would be assessed on their own merits.

What started as a drunken mishap, where he and Dudley could have been criminally charged for entertaining underage girls, ended up as an elegant temple of lubricity for the pleasure of the libertines and debauchees who could afford it. In the mean time the tire business was continuing to be a no surprise cash cow, the ravine more than half filled and approximately twenty acres more to be covered with a twenty foot layer of solidly packed scrap tires. Johnny estimated that the site would one day contain more than twenty five million scrap tires; at an average tipping fee of twenty five cents. Considering that there were hardly any expenses, this constituted the best business around; not bad for the runt of a Portuguese litter.

CHAPTER 14

"Nothing ventured nothing gained."

Time flies when you're busy and both Johnny and Dudley were busy getting the Saint Augustine Club started. Advertising on the radio or in the newspaper was out of the question. Word of mouth was the only way to go and while it doesn't cost much, it is not the fastest and most efficient advertising vehicle. Introductory free parties for potential customers, added up to a pretty penny, but got the ball rolling.

The members were chosen carefully and after six months, a regular flow of paying members and clients were attending the parties given every Friday and Saturday nights. The clients could eat, drink, gamble, seduce the hostesses, even be stupid, in which case they would be put to bed until the morning. Dudley was doing a great job, enjoying his new life as much as the custom made tuxedo he was wearing.

Johnny had not yet used his special movie equipment. He had been thinking of doing so for a while but was hesitating. Finally he decided to try it on himself and borrowing one of the cute hostesses, on a quiet Thursday night he activated the camera and did his thing. He was amazed at the detailed images and by the overall quality of the film. He looked at it once more and then burned it. Not a bad performance even though he had been conscious of the intrusion. For the first time he could see his naked body and had to agree that it was not one of the marvels of the world; eating more and weight lifting, he wondered.... The only organ he could be proud of was his over sized penis; what was it Emilie nicknamed him? "Little Priape".

-Can't have good looks and be smart. - He finally rationalized. Barcelo could rationalize most situations and come up for air.

Now was the time to launch phase two of the promotional program.

-Let's throw a party for all our scrap tire customers. After all, these guys have unknowingly bankrolled The Saint Augustine. - Dudley thought this idea brilliant and said that he could be ready in a week or even less.

-We'll need to send invitations, do this right and with class. – Both were aware that their scrap tire recycling bread and butter business lacked luster; Johnny would joke that disposing of carrion was a lot worse. If there are no dumb occupations some are better if left to others.

And they agreed on a date when their twenty some scrap tire clients would be treated to a party they were not about to forget. As it turned out, neither would the staff. Everything in the house would be free except the gambling room which was at the risk and peril of the guests.

-They'll keep their winnings and so will we. With a little luck the entire party will be sponsored and paid for by the gambling room winnings. -

Even Isaac was invited and Johnny told him to bring along some of his friends and associates. While he knew that it could jeopardize his future tranquility he also was aware that these people could bring in new customers from the big cities.

-Bring your friends from Boston and New York, and tell them to pack a bag for a couple of days. They won't regret it. - Isaac had reservations about introducing his underworld friends to Johnny. He finally agreed, thinking that it may enhance his prestige with both.

He also knew that they would try to muscle into Barcelo's business, like he had; this prospect pleased him as he owed one to Barcelo. Even if the imposed partnership was making him richer and richer, his pride had never recovered from the beating he had received on a stormy July evening.

-Why not, he thought, and may the best man win. - He surmised that either way, he Isaac, his favorite person, would come out a winner.

He had never disclosed to his partners the gruesome details surrounding the onset of his business venture with Barcelo. He felt less of a traitor to Johnny if their secret was kept; Barcelo would have a fighting chance if they were not aware of the considerable talent the little guy had for defending his assets. Furthermore his own pride and reputation would remain intact. May the best man win.

Two of Isaac's associates were deputized by the Familia. They would spend two days in Lisbon as Barcelo's guests. The fact that they traveled accompanied by body guards pleased Barcelo who did not want to deal with pawns.

The party was set for the entire weekend and the guests started to arrive around five on Friday; for anybody else the Club was closed. The accountant was a little grumpy until told that the gambling tables would be available. Accountants are paid for counting not for thinking. Joseph had no great imagination only cold hard facts prevailed in his calculating mind. He was good.

On that Friday, the most bizarre assortment of people one could dream of found its way to Lisbon Maine. Like a plane from Mars, unloading its creatures: some as skinny as Thanatos, others as chubby as sumo wrestlers, most had the tell tale dirty fingers that came with the business of dealing with scrap tires; most were dressed in new, poorly cut attires. The common denominator was that all were ill at ease in this luxurious and classy environment, surrounded with beautiful and deferentially courteous hostesses.

One in particular, Little John, married for almost twenty years to a nagging scare crow almost fainted when the hostess showed him to his room and touched his lips pretending that a speck of dirt had to be removed. "LJ" was a massive man of forty five weighing not less than three hundred pounds at a height of five feet and six inches. Little John was not a tender heart in business, but for all his strength, he was shy with girls and suffering greatly from the total lack of sexual interest his wife had developed since the birth of the last of their five daughters. Being a good Pentecostal Evangelical Christian she believed the only contraception method accepted by god was the Bush total abstinence. Not a problem for her. She had always preferred taking care of her own sexual needs, her Romeo being both speedy and unskilled.

The two special rooms with an introspective view from the outside were assigned to Isaac's associates. Johnny had decided that he would keep a souvenir of their passage in his establishment. When one is dealing the cards, prudence dictates that a few trumps are set aside for the dealer.

They had arrived in a large black limousine driven by one of the body guards; tinted glass on the outside and a glass separation between the front and rear seats preserving the privacy of the occupants. Very impressive, thought Johnny who was looking out for them from the window of Dudley's office.

The Saint Augustine Club could have been a monastery, perched on hill top, mature trees lining the hundred foot entrance; cobble stones paved the drive way which circled in front of the main entrance. A green canopy covered the wide stairway leading to the impressive oak double doors. A doorman, wearing the costume of a twelfth century Augustine friar, very smart and correct after several weeks of training, opened the back door as soon as the limousine came to a halt.

-Welcome to The Saint Augustine Club. We all hope you'll have a pleasant stay. – It had taken a good two days for him to learn the proper pronunciation of Saint Augustine.

He then went to the driver's side and offered to park the car. Deana, the hostess of the premises came down the five steps to meet these gentlemen. Flashing a smile as inviting as the rest of her body, she was dressed in a tight fitting navy blue costume, sober but allowing all to appraise the perfection of her body. A knotted cord was tied around her waist, similar to that of the Saint Augustine nuns.

After a six hour drive the two Italian gentlemen were happy to stretch their limbs for a minute before fully appreciating the view.

-Welcome gentlemen, if you will follow me I'll take you to Mister Barcelo's office. –

Alberto, the smaller of the two, was a typical Mafioso product, the kind you see depicted in Hollywood movies. His olive complexion was a dead give-away that he was born on the shore of the Mediterranean Sea. His face was well proportioned, and if it hadn't been for the pinkish scar zigzagging across his right cheek down to the corner of the lips, Alberto could have had the face of a beautiful girl. A beautiful girl with cold eyes, the coldest darkest eyes this side of hell thought Deana, who knew about hell. When he smiled, which was not often, one could see that his lower right canine was capped with gold.

Twenty years ago when only ten, he had landed in New York with his family: papa, mama and two older sisters. After the quarantine on the awful Ferris Island where dysentery almost killed him, he had quickly learned to take care of himself on the streets of New York where only the smartest kids could survive. Well honed by hardship and proud poverty, he fitted perfectly into this incubator.

One day, his older sister, a very nice Catholic and extremely proper young woman, came home from work looking as if she had been raped; she had. After extracting the truth from her, Alberto took her to a doctor, who confirmed that she had been abused sexually.

-She was raped as we can see by the tears inside her vagina. – The old doctor confirmed. He wanted to call the police but Alberto said that he did not want to follow this procedure.

-We have our way.- Grunted Alberto.

-I understand. It may even be better than ours. Good luck and be careful. - The doctor suggested knowing that blood would be spilled.

Going home, Alberto stopped the car and looking at his crying sister, he gave his directives.

-We both know what happened. Now, tell me who did this to you. Then you'll forget this incident as if it had never happened. You will not tell your sister, or mama or papa. You will not even tell the priest at confession because this is not a sin for you, just for the animal who raped you. Do you understand what I said? I want you to repeat it.-

And she did, word for word. Then, she told him who had raped her, how, where and the complete story: Following an often tested strategy, her supervisor had asked her to work over time, trapped her in the store room, attacked her from behind, raped her like he had raped half a dozen other girls and told her that it was her word against his.

-I'll want to fuck you again and you'll let me have my way if you want to keep your job. - The supervisor told her.

A few days later, she was only mildly surprised when the Irish supervisor didn't show up for work. -Not feeling well- was it reported. Some of the other girls, who had also been treated to the imperious libido of the Irish stud, cheered and hoped for a long lasting degenerative illness.

When he resurfaced two weeks later, the "randy shrew" as he was surnamed, was a changed man who had seen the light; courteous and even affable with his former victims, apologizing to some of them. His voice had lost its deep masculine tonality and he was no longer the former horny marsupial on the hunt for a new victim and a quick piece.

As it turned out, Alberto and one of his friends, had ambushed the Irish rapist, abducted him at gun point and taken him to an empty warehouse. There Alberto squeezed the head of the frightened man in a bench vise and promptly proceeded to emasculate him. When the victim had finished yelling, Alberto sat him down on the floor and explained the facts of this new existence about to begin.

-This is nothing compared to what I'll do to you if you go to the police or seek revenge from the girls. We know that you have raped all the good looking ones. From now on you'll be kind and compassionate with them all. - Kapisce?-

The friend who had assisted in the surgical removal of the rapist's manhood was impressed and reported the incident. From that moment, Alberto steadily climbed the rung of the organizational ladder. His coolness in the face of danger as well as his creativity when confronted with problems, changing near catastrophes into opportunities, appealed to the capo. He was now in charge of a large portion of the family's operation, of which scrap disposal was but a small fraction.

His reason for accepting Isaac's invitation was more by curiosity than for his continuous drive to expand. As far as he could determine this Barcelo was a smart enough cookie, diverting his scrap business into the more profitable area of bootlegging and pleasure. He thought he could get this Barcelo to associate with the family and accept its protection in return for some kind of profit sharing.

The other occupant of the back seat was a much larger and older man. At fifty five Mario was a long time survivor in this business: out of jail and alive, he was more an advisor than an executive type, in fact he was almost pensioned off for past services. He had paid his dues. The flat nose, scarred eye brow and the limp of his left leg were only a small part of the price he had paid to access his present position in the hierarchy of the family. Deana, doubling as his very special hostess for this weekend would later testify that he had what appeared to be three bullet holes in the back and a nasty scar on his left thigh.

Unscrupulous and totally amoral he would have sold his youngest daughter for the Familia. Over the more than thirty years of faithful and loyal services working for the organization, Mario had seen and done just about everything one could imagine: from brow beating, to kidnapping, torture and killing. Over the years he had improved on his early penchant for inflicting pain, to the point where he now was a close study to the famed Marquis de Sade.

As soon as they arrived, Johnny hurried to meet them at the door and while the body guards took care of the baggage, he took them for a small tour of the premises.

-The scrap tire business is good but boring; this place provides the excitement I need for now. We're very selective and careful about who we accept as customers. As you'll see this weekend, we can cater to most of the whims of our customers. -

While Johnny was going through his little speech, Mario was assessing the quality of the service and the unusually neat and professional appearance of the staff. He was surprised to find such refinement in Lisbon Maine. He thought that he could even bring his mother to a place like this one. The staff was wearing a costume less elaborate than the doorman's but retained the distinctive religious aura: for the men, white silk shirt with long sleeves, belted at the waist with a knotted flax cord hanging to mid leg; for the girls, a tightly molded ankle length slit skirt, topped by a short sleeved white silk blouse, also belted at the waist by a knotted flax cord hanging to mid leg. None of that debasing familiarity one usually finds in such places of business; the girls were competent, beautiful and slim; the men large and imposing while deferent and courteous.

-You've put a neat business together. We may have a proposal for you before we return home-. Said Alberto, feeling the water. - For now we need to clean up.-

Johnny signaled to Deana who had been following at a distance. She came over and escorted both men to their respective room: the famous suites with an inside view.

-I'd like to show you the recycling business before we eat. We could do that in an hour.- Alberto said that he would like that very much.

The little weasel could feel that a treasure had been unearthed. What they saw in West Bowdoin would confirm his opinion that Barcelo was a prime target for a quick take over. Both he and Mario sensed that he would not yield to black mail or be scared easily. It would have to be the quick and dirty old fashion method they favored.

The easy and more usual approach was simple; bully the poor slob until he cracks. However, this tactic, very efficient in larger cities might not work so well in Lisbon where the density of the population was not sufficient to provide the smokescreen this operation required. Furthermore, they had no experience in working in hick towns like Lewiston or Lisbon. Isaac, who had married Mario's niece, would be able to help identify any weak link in Barcelo's armor.

While they were going into their respective rooms, Johnny activated the special "imaging equipment" as the New York technician has named it. Preparation and prevention would allow him to be one move ahead of these two city slickers he would not trust more than Isaac. The wolves howl with the wolves. In this business he was aware that like a nasty mother in law, one of these days the mob would show up for dinner. Then better if the confrontation is on his terms and turf.

Waiting for his two guests he flagged Dudley and they went over the week end program; a program they had carefully prepared and rehearsed with the staff. When done, Johnny told him.

-We may have an offer from these WOPs. An offer we won't like. Having them come here was a calculated risk, maybe not such a smart gamble. Let's see if we can live with the consequences and turn the tables on them, as we have done with Isaac. -

Dudley knew what Johnny was talking about when he referred to Isaac but was not so quick at grasping the full implications. He thought that Johnny was speculating and his intuition at work more than his reason. But knowing where Isaac was coming from and the latent threat he represented, his guard was up.

-What kind of offer do you think they'll make; this place is not for sale is It.? If it was I'd like to bid for it even though I don't have all the cash I could borrow most of it. - Answered a now very concerned Dudley.

Johnny knew that he could borrow the huge sum, having made the most of the few months he had been managing The Saint Augustine. Very important and wealthy people were fascinated by illegality if it was risk free and could hide behind a trustworthy front man. What a good scheme to invest illegal cash. Dudley was the kind of person they would be comfortable with.

-If it was for sale I'd sell it to you, but it's not...yet. - He added quickly and continued...

-What I'm saying is, that these two gentlemen will try to steal our lunch box... take it from us, by force without paying, exactly like Isaac tried if you remember.-

He remembered well both, the lunch boxes in school and the Isaac aborted coup. Thinking about this for a minute, Dudley looked at Johnny and said slowly.

-I still have my Marlin. Anyone looking for trouble will find it.-

-Hopefully we won't have to get rough. Let me deal with it. Act as if you didn't know anything about this; nothing will happen this week end. They're out of their turf in a small village like Lisbon. If they make a move they'll go through Isaac, and we know how to deal with him don't we.-

-We sure do. - Replied Dudley smiling.

He raised his glass of tomato juice to Johnny and, in one fierce gulp swallowed the entire content as if he was removing all danger.

Dudley would be faithful. Trustworthy friends would be precious for the next few months. Speaking to Alberto and Mario gave Barcelo the shivers. These guys were in the super major league. Cold bloodied business men with rules of their own.

A few moments later, Alberto showed up in the bar and Johnny joined him for a quick drink while waiting for Mario. He was wearing one of the after shave lotions Johnny was allergic to.

-Very nice room Johnny and it looks like full comfort has been provided. - Said Alberto winking at one of the girl as she brushed by. As it turned out, winking would be his only foreplay to Helena.

-We try to please and so far we've been lucky to recruit smart and competent personnel. Of course it costs a lot but in the end it's worth it. -

Mario joined them and they were able to visit the recycling business site before the evening sat in. Not a word was said during the visit. As a full truck load was backing up over the half full ravine, Johnny could see from the corner of his eye that Alberto was taking in the view as if he was already the owner.

Not a chance my greenhorn fellows. As Mario turned to him he wondered if he had not been thinking loud. He was known to do that.

-You have the kind of business our organization likes to be part of. You may consider selling out or accepting us as partners. We could help you fill this hole in a few years. -

-I'll fill it in a few more months, but I'm open to any sound proposal you could come up with. I asked Isaac to invite you for that specific purpose. - May as well remove the pin from this grenade right now, thought Johnny. He smiled realizing that his subconscious, his other self was looking for trouble as usual.

Mario who had been listening attentively to Johnny's reply remained pensive for a while.

-We'd be happy to have you as our guest in New York as soon as possible. Alberto and I can make some decisions on our own but for the very important deal we rely on the boss. Our elders will want to meet with you. – He had used the word elders to give the group a family air.

- I'm just a country boy who needs to have his ducks in a row before even thinking about a deal. So if you don't mind, I'd like to know the kind of association you guys have in mind before I bother your boss in New York.- Johnny replied.

-I'm really not at liberty to make any kind of offer but I can tell you from earlier experience that you would benefit by an association with us. We're big and powerful. - Replied Mario.

I'll bet you're big and powerful and dangerous, but what about fair play and honesty, thought Johnny.

-Ok, let's talk next week to set a date.-

The rest of the week end was spent in fun and frolics; while the liquor bill alone could have bankrupted them, the gambling revenues more than compensated. But the staff would be happy to never again have to deal with that bunch of psychotic social misfits.

Little John had fallen asleep before achieving his goal, the wine and the cognac eradicating or anaesthetizing any trace of hormone in his body. He'd be in a position to swear to his wife that he had been faithful. Dudley wondered how this otherwise smart business man would explain having lost more than two thousand dollars playing blackjack like a beginner; but money was not his problem.

The most interesting behaviors were that of the two New Yorkers. Mario turned out to be a close study to the infamous marquis. Deana was physically injured as well as humiliated. Dudley had to take her to a doctor on Sunday morning. She had been tied sitting on a chair and Mario would plunge her face in a basin filled with water until she almost drowned. Then he would throw her on the bed and rape her. When he no longer could get an erection, he would use a wooden replica of a penis to pinch hit for him. After a few hours of this, he threw her out of the room with a hundred dollar bill inserted deep into her vagina. She had barely been able to make it to Dudley's room. The doctor who treated her said that she had been tortured by an expert and would suffer the consequences for a long while.

Alberto was more the professional, so thought Barcelo until he saw the home movie; it turned out he was as queer as his colleague, even though less turbulent.

CHAPTER 15

"If you go to war against a mouse, prepare as if it was against a lion."

It was Monday morning before Johnny could retrieve the action films. He was curious about the meeting Mario, Isaac and Alberto had had Sunday afternoon. The meeting had lasted only thirty minutes but Johnny knew that it would be of the utmost interest for the club's and his future.

Alone in Dudley's office, he set the equipment up and started what would be a long and mostly boring session at the movies. Well, not totally dull; some footage would turn out to be life saving and others educating.

In suite one, where Alberto was staying, turned out to be of little interest except for a telephone call to a certain Luigi in New York. This guy appeared to be the boss man. Checking the name in the little black book he had taken from Isaac he identified him as Luigi Rossini. The conversation lasted only a few minutes:

Alberto. - Luigi, we seem to have a live business here; several million dollars potential over the next several years; gambling, booze and sex, very classy with a touch of originality. The staff is dressed like monks and nuns. -

Luigi. - Nuns...What do we need to get a hold of this monastery? -

Alberto. - As usual I'd say. Barcelo is smart enough but I've asked Isaac to collect information regarding his family and routine. The best way would be that he's removed from the picture; he's the captain of this ship. Without him the others would be push-over's. -

Luigi. - Bring him to New York where we can supervise his removal, accidents happen and the farm still has the best disposal crew.-

Alberto. -Understood. See you Monday.-

Then Johnny had seen Alberto refuse to be tucked in by Helena but had masturbated, like a girl, having a penis the size of a large clitoris. During the event he was standing in front of the mirror. Weird, thought Johnny, one is a sadistic son of a bitch while the other won't have anything to do with girls because of a small penis. This picture would be a real hit with his macho Italian friends.

Mario's footage was more interesting in terms of being disgusting. The guy was a pervert, sexually and morally as Johnny knew already having been told of his prowess by Dudley. The sadistic Mario had gagged and tied Deana, then really worked on her for more than one hour, plunging her head into a basin of water until she almost drowned, then releasing her so she could be revived enough for him to enjoy another bout of the same game. He had stripped but for his shoes and had entered every orifices in her body, licked, pinched and kicked her before untying the almost unconscious girl. After stuffing a one hundred dollar bill into her vagina, he told her that silence was a guarantee to stay alive.

-If you talk you're dead. I'll do it personally making the fun last.- The poor girl was too sick to react and had crawled out of the room on all fours; which had amused Mario a great deal.

While Mario had not phoned anyone, Alberto came frequently to his room and this is where they had the meeting with Isaac. Isaac knew of Alberto's reputation and was obviously terrorized by his wife's uncle. He would do exactly what they expected of him and in a way seemed happy to finally have an opportunity to get back at this "Portuguese runt" as he called him several times during the meeting. Johnny was glad that Isaac omitted to tell about his earlier encounter in West Bowdoin. He went back and doubled checked. A good soldier would have told it as it was. More planning and care might have been deployed to pluck the Saint Augustin and the BRE INC. While viewing this interesting sequence Johnny was thinking about an old proverb: -If you go to war against a mouse prepare as if you were fighting a Lion.-

After Isaac's departure from the suite, Alberto and Mario elaborated and agreed on a strategy.

-Let's make a million dollar offer to this Barcelo. Nobody refuses to listen to such an offer. The condition will be that the deal is ratified in New York. There he'll have a mortal accident and be disposed of at the farm. The animals haven't been fed in a while. –

And they both laughed remembering the last meal served to the hyenas: one of the rank and files had been caught with his hands in the cookie jar.

An example had to be made; in front of several members of the confraternity, assembled at the farm for a business meeting, the imprudent thief had been judged and thrown live into the pen.

A sumptuous banquet had been offered to the group of capo. After the desert was served Luigi had made a speech on the importance of being trustworthy.

-I can still hear the terrible sounds he and they made. But... we never had another problem.- Said Mario who had enjoyed the show almost as much as Luigi's wife.

The offer of a million dollars was old news as Johnny had already received it the previous Sunday afternoon. He was less surprised at the mob's generosity when the entire plan was exposed. The meeting had been scheduled for the very next Saturday but Johnny had rescheduled for the following week, needing more time to prepare.

What was he to do? Before anything else he had to move Emilie out of the house as she would be a target no matter what he did. Would he confide in her and Dudley? He chose not to for the moment. A secret shared by three persons can remain a secret only if two of the three die. Even displacing Emilie could alert the enemy.

After several hours of intense cogitation he had established a priority list and the first draft of a plan: First, a meeting with Isaac; to know as much as possible about the organization. While he still had the phone numbers and addresses collected from Isaac's little black book, some changes were probable since that famous July evening. Another source of information would be the calls made from the Club's phone.

Action time was now; he had to engage otherwise the fear would stifle his will. Reaching for the phone he dialed Isaac's number. His wife answered and yes he would come to the phone she said with a very strong Bostonian accent.

Without the usual "How do you do", Johnny attacked immediately.

-You may or may not know about the offer I received from your partners. You've been the instigator of this deal and as such you're entitled to a ten percent commission. –

Why be stingy. The best defense against a lie is to make the liar believe you are caught in his web. Johnny had tried to sound happy and enthusiastic. Silence at the other end so he continued.

-I'll take a well earned vacation if this comes true. - It was essential that Isaac believed him.

More silence as Isaac was thinking about a way to also sound tickled at this news; which he knew to be a trap... even if Alberto had told him about the offer, Isaac was sure that the Familia would never pay a million dollars for anything. The trap would be set in New York and would be of the fatal variety. Tough luck he thought.

-A one hundred thousand dollars commission on this deal... wow, I'm speechless. - So you were told, thought Johnny. I'll bet you're speechless. - And he continued loud.

-Isaac... you'll always get what you deserve.... If I make money you make money, as you already know. How much have we paid you so far.? More than a hundred thousand I'll bet. - He had checked the numbers and knew that Isaac had so far received one hundred and twelve thousand crispy dollars in cold cash.

May as well give the rat heart burns with veiled threats of getting what he deserves. Then Johnny thought that Isaac may not have known the entire plan. Why would Mario or Alberto trust this lowly member of the organization? Replaying the movie in his mind he realized that Isaac did not know anything about his planned termination, nothing during his conversation with Mario and Alberto could have given him the inkling about what the entire plan was. On the other hand he knew that the mob was not as generous as to offer a million dollar for The Saint Augustine Club and the BRE recycling site. Isaac also knew of their ways and how they disposed of reluctant business targets. Yes, more powerful than the attraction of substantial gains, revenge was what Isaac was seeking.

-Before I go to New York, I'll need to meet with you. Understanding how this organization works is important for both of us. You wouldn't want me to abort this deal. You'd lose a commission of one hundred thousand dollars. You've been with them for a long time and to earn that ten percent commission you have to educate me. By the way they all seem to be Italian in this company, how did a good Jewish boy like you get in bed with Sicilians?-

-My wife is Italian. She's the niece of one of the bosses. - Answered Isaac.

-Very good, - replied Johnny, -then you know all there is to know about these future partners of mine. And by the way I am sure that they've asked you about me. I hope you haven't described the peculiar incident marking the beginning of our relationship.-

-Not a chance. - Isaac replied quickly. Quick enough for Johnny to know that it was the truth.

Johnny was pleased with this answer. He knew the Italians would think of him as a naïve country boy. Being underestimated is an ideal position; in any type of game. –Let them prepare to go to war against a mouse. - Thought Barcelo. He was not about to do the same thing.

-Let's meet tomorrow morning Isaac, I'll drive to Boston and be at your home around seven o'clock.-

And he hung up. -Surprised that I know where you live, aren't you. By ten o'clock tomorrow I'll know a lot more about you and your mob friends.- The "last scene", with Judas sitting at the table sprang to his mind.

It was only six o'clock; he gave Dudley a call. Now was the time to tell him. He would need his help for the next innings of this match.

-Hey Dud, let's have a short meeting. This offer I told you about is not as good as it sounds and I would like to clarify some of the.... finer points. -

Dud sounded relieved at hearing Johnny's voice. Ten minutes later they were sitting at their table, being served the best Atlantic smoked salmon this side of Mars. An inch thick T Bone steak would follow.

-Dud, we've been around for a while and so far we have a good batting average. We're making heaps of money which is very unusual for the two bums we were. I know you can get all the money you need to become the owner of The Saint Augustine, if you need to, but I am not yet ready to sell. You won't be surprised to learn that these good people from New York want the Club and the BRE recycling company. The only problem in dealing with guys like them is that you can't say no and have to accept their offer or be taken out. They could have guessed that I am not a push over and the offer they made is a death trap. I'm invited to come to New York so they can kill me on their turf. If the plan they have developed works out, I won't be coming back walking or... for that matter not coming back at all.- Johnny was thinking about the reference made to the disposal animals.

Dudley's eyes were fixed on Johnny's mouth. He continued fixing Barcelo's lips for a while without saying a word, expecting the lips to keep on talking. The information was sinking in.

-You're right, we've been together for quite a while and if I'm not as smart as you I've learned a few tricks during all these years. I'm not surprised at what you're telling me..... How in hell did you learn about their plan? How can you be so sure? Can't be Isaac... I'm sure he hates our guts. – Remarked Dud, waiting for an answer.

-Right, it couldn't be Isaac and it'll have to be my secret for now but I'm one hundred percent certain of what I told you. Not ninety nine, one hundred percent, totally without the smallest doubt. –

He needed to convince Dudley that he was not assuming or guessing. He continued.

-I'll need your help to turn this around. We've done it before and will do it again except that this time we're dealing with people more dangerous than any one you or I have ever known. We'll have to be smart, careful and if we need to, ruthless... I mean that we may have to kill to defend ourselves and what's ours.-

The last of the salmon disappeared in Dudley's mouth. Johnny had not yet started to eat, busy thinking and talking. Dudley was quick in answering.

-Tell me what you expect of me and I'll do it. - He said, his large frame leaning over the table to be closer to Johnny's eyes.

-I don't know yet but I'll have a complete plan before the day is over. Remember that my life is at stake, as will be yours if you agree to help. If they succeed in getting rid of me, they'll probably make you an offer to continue running The Club for a while.-

Barcelo tasted the salmon. Jeremiah was not bragging in vain when he had assured Johnny that he could make the very best smoked salmon.

-Until we're ready to move, don't change anything in your attitude. Isaac is part of their group and will have a role to play in this game. I'll try to use him. I'm meeting with him tomorrow morning. He may not be aware of the entire plan but he knows their ways and can guess the outcome. He was asked to collect information on me, my family, you and the accountant; we should cooperate. Let them think we're babes in the woods. After his last episode with us he should know better but, as you said he wants our hides and was stupid enough to not tell his partners about the famous last time. -

Dudley had stopped chewing on his piece of toast, always a proof that he was very attentive.

-Nobody will take this business away from us. I'll do exactly as you say. In the mean time let's eat I'm hungry. - Eating had always been a priority with Dudley.

Laughing, he finished the toast, the capers and had a glass of red wine which he didn't consider to be an alcoholic beverage. It was the same color as the tomato juice and with his size; a few glasses did not give him much of a buzz.

-What I'll need from you is a complete list of the available muscle inventory we can count on: female or male, with their specialties if they have one. Also buy the following articles, in Portland, not in Lewiston and make sure not to be recognized. Wear a hat and an outfit that you'll get rid of after the purchase. Pay cash for everything.-

Johnny took out from his pocket a long list of articles which read:

One case of dynamite and caps, five .45 caliber handguns, one with a silencer, two pumping action shot guns, five stilettos, one cross bow with arrows, seven wigs of different colors, six false mustaches and seven blue coveralls, the kind the garage repairmen wear, rubber gloves, ammunitions in sufficient quantity.

-I forgot to include handcuffs, please get five of them as well and chloroform. - Dudley studied the list for a while.

-Do you intend to start the third world war?-

As Johnny was not replying, back in his planning mode, Dud quickly added that he would have the material in two or three suit cases by tomorrow night.

-Okay then, let's meet again tomorrow night. - Johnny said.

-I haven't been excited like this since that famous July evening. What a tale to tell our grand children if we survive. - Replied Dudley.

-We'll survive. To us my good friend. - Johnny said as he raised his glass in a toast.

CHAPTER 16

"Take the war to your enemy if you can't avoid it"

After a night of turning and tossing, getting up at four was a relief. The walls and the ceiling had been closing in on him during most of the night: panic, not because he was afraid of what the next week had in store for him but because he could feel the cold tentacles of this ugly malice squeezing him. Having a death sentence decreed by a criminal group because you own something they desire, would have disturbed most people he knew. He couldn't help making the analogy with the MacFarlane kid who would steal his hand made toys.

Dawn brought respite and his anger provided the antidote. His entire being was in a whirlwind, reshuffling several scenarios he had been elaborating during the night. Some of them completely out of reach, others improbable and a few that could succeed because of their simplicity. He elected to stick to a strategy that would be uncomplicated.

The question was straightforward: How did he want this adventure to end? Answer: He wished this misfortune to become an opportunity; one that would save his ass, his business and his future. A gross schema of his plan was delineated by three in the morning; he then spent the rest of the short night analyzing each steps in view of removing any and all elements not absolutely essential. The three hours driving time to Boston provided the right environment to finalize a strategy that could work. It would work because it was simple, unexpected and yet, audacious beyond the imagination of these hoodlums.

Finding the Weinstein's home was easy. A neat New England two story wooden house with a pointed roof under which a large balcony opened on what was certainly the master bedroom. Freshly painted in white with green trim around the windows, the doors and the roof lines, it had character and warmth. A white fence surrounded the property, hemming in an array of well kept flower beds.

The door opened before he could ring the old fashioned copper door-bell. Looking at him with large dark piercing eyes was a little girl of around seven, neatly dressed in a navy blue costume, a red bow in her well groomed jet-black hair; she stared at him for a long moment.

-Please come in Mister Barcelo, I know who you are-.

-What's your name little miss. - Bowing to the little girl who giggled before answering that she was Anna Maria Weinstein.

-I can speak Italian and some Yiddish, although not well. - She admitted.

-That's a lot more than I can. - Answered Johnny as he came in the door almost running into Mrs. Weinstein. He had met her at his wedding but did not remember her as being so pretty, very Italian, well proportioned and petite, with eyes as dark and piercing as her daughter's.

-Sorry to intrude so early but Isaac and I have some important business to talk about and very little time to do it.-

-You're welcome in my home. Isaac won't be long, in the mean time come in and have a cup of coffee while I make breakfast. Bacon and eggs ok?-

-Just great. - He answered, and sat down at the kitchen table wondering why such a nice lady would marry a bum like Isaac.

Looking intensely into her eyes, he could not detect any trickery; Anna Maria Weinstein was not aware of the scenario being developed by her husband.

He could hear Isaac flushing the toilet one story up. He would be nervous and skittish. Past experience had taught Isaac what could be dished out in retaliation for treason. He would remember about Herb and the signed statement indicting him for the murder of his employee Herbert. Now that he thought the shit could hit the fan, he must have been thinking about a way to reclaim this document. He also must have prepared options. Johnny was wondering what these would be; or was his desire to exact revenge so strong that he did not care about repercussions. Isaac was a gambler and loosing could be as exciting as winning. For that matter so was he, he had to admit.

Sporting a razor cut on his chin, Isaac entered the kitchen where Johnny was sipping a cup of excellent coffee; Italians do make the best. Sitting down at the table he extended a sweaty hand to Johnny.

-Congratulations. A hell of a proposal my friends made. It's not usual for them to pay as much for start-up companies. Very generous I must say. - There might have been a word of caution in this statement; his conscience speaking out of turn.

Anna Maria was listening while frying the eggs. From the corner of his eye, Johnny saw her surprised expression when the word generous was mentioned. Uncle Mario never had a generous bone in his miserable body, and while Anna Maria ignored the lurid details of the business, she was well aware of the dangers dealing with the mob represented. For a moment she locked eyes with Barcelo.

-I don't have the money in my bank account yet and both my businesses are already making lots of money as you know, so we're not looking at start-ups, but this offer looks real enough and I suppose these people are honest and trustworthy.-

He had difficulty keeping a straight face while pronouncing the words honest and trustworthy. The smug smile on Isaac's face confirmed that the bastard had sold him. Too bad for his family, he might get hurt playing with big boys and Anna Maria might be made a young widow. Johnny had kept monitoring her facial expression and was amused at the grimace she made when the words –honest and trustworthy- were pronounced.

-As much as I can tell. They've always been square and fair with me. - Was the non equivocal answer.

Eyes turning left while talking, creativity was used, and therefore a lie was being fabricated. Isaac was looking to his left shoe as he talked. Not only was he lying but not proud of it.

-Very well, if you don't mind I'd like to know more about this organization. A deal is only done when the money is paid out. Mario and Alberto are great guys but as they admitted they don't decide on transactions that size. -

-Ask away. - Said Isaac. He had decided to answer Johnny's questions. Dead people are good at keeping secrets.

One hour later Johnny knew what he needed to know. His game plan was not complicated: First assert a dominant position in the negotiation by a clear show of force; then convince these business men that they would fare better financially by leaving him and his business alone; and the last, was to increase the flow of scrap tires to the BRE INC. While listening to Isaac and getting acquainted with the Rossini organization he had put the final touch to his plan.

Thanking Anna Maria for the excellent breakfast, he asked her which one of the bosses was her uncle. It turned out that she was Mario's niece. She expressed open aversion for the old sadist and averted Johnny's eyes when she answered. Her blushing face gave away the secret that only she and Mario shared or was it that she had guessed that Barcelo would soon be a departed acquaintance; or both.

Johnny could see how Uncle Mario would not be grieved by this girl. In the final version of the plan, Mario was to be the example and provide the show of force. The son of a bitch had it coming. His distorted sexual fantasies made him a perfect target for an unhappy former romping partner.

Some girls don't have a sense of humor. Deana did not. She had kept the hundred dollar bill the old doctor had removed from her uterus and intended to shove it deep into the anal canal of the pervert. Johnny had laughed, wondering what the pathologist would have to say about this when autopsying the murdered old man. On this lighter thought, he had been able to sleep a few hours the previous night.

Recapitulating the information he had received from Isaac, Johnny had learned that Mario was a respected advisor and that Alberto was an executive honed to go up in the organization. The real Boss was this Luigi Rossini, whose son was being groomed to succeed him and was therefore Alberto's rival. The Familia owned several hotels, factories and various other businesses that were useful in laundering substantial illegal revenues from boot legging, prostitution and gambling.

The Rossinis were living on a large estate in New Jersey and raised horses, as well as other exotic animals, Isaac had said with a sly smile thinking about the infamous hyenas and remembering how they had devoured dim-witted Bruce. The poor slob had only taken four hundred dollars and said that he was to return it. His honor and the death of Herb would be properly avenged.

The three hour return trip was used to review and adapt the plan to the space-time reality. It would be a succession of surprise to his foes, always a step ahead, a quick succession of well orchestrated moves, never leaving anything to chance; hitting first and hard. This costly cinematographic equipment was now proving to be a life saving investment. Who said paranoia was not useful?

First the meeting schedule would be delayed one more week. They would not be annoyed as Isaac had undoubtedly been reporting their conversation to Alberto or Mario. Johnny needed the extra week to train and prepare his crew. Since the very beginning of the Saint Augustine caper, Barcelo and Dudley had hired people who would be substantially upgraded in working for them: honest people capable of dedication. For these qualities salaries almost fifty percent higher than the industry standard were paid. In return The Saint Augustine received total loyalty.

This strike force, as he now called his team, would be arriving in New York one day prior to the meeting date, staying in the hotel where his doom was to be sealed. He had logically surmised that he was to be kidnapped rather than killed in the hotel suite; he needed to be kept alive for the disposal animals. But that detail was not important as the table would be reversed on the kidnappers while in the act. Simultaneously Mario would be taken out and dealt with in a manner befitting his life style and taste for the sordid. The final negotiation with Luigi Rossini, the real boss, would then take place in his home, in this infamous farm, and, either culminates in a blood bath or a reasonably secured and mutually satisfactory agreement for everyone except for Isaac and Mario.

Verification of all addresses and routine for the Rossinis, Alberto and Mario would take a few days. Isaac had confirmed that the addresses in his little black book were still current but extreme paranoia was to be exercised. Johnny would use the services of a one man detective agency from the Boston area to double check. For a healthy supplement he was guaranteed that the job would be done within the next seventy two hours.

-Try to know as much as possible about this Mario Santini's daily routine. We want to know when he gets up, pees, defecates, eats and other occupations he might have during the course of a day.- Had stipulated Johnny as he was paying up front.

The detective, an old gumshoe prepared to do almost anything for the right price said that he would do his best. Johnny was even given to understand that a fatal accident could be arranged if the price was right.

-You'll get a bonus if we can use the extra information but we are not planning anything illegal.- Replied Johnny. This was not a fib as he would be acting in self defense.

Now that the plan was taking form the most critical remained: select the strike force and carefully and thoroughly rehearse the game plan until it becomes as natural as eating. The dices were rolling as from Boston he had confirmed the meeting for the next week; Alberto was pleased, obviously wanting to get this out of the way as soon as possible. After all, every day that went by was a loss of revenue for the Familia.

-Your hotel reservation has been confirmed at the Park Plaza hotel, we're expecting you Friday night next week before six in the afternoon.- Said Alberto.

Immediately Johnny phoned the same hotel and, under a false name, reserved three other suites for the previous day and two for that fatidic Friday night. He and his team would register on Thursday night, under different names and disguised. He would then arrive as expected on Friday evening for the meeting. Occupy the terrain and get comfortable with the scene; there should be no surprises on D Day.

The plan was simple enough and should work because of the complete surprise element. Coming into his room, to abduct or kill him on Friday night, the kidnappers would be ambushed and taken prisoners. The linchpin of the plan was that all actions should be synchronized as of the kidnapping moment. As Alberto had not fixed a place or a time for the meeting on Saturday morning Johnny was reasonably sure that they had planned his execution for Friday evening. He still did not know which animal species would be disposing of his carcass; what could it be, he had heard of cadavers being grinded and fed to chicken or pigs, alligators could also do a job.

As he walked into The Club, Dudley came to meet him.

-Everything is purchased and stored in three large trunks. I couldn't buy a silencer but I'm having Harvey the tool maker making a couple. Ready tomorrow he promised.–

-What about the people. – Asked Johnny.

-We have five employees we can count on.-

And they went over the list: four of the most trustworthy male employees plus one female, Deana, Mario's play thing. She would have a chance to return the hundred dollar bill in the spirit of "Pay your debt keep your friends". The four fighting monks had been working for The Saint Augustine since opening day and would all be handsomely compensated. All of them realized that they had good jobs and would do anything for Dudley.

-We have a few days to prepare, have you talked to the men. - Asked Johnny.

-I was doing just that when you came in. All of them are unmarried and have been working for us since day one. The guys are mostly farm boys, former soldiers and familiar with most weapons. Deana is tough enough and while she does not yet know what we plan exactly, would not have a second thought about closing this pervert's eyes forever.

-I suppose that they're still here. – Dudley nodded. –Let's brief them. I'll go through the plan with them and you. Then practice and rehearse every step during the next few days and again early next week until just before we leave for the real thing. That will include actual firing the guns on the BRE site, double checking the equipment, train to change their appearances and go over each step of the plan until it's perfect. We don't have much time but in a way this is good, no one will have time to think about it and get nervous. We'll need to be ready by next Thursday morning around five o'clock. In the mean time The Club stays opened as usual but these five are to rest all day next Wednesday. They'll each receive five hundred dollars for that job. No booze for any one until this is over. There will be one thousand for you and, from now on, ten percent of the net revenues the good Saint earns for us.-

Dudley's face lit up at the ten percent participation. He was becoming a partner in The Club. The thousand was not bad but he would have helped for free.

Starting the next day, the strike force had daily sessions of gun handling, preparation drills, disguising and finally game playing of all the incidents and accidents that could and would occur.

-Anyone having second thoughts about having to use the guns you'll be issued? - Asked Johnny.

They did not think it would be a problem but having never shot any one before, they could not answer with certainty.

-You've been poaching and you've killed deer's and bears and moose. This will be easier as the people you'll face are meaner than any animals you have dealt with. Chances are that you'll not have to go to this extreme. If it becomes necessary Dudley or I will do it. - He knew about poaching and so did all of them except Deana. But she was ahead of the class because of hands on experience the others never even dreamed about.

Johnny had a long private chat with each of the members and was satisfied that they would perform as required but more important, they would be tight lipped. They only had a vague idea of the real objective and would not be told anything unless absolutely necessary. In a year or so they would not remember any of the details, only the buzz would linger on.

Thursday morning the following week, they left at five o'clock and arrived in New York on schedule at four in the afternoon. Johnny, Dudley and Deana were disguised beyond recognition. During the previous week, Barcelo had grown a thin black moustache and was wearing a light blue silk shirt under an expensive black leather jacket. A blue beret covering a black curly wig contributed to improve his looks to the point where he resembled a known European film director.

Dudley was also sporting a moustache; a walrus moustache more befitting his massive build. Wig and dark glasses made him unrecognizable to even his mother. He had tried it on the woman and was still laughing at the face the old girl did when he peeled off his mustache.

Deana had been easy. Trimming and dying her hair blond had done the trick. A smart costume and a briefcase contributed to giving her the allure of a private secretary travelling with this off beat movie director and his body guard. Nobody but Mario had really looked at her and he would not have much of a chance to tell.

Johnny and Deana registered as Mister and Mrs. Davison for one night only; while the others shared three rooms. Inventing a weird story Dudley had been able to rent the suite 301 across from suite 300 reserved for Barcelo by Alberto. Johnny had insisted on knowing the number of the suite he would occupy at the Plaza: saying that he was expecting to interview a New York accountant for the Club on the following Saturday morning. Not surprisingly suite 300 was right next to the fire exit and the service elevator. Johnny had learned from the Boston gum shoe that the Park Plaza was owned by the Rossini Familia.

-Let's eat in groups of two. - Ordered Dudley who had taken over the day to day organization.

M. and Mrs. Davison went out early for a good dinner at the Four Seasons. Other than having seen how she could handle a gun and admire her street smartness, Johnny didn't know this girl from Eve. She was to play a key role in this caper and while Dudley thought that she was – right for the job-...

-How did you end up as a hostess in The Saint Augustine?-There is nothing like a direct approach if you want straight forward answers. She looked at him with her deep dark eyes, trying to guess what he wanted to hear.

-Difficult to get a job if you've done time. Dudley knows about my past. I thought he had told you about me and the others. –

-I trust Dudley, we go back a long long time, if he thought you were fit for the job you are.-

-Okay. I'll give you a short version of my life up to now, if you want more details, ask. My father died during the last war and I was left an orphan with a younger sister. Mom did her best but couldn't make ends meet. She met someone and married. I was ten at the time and my sister only five. It wasn't long before I discovered that our step father liked ten year old girls. He started abusing me after school when mom was working. This lasted several years. I didn't know better and believed him when he said that my mother would die of a broken heart if I told. She had cried enough when the telegram was received advising her of our father's death and I wanted to protect her from more grief. Up until that time Henry had been gentle with mom and had left Jodie alone. She's my younger sister.-

She took a sip of water to catch her breath.

-When he started being violent with mom and pawing Jodie I had to do something. One night that he had been out drinking heavily as usual, I waited for him outside the house. It was easy to have him follow me behind an abandoned shed where I had hidden a baseball bat and a sharp knife. As he unzipped to pee before fucking me, I let him have it on the head with the baseball bat; then while he was unconscious I cut his balls and broke both his legs with the bat. They found him in the morning when someone heard his moans. The police came but he never laid charges, saying that he had not seen his assailants.-

-I'm sorry, I didn't know. I can better understand that what this pervert did to you last week was salt on an open wound. - Cut in Johnny.

-Don't worry about me, we all have our secrets and I like being a hostess for you at The Saint Augustine as long as I don't draw numbers like this pervert. After being screwed from age ten to sixteen by my step father, prostitution is not a moral problem. It's a job, like washing dishes or typing letters. I don't take any pleasure out of it and never have. They say it's the oldest profession in the world and during my stay in jail, because that's where I landed for shoplifting when I was seventeen, I had time to read and learned that the Greeks or was it the Romans, had nuns in their temples, sexually accommodating the visitors and probably the priests as well. Vestals they called them. –

-Vestals, Johnny repeated; I guess we could call the hostesses, Vestals and the Club could be renamed the Temple or the monastery of Saint Augustine. - Said Johnny. –Vestal has more class than Hostess and would give the place a spiritual atmosphere, more suited to the garb, wouldn't it.?-

She giggled at the mention of spirituality.

-Yes, that would be better; although some of the girls are far from being spiritually motivated-She quipped.

-This job is important for The Club as you can imagine. I made a mistake in thinking that the mob could be client but not predators. - Continued Johnny who wanted to further reassure himself that this girl would be as trustworthy as Dudley believed.

-I gathered this much and we're all very pleased to be able to help. And-, she continued, - the money is not bad, I intend to buy myself a car with the five hundred....I would've done it for free in order to have a crack at this pig. I have a few instruments I'd like to ram up his pervert ass hole. You'll let me deal with him won't you?-

-He'll be all yours and we want him to be ... taken out as Dudley told you. It'll look as if one of his former sexual toys has come back for revenge. In a sense that's what it will be. –

There, it was said. Johnny wanted to know how she would react; she continued to sip her tea for a second before replying.

-Taken out means executed doesn't it.? ...- He nodded. -That wouldn't be the first time. I've done it before...., in jail. -

She glanced at Johnny. He nodded that he wanted to know this detail. She related in a monotone voice how when in jail at seventeen, she had been sold by the prison guards to a bulldagger, and had killed her in the showers by fracturing her wind pipe, keeping her head under the spray of water until she stopped moving. Throughout the incident the other inmates had watched silently preventing one of the lesbian's cronies from interfering.

Johnny was beginning to like this tall beautiful young woman.

-Let's go home, and by the way I don't expect any sexual favors from you even if we'll sleep as man and wife.-

She looked at him with a smile and murmured.

-We'll see about that Mister Barcelo, what we're doing may be the only type of arousal still getting to me. We'll see about that.-

At eleven they were back in the room and while Johnny was talking to Dudley in the hallway, Deana took a shower and was in bed when he came back.

He cleaned his gun and hers and felt the edge of the dagger she would be using. The shotguns were in Dudley's room and for now everything seemed in order. He showered and crawled carefully in bed paying attention not to awaken Deana who seemed asleep.

CHAPTER 17

"In war as in love, you have to get close to end it."

Friday was a morose type of a day; appropriate for starting a world war or to be on the receiving end of a large meteorite. There was no need to get up before eight. Drinking his first cup of a bad coffee, Dudley reviewed the plan one last time. Satisfied that every player understood his role, he had a healthy breakfast and advised his group of mercenaries to do the same.

-This meal will be the last you'll take sitting down today. –

Even though tempted to have a final rehearsal in the late morning, he decided that too much is sometimes worse than not enough. Next would be the real thing. They were ready for the grand opening.

Mister and Mrs. Davison checked out of their room. Later on that day, without the wig and the moustache, Johnny Barcelo would be back to register under his own name. In the mean time, he, Deana and Dudley would pay a visit to "Perv" Mario, as Deana had nicknamed him. On the check list of things to do, he was the first assignment. The success of this operation depended on the next few hours.

Mario Santini was living in one of the luxurious apartments flanking the Hudson River. All the trimmings: Doorman, underground garage, in house phone, main entrance invaded by tropical plants of all sorts, wealthy neighbors, security and all other modern conveniences money can buy. The detective Johnny had hired reported that one of the extravagances Mario indulged into was a daily massage at three o'clock sharp. His regular therapist would come to his apartment and work on him during one hour. No one can serve the Mafia for as long as he had without carrying forward a multitude of aches and pains. The private detective had been able to provide the address, the description and other important details of the therapist. For instance that she would walk from her apartment to Mario's carrying an old duffel bag. -You'll recognize her from this duffel bag; otherwise she is ordinary, fortyish, Porto Rican, wearing glasses and in good shape. -.

On this day, as always, Claudia started her ten minute walk to Mario's apartment at two fifty on the dot. Five minutes later she was picked up, chloroformed, gagged and tied before being thrown into the trunk of the car. Later they would transfer her into Mario's vehicle from where she would be released later. They had indeed identified her by the duffel bag containing her professional ware. The bag was immediately brought to Deana waiting to enter the building.

Her blond hair and makeup would fool Mario as it had tricked Dudley. Posing as the replacement physiotherapist, Deana waltzed through the imposing front door staying a minute longer under the inspection of the in-house video surveillance system. Flashing a quaint smile she easily convinced the doorman that she was replacing Claudia who was sick.

-She has a problem with her sciatic nerve and can't move. – The retired New York City police officer picked up the phone and repeated the tale to Mario.

Mario didn't like changes of any kind to his daily routine and was about to refuse when the doorman told him that: –This one is "quite a Looker" and carries the same old beaten up bag your regular drags around. Take a look at the video and you may change your mind.- That got Mario's attention. – She is? The same bag? Are you sure?- OK I don't have to look at the video; let her come up, a little change could be fun.-

The doorman grinned at Deana before showing her to the lift. He punched number four for her. – Number 411 to the right, good luck. - He knew she would have to be lucky if Mario was in his usual horny disposition.

On the way up Deana opened the bag to have easy access to the silenced 45 revolver she had hidden inside. Apartment 411 was a large corner residence looking down on the Henry Hudson river; Deana's pulsation was approaching the tachycardia max when she rang the bell, bending her head so Mario could see her blond hair and not recognize her through the peep hole. She heard shuffling and during an eternity, like a blast of cold air, she felt the inspection on the other side of the heavy oak door; the door opened; she walked in. Mario had opened the door staying behind the door as she walked in.

She had anticipated that he would be behind the door and dangerously close. As soon as she heard the door snap closed, she went forward a few feet and pivoted as she dropped the bag; her left hand holding the big silenced forty five aimed at Mario's belly. Not a word had been said. Deana could smell the acrid breath of the old man. Wide eyed he was staring at her then at the gun, his hands starting to move forward.

-Turn around and kneel. - She growled. –The hammer is pulled back and I won't hesitate a moment to squeeze the trigger and open a hole the size of the Lincoln tunnel in your flabby stomach. Do it now. - She repeated.

Mario had the kind of experience you acquire during several years of tempting the devil. The sound of her voice was a sure warning; this girl would enjoy shooting him. His white bath robe, opened at the waist allowing a large white belly to protrude, was hanging loose over his knobby knees and chicken legs. He felt ridiculous but his instinct advised against any sudden moves. The girl was tall and strong, but what stopped him were the determination he could feel and the mention of the hammer being cocked. Looking at the big silenced gun and then at the woman, he could vaguely remember that face. During their last encounter, the hair was dark and longer, she was naked and on all four; he had spent more time looking at her breasts and ass than at her face.

A shot fired would not be heard as the silencer was of the right size; he knew a lot about guns and silencers. Obediently, he turned around and started to kneel as ordered while muttering:

-Who the fuck are you. What do you want from me? Do you know who I am.? – His voice wanted to be firm but the sounds came out as a whine.

He was slow at kneeling, his right knee stiff from an old wound. Deana kicked him above the calf and without resting her leg on the floor, cocked it again to wham him in the kidney as he was falling on his knees; which made him crashed down with a grunt; as he could not jut out his hands fast enough, Mario smashed his nose on the carpeted floor. Red blood on a white carpet; Deana was amazed at becoming aware of the contrast.

- What's important is that I know who you are. If I wanted to kill you … Stay cool and everything will be fine. - She now wanted to reassure him, no hurry, no need for useless bravado.

The house phone rang; she found it close to the door and answered. The doorman was announcing two visitors. Pretending to ask Mario she came back to the phone.

-He says to send them up, they're expected. -

She backed a few steps and opened the door while Mario was nursing his bleeding nose. A moment later Johnny and Dudley walked in. From the floor, Mario glanced up and recognized Barcelo who had come in removing his curly black wig.

-Surprise, surprise, Mario. My little finger told me what you were planning for this sucker Barcelo. I didn't like what I heard. - Whispered Johnny as he lowered his face close enough for Mario to recognize him.

Mario had been in several tight spots during his tempestuous life but this time, he knew his ass to be in a precarious sling. While Barcelo was being civil and introducing himself, Dudley was checking the three large rooms in the apartment: a lavishly furnished living room, the kitchen in disarray and finally the bedroom where he was surprised to find a very young girl lying naked on the king size bed.

Naughty Mario had been up to his daily fun and games. On her back, the girl seemed to be sleeping or unconscious, probably drugged. Each foot was cuffed to the bed posts but her hands were free.

-What do we have here? Back to your old tricks? Very nasty of you to continue hurting young girls the way you do. How many have you destroyed like this one? You're a depraved old monkey. - He continued.

-Have you recognized Deana? She didn't appreciate your unusual love-making style. She would like to get back at you.-.

Mario was now fully aware of who these three were. His neurons firing to the limit could not understand how Barcelo had been able to outguess him.

-You're all crazy, I'm one of the most important person in the Mafia. I'll have you all killed. –

Then looking at Johnny and realizing that what he had said could only worsen his already precarious destiny he decided to play the slighted business man.

-I thought you were coming over to sign a contract with Luigi, what's the matter with you, we had a million dollar check for you. –

Barcelo would have enjoyed this little game but time was of the essence.

-We don't have all day Mario, so I'll tell you my little secret. You were filmed and heard during your visit to my Club and I know what my fate is going to be if I let you have your way. The best defense is the attack.-

Dudley was within hearing and raised his arms to the ceiling.

-That's how you knew so much about their plans... How did you ever get to film them.-

Being filmed.... Mario never imagined these hillbillies would be as sophisticated. By this time Dudley had shackled his hands and feet while Deana was holding her gun to his head ready to muffle any sound.

They grabbed Mario by the feet and arms and tossed him on the large bed, alongside the immobile nymphet.

-Make sure she won't be able to recognize any of us. No more name. Stick wet paper into her ears and pull the blanket over her head. Gag her as well.-

Deana did as instructed and also gagged Mario with the girl's pink string panties shoving them into the gaping and toothless mouth before taping the lips together.

-You'll go out in a style you're accustomed to. -Said Deana.

Until then Mario had nurtured the hope that he could speak his way out. Gagged, he understood that he had abused his last human being and ejaculated his last droplet of sperm. Pathetically writhing and twisting on the bed, he kept trying to emit sounds.

-Find the key for the girl's cuffs and release her. Give her a little more of that chloroform she was administered. We want her to be asleep for another three hours.- And let's take a picture souvenir of Mario with his latest conquest. – Continued Johnny.

They propped Mario and placed his head between the sleeping beauty's thighs. For a few seconds his gag was removed and the picture taken. Then the roll was removed from the camera and inserted in Mario's anal canal.

–Don't use any Vaseline he didn't with me the filthy pig. - Grunted Deana.

-You're on stage next if you feel up to it. ? - Said Johnny looking at Deana.

She was angry enough to do this bastard in but not while he was tied up; with the silenced gun maybe.... but like that, coldly .... Johnny saw her hesitation.

-Give me that hundred and wait in the next room.

As she was walking out of the room, Barcelo slowly placed the point of his stiletto under Mario's chin and pushed at a slight angle until it reached the cerebellum. The body stiffened, the eyes closed and death was instantaneous; almost bloodless. He then pulled the dead man's pants down to his knees, cut off his penis and testicles which he stuffed in his mouth after having removed the gag. On the belly he wrote with the razor-sharp point of the stiletto: « Sadistic PIG ». He then rolled the hundred dollar bill and inserted it in Mario's anus, crowding the roll of film further up the colon.

He did not feel any remorse. As with Herb, Isaac's hit man, he was only serving justice, his kind of justice. After carefully wiping the blood off the blade of his knife, he walked out of the room.

-Is there anything in here that could be useful? Where he's going, Mario won't need the money. It will help pay the expenses. -

A little black address book was taped under one of the drawers in the kitchen. Johnny pocketed it and after further searching the place they found an envelope with five thousand dollars. He took that as well. Throughout the apartment, there were several black and white and colored photographs depicting various events in Mario's life; in the living room, alone on one of the walls, a small painting hanging under a powerful spotlight attracted Deana's attention; she cut it off alongside the frame, rolled it and placed it in the duffel bag with the address book, the Rolex watch and the money. Johnny was looking on and stepped in: -Not the Rolex; it could be traced.-.

He unrolled the painting and could not make out the signature: something like *" E. Ma.e."* He could not make out the third and the last letter; but it was very old. - Let's keep it could be useful.-

The key and registration of Mario's car were on a table near the entrance. It would be easier to come up to Luigi's house if Mario's car was used; and Claudia, the physiotherapist had to be transferred. An additional decoy, one of Mario's famous hat was snatched.

-We're done, let's go.-

Using the fire exit, they reached the garage and were off in Mario's car, dropping Dudley near his own car a few blocks away; where Claudia was made as comfortable as possible in Mario's car trunk, after a little more sleeping agent. She had to stay under full control until the end. It was three forty; the entire operation had lasted less than forty minutes.

Back in the apartment, the teen aged girl would wake up in a few hours and probably scramble out as fast as her still weak legs would allow. She would not go to the police. Johnny had placed one hundred dollars on top of her clothing and she would most likely be delighted to see her tormentor cold and dead. If she was questioned by the cops, the pictures retrieved from Mario's ass hole would clear her. How could she be taking a picture of herself and of Mario while tied to the bed posts?

Back to the Plaza hotel, Johnny signed in. Expecting him, the clerk phoned the manager. After listening she hung up and gave Johnny the key to what she said was the very special suite.

-Suite 300 Mister Barcelo. The bell boy will accompany you.- And she pointed to a sinister looking individual sitting in a corner of the lobby.

-Thanks but not just now, - answered Johnny, -I have a few errands to run-. He pocketed the key and went out.

The manager, who had walked out of his office, was obviously annoyed at this unexpected change of plan but could make his move when his guest came back. They would be waiting. He waived to the grumpy looking bellboy who returned to his seat. As usual a large bonus depended upon the happy conclusion of this special business.

Johnny got back into his car, drove around the corner twice to make sure no one was following and stopped at a parking lot where Dudley and Deana were waiting in Mario's car.

-It's room 300 as I was told two days ago by Alberto. They're obviously waiting for me. The manager seems to be in this action and the big bellboy is probably the guy who will do whatever needs to be done. –

-It could happen as soon as I enter my room. It's important that you guys should be there before me. Remember to assume that the mirrors are two ways and that they could be listening. – Continued Johnny as he gave his room key to Dudley.

-So here is how it goes: I sneak past the bellboy, go up to my room at exactly seven o'clock. Dudley and three of his team are already there hidden in the wardrobe closet and bath room which is close to the door. Deana is in room 301 where she keeps an eye on things from the peep hole. –

-Remember, I am now in suite 300 while you are hiding in the closet and bath room. From the suite I call the manager to complain about something. He's very surprised to have missed me and he'll be there with the bellboy in a few minutes or my name is Albert Einstein. When they enter the room, you come out of the closet and take them to room 301. Expect two but there could be three of them. –

Again he repeated the scenario and made sure that Dudley and Deana had taken all this in.

-Then I'll join you in room 301 and we'll have a friendly conversation with our hosts. The manager will phone Luigi Gnocchini to give him the good news and we should be on our way to meet the great man.-

-The loose end in this is Alberto. Hopefully he'll be at the farm, if not, we can get Luigi to invite him over. We know Mario won't cause any trouble.–

At seven ten, Johnny walked into room 300. Dudley had left the door open and was hiding in the bathroom and closet with three of his squad. From room 301 Deana was monitoring the action. Walking casually into the room, Johnny threw his valise on the bed and called the manager about the television being broken.

-I'll be right with you Mister Barcelo.-

Arriganello was obviously surprised to have not seen him come in. How could he, Johnny was wearing his black curly wig and a top coat.

Less than two minutes later, Johnny heard the service elevator rumbling to a halt; the elevator doors opening and not closing, jammed opened for quick access.

A subtle knock on the door by Arriganello; behind him the colossal bell boy; a smaller individual, dressed up in his Sunday's best was at the back. The plan was to ram the door as soon as it cracked open.

From room 301 across the hall, her eye to the peep hole, Deana saw this third person and motioned to Steven behind her. She showed him three fingers while grabbing her silenced 45. He did the same and when the door of room 300 opened, and the bell boy and Arriganello busted in, they stepped out and dragged this third guy into room 301. Barcelo had unlocked the door and then backed away allowing the two kidnappers to come in as Dudley and his mates were exploding out of the bath room and closet easily overpowering them.

In case there was a two way mirror, the full sequence had taken place in the entrance of the suite 300. As in a football melee they were surrounded, pushed back out in the hallway by Dudley and his three friends to be sucked into room 301 by Steven and Deana.

Johnny stayed a while in his room listening for unusual noises coming from behind the mirror; nothing. He crossed over to join the party.

For a minute only heavy breathing could be heard. Like yesterday's pancake, the three would be kidnappers had been flattened on the floor. Face down, stupefied and silent. What could they say anyway as there were five large men and a woman standing over them; not counting Johnny?

-Mister Arriganello I wouldn't want to be in your shoes right now. - Said Johnny.

The three of them were having their hands cuffed behind their back. Soon their feet were duck taped as well.

-Sit Arriganello down on this chair. – Commanded Johnny.

Two strong arms grabbed the small man and sat him down on a straight chair. The other two were gagged and their mouths taped solidly before they were rolled over to stare at the ceiling. So far the surprise had been complete, not a sound and the operation done in less than two minutes.

-Who might this other gentleman be Mister Arriganello? And why are you all packing a gun and this wicked little blade I wonder.-

Searching the pockets of the three men had produced three hand guns and a wicked knife with a twisted six inch blade. Arriganello had recovered some of his cool and managed to say:

-I don't understand your action Mister Barcelo, I was only coming to your room because you called me.-

-That's why you left the elevator door jammed opened, and also why you came with a dirty linen cart.... You didn't need to show up with two accomplices for a broken TV. - Snapped Johnny. – Enough of that.-

He winked at Dudley who understood and placed his large hand on Arriganello's mouth while taking a pair of tongs out of the duffel bag containing their arsenal. After showing it to Arriganello, he carefully placed Arriganello's pinky between the pincers of the blacksmith's tongs. He glanced again at Johnny and snapped closed the tongs. The sound of the bone cracking could be heard in the now stilled room. Eyes wide opened but unable to yell because of Dudley's hand, Arriganello stiffened for a moment before his body relaxed completely.

-Give him a large Bourbon it will kill the pain and get him talking.-

-We react strongly when told lies. May this be a lesson. The next time you fib you can kiss goodbye to one of your testicles, and so on, until you learn to tell the truth and nothing but the truth. - Said Johnny slowly, separating all the words carefully.

As he was finishing his little speech, Deana was pouring a large Bourbon in Arriganello's open mouth. Then she untied his belt, pulled his trousers down to the knees. The cute boxer shorts, pink with blood red dots were left in place for now.

-As you understand we don't have much time. I'll repeat the question once more. Who is this well dressed boy? We know that you were to kill me and make me vanish, so let's stop this game.-

Looking at his flattened, bleeding and throbbing little finger, he could see several bone splinters protruding from the broken skin. Then he glanced at the smaller guy. Barcelo already knew who he was; the contents of his pocket had identified him as Mariano Rossini most likely the heir to the family.

-One more chance, Dario, why is he here and who hired him to kill me.?-

While asking the question he was opening and closing the tongs. Deana's gloved hands were yanking the boxer shorts down to Dario's knees, exposing a flaccid penis.

Arriganello was not stupid and realized that they were not threatening in vain. They would cut his balls and more if he did not tell them what they would easily learn from looking into the wallet they had retrieved. His only chance to survive in one piece was to answer the question. He did.

-He was sent by Luigi Rossini to escort you to his house. A sort of body guard for your protection. - Replied Arriganello.

-Give him another large bourbon; he'll need it when we crush his left ball. - Said Johnny to Deana while he continued.

-I repeat: I am fully aware that you're here to kill me. We have filmed Mario's conversation with Alberto when they were my guests last week. So unless you're a dim witted masochist and enjoy having your body pulled apart with a pair of blacksmith's pincers, tell it exactly as it is. One last time: Who is this gentleman and what were your plans for this evening's enjoyment.?-

Looking at the pincers and then at the two bodies on the floor, gagged and bound like two live monkeys being served at a Japanese banquet, Arriganello made up his mind that it was better for him to face the ire of his Mafia boss than this immediate and very real danger of being torn into shreds by this very angry human being they were supposed to kill.

-Ok, I'll talk but...- and he looked at the other two on the floor.

-Done, - Replied Johnny as he motioned to Steven to have the two monkeys removed and transported into the bedroom.

-Stay with them and watch them like a mother bear would watch her cubs. - He told Steven.

The door closed. Dario breathed heavily and twisted on his chair, uncomfortable with his pants down to his knees.

-The smaller man is Luigi's oldest son and the larger guy is... was the hit man. They were supposed to kill you in room 300, and move you out through the service elevator in the dirty linen cart already in place as you know.-

-Are the mirrors two ways in room 300.-? Asked Johnny.

-Yes they are but there was no need to have anyone watching as we thought the job would be easy. -

-Is this the key to the lookout room? - Asked John pointing to a key.

-Yes that's a pass for all doors in the hotel. Room 302 is the lookout station but there is no one there. - He repeated.

Johnny put the precious key in his pocket, then, having a second thought, removed it and gave it to Dudley.

-Could you please check it out, trust is at a low level today and should never prevent control. Assume that there is someone inside the room. – He returned to Arriganello.

-Tell me about Luigi's place now. How many persons in the family and how many servants?-

-It's a farm with several horses. A large stable and two man servants as well as a girl. Luigi lives with his wife and a daughter. His son Mariano is usually there also but you know where he is now. The security is linked to the local police. They're on his pay roll. - Answered Arriganello.

-You've been cooperative and I'll let you live. The only casualty so far is Mario. I killed him to show that we're serious and ready to go to any extreme if pushed hard enough. Willing to lose our lives in order to keep what's ours. We'll now all go to Luigi Rossini's place without one.-

Johnny continued.

-Your hit man will be taken out. You don't want any witness to this failure. His body will take my place in the cart. Nothing is to be changed: you'll drive the car you were supposed to use and dispose of the body as you were to dispose of mine. You'll be accompanied by two of my guys so that the head count is right. Were you supposed to phone Luigi to tell him that the mission was accomplished?-

-Mariano was supposed to do this. - Replied Arriganello.

-He'll do it from here. By the way did you know that Mario was drugging pre-teen girls to abuse them sexually?-

Arriganello didn't answer but he knew well enough as Johnny learned later; his daughter had been savagely raped by Mario last month. That explained the pleased look at learning that he had been killed. As for his niece Anna Maria, all file and rank's daughters were abused by Mario. He would apologize after the facts, pretending that he was sick and addicted to sex.

Taking the small man under his arm like a grocery bag, Dudley carried Mariano Gnocchini into the living room and sat him on a sofa facing Arriganello. Arrogant, flushed and furious as one would expect of a don's son, he hardly paid attention to the bleeding and broken finger, stared in disgust at his undressed bottom section and then looked hard in the eyes of Dario Arriganello. The message was clear, Arriganello was a walking corpse.

-You'll phone your father and tell him that the mission has been a success. You're coming to the farm with Dario because your car has broken down -. Johnny said.

The reaction was predictable.

-Up yours Barcelo, you'll find that I don't sing as easily as Arriganello. I won't tell my father anything but the truth and you guys are as good as buried.-

Barcelo was expecting that answer and ready.

-You're talking about mass burial. I hope the tomb is large enough for all of us. You'll be the first casualty. Now let's go over some facts. Fact number one, Mario is dead; fact number two, we will not kill any of you if you cooperate; fact number three, we're acting in self defense, after being pushed by your father as the result of Alberto's and Mario's report; and finally fact number four, your hit man will die in a minute. –

Silence for a moment, and then Johnny continued.

-Let's get this out of the way so that you'll understand we mean business. - Silence in the room for a calculated full minute. Then to Dudley:

-Dudley would you mind trying out the silencer on this gun.-

Dudley picked up the hit man's gun: a 25 caliber Beretta with a silencer. He walked into the bedroom where the big hit man was lying on his back rolling his eyes and trying to break out of his cuffs, having heard the conversation.

On cue from Barcelo, Steven and Paul picked up Mariano and stood him up so that he could see the execution. Dudley walked to the bed, pointed the gun: three swishing sounds, like muffled farts, the odor of powder overwhelming. A couple of jerks and life was snuffed out.

-Bring him over so that he can see that we're not faking.-

-You bastards, I'll have you killed for this in such a way that you'll take several days to die.-

-If this is the way you feel the other three bullets in the Beretta will be used on you. Enough bravado and let's get this over with, one way or the other we have little time and even a shorter fuse. –

Then in a very low voice, again separating every word, he continued.

-But you should know that if you force us to kill you, we'll have to dispose of your entire family as well; mother, sister, father. Complete extermination including Dario and Alberto would be the only safe way for us. -

Mariano's eyes were glued on the large corpse. Alex was large even in death. For a long moment Mariano stood there, the others remaining silent. Finally coming out of his trance, he slowly took in the scene for the first time since he had been dragged into this room. Barcelo's aim in terminating the hired gun had been to show his determination. The message had been understood.

As if snapping out of a bad dream, Mariano clearly saw that the table was completely turned on them. He could see how Barcelo could kill all members of his family; no one would know much about who did it if the Weinstein and Alberto were included in the casualties.

Mario's death was not a great loss, he had always hated the pervert; Alex was a soldier and soldiers died during wars. Saving his and his family's hides was a priority. At a later date, revenge could be exacted from this Barcelo. On the other end, Barcelo had not started the hostilities; he was defending his life and doing a great job.

Almost choking on the first word, he heard himself say.

-I'll play ball. You're doing what I'd do in your shoes. –

-Let's move it then. - Said Johnny breathing a sigh of relief.

It never had been his intention to become a mass killer, which is what he would have had to be in order to erase all traces: Alberto, the Weinstein family, the Rossini family, Arriganello and all servants and hired help at the Rossini estate.

-Bring the phone and dial the number. –

Deana dialed the number as dictated by Mariano. She then placed the phone close to hers and Mariano's head. A gruffly crackling voice answered.

-The job is done. - Mariano said and explained that his car had broken. The line went dead at the other end. Deana hung up.

The dirty linen carriage was brought in and Alex's still compliant large cadaver twisted and crammed into it. Arriganello's hands were unshackled and he got the job of pushing the cart into the elevator and then into the waiting panel truck in the garage. Mariano's feet were also untied. Closing ranks was Dudley with the sawed off shot gun under his coat and a forty five in his belt. Steven and Paul were leading the way with the other shot guns.

Waiting in the garage were Deana and Johnny wearing his wig, they had preceded the convoy. The other members of the task force were waiting outside in two cars. The garage was empty but for one lady driving out after waiving at Arriganello.

-A secretary from the pool. - Arriganello quickly said fearing a misunderstanding.

He kept on mumbling looking dejectedly at his crushed little finger. – Nothing we could do. They waited for us and had six well armed men.-

-What are you talking about? – Asked Barcelo.

-Nothing, nothing... I guess I'm preparing my defense to Luigi.... He'll have my head for sure. Fucking up this job, how could I be so stupid.-

-You weren't the weak link in this job, Isaac, Mario and Alberto were the real bunglers. Isaac for not telling what he knew about my ...methods, and as for Mario and Alberto, they prepared to go to war against a mouse and found a lion. - Said Barcelo.

He then exploded in a loud laugh which relieved the tension all around. Everyone laughed with him including Arriganello who was now seeing a way out of his failure. He had a good job at the Park and did not want to lose it... or his life.

As Johnny's corpse was to be fed to the Rossini`s waste disposal animals to be consumed as edible evidence, the panel truck was expected to travel to the estate. Dudley was driving, with Mariano sitting in front, Arriganello in the back with three team members and the stiff. Johnny was following with Deana and the last one of his monks.

-As soon as you get to the gate, Steven will switch place with the guard who will be gagged, cuffed, put to sleep and pulled into the panel to be stuffed over the dead man's body.-

The traffic was fluid; soon they were driving along a winding road in the New Jersey country side. As directed by Mariano, Dudley turned right between two impressive field stone colonnades with brass coat of arms, sporting a motto written in Latin. From here on said Mariano with some pride, this land is ours. A mile down the narrow side road they came to a red and white barricade closing the lane. On the left side leaning over the barricade, a small guard house; checking the oncoming traffic, a gate keeper stuck his head out.

Unseen from the sentry box, Steven had jumped from the still moving panel truck, jogging close behind it. As the truck stopped at the station, Steven sneaked out of the back between the now immobile panel truck and the guard house. While Mariano was talking to the sentinel, Steven reached out and tapped the guard on the head; he pulled him out easily and dragged the unconscious sentinel to the back door of the truck; where he was cuffed and anaesthetized. As the truck started moving again he was stuffed over the dead assassin in the linen cart. In the rear view mirror, Dudley could see Steven in the sentry box wearing the guard's cap and coat.

About another mile further, coming out of a curve, the estate suddenly materialized: a sight out of a Walt Disney film. A large three story cut stone castle of a nondescript style, sporting two large towers looming over the massive structure protected by sixteenth century turrets and windows with a clear view over the country side, the entire structure covered partially with vines. Old oak trees flanking it on three sides made it look smaller than it was. The fields around the house were smartly quartered into several paddocks; horses were still grazing at this time of the evening. The cobblestone road leading to the house, after circling in front of a preposterous Versailles like portal, was continuing toward a very large barn-stable arrangement surrounded by a double row of tall poplars standing straight.

-Impressive, royal.... – Said Johnny. Then more businesslike. - What are we to expect in the barn?-.

Johnny had boarded the panel and was standing behind Mariano; leaving Deana to drive his car and follow them to the barn.

-Well ... began Mariano and then he seemed to have second thoughts.

-Mariano, don't change the scenario, this is where I'm the most likely to make snap decisions.- Growled Barcelo the silenced forty five suddenly in his hand and pointing in the general direction of the future Don's balls.

Feeling more audacious now that he was on his turf, Mariano had hesitated for a moment. Looking down the huge dark opening at the end of the .45, and remembering the ease with which Alex had been taken out, he decided against a change of plans and gave the information.

-You're right no change... One stable hand, only one. There, you can see him by that side door.... This is where we keep the hyenas. He's armed and has more guts than brain. Better let me out first. You can come in after me. He's old and has been with the family for more than twenty five years, his life is less important than his honor.-

So, thought Johnny, hyenas are the waste disposal wonders I was to be fed to....The bastards.... And then he continued.

-Stop about twenty feet from the door and we'll get out from the back door while you step out from the front. No false moves, you'll be covered all the way. -

The stable hand was about sixty five, wearing a face so rugged that it seemed engraved like a copper sculpture, tarnished by sun, sea water, wind and time; no doubt a farmer, a poacher, a killer all of his life. Smoking an ugly and foul smelling cigarillo he was leaning against the wall with an air of utter contentment. Like an aficionado waiting to see a bull fight, he was obviously savoring in advance the spectacle he had seen several times before. These hyenas were his pets. He alone would dare walk in their den. They had accepted him as their master, the person providing them with the only important element in their life: food.

-Alfredo, bona sera.- Mariano said as he stepped out, - Come va compadre.-

At the same time, Johnny and Paul one of his disciples holding the sawed off shotgun materialized from the back of the panel; with speed not to be expected from such an old man Alfredo reached for his piece.

Looking down the barrel of a sawed off shot gun didn't seem to change his mind and Mariano had to step in the firing line to prevent that a shot be fired.

-Do as I tell you Alfredo, and it will be ok. - Mariano said. In a second Johnny was holding the silenced forty five to Alfredo's head and grabbing the old soldier's Gluck from his right hand. Dudley had jumped out of the truck; reaching over he connected with a direct to the jaw putting the old soldier out of his misery; Deana was soon cuffing his hands and feet and placing the chloroform impregnated sponge on his face.

-Very good so far Mariano, call your father and ask him if he wants to join the party. If he says no, tell him that you'll be over in a moment. - Johnny said, pointing to a house phone.

Luigi Rossini wanted to get out of the house if only to smoke a cigar; his wife did not allow any smoking in the house. He arrived as the cart was being unloaded and was surprised to see his son actually pushing the cart and more surprised when Deana silently appeared behind him with her forty five and told him to stay still while he was being frisked. A snub nosed 38 caliber was removed from his belt and he was cuffed before he could snap out of his surprise.

-Not to tight I hope Mister Rossini- Asked Johnny appearing in the door way, and he continued:

-I am the dumb Portuguese runt you were supposed to pluck and feed to your hyenas tonight. They'll be fed but I won't be on the menu. -

At that moment, Luigi Rossini was certain that he was the intended replacement. That's what he would have done. As a last and futile attempt to save his ass, he started to open his mouth to yell. Deana who was still close enough and expecting this move, pushed her gun barrel into Luigi's mouth making him puke his dinner, breaking a tooth as a bonus. Mariano was then pushed into the light; kneeling close to his father's head, which was now between his knees, told him to remain quiet that everything would be OK.

-We were beaten like school kids; the only way to survive is to play their game. Are you listening to me? – Luigi nodded between spitting bits of fragmented tooth. - Mario and Alex are both dead. We will all be killed if we don't play ball. Kapitche? - The older Rossini looked up, then around and signaled that he had understood. Then he spat out another loose piece of his front tooth.

-Deana, stay close to the Rossinis. You too Paul, help her and don't let them out of your sights. Now let's not make the hyenas wait for their meals.-

-By the way how in hell did you get a hold of these hyenas? - Asked John who could not believe what he had just learned.

Coming out of the end of the stable, about a hundred feet from where they were, this lugubrious and bone chilling laughter that had nothing in common with joy, startled him as it did every one. For having been exposed to this dissonant cacophonous sound in -*Tarzan the ape man*- films, he knew, that somewhere in this barn, there were real African hyenas. Until this moment he could not believe that African hyenas could be found anywhere but on the African plains or in a zoo.

Slowly getting up, his cuffed hands behind his back and pale as death under his Mediterranean complexion, the older Rossini took heed from his son. Always on alert, knowing that changing the focus is the best strategy, he decided to answer the question about his menagerie. With a weak and broken voice he recited a story that he had told hundreds of times before.

-About eight years ago, one of our friends imported two of these beauties from Africa. They are spotted African hyenas, *crocuta crocuta* for the Scientifics. - He was proud to add as if it mattered. He continued with more assurance, getting used to his broken tooth; he had had difficulty in pronouncing crocuta.

-When this friend died, his wife was going to either give them to a ZOO or have them killed. Out of respect for my dead friend I took them in.- He omitted to say that he made this woman a widow, her husband having had the misfortune to be a hurdle he had to jump over.

-Did you know that they can crush any bones in a human body and digest them? No other animal can digest bones. Not a scrap is left. Their jaws are the strongest there are. Even the lions think twice before messing with them. With three tons per square centimeter of crushing power, elephant or rhino bones will be pulverized; the gastric juices will do the rest. - Then with some pride he added.

-From two they became twelve and we now have the very best way to dispose of damaging edible evidence. – He looked around fearing to have been saying too much.

Deana made a face and looked away disgusted. She thought she had seen and heard the worst of mankind.

As they got nearer, the loud staccato laughing sounds coming from a large pen at the rear of the stable made it clear that the crocuta hyenas were waiting and hungry. The stalls lining the entire length of the stable leading to the hyenas were occupied by beautiful horses munching away at their evening meals; obviously used to their unusual neighbors and reassured that they would not come out of their pen.

The cart was wheeled down the aisle between the rows of stalls. As they got closer to the pen, the dank, decaying odor of the jungle became overpowering. For a North American, the offbeat sight of these hyenas, with their incredibly strong jaws, able to crush any bone that will fit into their gaping mouths was terrifying. Their eyes, like cinders, their huge mouths lined with enormous teeth, gaping and salivating, all twelve of them fighting for a better place at the table. The old matriarch lining up first for the feast they had been prepared for by a two day fast became one more recurrent nightmare Deana would replay the rest of her life.

As if reviewing a Sunday morning buffet in a good restaurant, the animals seemed to be making their selection out of the smorgasbord of heads that suddenly appeared over the wall of their lair. Johnny was perspiring and dizzy at the thought that he had been the intended dinner. Was it planned that he would have been dead or alive going in....?

-You son of a bitch, you were to feed me to these animals....; dead or alive? - He didn't expect an answer.

First sighting of a live hyena, let alone twelve of the beasts; Luigi looked down and said nothing. Dario muttered that this was their way of doing business.

-Your business ethic will never fail to surprise me. - Mumbled Barcelo, shivering at the thought of having been dismembered by these monstrous jaws.

Like a kid at the Zoo, Dudley was amused, almost hypnotized by the pack and getting dangerously close to the pen. Deana pulled him back as the old matriarch was getting bolder.

-Let's not make them wait. – Said Johnny.

The now stiff and dead Alex was quickly stripped of all his clothing and thrown to the waiting jaws. He landed on his back, eyes opened, looking like a charcoal black Michel Angelo's David off its pedestal. The hyenas backed off a few feet and waited for the matriarch to give the signal. Then, pushing and fighting they lunged at the large hunk of flesh. Less than five minutes later not much remained but the cranium, the pelvic and femur bones being attacked by the bone crushing jaws. Another three minutes of bone cracking and it was all over. Nothing left of the more than two hundred and fifty pound hit man;

back to the earth via hyenas' digestive tracks; a rare sepulture. Johnny was astonished that nothing was left; better and faster than fire.

-I'll bet that you've thrown live men in there.- Snapped Johnny still shocked.

Nobody answered but the silence was admission. Taking his eyes away from the hyenas, by now ready for more of the same he continued.

-Are you expecting any one tonight Mister Gnocchini.? Tell me the truth if you want this caper to end favorably for everyone. After seeing your disposal unit at work for the last five minutes you'll understand that I'm not in a gentle mood. Nothing prevents me from killing the whole lot of you and feeding your animals for a week.... – While talking he was trying to find leftovers of the big guy and couldn't find any... - By the look of it.... nobody would find any trace of the corpses. -

-No, I'm not expecting any one. –Luigi Rossini was quick to answer. - Only my family is at home. My wife and my daughter, as well as Mireille the maid and my chauffeur. -

-Call the Chauffeur and tell him to join us over here.- Ordered Johnny.

He did and a few minutes later a burly man of around forty made his way on foot towards the stable. As he came in he was overpowered, promptly cuffed and put to sleep. He would be quiet for a few hours in the horse stall where the gate guard and the stable hand were already resting. The tenant of the stall was a nice not so young anymore warm-blood mare, used by the nephews and nieces for their introduction to the noble sport of horse riding. -Mona-, that was the name on the brass plate screwed on the stall, hardly stopped eating her hay during the intrusion, enjoying the company, looking at every one in turn.

-Lets go to the house where we can sit and talk about this... misunder-standing. - Said Johnny.

-Yes, yes, truly a misunderstanding,- Muttered Luigi. - That bum Alberto didn't do his job properly. I'll have his ass kicked.-

-Alberto, yes. - Repeated Johnny. -By the way, call him. You and I don't want him to play hero in this drama. He's got to join the party. I figure that it would be in his best interest to have you all killed. Who would be the new boss? - Insinuated Barcelo.

-Jesus Christ, you're so right. – Luigi, the old schemer, did not take long to see the possibilities for Alberto; he would inherit the job.

Led to the phone, he dialed Alberto's number. John removed the receiver from Luigi's hand, listened until he could recognize Alberto's soft voice then gave the receiver back to Luigi.

-Alberto, come over right now, I need you for something important we can't discuss over the phone.-

Like a docile warrior, Alberto answered that he would be at the estate in less than thirty minutes.

-Now dial the main gate. –Johnny said.

-Steven, Alberto will show up in thirty minutes. I'll send two of your friends to help you organize a proper welcoming committee. As usual, cuff him and bring him over to the house. Leave one of the fellows at the gate. ....Yes everything went fine here. And don't forget the ankle gun and the knife on his arm.-

The procession got going to the house where they would meet Signora and Signorina Rossini. Dario and his father Luigi led the march followed by Arriganello and Dudley; flanking the group, two of the monks and, at the rear, Deana and Johnny. Before entering the house, Johnny had had the cuffs removed from the Rossinis.

-Appreciate that I don't humiliate you in front of your family. But if I have the slightest doubt, we start firing and no one will survive, not even your daughter. We'll feed the cadavers to the hyenas and torch the place. Nothing would remain, we brought dynamite and I'm sure that you have plenty of kerosene. The cops would think a rival gang did the job. -

Luigi Rossini was as much a pragmatic as he was a coward, two qualities essential to survive in a dangerous world. He would not attempt to reverse a situation, against odds so clearly in his disfavor. This Barcelo was not as bad a person as he would have been, in a similar context. Barcelo was also civilized, as he had shown by freeing his hands. Regina would bring back this moment several times during the rest of his life. Cuffed hands would have been unbearable. He was now certain that unless something drastic forced Barcelo to open fire, they would all live to talk about it. He nodded that he had understood and agreed.

-Don't worry I'm not suicidal.-

—— CHAPTER 18 ——

"Man cannot be too careful in choosing his enemies."
Oscar Wilde

La Signora Rossini was a monument of flesh and blubber. Draped in a pink dress, garnished with laced trimmings, her swollen feet overflowing purple slippers; moon face with a dark complexion, out of which sparkled two little green eyes, not unlike the deeply ensconced eyes of the matriarch hyena. Her rounded shoulders supporting a twenty pound hump in the back of her neck, similar to that of the fat reserve found on the shoulders of Brahma cows gave her an egg shaped silhouette. Severe *Rosacea* coloring the olive dark skin texture of her cheeks and extending over the lips, created a new shade on the color map. Her hair however was flamboyant, like a tropical plant: healthy dark ebony tied in a huge bun; must have flowed down to her knees when unpinned. Almost bald Johnny estimated at least twenty years of growth.

To see such a contingent of people walking in her living room, most of them strangers raised a red flag. She had lived through the worse and would not be easily surprised but locking eyes with her husband, easily spotted that he was not in command of this group; nonchalantly she wiggled her weight and reached under her seat where she kept a gun. Signora Rossini was the daughter of a Sicilian don and had seen more blood than a hip surgeon.

-It's fine Regina, these people are friends. - Swiftly said Luigi who knew too well what she was reaching for.

This was one of the possible accidents that could have ignited the fuse. Weighing Luigi's advice, she opted to calm down. Fighting gravity, she tried to get out of her easy-chair; the leather retaliated, sucking her back in and for a few seconds it was not certain who or what would win the bout; until a final and desperate assault gave Regina the advantage.

Luigi Rossini was or rather had been a smart looking young man. He had been coerced into marrying Regina; the price to pay for his vertiginous ascension in the Familia. For the godfather turned father in law, Regina was a spy behind the enemy lines. As in most businesses, in the Mafia world, a friend is never anything more than half a traitor.

However ugly and disfigured, Regina was an intelligent person who gave sound advice to her husband. Kept abreast of all deals, she was a faithful and careful advisor in all matters. Several generations of interbreeding Mafiosi leave a strong genetic imprint. Regina was a mutant from the human race and had mutated into this Homo Mafioso hominid sub specie.

Being pragmatic and intelligent, she recognized and accepted her esthetic fact. She could always stay ahead of the game by choosing carefully her husband's live-in mistresses, doubling as maids. This way there would be less risk of an emotional attachment on the part of her husband or on her part as well.

She always arranged all the details of the work schedule. What Luigi Rossini did not know was that she would also use the maid as her lover, getting an equal shake in the arrangement. Once in a while, for the gallery, she extracted a few milliliters of sperm from Luigi, who had to perform using his imagination and closing his eyes.

Mireille, the present maid mistress combination was a beautiful brunette of twenty some years, salvaged from a pimp who was beating her and selling her to several customers per day. The pimp had been convinced to let her go and Mireille had been grateful for the sinecure she was offered, being paid handsomely to boot.

Upon entering the house, the faint singing sound they had heard on the pathway from the stable, turned out to be a beautiful Cantata.

-I know this number. I heard it on the radio and liked it so much that I remember the title and the author. - Said Johnny.

-It's from Bach, - "I have had enough"-. Jesus on the cross, lamenting that he's fed up and discouraged. – Answered Luigi, again not a little proud of his culture. Versatile as hell thought Barcelo, equally at ease with the Crocuta and the Cantata.

Listening to the vibrant and emotionally charged voice, Johnny could not help but draw a parallel between the hyenas' crackling cacophony and this voice from heaven, both performing in the ante-chamber of hell.

-My daughter is a professional singer. Singing is her life and she practices eight hours a day. - Luigi said, almost apologizing. He continued:

-We're fond of her singing, it reminds my wife of Sicily, where people sing a lot more than here. - And he continued.

-If you could leave her out of this.... She's a complete stranger to the family's operation or anything that is not musical or equine. She loves horses as well and, like my brother was saying: - "if it doesn't fart, eat hay or looks like a musical partition, she's not interested"-. She will not come out of her room for another hour and even then, wouldn't know which end of a gun to point.-

-Not a good idea.... –Johnny said after a moment, - she could phone the cops or someone else. Our entire carefully planned scenario would then be modified. It's better for us all if you could call her on the intercom and ask her to come down. We won't be long if everyone cooperates. Call the maid also while you're at it.-

-Luigi tell me that what I see is not real. - Said Regina Rossini.

-you're smart. You understand quickly. This is the John Barcelo we were supposed to feed to the hyenas. He has learned of our intentions and caught us by surprise. Alberto was tricked, Mario and Alex are dead. We'll live and be able to learn from our mistake if we cooperate and agree to the terms of a deal that I am not yet aware of.- Said Luigi looking at the tip of his shoes, carefully averting her eyes.

The only indication Johnny had that she was as angry as mother Theresa not being canonized while still breathing was by the increasing redness of her cheeks. Rosacea reacts to anger and elevated body temperature. Not opening her thin lips, Regina looked long and hard at her husband and then at Johnny.

Her sow's eyes, cold and calculating, told Johnny that if there was to be any trouble that's where it would come from. After a long moment of silence during which she glanced twice at her leather chair, she came to the conclusion that the muscle power was not in their camp at this time and that she should cooperate, at least for the moment.

-This plan has never been a good one and Alberto is too smart for his own good. I hope you'll do something about him. As far as Mario is concerned, may the devil have his rotten soul. What do you want from us Signor Barcelo? - Her English had suddenly improved to the point that it was in the best of Oxfordian accent.

-I want your word of honor that I'll be left alone and in peace. Let's wait for Alberto to arrive, we can rapidly come to a satisfactory arrangement; mutually satisfactory as you'll see, as long as you stay away from my business, and..... Your leather chair. - Replied Barcelo.

Smiling, he went over, and sliding his hand under the seat, came out with a twenty five year old snub nose .45.

- I'll give it back when we leave. It has to be an old souvenir. - She nodded.

Alberto arrived twenty minutes later. Surprised to be manhandled by a gateman he recognized as a Barcelo employee from The Saint Augustine Club in Lisbon, he thought his last day had finally arrived. He never had a chance to use his gun as he was looking down the dark muzzles of a double barreled shot gun when he stopped at the gate. Gunning the car was out of the question, he would have had to shift and this action would have given enough time to be on the receiving end of two 12 gauge buck shot loads.

Extracted from his vehicle through the window he was quickly cuffed, while being frisked. His .44 caliber removed from its holster, as well as the ankle gun, a .32 Smith and Wesson. But he was astonished when the thin knife strapped to his fore arm was also taken; as if they knew where to search. The film had shown that Alberto had three weapons, where and what they were. The film also had shown Alberto tying a money belt around his waist and it was removed along with the two thousand in cash it contained. In the end, Barcelo's expenses would be totally reimbursed by the booty.

Steven pushed Alberto back in his car and slid into the driver's seat; nothing less than a Ferrari for the future Don. For Steven it was the first and last time he'd drive one of those; a few minutes later he screeched to a halt in front of the mansion, not answering any of the questions the little Italian rooster was barking at him.

The door opened as he stopped the car and one of the monks came running to escort the yapping prisoner into the house. At this point it was becoming clear to Alberto that the Barcelo caper would be remembered as a fiasco. He didn't know which to fear the most, Barcelo or Luigi. Failure is not tolerated in certain organization.

His cuffs were not removed and he was pushed roughly onto a sofa before his legs were also secured.

-Everybody is here. We can officially open this meeting. Please get your daughter into the kitchen with the maid; they don't have to know the details of this arrangement. If you feel that Arriganello and Alberto should also be left out of this... friendly conversation let it be so.- John said ignoring Alberto swearing profusely in Italian.

Luigi had been throwing darts at Alberto and finally could not contain his anger any longer.

-Alberto, shut the fuck up... subito. - And then Luigi, calmer, continued. -This business only concerns my family. The others have to leave the room. -

Regina's daughter was still singing. She had quite a repertoire and her voice held the promise of excellence in a few years. Looking at Regina, Johnny said.

-You must be proud of your daughter's gift.-

She nodded, accepting the praise; her daughter Carla had all she would have wanted for herself; a genetic fluke, a miracle for which she thanked God daily. But then her maternal instinct raised a red flag, could this be an implied threat? Johnny felt her concern and added.

-We wouldn't touch a hair on her head as long as you don't force us to do so.- Then after a moment he continued, - I would like you to be a part of this meeting Signora. –

Johnny had recognized that she was the real boss; the Rossini family was matriarchal as in the Hyena world. She nodded; having never thought that she would not.

Deana went up the stairs and met Carla as she was coming down the stairway, having been called by her mother on the interphone. Ill at ease with this crowd, the surprisingly beautiful daughter of these two very ordinary persons, made a slight movement of her head, obeying her mother. Deana escorted her into the library where Alberto and Arriganello were already arguing complimenting each other in Italian. Steven settled the argument by telling them they would be anaesthetized. Arriganello brought Alberto up to par.

-Take them seriously; they've killed Mario and the hit man.... They're also making you look like an amateur. - And he sadistically told Alberto about the hidden camera spying on his every action in the privacy of his room when staying at the Saint Augustine Club. That got Alberto to shut up immediately.

Johnny and Dudley remained with the Rossini family.

-I won't go into the facts as everyone seems to know them including the Signora.- She nodded and Johnny continued.

- We're left with two choices; one is that we kill everyone and hope that your associates will not know who to retaliate against. With the participation of the hyenas... – He didn't finish the sentence.

-The second option is that we resume our lives as they were before this unfortunate decision was made to deprive me of my property, of my bread and butter business and to feed me to these monsters. - He paused and looked at Luigi and Regina for a long moment.

-The last one is the solution I prefer. I'll go one notch further and transfer to you all commissions I am now giving to Weinstein for the business he has been bringing. I'll extend the same business offer for all disposal business you'll bring to me. In return I'll not want to see any one of your group in The Club or sniffing at my heels, ever. If later you decide to double cross me, bear in mind that if I'm killed, there is a contract on your life Luigi; half of the money has been paid and the other half would be paid upon your execution. –

The gum shoe from Boston had been only too happy to accept the advance, with the name of the lawyer to contact in case of Barcelo' s untimely departure.

Waiting for this to sink in, Johnny looked at Regina first then at Luigi and finally at Mariano. They were astonished to be let off the hook so easily. They would have asked for a very large ransom. For a moment, they talked in Italian, this family confabulation lasted only a minute and Luigi nodded to Johnny that this was accepted by the family. Then he continued.

-Tell me more about the commission Mario's son in law was getting from you behind our backs.-

Johnny told him and also said that because he felt that Weinstein had double crossed him, he had to either kill him or exact a punishment for his action. The loss of more than one hundred thousand dollars per year would hurt him enough. If Isaac was not to accept this decision, the family should convince him. Any noise from him should be dealt with by Luigi.

-We'll take care of Isaac as he deserves. If he has double crossed us once he'll do it again. - Said Luigi.

-I'm getting a large volume of business from Isaac and I wouldn't want that to cease because of some nasty accident. - Replied Johnny. – Let me tell you something that may convince you of the uselessness of shooting ourselves in the foot.-

And he told them about the July incident, where Herb was stewed and canned for posterity while Isaac kept his life because he had a useful purpose.

-I see what you mean; business is the name of the game. Right, we won't remove him but he'll be under close surveillance. - Then Luigi continued. – That he forgot to tell us about the commissions is not as serious as the fact that the little fart should have told us about you. Either we would have left you alone or been more careful. He's dangerous because... he's proud, greedy and stupid. –

-Amen to that. We'll leave now. One last thing, we're on thin ice until we're back home. We would feel more comfortable if your son would accompany us until we reach New York. He'll then come back with Mario's car left in the hotel parking lot. Don't forget to release the therapist from the trunk; she may start to be uncomfortable. -

A few minutes later they were on their way back to New York, Mariano sitting comfortably between Deana and Steven in the back seat of Johnny's car, Dudley driving with Johnny at his side.

Back at the farm, Luigi was kicking asses. Alberto and Arrigano would not be sitting down comfortably for a while; but all in all as Regina said:

-This is for the best. We get rid of Mario, increase our revenues substantially and don't have to spend an ounce of energy. Too bad this Barcelo is not Sicilian, I like his style. -

—— CHAPTER 19 ——

"Lorsque le crime devient maladie, l'exécution devient opération."
Junger

Year 2000 back in the hospital

Barcelo had not seen or heard of the good father Donnelly for more than two days. Could he have shocked him he wondered. He didn't think so, Donnelly seemed to have welcomed the discussion; different from his day to day church mouse soul searching discussions. These questions were not new, they had been asked for the last sixty some thousand years; the very basis of all religions and of all philosophies. -*Who are we, where are we from, and where are we going*? - Philosophia perennis transmitted from mouth to mouth and now part of our genetic baggage.

-Who do we have in here? - At this very moment, Johnny heard a deep throated voice asking a nurse walking by.

-Mister Barcelo is still with us but... leaving tomorrow. – She seemed relieved.

And then Johnny saw the head of the good father peep through the half open door. He looked as if he had fought with Satan to wrestle the soul of some being from eternal damnation.

-Excuse me for being so frank, but you don't look good father. What happened to you? - Inquired Johnny shocked by the pallid skin texture of the priest, further accentuated by the black shirt he was wearing.

-You're as white as your roman collar, not mentioning the black and blue circles under your eyes. Must have been a hell of a party.-

-Cold, the common cold can hit every one, even those who don't deserve it. I suffered enough already. - Responded the saintly priest. But this was a half hearted joke.

-Come on in if you're no longer contagious, but just in case we'll skip kissing.-

-What disappointment. – Replied the priest as he came in laughing for the first time in several days.

He could never see himself being a homosexual and certainly not with a rhesus monkey like Johnny as a first date. He was carrying his little black bag and had obviously been catering to a dying patient in need of the last rites.

-How's business father. I see that you're dressed up for the worse and I know it's not for me. Is some poor blip on the way to being rubbed off the screen? - Johnny said, remembering the analogy Tim had made, that death was the disappearance of one's –blip- from the screen of life.

-Right and a lot better off he'll be, suffering like he has been for the last several days, refusing all pain killers thinking that pain would buy him a better place in paradise. Nothing to do with the love of God, just thinking he's buying a better place with his suffering. Superstition..... –

-Any truth to that father? - Inquired Johnny cynically.

-As they say in the movies, don't fuck with my brain Barcelo. Pain is as unnecessary to man as life, its origin.... Sorry about that, death always depresses me while it should be the opposite, according to what I preach: paradise, eternal happiness....-

Sitting down on the only chair in the room, he opened his black brief case and took out the infamous gourd from which he poured a stiff drink for Johnny and himself.

-I need this more than breathing right now and it has nothing to do with this poor soul's timely departure. Here's to your miraculous recovery. – And he emptied his plastic glass in one gulp before refilling.

Mildly surprised at the priest's opening speech Johnny took a sip and found that it had a slightly mellower taste than the Glenfiddisch he had sampled a few days before.

-What's the problem father, one more death is surely not the only reason for this gloomy state of mind, there's got to be something a lot more serious. Tell me about it.- Offered Johnny feeling sorry for the poor man who looked as Jesus might have looked, on this celebrated Friday morning when he learned that he would be crucified, having been caught at his own game of playing Messiah and King of the Jews.

Tim looked at Johnny then remained silent for a long minute. Why not he thought, there is no way he can ever guess; and he related one of these awful stories only priests, cops and psychologists have access to.

-In my job, the worse is to be told secrets you cannot divulge or, be made aware of situations you can't redress even if the injustice and the wrong disclosed to you is satanic, fiendish....... I've been made aware of another such nightmare. I just can't chase it out of my mind, I wake up in the middle of the night and can't go back to sleep imagining the worse for these kids. –

Taking a sip, he looked at Johnny and asked.

-Are you sure you want to share this disturbing confidence with me? I won't be transgressing any confessional secret as you'll see but it will haunt you forever.-

Johnny nodded, thinking that knowing of someone in a worse way than he, might restore some of the confidence he had lost over the last years. Little did he know that this would occupy his mind and his body for a while, a long while as it turned out.

-You're asking for it. Last Saturday morning I was finishing breakfast when I heard a faint knock at the back door of the presbytery. Usually people come to the front door and use the bell. I opened the door to a frightened little girl of about eight, already turning to run away. I recognized her, one of four children in a good Irish family, member of my community. –

-Are you father Tim? – She asked in a whisper, still facing the other direction.

-I told her I was and she quickly came in after a quick look over her shoulder, as if afraid someone would have followed her. –

I was surprised and ill at ease. You know, people's minds are so distorted that nobody dares being alone with a kid in a house nowadays, particularly if you're a man of the cloth, there have been so many of us abusing children..... Well... There wasn't much I could do other than throw her out and I didn't have the heart. So I offered her a hot chocolate which she politely refused.-

-Mrs. Langendonck- she started timidly, - my teacher, told me that I should come to your house and talk to you about my mother's new boy friend. He's hurting us and... -looking for her word, she looked around as if to find the words and the courage... then she continued, -He makes us all get naked and sin. He makes us do bad things and he says that he'll kill our mother if we tell. We love our mother.- She continued: -Mrs. Langendonck told me that it was okay not to tell her why I was crying so much in school but that I should tell you and that you'd make the problem go away. -

-She stopped and looked at me with such distressed eyes that I haven't been able to chase that look out of my mind. - Sighed Tim.

-Please make him go away.- She said as she started crying and sobbing so hard, I couldn't help crying myself.-

And Johnny thought he saw a tear slowly running from Tim's left eye. Turning away to hide this tear, he continued.

-This is not the first time I've heard about these pathetic situations where an entire family becomes sexual slaves to some pervert, sometimes the father, a brother, or as in this case the new boy friend of the often hard working mother. There's never much we can do. The law acts slowly and often the victim who came out and told is savagely beaten or even worse-

-Anyway, to make a long and sad story short, this son of a bitch moved in a few months ago and has systematically been molesting the four kids in this family on a regular basis when the mom is working. The mother is unaware as he keeps telling the kids that he'll kill them and her, if one of them rats out. This little girl couldn't take it any longer and said that she would rather die than submit to –that- forever as she said. The children are three girls age six, eight and ten and a boy eleven. The girl who came to me is the eight year old. She said that when other men started coming in their home to also touch them and do bad things as she said, she decided to take Mrs. Langendonck's advice and come to me.-

-Why can't you go to the police? – Interjected Johnny.

-True, I thought I could unload on the police but I then decided to do a little investigative work of my own. You never know with kids. So for two days I arrived at a vantage point overlooking the house an hour or so after the mother left. During the approximately six hours I watched the house, three men and a women rang the bell and stayed in for about three hours each time. That was enough corroboration and I was satisfied that Jody had not lied. However and this is where the plot thickens, two of the visitors are citizens of this community. One of them employed by the State. The other is a business man, owner of a motel. As for the other three, if their automobiles are any indication of their status, they have what it takes to hire good lawyers.... Yes I have their plate numbers and also pictures I have taken with my telescopic lens. One of my hobbies.... You can see my dilemma.-

As Johnny was not saying a word processing this information in his mind, Tim continued :

-I fear the system will be slow. In the mean time an accident can happen or the kids could opt to clam up; fear is nasty and their mother is threatened here, not mentioning their own lives. –

Stopping to drain his plastic cup, he continued.

-There's more. This guy could have taught the Nazis a few tricks.... He choked the family cat in front of the kids in order to drive his point home. He also brought a rabbit home and cut all four legs with a branch cutter, then further tortured the dying animal. All of this is on film apparently. Before leaving, Jody told me that he was continually filming their activities, further threatening to show the video to their mother and their friends at school. –

-Wow ...- Was all Johnny could reply, thinking of his own five year old. -I never heard of such... - and he couldn't think of a proper name for the kind of bastard who would sink that low.

-Obviously this guy is in business and intends to sell the footage to other pedophiles as well as selling the kids to the highest bidders. - John said and continued.

-I see what you mean when you fear that he would make them all disappear in a fire or something of the kind. -

There was a long silence. Both assessing the situation and obviously not coming to any decision. The obvious was to go to the police or to the youth protection agency; often these agencies were so starched up with red tape that they could cause more harm than good taking forever to act. In this case it would have given the predator all the time in the world to either disappear himself or make the witnesses vanish.

-I have to do something about this, I haven't been able to sleep for the last three days. I'll go to the police and tell the tale. I run the risk of having the kids deny it, even Jody might clam up. It took all her courage to come to me and when confronted by her own siblings she might rescind. The life of the mother is threatened by this animal. And, don't forget that she came to me thinking that I could make the problem go away. I'll lose her trust if I go to the police. If I don't do the right thing, it's worse.–

Tim continued as if to convince himself that going to the police was the only viable alternative.

-I didn't believe it at first but after careful questioning I came to the conclusion that this child was either well read or had had some hands on experience. I am certain that she was telling the truth. After stalking the house and seeing with my own eyes the visitors who could be pedophiles, I no longer doubt Jody's confession .... Believe it or not she was concerned about forgiveness from Jesus. I told you, good Irish family..... I'm on my way to the cops.-

Johnny hesitated a moment before muttering between his teeth almost inaudibly.

-Maybe not a good idea. You probably hit it right on when you expressed fear for the kids' life or that they would clam up. Give me another shot of that elixir which enhances my imagination and boosts my will power... please close the door as I'm about to confess sins not yet committed.-

Tim closed the door. He seemed relieved for having told his frightening story, sharing it with someone else. Some truths are too much for only one to bear. His mind was made up and he could see that going to the authorities was the only way out; maybe not the best solution but the only one; better than not doing anything. He should have done it before but deciding had always been arduous for Tim; that's why he was still a priest.

-What do you have in mind Johnny, is there another solution to this problem which has to be resolved by tomorrow morning? The mom is not working today and nothing will happen to these poor kids until she goes back to work tomorrow. Can you imagine the panic when they see her leave? –

Barcelo had closed his eyes and was obviously processing some very profound thoughts. He kept going back to Henrietta. He could still, after sixty years, see her being raped by his two brothers and Andres. Righting a wrong would not make her a happier dead person but it would make him feel as if all this mess had served a purpose. It would also put a cap on his life; give it a sense, a final touch of class before he allowed his –blip- to be cancelled from the big screen. Enhancing his tarnished image was a strong motivation. Of course he felt compassion for the kids but this alone would not have sufficed. A hands-on participation in a grandiose offbeat project was the nudge he needed to rise up to this otherwise senseless mission. All his life he had been on the assignment of pleasing his ego; this would not be different except that it would serve a worthy purpose this time.

Tim had been silent, intently watching Barcelo's emaciated face protruding from an over sized hospital gown. After a few more minutes Johnny finally opened his eyes.

-I appeal to you as a father confessor so that you'll not have to answer any question if asked about my involvement in this affair. I suppose that like lawyers you can invoke soul-priest confidentiality-.

-What do you mean involvement...-?

And then Tim understood where this could lead. He had touched the deep rooted rebellious fiber in Barcelo's soul. The sleeping champion of lost causes, of mountains to climb was stirring and would soon awaken, and one last time, make waves and please this huge ego everyone thought broken by alcohol and battle fatigue.

Tim continued: -Tell me you're not serious; do I understand that you want to be the hand of God in this matter? You want to be the avenging angel....? I can't believe it... ; yet... I know what you've accomplished in your life....-

-The Avenging angel. Why not, if he exists, which you and I don't believe. What I want to do is make sure that these bastards will be stopped, that these kids will not be deprived of their futures, whatever is left of it after two months of this ordeal. Maybe children have enough resources to spring back if their honor is salvaged. If the culprits walk, they'll never outlive this hell; on the other hand if they can be part of the revenge party, I'll bet whatever teeth I have left that they'll forget most of it and.... maybe, turn out to become stronger persons for it. This is where you'll have to intervene, after the bad guys are taken out. –

-Taken out.... You mean taken out like in... rubbing out their –*blip*- from the big screen? How? How do you intend to do that? - Asked Tim, scared to hear the answer but his curiosity getting the upper hand on his judgment.

He knew that he should not have paid attention to these divagations; talk, people talk, say anything, dream, then find excuses for not proceeding; nothing would come out of this intention, a good one but far from the action stage.

-I'm not yet finished thinking my plan but I'll tell you how it will end for the bad guys. As you know, when I'm not involved in philosophical conversations with you or dreaming of this cute nurse's long legs, there is sweet nothing to do but read. Just yesterday I was reading a book, - The story of civilization by Will Durant-, which I found in the hospital library. By the way, I recommend that you read the entire nine volumes. But back to our perverts; let me relate the final seventeen days in the life of Mithridate the soldier, as it was reported by Plutarque.-

« Mithridate, a soldier living approximately 600 years before our era and serving under King Artaxerces the second, had been drinking heavily one day and was heard bragging that it was he, and not the king who had killed Cyrus the young, at the battle of Cunaxe.

It may well have been him but as the king had already claimed this honor, the fate of the good soldier was sealed. An exemplary punishment was decided: Mithridate would be put to « death in the two boats », which is done according to the following scenario:

Two wooden boats of exactly the same dimension, which can be super-imposed upon each other, are chosen for the occasion. In one of the boats the criminal is placed on his back and is promptly covered with the other boat, his head and four limbs being left hanging outside the now super imposed boats, the rest of the body being completely inside this clam-like arrangement. He is then force-fed. If he refuses, he's coerced into eating by having his eyes pricked by a needle. After he ate, his face is smeared with a mixture of honey and milk.

Positioned so he faces the sun, soon flies and insects of all sorts cover his face. Inside the shell formed by the two boats he has to carry on the usual bodily functions of persons eating and drinking, his excrements soon incubating innumerable parasites, maggots which migrate inside his intestine via the anus and other body orifices, devouring him alive from without and within.

When finally the prisoner is dead and the top boat is removed, the flesh and skin of the criminal is gnawed and consumed by millions of filthy and vile crawling animals which continue to feed on this corpse. The good soldier Mithridate survived seventeen days before dying. »

Tim looked long and hard at Johnny. It appeared that neither knew how this caper would begin but Barcelo had the finale organized.... and the little guy had established his reputation as a serious entrepreneur.

-I didn't know you could be a sadist Mister Barcelo. I agree that this pervert deserves all of it but I can't sanction this approach..... Unless ... it could scare the shit out of others like him. I wonder if this could be taped and projected on the internet pedophile network?-

Tim had often thought of taking matters in his own hands; could never summon the courage; maybe this time he could be a part of a justice system ..... More efficient, more poetic....simpler. Barcelo picked up immediately on the "mediatization" of the project.

-Yea... Internet or even TV. That's a great idea. Everything is possible but give me until tomorrow morning to organize before you do anything with the police. You can be sure that your pervert will be out of the house by nine o'clock Monday morning. Now get out of here I have some serious planning to do. - Barcelo said, suddenly a superman.

CHAPTER 20

"We are condemned to be free; which means responsible for our actions."
JP Sartre

When Lieutenant Paterson came once again to ask Johnny about these bogus checks cashed around town by a woman, Johnny had signed himself out. The psychiatric nurse who knew Paterson related:

-Right after Father Donnelly left his room, Barcelo got busy dressing up, went down to the reception and signed himself out. He looked completely possessed by some idea and was determined to get out of here even though his health is far from being completely back to normal. Probably never will.-

Hospital staff gets attached to their patients, as a banker to your deposit. But this patient knew that they could not keep him against his will. Paterson thought that Barcelo's decision was smart enough; if you're well enough to fight the staff and the administration you're well enough to be on the street.

Excited and still reeling from the bold decision he had made, Johnny had politely told the hospital administration to kiss his indigent bottom goodbye. The magnitude of his new project escaped him for the moment but he could feel that it would fulfill what was left of his life; aware that he would not be breaking any record of longevity. Soon his time would come, and going in style, performing a useful task had always been his goal, unattainable until now. He came to this world without having been consulted; the least he could do was to go out in style when good and ready, performing a last flamboyant action for which he would be remembered.

The task at hand, although illegal, was honorable and very much in line with his life philosophy. His self esteem needed a boost and this job was it. Some people build empires, others win wars; he had built a modest empire, lost it and now he would remove a sadistic pedophile from the earth while hopefully scaring others of the same breed. The main objective was to bail four kids and their mother out of hell. Yes, he'd do it and enjoy every minute.

There was a pay phone in the hospital lobby and from there he phoned Dudley. Dudley was living in Auburn, across the Androscoggin River, just a few minutes away. Even though their lives had parted when he fell into the bottle, they had always respected each other. Dudley had bought the Saint Augustine Club from Johnny and had managed it so well that soon he opened a second, then a third one. He then started a restaurant chain which Deana, now his wife was running like a pro.

Deana had always been grateful for the confidence shown her almost forty years ago and had been a faithful and understanding companion for Dudley. Her only regret was that she could not have children; something to do with the abuses she had suffered in her childhood.

-Dudley, my old friend, what have you been up to?-

Dudley recognized the deep gravelly voice. He had been expecting this phone call for at least five years. He had realized long since that Johnny was directly responsible for his emergence from misery and poverty and was looking forward to helping him out of this dreadful period as soon as he would dry out enough to regain control of his reason. Often over the last years he had left an envelope in Johnny's mail box. Not much, yet too much for the use the money would have.

-Hey, happy to hear from you. How have you been?

Johnny told him about his bad health and said that he wanted to see him.

-Come on over if you don't mind crossing the river. Better still let me pick you up, where are you?-

-I'll grab a cab and be at your place in fifteen.- Johnny said and hung up.

Less than fifteen minutes later he was at the doorstep of a plush and comfortable bourgeois mansion enclosed in a well manicured lawn and a cedar edge. The door opened before he could reach the bell.

His old friend was still in excellent shape. It had been almost eight years since he had run into him by accident; drunk as always during that period. Even then, he remembered that Dudley had shown him respect and had offered help.

Looking at him for a moment, Dudley didn't know whether to laugh or cry. He had in front of him a sick and fragile little man. Still, the eyes were burning into his and the spirit seemed as high as it had ever been.

-I'll be honest Johnny, you look as if you could do with a six month cure in some mountain hideout. Are you sick?-

-I was... but I'm fine now. You should have seen me last week. –He replied with his crooked smile.

-Let's talk Dudley, there's something I want to do but I can't do it alone. I'll need your help. It's dangerous but the cause is worth it. By the way I'm off the booze.–

-I'm listening. To tell you the truth, being retired is not my idea of a good time and any action would be welcomed. Come sit down in the Gym, Deana will join us unless you want to keep her out of this.–

-Deana... she's fine and we'll need her as well.-

He called for her and from somewhere nearby she told him that she would be but a minute.

-Let's have a coffee while we wait.-

They proceeded into the Gym as Dudley had called it and Johnny was not too surprised to see an exercise room equipped with the best of equipment. On a bench there was a forty five pound bar with at each ends two forty five pounds weights for a total of two hundred and twenty five pounds.

–You're still as strong as an ox at sixty seven. - Johnny had always been a little jealous of Dudley's strength.

They were half way through drinking their coffee when Deana came in the room. Statuesque, she must be working out as well, thought Johnny. Wide shoulders, and as flat a belly as Johnny had seen on any Olympic-class athlete. She radiated strength, suppleness and assurance, oozing mature ... yes that's what it was... mature sexuality. Calculating quickly in his head he figured that she was no less than fifty eight; yet looked hardly forty. An eternity had passed since the Italian caper.

Awkwardly the sickly little guy jumped out of his seat. She came close to picking him up in her arms fearing that he would slump to the floor. Planting two loud kisses on his emaciated cheeks, she backed away to have a full view of this ghost.

-You look like you could use a large meal and a good night sleep. Johnny what happened to you? –

-Nothing much except that I almost met my creator or whoever is responsible for my passage on this earth. I feel fine now that I have a purpose and you'll see the results in just a few days. Let's sit down, I have something to tell you and a request to make.-

During the next hour, sometimes out of breath, he told them the entire story, beginning with Father Tim's first visit and then the second one that morning. A long silence followed. Looking at Deana, then getting up and pacing the room for a moment, Dudley went back to his seat. He had always done this little dance whenever stirred.

-This is out of a horror movie. Something to scare little children with... the part about the strangulation of the family cat in front of the kids is unbelievable. So unbelievable that it has to be true, no eight year old would be able to make this up. I'm sure this eight year old girl is not making this up; but it has been done before and we would look stupid if it wasn't true. –

-I agree and have grilled Tim on this. He was also hesitant at first but after sitting down in his car for several hours in front of the house and questioning the teacher who had sent this Jody to him, he now feels that the possibility of a frame-up is remote. We would not do anything to this guy without some solid proof, like video clips and hard evidence from the kids themselves.-

-True that the law would have to play it by the book and the kids could clam up, - said Deana, -but tell me again why the kids are so ...petrified that they won't tell their mother, that part isn't' t clear. -

Johnny had omitted to relate the episode of the rabbit being tortured, amputated of its four limbs and left to die as a demonstration of what would happen to anyone ratting. Deana looked at Barcelo in horror and remained silent for a long moment.

-That would terrify any one let alone kids. I'm scared. What kind of psychopath can conceive such demented torments, let alone carry them out.-

Deana and Dudley, like most close friends, did not have to articulate their thoughts. Telepathy exists between old couples and words are often superfluous. Finally Dudley said.

-Tell us more; what is your plan, I'm sure you have one. –

Johnny smiled, satisfied that he had found the allies he needed to achieve his new goal, more a calling, a vocation.

-My plan is as simple as preparing breakfast in the morning. We dress up as Jehovah's witnesses, ring the door bell at eight fifteen tomorrow morning, crash in, look for evidence, abduct the psycho after we're convinced he's guilty and bring him to this cave I prepared more than forty years ago.- He looked at them before continuing.- I call it my Ali Baba cave. It's actually at the bottom of the ravine in Bowdoin. About ten feet from the bottom a small entrance opens up into a large cave which I have organized thinking it could, one day, serve a purpose. With the Mafia incident, it could have been useful. - He took a deep breath before continuing.

-It turned out that I never used it for purposes other than storing documents; like the Weinstein's confession and the second set of accounting books for the tire dump. We access it from a two hundred feet tunnel made of six foot diameter cement pipes running under more than a hundred feet of scrap tires. The entrance of the tunnel is camouflaged under truck tires which can be easily moved. -

He stopped again to catch his breath. He had a cortisone inhalator pump in his pocket and used it to resume breathing quasi normally. So far no one seemed hesitant; Deana and Dudley had done stunts a lot more dangerous in the past and they looked like a little action would make life interesting again. Deana cut in.

-I follow you up to where you have him in this cave. What then?-

-Let me tell you about the entire plan if you have not decided to dismiss me as an old fool. Other than to free the four kids and the mom from this enslavement and maybe certain death, the purpose is to give a lesson to other pedophiles. The sentence should be so unusual... well let's not mince words... cruel and cold blooded, that it would leave a lasting impression. You know how thieving is reduced in countries where the penalty is the amputation of limb. We are too civilized to go to these extremes for thieving but, to punish torture and slavery, we are justified to revert to the -lex talionis- approach.: an eye for an eye.-

He then told the astonished couple how the soldier Mithridate was punished. Taking his time and going into the finer details of this poor martyr's ordeal. As he had already been rehearsing with Tim, he could work strong dramatic effects into the right places. Deana's facial reaction was the perfect barometer. She made such a face when he described how the little man eaters would enter the body of the good soldier using the back door, that he could not help but stop a minute and asked her if she had grasped the fine points. –You're an old sadist Barcelo. I always knew it. - She murmured.

-This is the program I propose for this animal. We don't have to use boats, we can choose a slightly improved version of this torment which was done by adepts of -stoicism-. I read they would freely choose to die this way in order to expiate their sins and achieve Nirvana. They simply dug a hole in the ground or into the walls of a cave and squeezed into it to never again come out; being fed as often as possible in order to produce nourishment for the ultimate recyclers. Same results as with a boat but without the sun. Videotaping this hellish torment might impress pedophiles of the world. -

-Jesus Christ Johnny, you're a real artist. I never doubted it but now I know it. - Deana managed to say still grimacing. Dudley's face was impassive but his eyes were going from Deana to Barcelo.

-Tell me about this Ali Baba cave. If this is going to be the center of the operation ...- Asked Dudley always the practical "hands on" business man.

-I have not been in this cavern for a good ten years. The last time I went down, there was electricity and it was dry and sound proofed; not a noise would filter out to the surface. Don't forget that it is approximately ninety feet under the surface which is covered with a thirty foot layer of hard packed tires. The camouflage has certainly improved over the years. We access it through a tunnel made of six foot cement pipes. As I said earlier, the pipes tunnel under more than one hundred feet of tires and gravel. The only guy who knew about it was Ed, the former owner of this piece of land; this is where he had hidden the dogs that killed his father. I told you about this. Ed died several years ago. I don't think he ever told anyone but me and his aunt Suzanne.-

His lungs were collapsing again. The excitement and the conference he was giving were draining the last ounces of energy. The inhalation pump reopened his alveolar and he could continue.

-When you say that we should be careful, that Jody could have been lying, you're right on. But frankly, I don't believe she did. Too many bloody and horrible details for a kid to even have nightmares about.- He continued,

-But we'll also take all films and videos that he must have in the house. Who knows what will transpire from these clips. Tim said that he had recognized some local people visiting the house-.

Again, without a word, Dudley looked at Deana. They both knew that once into this sordid, although philanthropic affair, there would be no easy way out. Were they willing to risk their freedom, their comfort, for some family they had never heard of? Finally it was Deana who answered for both of them.

-Sounds easier than some of the jobs we pulled earlier. And the cause, well ... nothing to say about its merit. Believe me I know what these kids are feeling.........- She could empathize with these kids. -Yes, I'll, do it- She answered.

-Hey what about me.- Dudley said,- I' m in. -

For a few minutes Barcelo closed his eyes and remained speechless, recharging his battery. In less than an hour they were done fine tuning the plan. Simplicity had worked for them once before. Remaining anonymous and not to be seen going into the cave was Dudley's main concern. A long list of things to do: Disguises with wigs and Kryolan makeup; borrowing a minivan; buying video equipment, various tools, food, lots of food for the little creatures. Deana, the practical member of the group, came out with a culinary winner: olive oil, black beans, brown sugar, salt, water, mixed properly and administered from gavage bags... Yum Yum.

-I'd like to taste it- said Dudley, -maybe we can market this potion for nagging wives.-

CHAPTER 21

"Men think they are free because they are conscious of their volition's but not of the causes that prompt them to desire."
Spinoza

Monday, eight fifteen, grayish and dull. A man and a woman dressed in black, step out of a gray minivan. The man is tall and large, wears a wide brim black hat and dark clothing; the woman is dressed in a knee length navy blue skirt half covered by a double breasted top coat, she's also tall and her face is stern, severe. Typical Jehovah's witnesses carrying little black briefcases; as Clara the nosy neighbor would later describe them, when interrogated by Lieutenant Patterson.

After climbing the five steps leading to the front door, they ring the bell of number fifty two. By the third ring a child cracks the door open. Deana can guess this nice little girl would be Jody; her head squeezes out of the opening. Looking up at the very tall man and the somber looking woman, she is afraid that it might be the visitors Steven told them would be coming this morning. He called them –clients-.

-My mother is away and Steven is in the shower. Please go away. - And she tries to slam the heavy door closed.

Deana had been expecting her reaction and jams the door with her foot, smiling as she bends down.

-We won't hurt you little girl. Jody is it? You see I even know your name. We're sent by father Donnelly.- Whispers Deana as she gently pushes the door open and walks in followed by Dudley.

Terrified, Jody backs away from the door and looks at both of them standing even taller inside the exiguous hallway. Disconcerted, Jody doesn't know what to do. Her mouth opens up, and then closes, she looks over her shoulder, hesitating but desperately hoping to see freedom and deliverance in these two tall strangers. She remembers other strangers coming in the house and hurting them after they had pretended to be friends. But the lady said she knew the priest.

Deana picks her up and repeats that father Tim has sent them: - To make the problem go away-.

-Where is the problem Jody, where is Steven. Would you like to see him go away? - Tell me where he is. Take us to him. –

Jody's blue eyes are looking for the truth in Deana's eyes; she breaths deeply trying to regain confidence. The mention of the name Donnelly brings a flicker of hope in her eyes. She makes up her mind.

-Follow me please. - She says hesitatingly, still not sure but her hopes getting the better of her fear. –He's in the shower with Don. He's hurting him.... we can hear Don crying. Come quick before he comes out.-

She quickly climbs a stair and walks into a large bedroom. On the far wall a closed door opens on a bathroom from where could be heard the sound of water splashing on the shower walls. Listening more closely Deana could also hear a child sobbing.

Dudley is behind her; she side steps to let him go through. He tries the bathroom door; it is locked from the inside. Backing off a few feet he raises his right foot and directs a stiff kick under the handle. The door crashes open with the first try. He moves in quickly. The shower is a glass enclosure partially fogged up, but through which can be discerned a vague mass.

Before Steven can even know what was happening because of the noise made by the water and of the intensity devoted to the onanism he is perform-ing on the eleven year old Don, two powerful hands grab his long salt and pepper hair and pull him outside the shower cubicle, his penis still erected his hands trying to hold on to the boy.

Soaking wet, his fat flesh glistening under the light, Steven is lying on his back in the middle of the bath room floor. His feet are still in the shower cubicle where the water is still splashing. Steven is now rolling frightened eyes, trying to focus on this giant holding his wet hair in one hand and slowly squeezing his throat with the other.

In the mean time Don has been able to roll over and gets up, moving quickly out of the bathroom while Dudley is concentrating his fury on Steven's neck, gradually increasing the pressure and enjoying every second of the procedure.

-Don't kill him, follow the plan. - Said Deana handing over a piece of cloth impregnated with chloroform while intercepting Don who was heading out of the bathroom.

- Right, let's wait. Johnny's recipe is what this rat deserves. - And he applies the cloth to the face of the already sagging larva.

In the mean time Deana has thrown a towel to Don and is directing him into the bedroom where his three sisters are silently watching.

-They're sent by father Tim- Says Jody to the others. –They're here to save us. - She's proud and takes over, having the proof that she made the right move.

-Sit down on the bed, all of you. I'll tell you what we're doing. -Said Deana trying to appear calm and relaxed. Which she was far from being, having never been so angry.

They all sat and watched as Dudley was dragging Steven out of the bathroom, his body, like a snail, leaving a trail of water on the floor. Picking him up with difficulty as he is wet and slippery, Dudley throws him on the bed. As if burned on a hot stove, the kids recoil and retreat to the far side of the room.

-Don't worry, never again will he touch any of you. - Says Dudley in a voice which he was trying to make gentle.

He could have used Johnny's inhalator to catch his breath if it worked against anger. His mind was in a melt down and no longer in charge.

-Sit on the floor if you don't want to be near him- Said Deana.

Still looking at the limp fat body of their tormentor, they obey and sit on the floor leaning on the far wall. In the mean time Dudley is duct taping the hands and feet of the naked Steven. A piece of tape is also placed on his mouth and another over his eyes. He now looks more like a Christmas turkey than like the predator he was just a moment ago.

-Your sister is right, we're sent by god. None of you should ever mention that we are sent by anyone other than god. You understand don't you? – If there was a God he should have done exactly what they were doing thought Deana as she was talking.

That was the only loose end in this scenario. Father Tim was known by Jody and she could tell the police about him if questioned.

-We'll take Steven away in a minute, but before, we want all the movies, the video clips he has taken of you and of these bad people. Who can tell me where they are.-?

As she is speaking Deana is scrutinizing the faces of the four scared children. Jody is jubilant, a large smile on her face. The sight of Steven all tied up like a sausage, was turning them back into thinking human beings. Hypnotized, they could not lift their eyes from this pathetic carcass. This monster was now a pathetic heap of wet blubber.

Don was the first to speak and told them that the clips were in the trunk of the car parked in the garage. The video camera was ready to roll in an adjacent room and it became obvious that some action was expected that day. Lights were placed around the room and a bed covered with a white sheet had been moved to occupy the center of the space.

-Anyone knows when the first visitor is expected.-? Asked Deana.

Karen, the older girl, had heard a telephone conversation and thought that it was around ten thirty.

Dudley looked at his watch: nine o'clock, more than an hour to go. Looking at Deana he took his cell phone and dialed Johnny's number. Sitting in the mini van a few streets away, Johnny picked up.

-All is clear over here but we're expecting visitors around ten thirty. - Said Dudley. -Do you want to make this a double or do we stay as is-.

-The kids will be in the house so there's danger for them. We could ask Tim to pay a parish call or they could not open the door..... Let's leave now with what we have.-

Dudley interrupted the conversation and signaled to Deana that they would leave now.

-Here is the plan children: we'll take Steven away with us and he'll never be back to hurt you. He'll be punished for what he has done to you. Until your mom comes home you'll be locked in a room. In an hour we'll call your mother at work and tell her to come and release you. Your mother doesn't know what Steven has done to you so you'll have to tell her. She may find it difficult to believe you so we'll leave one of the clip for you to show her. Don could you bring all the clips inside before we leave. We want to identify those other bad people and punish them as well. –

Don got up, dressed and went downstairs into the garage where he opened the car trunk and came back with a large box containing several video clips. Deana fished one out of the lot and threw it on the bed.

-We'll leave this one for your mother. After she has seen it, destroy it, don't ask her, just do it. It's easy, just pull all the film in a bundle and light a match to it in the fire place. – She stopped and looked at each one of the children. Speaking slowly she continued.

-Will you be able to do what we asked.-? We need your help to deal with this situation. You'll need to be brave. The police will come. They'll want to know who we are. Don't tell them anything about us, say that we were disguised. – Again she stopped and with a smile continued. –In fact we are disguised and we don't look at all like what you see now. You can tell the police that you don't remember anything. - They all nodded their heads.

No longer able to touch this disgusting bare skin, Dudley rolled Steven in a blanket and transported the package down to the garage using the connecting door. He used the keys Don had given him to move Steven's car out on the street so that Johnny could back the minivan inside the garage.

-Come in Johnny. The garage is clear and you can back into it.-

Deana went into the fridge and brought enough juice and water for the kids to drink during the next hour.

-The door bell will ring but you won't be able to open it. Your mother has her own keys and she'll be here with you in less than two hours. –

Looking at the older girl, Deana said.

-Tell your mother that we'll phone her this morning. Ask her to keep the police out of this until we talk. Can you do that for me? – Karen nodded.

Deana jammed the bedroom door from the outside and went down to the garage as Johnny was backing the van. He couldn't enter the garage with the minivan, but could open the rear door into the entrance so that they could load their parcel without being seen; as was later reported to lieutenant Paterson by the nosy neighbor.

The minivan had conveniently been stolen from one of Dudley's friend, away for the next two weeks. The entire operation took less than thirty minutes. Fifteen more minutes and they were stopping in a wooded area near the former Barcelo Recycling Enterprise. The site had been abandoned with more than twenty five million scrap tires, making it the largest Maine Department of Environmental Protection tire dump site. For all intents and purposes they still owned it as the city of West Bowdoin did not want to take it for non payment of back taxes. The cost of cleaning up this mess was estimated at about one dollar per tire or twenty five million dollars; good enough reason to not want the ownership.

Steven's carcass was transferred into Barcelo's four by four ATV, dragging a trailer into which Steven fitted very nicely. Driving between two twenty foot walls of scrap tires, they soon reached the rear of the property.

It took a while to find the entrance to the cave; several years of growth had improved the camouflage. After some probing and a few well chosen swear words, Johnny found the cement pipes tunnel leading to the cave. Soon they were dragging Steven's fat carcass through the musty and damp tunnel. After what seemed to be an eternity, the tunnel opened into a spacious cave. Changing the light bulbs took another minute and they were all happy to see that the old electric wire had not been chewed up by rodents.

Steven was starting to come to.

-Should we remove the duct tape- asked Dudley, - I'm dying to hear what this gentleman has to say in his defense.-

-He won't convince me but fine with me if you want to hear his story. - Said Deana as she was installing the video and the screen they had brought.

-We should be able to start viewing the clips in a minute or so. –

As Dudley roughly yanked off the duck tape covering the eyes and the mouth of Steven, Johnny was bringing in the box filled with the clips. He gave it to Deana.

-There are fifteen of these clips. We'll be looking at them for ever but I think it's worthwhile. The spectacle will make us all sick as we'll see what some of the worse bastards living on earth can do. - Said Johnny.

Deana was already loading the first clip while Dudley was installing Steven in a chair placed squarely in front of the screen. The chair had arm rests onto which Steven's arms were taped solidly. His lower extremities were also taped to the legs of the chair, which was then inclined at a thirty degree angle.

So far not a word from the alleged pedophile; his bare skin was shivering and covered with goose bumps making him look like a Thanksgiving turkey. Still recovering from the chloroform and the partial choking, he hadn't yet fully realized what was happening. From the warmth of the shower, his idea of what paradise should be, he had been half choked by a giant wearing a wide brim black hat, put to sleep with chloroform and was now somewhere in a prehistoric cave, with three judges who were preparing to view his video clips. His heart was beating a frenzied number. He could feel the adrenaline flowing by the liter in his bare ass body.

-We wouldn't want our star to miss any of the action. We're also counting on him to tell us about the names and addresses of the other players.- Whispered Johnny in Steven's ear, while opening and closing a pair of pliers, blacksmiths use to clip the hoofs of horses to be shod.

Pliers had worked efficiently once before with Arriganello, why invent a new mode of persuasion.

-We'll look at all the clips, starting with the first one as they are conveniently numbered. You'll tell us the names and addresses of your guests. - Continued Johnny touching Steven's nose with the pliers.

-Ready to roll-. Said Deana as she pushed the start button.

The first clip was showing the kids, naked, gauche and clumsily parading in front of the camera. All were sobbing, tears streaking down their puffed up faces. Their lower backs and arms streaked with red stripes as if they had been beaten. No adults were seen on this first one. In retrospect the second one was the worse; it was featuring Steven raping each of the children. He was training and preparing his victims for his paying customers. Then all the others were of the paying customers. Under Barcelo's gentle coaxing, Steven identified each and every one of them. Two of them were from the area, while the others were from Boston and New Jersey.

-Were they aware that you were taping?- Asked Deana

-Yes. Answered Steven. - After being shown the tongs. He continued, - But they didn't know I was keeping a copy. –

-So the original will be found in their homes-. Reflected Deana.

At ten thirty, using the cell phone they had found in the stolen van, Johnny phoned Maureen O'Reilly at work and told her to get home immediately. He hung up after telling her that he would phone back in fifteen minutes to explain what was going on. Fifteen minutes later he phoned the O'reilly home and told a panicking mother what had been happening under her nose and to watch the clip for proof.

-We have fourteen other clips, similar to the one you should look at; we can give them to the police if... this is what you want. I'll get back to you tomorrow morning. In the mean time don't feel guilty, you have all been abused. You can go on with your lives if you stick together. Steven will never bother you or your family again; we have him and will never release him. - He could hear the kids talking all at once in the back ground. That was a good sign.

It took more than two hours to watch the fourteen clips. Six names and addresses had been obtained from Steven, who was now shivering from head to toes.

-Let's throw a blanket over his shoulders and let's feed him, - suggested Johnny –we want him to be around for as long as possible. This man has a task to fulfill. –

By now, Steven was rolling panic stricken eyes and had no illusions about his immediate future.

-What will you do to me? I haven't done anything to you. Let me go and I won't press charges.-

The words were difficult to grasp, partly covered by the castanets sounds made by his chattering teeth. Not bothering to answer, Deana, expertly pinching his nose shut, inserted the gavage tubing into his mouth, down the pharynx and proceeded to eject a generous portion by squeezing the bag. The concoction was not appreciated by Steven who tried to spit the tubing out of his mouth. Deana pushed it further into the esophagus and was able to empty the bag completely.

-The olive oil is good for your heart -. Said Deana.

-He should also drink a little – Johnny said before continuing. - There's another aspect of this caper we haven't covered, flies, there are no flies in here, we'll have to import some and raise the temperature so they'll reproduce. –

-It will be hot enough in here once the flood lights have been on for an hour. As for the flies I have an idea. – Said Dudley.

By now Steven was starting to see the broader picture of his predicament. Fully recovered from the chloroforming, fear had taken all of the space available in his brain. Over the years he had come to be able to justify his very different sexuality. He was well read on the subject; several others had paved the way. This kind of psychopathic behavior was well documented if you knew where to look. The famous marquis de Sade and even a close associate of Joan of Arc, the count de Rais, to name just two of several thousands. The count de Rais had been a model for Steven, raping, torturing and killing several hundred children before he was condemned by the church and burned for his actions. The clergy will only go so far in tolerating these sick but otherwise useful individuals. This count must have been very useful to have been allowed such depravity with impunity for several years.

Steven was amoral, aroused by the enslavement and raping of children. Over the years he had perfected a pattern and could live without remorse. The destruction of the children's lives, their submission to his will, were his ultimate aphrodisiac. Now that the table was turned, he could not find the slightest hint of pleasure in his own enslavement. He was now absolutely certain of not being a masochist.

Whining in as high a pitch as he could command, he blurted out.

-My rights are violated. I want to be turned over to the police. This is what you should have done immediately not kidnapped me in my shower. You have no rights to render justice.-

Johnny's blood was boiling with anger.

-We found you raping an eleven year old boy; you have been raping each and every one of these poor kids; you have sold them to your friends and in the process have ruined their lives as surely as if you had killed them. At least killing them would have left them their pride and put an end to the humiliation. You're the lowest form of life and we'll let the lowest forms of life deal with you.-

Johnny stopped and looked at Steven a moment so that the last words would sink in. He was pleased with the analogy.

-Let me tell you a secret that I know you won't repeat. In expiation, you will suffer the fate of the famous soldier Mithridate..... As you'll see, this is what I meant by having the lowest forms of life deal with your punishment. You enjoyed entering kids' anus... well, let's see how you'll feel having thousands of maggots entering yours and devour you from the inside. -

As Johnny was pausing to suck on his pump, out of breath for having done so much, Steven yelled back at him.

-Mithridate, who the fuck is he, I never heard of this ass hole. -

-Appropriate that we should share this story with you. After all you'll be re-enacting this historical incident. - Said Barcelo, able to breathe again.

And Johnny told him in details the story of the poor soldier, carefully pronouncing each word and stopping frequently so the entire atrocious picture could be imprinted in Steven's neurons. When the tale had progressed to the seventeenth day, Steven was screaming at the top of his voice, horrified at the thought that he would be put through this torture.

-Yell all you can, no one will hear you. – Cut in Johnny, -This place is perfectly sound proofed: on top, ninety feet of soil and twenty feet of scrap tires, on the sides, more than one hundred feet of scrap tires. All sound waves will be rubbed out before they travel one tenth of the distance. – And he continued. -The only ingredient missing are the flies. We'll have to bring some from the surface. Also there will be a slight variation. We don't have boats and will have to be imaginative; trust us we will be.-

-Oh. I almost forgot: during the entire expiatory period; elegant choice of words isn't it? You will be filmed and the whole world will be able to look at you while you prepare for your next life. Hopefully, this spectacle will cause some of your pedophile associates to change their minds, convert and seek treatment.-

-You're crazy, you can't do that to a human being. You have no right to judge me. - Steven was sobbing.

-We know that the justice system would play it by the rules and give you a fairer chance than what you have given your victims. Your lawyer would question these kids, scare them once more, abuse them again and find loop holes in the legal system; you would be freed on bail so you could also scare your accusers and continue your activities. This is precisely why we have decided to bypass the system. You could also say that while the state cannot run the risk of making errors, which they do anyway, we, as individuals have decided to act without all the usual rails and guidelines, if convinced of the culpability of the accused. In your case we are. You have been judged, sentenced and the penalty will be applied. I only hope that you'll be strong enough to last as long as the good soldier Mithridate. If you remember he lasted seventeen days..... –

-Seventeen days, seventeen days, tied to four pegs in the ground, under flood lights, being eaten alive by maggots.....unable to chase them away, feeling their teeth sucking at my skin, piercing it, their wiggling slimy tube bodies entering my anus, my mouth, my nose, my eyes.... Nobody can be cruel enough to do that. Don't do this to me...What can I do? - Pleaded Steven who by now had a clear vision of what was in store for him. Johnny had been very vivid in his description.

-We saw little eight year old Jody pleading before you raped her, all the children in this family have implored and cried before you .... Did you enjoy watching these kids being humiliated and hurt by your customers? What about the cat you strangled, the rabbit you amputated and then skinned alive to scare the kids into submission, what about the daily physical and mental torture you imposed on your victims? What about the way out of this affair? Isn't it true that after some weeks you would have killed them all including the mother. Did you have another choice? No you didn't and how often before today have you taken over entire families and destroyed their minds and their lives? You deserve more than the treatment we have chosen, unfortunately we couldn't come up with anything worse.... You.... - Deana could not finish, she was really enraged.

-If we can prevent one child molester from hurting only one victim, we will have accomplished our goal. Don't feel singled out, your customers and friends shown in these clips will be joining you soon. The good news is that you'll die before they do having started one day earlier. - Deana was flushed and Steven knew that mercy would not be coming from this girl.

Dudley and Johnny had stopped and were listening, surprised at so much anger. Dudley had always known that there was a dark side in his wife's soul, so dark that he could be crushed by its intensity, so frightful that even she didn't dare explore it completely.

Frightened by the intensity and the hatred expressed by Deana, Steven was terrified and knew that she had been abused by the likes of him and would seek revenge. Maybe one of the men.... Hope, only hope, and very little of it was left for him. Right then, nothing he could think of doing could put an end to this nightmare. Suicide, the ultimate salvation, was also out of the question; how could he kill himself without the use of his hands or feet, he could not even starve himself to death, gavage would keep him well fed until the maggots had gnawed their way into his guts, slowly causing a massive infection. He felt an enormous weight crushing his chest, a sense of total helplessness, already nibbling at his bowels, in preparation for the maggots' feast. He had to react, do something. Screaming was the only action possible and he did, at the top of his lungs.

For the next several minutes the cave walls were amplifying and giving considerable dimension to these sound waves. Johnny's tortuous intellect thought that a recording of this horrible a-cappella tune could find an audience. Exhausted after ten minutes of this concert, Steven gradually stopped and started to shake so much that Deana feared he would die of a heart attack. She did not want his death to be so easy. A full glass of whisky forced down his throat calmed him.

During that time, Dudley had been organizing the stage. First he laid a thick clear plastic film on the ground, in order to keep all the body juices basting around the naked body. He then untied Steven's legs and arms from the chair and positioned his wiggling body in the middle of this plastic sheet.

He then secured the wrists and legs to four deeply set steel pegs. Steven would look like Jesus Christ on the cross, but horizontally. He then covered the body with another plastic sheet spread loosely, so that it would create a hot house effect and facilitate the biological process. Clipping the sides together around the neck, arms and ankles would provide the right climate for the festivities that would take place under this improvised cocoon.

Flood lights were positioned on each side of the stage and the wide angle camera covering the entire scene was ready to roll. The strong flood lights would raise the temperature in the cave providing the right incubating environment to hatch the flies' eggs into hungry maggots.

-Let's start rolling. –

And Deana pulled another gavage unit from the carton and forced its content into Steven's stomach; not unlike the procedure used to force feed ducks or geese being prepared for "foie gras". They left after promising to return later that day with a fly producing carcass, and, every day thereafter to feed him until his body was completely eaten by the maggots born out of and feeding on his decaying body.

The video camera was rolling slowly and all Steven could hear when they had left was the slight buzz of the motor turning the film which would immortalize his last days on earth. He started screaming again in the hope that someone would hear. His voice remained captive in the cave, but yelling relieved some of the tension and exhausted him. After thirty minutes he fell asleep for a few minutes. These few minutes would become the only relief he would get for the next several days, yelling himself to sleep every thirty minutes or so.

CHAPTER 22

"Nous nous consolons rarement des grandes humiliations, nous les oublions."
Vauvenargues

Lieutenant Paterson, was available when Maureen O'Reilly called the precinct, he took the call. In the morning, after the mysterious phone call received at work, Maureen had come home immediately. She had opened the front door with her keys as no one answered her repeated ringing. Surprised that Steven was not at home she had released her children from the master bedroom and for a few minutes, was unable to make any sense out of what they were saying. Then she grasped the horror of the situation. Without further thinking she reached for the phone and dialed the police number which was scotched to the wall above the phone.

-I have something awful to report. - She had already given her name and address to Paterson.

Then Don, who was following her, took the phone from her and guided her in the living room after interrupting the communication.

-The woman said that you should look at this before you phone the police. –

He had already set up the projection equipment. The first few images fitted all the pieces of this horrendous puzzle in their proper places. For several minutes she saw Lisa being the sexual object of this couple. Maureen stopped breathing, almost fainting.

-Destroy this film. Burn it immediately. I have seen enough. - Said the crying mother.

Now that she had seen this horrible clip, she was not at all certain that getting the police involved would serve any purpose, other than to smear her children a little more, raping them again and again every time the clip was played to police officers, lawyers, judges or jury members, among them, some pedophiles, enjoying the show. She and Lisa had cried so much, the other children cried also, partly in relief that it was finished partly to vent out some of the frustration. All that was left in their souls was an intense hatred, a primeval need to obtain revenge, to kill, to torture, to tear the flesh of these animals as they had done to them, to the cat and to the rabbit.

Not the least of Maureen's sorrow was Steven's deceit. The friendship, the love and the trust she had accorded to this individual were genuine and whole. Maureen was deeply wounded in the most intimate part of her soul; a wound that would never heal. It was obvious that he had feigned love to trap her children, to have free and continuous access to children, his only passion. He had never cared for her, never meant these passionate words, targeting the children from the very beginning. She could see it clearly now.

She had been gullible and being gullible is always the easy way out of a decision; but then total skepticism is not better. After the facts she could blame herself for not looking further and beyond the fiery phrases pronounced by this fucking snake. She should have conducted an investigation. This catastrophe would change everybody's life, forever, but the survival of her children demanded that she grabbed the fragile thread hanging from over the edge and heaved her family out of this cesspool.

Patterson had found it weird that the communication had ended and had phoned back. The police was alerted and Paterson came to the house. Maureen formerly accused her former common law husband of having sexually assaulted her children.

-No we don't have any physical proof and no I will not ask my daughters and my son to submit to a medical examination at this time. - Had she answered Paterson when he explained to her what the procedure was.

-If you have children of your own, lieutenant Paterson you will understand that I want to protect them from further trauma.-

-You're right but consider the damage a person like the one you have described can go on inflicting to other kids. - Had argued Paterson.

Yes said Maureen but she continued to be hesitant. It would be wise to have the advice of a lawyer before making further decisions; she said. The clip had been destroyed, burned in the fire place. There was no evidence left other than the bodies of her children. And yes, upon examination the doctor would report that they had all been raped repeatedly.

Knowing precisely what the procedure would be was a must. Then she could make the decision. A bad decision had been made by trusting Steven; from now on she would be careful.

-More than anything else, I want to shield my children from further shame and degradation. How can these animals be allowed to live with the rest of the world. - She was aggressive.

-I understand your concern but, I can't do much on what you've told me. We need more tangible proof. You'd be surprised how many accusations are .... Where is this person? Is he still around here and is there any danger that he'll be a threat to you?-

Don, who had been listening intently to the conversation, could not keep his tongue.

-Oh no, he won't be back, we know.... – Then realizing that he had spoken out of turn, he corrected his statement. -He left this morning and said that he wouldn't be back.-

Paterson looked at the young boy and understood that the kids knew but would never tell. He had seen this reaction before; traumatism so violent that the mind hides it in the confine of the brain. There was a lot more to this affair than met the trained eye of the detective: Steven's car was still on the street. How did he leave?; on foot or with somebody else? Better still why had he left; what had scared him into leaving what could have been a paradise for a pedophile; questions but no answers. And the eyes of every one were puffed out. Paterson could tell that they had cried all the tears in their bodies. He had seen eyes like these numerous times. Miseries, hardships and depravation were some of life's shortcomings he knew too well. He pursued a little sarcastically.

-He left on foot I suppose; his car is still parked on the street. -

Nobody answered his question and he could see that the mother was telepathically telling her son to shut up. He did and went out of the room averting Paterson's stare.

-I can't force you to tell me what happened. I'll leave now and be back tomorrow. In the mean time we'll check on Steven and see if he has a criminal record. Give me an object which he alone had touched and I'll get the vehicle impounded. -

Maureen pointed to a bottle of gin.

-No one else touched this bottle. –

-These finger prints and the license plate on the car might yield his secret. - Said Paterson as he was bagging the bottle.

As soon as Paterson had departed, Maureen took Don aside and asked him for the complete unabridged story. Don was reluctant at first.

-Don, if I'm to make the right decision I need to know what happened in …. details. –

Don looked at her as if she was asking him to walk on red hot cinders.

-I'm ashamed to talk about this, I want to forget the last two months. … But I suppose I have to tell you. … But to nobody else, ever. -

He then lowered his head between his knees, his forearm on his thighs, and in a low monotonous voice, like a robot, he told her the complete awful, nightmarish story of their ordeal, including the threats against her life, the cat, the rabbit and the other things as well. Maureen had closed her eyes and reopened them when he was done, tears silently flowing on her cheeks from the beginning to the end of the narration.

From the first days Steven had been working towards his objective, being friendly with Don and flirting with the girls. He would also exercise unnecessary authority on the children asserting his position as the dominant male, slowly browbeating them into submission. Little things at first; like when you train a dog, ask the animal to sit as he is about to sit; then reward it. Steven was shrewd, Machiavellian, a master at his art.

When he finally made his intentions obvious, he told the kids what he expected of them and, to drive his point home, strangled the family cat and tortured a rabbit during several minutes, repeating that this was the fate of any one ratting. He said that he would also kill - your mommy-, tearing her apart like this rabbit, if any one told about their private business, as he was now calling their association.

He then undressed and abused each child, smearing them with the blood of the rabbit, while the others, locked in a room, waited their turn listening to the sobbing and protestations of their sibling. It became a routine and every time Maureen would leave for work he would train them as he said, in the fine art of making adults happy. Later, strangers started to visit and after the children had paraded in front of them, one would be chosen.

That morning, he had been chosen to take a shower with Steven and while he was ….being hurt by Steven, the door of the shower was crashed opened and a tall man had grabbed Steven by the hair and pulled him out of the shower. The man was choking him when a woman came in and told him to stop, that they needed him alive. She then handed over some gray tape and a towel smelling funny.

He continued, - It went quickly after that: She gave me a towel, asked me to sit on the bed with the girls. Steven was thrown on the bed, taped up all over, wet and naked. The tall lady then asked to not remember their faces, but that it didn't matter much as they were disguised. The most important thing she said was that: - Steven will never hurt any of you again. You will never see Steven again. -

Relieved, Don started crying. Maureen took him in her arms, rocking him as she had done when he was just a baby. In time he regained enough composure to stand up.

-I wanted to kill him but he was always careful, never turning his back, never leaving hammers or knives around. -Said the poor kid. –We couldn't tell you. He said you would be the first to die.... Like the rabbit... I dream about the rabbit : I see the four legs cut up, the blood gushing, Steven tearing the flesh with the branch cutter and the awful yelling of the poor white rabbit.-

She ran to the bathroom and vomited. What a mess. Where is Steven now, can he still hurt them? Who are these angels? Any time she would ask a question about the strangers, the kids would clam up. They kept repeating that they had been sent by god and were disguised. Could not remember their faces anyway as they were too scared. The only description was that the man was very tall and the lady had a soft voice, little Jody said, still so pleased with herself.

Just then the telephone rang. Scared, Maureen hesitated a moment, but answered.

-Maureen O'Reilly, - the same voice that had phoned her at work. –Are you free to talk; are the cops still with you?-

-No, he just left... who you are ....and thank you- She began crying again.

-No thanks necessary, and no talk on the phone. I don't think your phone is tapped now but it might be tomorrow. I just wanted to tell you that your children and yourself are safe and will be avenged. Steven has already started expiating his crimes. You'll be able to see him soon, either on a special web site or on television. We have fifteen other clips similar to the one you must have seen. One set will be delivered to you tomorrow if this is what you want. You can destroy them or give them to the police. – Johnny paused for a minute to let this sink in.

-However, you or they, the police, won't be able to have access to Steven or to punish him more than we're doing. His fate is sealed and he'll die for his crimes. You may want to go after the others, if so we have the addresses and full identities. If you do decide to let the police take care of this matter, we won't pursue the others, but if you want us to continue this action, they'll be dealt with more severely than they would by the law. Without your children having to testify and be raped virtually all over again. - He paused. She could hear his arduous breathing.

-You must know that as soon as you decide to press charges against the others, your life and your children's lives will be in danger as well as very disturbed. Medical examinations, questioning by cops, lawyers, judges, psychiatrists, the clips will be seen by a number of persons and more shit like that.-

Silence for a while. Maureen was processing these facts with as much detachment as she could. Think with your brain, process the facts and answer only when you are certain the proper decision has been made; easier said than done.

-My kids have been traumatized enough as it is and if this can be dealt without them being involved in court or elsewhere, so much the better as long as these others are punished and prevented from doing more of the same to other kids. - She finally answered.

-I hear you. I'll destroy these other clips. As for payback, you'll be able to follow the step by step action we have taken. You see Mrs. O'Reilly, we want to give an example to other pedophiles. Good bye and good luck with your life, we have done what we could. By the way a man of the cloth might be of help in a case like this one. Jody knows one. – And the phone went dead.

For a long minute, Maureen kept the receiver on her chest. This stranger had saved her family and she didn't know his name. How did he get to know about this situation while she, living here, had not had a clue? Not now, but later she would question the children; they had the answer; she needed to know in order to forget. Correction, forgetting was out of the question, it was more a situation that she would have to learn to live with, to deal with.

-Who was it mommy? - Asked little Jody.

-I think it was God or the archangel Gabriel. - She answered. –It was one of the men who came this morning, he wanted to know how we all were.-

Jody nodded and said gravely that:-It was God who sent them. They were angels. Big strong angels, dressed in black-. She continued:

-Steven looked so stupid, all tied up like a sausage with his penis hanging ...- And she giggled, something she had not done for a while.

Revenge is a wonderful therapy, thought Maureen, and while life would never be the same, it would go on if further trauma could be prevented. She would see to that; her mind was made up, the police were out of this scene. They would need to involve and question the kids, show them the clips, have lawyers interrogate them to exclude that they could be framing some one, bring them to the witness box and have them relive their horrible experiences. Furthermore, and that would be the worse in this scenario, the whole world would look at these awful clips, every time a piece of their souls being destroyed, like the prions destroying the neurons of the patients afflicted by the -mad cow disease-. She could not help reacting strongly at the thought that some of the lawyers, judges, doctors, policemen, jury persons, looking at the evidence, were pedophiles being aroused by the clips being shown as evidence. That would give the final blow to their self esteem. Never. The clips would be destroyed by the angels; this crime cried for terrible vengeance and it would be exacted by Gabriel the archangel.

-A man of the cloth could help-. As Gabriel had recommended. Maybe a good idea, but not today.

With this ability found only in people with a long history of suffering, Maureen O'Reilly turned the page. After eating a monstrous pizza with cokes unlimited, they all went to bed in Maureen's bed, seeking reassurance and the oblivion sleep brings; well ... most of the time. Not tonight though, Maureen could not sleep, she kept seeing the image of these two strangers violating her daughter's body and mind.

-Don't let me down Gabriel.-

Careful not to awaken the kids who seemed to be sleeping peacefully, she got up and, like a zombie out of voodoo land tip toed to the fridge and filled the tumbler in her hand with ice cubes. Sipping the whisky, looking out the living room window, on the deserted street, searching for the shadow of Steven, she realized how vulnerable they were. She would buy a hand gun first thing in the morning; it was in her Irish cultural background to be able to defend her loved ones; she would be ready next time. After emptying her glass she went back to bed and reclaimed her place. Jody had moved in and kept it warm for her. She too was an angel, what if she had not ..... Before she drowned into deep sleep, a clearer picture was emerging. Then she dreamt that Steven was boiling in a large pot. The four kids were skinning the bastard alive. Little did she know that the vigilantes Angels were doing a lot better than that.

CHAPTER 23

Avenging angels at work do not disturb.

Back in Auburn, Johnny and his friends had once more endured through the fourteen video clips and had printed pictures of the five pedophiles. Deana bailed out after the second one; she couldn't go through the ordeal twice during the same day. Coupling these pictures with the addresses they had obtained from Steven, the beginning of what would soon be a complete personal file on the five targets was laid down. The actors in the clips were now identified and could be tracked down one by one until all had been neutralized. If only for this purpose the O'Reilly tragedy would have served a cause. But it would go beyond taking out these five animals; a strong message would be given to the perverts of the world.

Two of the aggressors were living in the immediate area and they would be the first to join Steven. The other three were domiciled in Boston and the state of New Jersey.

Over the years, Deana had turned out to be a good little hacker and was of the opinion that the daily footage being taken of Steven's expiation could be relayed via so many unrelated transmitters that no one could find the primary source of the emission.

A sixty minute résumé of the first 24 hour clip could be made available starting tomorrow, and upgraded every 24 hours. A short introduction relating the events would also be available: scenes taken out of the clips, showing a child being abused, face blotted out, would justify the severity of the sentence to the viewers. It was necessary to continually justify the harshness of Steven's sentence. The general public was as good a judge as any judge; the general public had to be given all the facts. Deana felt that if it was possible for pedophilic and pornographic material to be shown and sold anonymously on the internet, this counter-measure had right to equal time opportunity.

Dudley, who was totally unfamiliar with Internet, could not be convinced that the emitter of the series could remain anonymous; what if some smart FBI computer whiz could back track to the cave; what if they were caught? He remembered having read about these smart ass kids creating havoc in the computers of others, some of these being as prominently safe and secured as the USA Army and the Government.

-Let's think this over. I'm not satisfied that we'd be safe. - Said Dudley ending this discussion.

They agreed that more data was needed before a completely smart decision could be made. Any mistake would be costly and they left the decision hanging until the next day.

Barcelo recapitulated the schedule for the next day:

-Eight o'clock tomorrow morning; we change the film at the cave. The flies will be introduced to the equation; no flies no maggots. The Deana gastronomic concoction of water, beans and olive oil given in large quantities should have already started to yield the expected results. – He stopped, taking a deep breath before continuing,

-Then we'll pick up the other two gentlemen and bring them over to the cave. This way Stephen will have some company. I still don't know whether we should treat the others in the same fashion. They may not be as guilty. – Johnny was getting soft.

-They're all mad dogs and perverts. There is no question in my mind; we should treat them as mad dogs. - Snapped Deana. -Furthermore how can we let them live if we abduct them, our security would be at risk. Can't do that.-

-Right you are my dear.- Echoed Dudley who was loading his colt .45.

The very same piece he had used during the Rossini incident several years ago. Deana had also kept hers and had been practicing regularly taking some pride in being one of the better shot around Auburn. With the silencer she could practice in her basement without scaring the neighbors. It had been decided that they could use the Mini Van one more time before ditching it. Dudley's friend would not be back before another week.

It was raining and a good day to be kidnapping a pervert or two, quipped Deana. They approached the Barcelo Recycling Enterprise site from Lisbon Falls having driven south on rte 136 from Auburn. Travelling on different roads and not keeping the same vehicle more than a few days would keep them incognito to the neighbors for a little while. Ten days maybe fifteen if lucky and careful. It was unlikely that these weaklings would have Mithridate's staying power; soldiers of this era would have been in terrific physical shape.

As soon as they entered the tunnel leading to the cave, they could vaguely make out muffled screams. As they advanced the wailing and whining became more distinct, like a crescendo in an opera partition. Upon entering the cave the full blast of the sound hit them like a wave during a storm; Johnny had never experienced such an eerie sensation, like entering a cathedral on a Sunday morning while the Mormon tabernacle choir is hitting high notes of Haydn's Messiah. Pain had a tangible substance, a presence which could be palpated. They froze for a moment and Deana was the first to regain control.

-If one can make so much noise, three could be heard from outside the cave. - Said Deana to break this awkward silence. –We'll have to gag them.-

Steven sensed their presence, heard Deana and stopped breathing listening intensely. He was welcoming their arrival; the solitude was the most awful torment. He could understand that abused women often stayed with their brutal husband, afraid to be alone, preferring brutality to loneliness. He had used this very fear to hook his victims. One had admitted so much. Little did he know that his solitude would be broken by little hungry maggots in a few days?

-Don't stop your exercise in vocalization on our behalf, we won't be long, just the time needed to feed you. – Said Deana.

The contraption engineered by Dudley had successfully sustained Steven's constant assaults. Only the wrists and ankles were bleeding, the steel pegs had not budged. Focusing his squinting eyes, Steven tried to look beyond the flood lights illuminating the stage. He managed to say.

-You can't go through with this, it's inhumane. Even what I've done doesn't warrant this. I don't believe you're cruel enough to continue. I repent my actions; never again, I swear it. –

Johnny was the weakest of the three and would have been in favor of putting the critter out of his misery. But then he had been dreaming about the inferno the O'Reilly kids had been living. Every time he felt some compassion for Steven he would replay in his mind a particular horrible scene where Steven was satanically enjoying hurting little Jody. The rictus distorting his lips, the wickedness in his eyes, the pure delight he seemed to be enjoying; that would forever prevent Johnny or any of the group to feel pity for this creature.

-Kill me now but please don't let me last seventeen days as this Thridate soldier did. There are rats in here... they bite my hands and feet when I fall asleep. They're so big I thought they were cats at first.... I am so afraid of rats, have always been. Look at my fingers they're bitten and bleeding. Even if I yell at them they keep on nibbling at my skin. They know I can't move.–

The poor guy was crying like a baby; or maybe like the rabbit he had tortured to death in front of the kids to obtain their submission or maybe like Don, Jody and all these other kids he had enjoyed hurting ....

-Think about the pleasure you had in torturing the rabbit, strangling the cat or raping the O'Reilly children. You might be able to forget your present situation and feel good about the pleasure of suffering in expiation. Offer your sufferings to God; he may absolve you of your sins. We won't release you. Save your breath. –

Deana was by far the toughest of the three. She had been used and abused during most of her childhood. Some bad souvenirs can be forgotten only when vengeance is exacted. Dudley was very much aware that while she could be tender and even docile at times, Deana was a potential hurricane.

She had bought a full carton of gavage units. Her special preparation of blended black beans, water and olive oil was making the gavage bag look like a balloon. Taking a half inch tube out of a sterile pouch, she fixed it to the gavage bag and after inserting it deep inside the esophagus of this modern Mithridate, being careful not to enter the larynx, she pressed slowly on the bag emptying the entire content into Steven's stomach.

Nothing he could do to stop the run of the awful potion which had already given expected results judging from the foul smell emanating from within the plastic incubator. His entire body was now covered with feces and other material. No wonder the rats were attracted. They would have to close the entrance of the cave as dogs could also be following the fragrance.

Dudley had changed the film and they left after having forced almost a liter of a sugar and saline water solution down Steven's throat. He could die of dehydration faster than of starvation. They were accompanied to the entrance of the tunnel by Steven's good wishes. He was now showing his true colors.

-I don't know if I'll be able to go all the way with this, - Said Johnny. -I think Dudley feels the same.-

-If you ever feel like ending his torment, go back and view the clip where he rapes this eight year old and you'll change your mind. I won't change mine, having lived a similar experience several times when I was about that age.- Snapped Deana looking at both of them with eyes a tiger might have backed away from. She continued.

-Remember that the name of this game is not to amuse ourselves or seek vengeance. If we can prevent only one child from similar abuses by animals like this Steven, his torture will have been worth it. I don't feel sorry for him. In a day or so he won't be conscious most of the time but these O'Reilly kids will dream about these two months in hell until they die. Chances are good that their lives will be fucked up. They'll suffer sixty, seventy years. Don't you guys be fucking wimps or I'll deal with you. –

-You're right- said Dudley, - but coming back here every day will be as bad for us as it will be for him. Could we send for pizza to be delivered?-

She looked at him and punched him in the gut knowing that it would hurt him as badly as a kiss on the forehead.

-Let's get going before this holy fire is snuffed out by our collective conscience. - Said Johnny leading the way out.

CHAPTER 24

"Right and wrong, vices and virtues often dance togehter"

-The fun part will now begin. Surprising these bastards in their universe will be a real pleasure. Can you image the surprise they'll have when they come to understand that the gig is up. No more impunity. - Deana had commented as they were leaving for their first house call. She had pit bull dedication.

The first on the list was a retired civil servant living in Lewiston. Deana and Dudley knew of Harry Gorsky, a good republican, Christian fundamentalist, known for his participation in community services and a passable tenor in the Sunday choir.

They could not believe that this pillar of the society and the sick and depraved human being they had seen on the screen were the same person. The clip was double checked, the picture enlarged and carefully examined before being reassured that it was really the same person performing these sadistic sexual acts on two of the O'Reilly children. His name and address had been confirmed by Steven. Recovering the clips featuring his performance would be crucial; otherwise the police would recognize and question the O'Reilly kids. In any event his and the identities of all the abusers in the O'Reilly tragedy would be shown either on the net or on Television.

On this day, Gorsky's wife was away visiting one of her sister and would not be back before early afternoon. Deana had checked at her place of work where she knew one of the employees.

Full disguise this time as they would be abducting a person they knew. Johnny being less likely to be identified would accompany Dudley. Dressed in blue overalls, they would casually ring the front door bell, Dudley would hit Harry on the chin, and they would walk in, gas the guy, search the place for the clip and leave with a roll of carpet in the middle of which Harry would be cocooned. A simple operation if nobody else was in the house; time of execution, less than fifteen minutes. Should they not be able to find the clip, the house would be torched.

Deana was driving and remained in the van while Dudley and Johnny walked up the steps. They had to ring the bell three times before Gorsky, a man of about sixty, middle height, mildly obese, balding with a crown of sores above his eye brows, opened the door. Surprised he started to close the door, not feeling right about what he saw.

Not quick enough, Dudley had time to insert his foot in the door and push it open, following with a short jab to the chin of the shorter man. Harry dropped for the count. They listened carefully for a full minute, not a sound in the house, Gorsky was alone. Johnny phoned Deana.

-OK to come in. - Then he continued looking at Dudley.

-It would be easier to question Harry about his little secrets; finding the clip may be a long process otherwise. – Suggested Johnny – Let's keep him awake until we've obtained some cooperation. First let's make absolutely certain we're dealing with the right bastard. I wouldn't want to make a mistake.-

-He's the right gentleman, but you're right. - Replied Dudley continuing to tape Harry's mouth, hands and feet.

Deana had parked the van as close to the front door as possible and came in. Not wasting any time she went quickly upstairs to double check that they were alone on the premises. She was able to enter every room except one.

-Second floor is safe except for one locked room. Dud darling, I'll need you for this.-

-He climbed the stairs and with his usual deftness, kicked the door opened. The room was Harry's private office, more a den than an office. On a large desk, a video was on and paused on a scene where he was the star performer with a different kid; a little girl of about ten judging from her budding breasts.

-Culpability won't be a question. - Said Deana. –Let's leave this clip on the video. We should not be long in finding the one we're looking for.-

They did indeed find it along with several others all lined up in a safe which he had left opened while answering the door. But why had he opened the door so stupidly, Deana wondered. And it dawned on her.

-He was expecting someone. Let's watch out for a visitor Johnny, he opened the door without taking any precaution because he was expecting someone. –

She's right, thought Johnny, we will have a visitor, that's why he tried to close the door when he realized that he had opened the door to strangers.

While Johnny was keeping an eye out, they revived Harry. It was important that they should recuperate all the video clips involving the O'Reilly family, copies could have been made that would be worth their weight in gold in this market. But more important, the law would identify the O'Reilly children and Johnny did not want this to happen.

Less than ten minutes had elapsed since they had crashed in and Gorsky was starting to stir. Dudley yanked the tape covering his mouth. Deana was standing over the little man.

-You know why we're here. – He knew but kept his mouth shut. She continued. -We don't have all day.... Two questions... First one: who are you expecting now? And, second question: where are the other copies of the O'Reilly video clips... I'll count until three before I start smashing your fingers with this hammer.-

She had found a two pound hammer on his desk and was holding it over Harry's hand which Dudley was keeping immobile on the desk top.

-You're cra...-

He didn't finish, his pinky having been reduced to a pulp, blood gushing around the cracked nail. Deana had not even waited for the complete negative answer. Dudley looked at her and thought he saw pleasure in her eyes.

After Harry had finished emitting a muffled scream, mostly choked by Dudley's large hand, Deana said, candidly smiling.

-Let's try again. - While she raised the bloodied hammer over the pinned index.

He looked at her, then at him, and knew he should come clean if he was to retain any fingers at all.

-You bitch..., two more copies in the drawer to the left. But you won't get away with this, I know who you are.- He then realized that he had made a mistake in admitting that he knew her; he clammed up.

She opened the drawer and found several copies of pedophilic video clips, meticulously arranged in alphabetical order. Under O'Reilly she found two clips. OK for that. She trotted down.

-Next question: who's coming to visit you this morning.?-

-No one, I'm expecting no one.-

She looked at Dudley and raised the hammer over the index.

-Think again and quickly as I'm taking aim. You'd make my day by not answering.-

He knew she would enjoy hitting him again. He quickly gargled.

-A friend, a business associate. He'll be here in a few minutes. -He said looking at the wall clock.

-What's his name and what kind of business are we talking about. Weren't you getting ready to show him some of your little treasures?-

Again she was preparing to smash his finger. He was not the most stoic person. Pain was something he enjoyed only when he was giving it.

-His name is David Smith, the owner of the Venus Motel. He's a photographer and wants to see what we've been taping.-

Dudley knew who he was. He had spent three years in jail for indecent exposure and pornographic films showing under age girls and boys. But better still he was the other person identified on the clips and was targeted to be picked up in the afternoon.

-Well, well, isn't that just great. We're looking for this gentleman and here he comes. – Said Dudley as he placed a fresh tape on Harry's mouth.

As a matter of fact he thought, why not put him to sleep now so that we can deal with the other gentleman without interference. And he opened the chloroform bottle. After a short struggle Gorsky was unconscious.

-Let's receive Smith with open arms.-

Johnny was amazed that the visitor was none other than the second Lewiston pedophile.

-Too much luck, - he said. -I don't like it-.

- Or maybe somebody up there likes what we're doing. It's a wonder that these barbaric actions are allowed at all by the great overall architect deciding all events on this earth. Bunch of crap. - Replied Deana.

They waited ten minutes before a dark green Pontiac came to a stop in front of the house. A tall, fortyish man came out carrying a black brief case. His vigorous stride implied that he was in better physical shape than Steven or Harry; former inmates are usually in good shape; nothing but weight lifting and physical training to pass the time.

He stopped and glanced at the mini van but thought nothing of it. Confirming his superior physical condition he came up the steps two by two and rang the door bell with a fury.

Deana had found an apron in the kitchen and looked the perfect little house wife when she opened the door.

-You're Mister Smith. Harry is expecting you upstairs in his office, he's on the phone but won't be a minute.-

He was surprised that a woman answered the door; Harry had told him that his wife was away for the day. But he could take care of himself against a mere woman; Deana closed the door behind him. Dudley immediately stepped out from the entrance closet and collared Smith around the neck with one hand while the other was pressing the barrel of his .45 on Smith's spine just above his belt.

-One move and you're a quadriplegic for life. Gently kneel and place your hands behind you.-

Not waiting for the execution of the order he had given, with his left foot, Dudley kicked viciously the back of the right knee at a forty five degree angle while pushing in the same direction. At the same time Deana had pivoted and was holding tightly on Smith's coat sleeves hindering arms movements. As soon as he was kneeling on the floor, Dudley motioned to Deana to come around and cuff his hands. As Deana released the hold she had on Smith's arms he made a move to grab the .45 and turn it away from him. Dudley was almost taken by surprise but not quite; bending his knees he crashed his left elbow on the top of Smith's head putting an end to the commotion.

Going through Smith's pocket she found the car keys, a little black book with addresses, a wallet and a Bull Dog snub nose .45, tucked in his belt. Good job she had grabbed his arms otherwise there could have been some blood spilled; of the kind Dudley was attached to.

He was looking on as Deana was completing the search and he frowned when he saw the nasty snub nose.

-You may have saved the day, this bastard was not about to let himself be caught without a fight and he could have easily shot me with this little cannon. – He was holding the mean little piece.

-Johnny can move the Pontiac down the road or leave it here. Leaving it here might be the best option but let's search it before we go. - And she continued. –We're done here, let's get on with our lives. Lots to do at the mine.-

Johnny had been looking on from the kitchen. He walked into the living room and moved chairs and sofa away from the carpet, which was just about large enough for Smith. Deana was chloroforming him and helped rolling the large limp body into the snug comfort of the expensive silk carpet.

-I'll back the van a little closer to the door, this guy is heavy.- Johnny was breathing hard and perspiring profusely; more because of the averted catastrophe than because of the physical effort.

-Wait-. And Deana followed him to search the Pontiac. Nothing much but another little black bag which she threw in the Van before going back to help Dudley move the two bodies.

They were soon on their way, both carpets in the back of the minivan. As far as they knew, no one had witnessed their raid. Gorski's house was an old and comfortable residence surrounded by a high cedar edge.

This time they approached the cave from rte 9 and 125; the only two possible routings to reach the cave. Nothing much they could do about it other than keep a low profile, change vehicles and wear a disguise.

The Van was driven far into the rear where the Honda four by four had been parked. As two trips had to be made Johnny remained in the van with Harry while Deana and Dudley move the bigger and more dangerous David Smith. They were soon back and found the difference in weight to be a great relief. –I'm not getting any younger-. Murmured Dudley.

Johnny followed on foot, still breathing hard but improving. When entering the tunnel he could smell the putrid odor emanating from the cave. Just breathing this nauseating mixture of decaying feces and urine was enough to cure any one from a wide range of diseases, including cancer and hopefully pedophilia.

-We'll need to leave a change of clothing here and do like the farmers coming home from the barn. This could be a dead give away. Face mask might help or we're likely to die before they do. Don't forget that your Mithridate was on the sea shore, the wind sweeping most of the stench away. - Johnny had difficulty to finish reciting his recommendations.

The two prisoners were still in their silk wrappings but slight movements could be detected. Steven had been in one of his short sleeping phase when they came in. Other than the buzzing of the camera, not a sound could be heard from the stage. He opened one eye when Johnny kicked his foot and immediately started yelling, thinking a rat was nibbling at his bare foot. Nothing he was saying made any sense; he was probably starting to loose it.

-We brought you company. The rats will have a better choice of menu. – Johnny was becoming a true sadist.

-They're awake so let's get moving, I don't think I'll be able to stay here long before being sick. – Complained Deana.

The first one to be processed was Harry. Stripped, he was inserted in one of this plastic sweat suit, tightly fitting around the neck, ankles and wrists. Dudley had purchased five of these. The excrements would accumulate nicely in this warm bio environment; the suit was slashed at one ankle and wrist to provide an access to the flies. Harry was tied like Steven, so that his hands or feet could not touch any part of his body. He remained gagged as the chorus made by the three of them could have been heard from outside the cave. Johnny's devious mind had come to the conclusion that leaving Steven free to speak would contribute further to exorcise the evil out of the other two.

Steven had some pretty awful tales to share. The three would be disposed head to head in a star like pattern. The camera had a clear view of the area and Dudley had figured that five of them would fit in the allotted space.

David Smith, convicted pedophile, was then stripped of his clothing and fitted into the larger sweat suit, before joining his companions on the stage. He was beginning to regain consciousness. Eyes rolling, trying to understand where he was, not able to emit a sound because of that damned duct tape and not able to move because of the cuffs, panic had replaced the anger. Used to dealing with organized and disciplined police forces, his rights had always been protected and up to now had been able to slip through the numerous legal loopholes. A good lawyer would always ask the right questions and confuse a witness to the point where the answers would come out blurred or counter productive. Isn't it what had saved his ass from a twenty year sentence the last time. His lawyer had so confused the mother and the kid that the jury had doubts about the real motives and the implied complicity of the mother.

Now was different, he realized that he was facing a group as immoral in their desire to punish and obtain justice as he was in pursuing his victims. He was in trouble and all his senses were alerted to find a way out.

From somewhere, a voice, amplified by the walls of the cave, brought him back totally to this new reality.

-You may be wondering where you are and what will happen to you. Let's not keep this secret any longer-. Johnny said. - David Smith, Harry Gorsky, you have been found to be incurable pedophiles and child molesters. You've been brought here to die. Not an ordinary death, not a bullet in the head, this would be too soft, but a slow and cruel death, a punishment justified by your crime. The ultimate purpose of this punishment is to dissuade some of your child molesting friends. We think that it could make them hesitate before abusing another child. You should feel some pride that your death will not be wasted if it saves other poor kids from pedophiles like you.-

Not wasting time, Deana had filled the gavage bags with her concoction. Without waiting for Johnny to finish his welcoming speech, she proceeded to force feed her three patients. A small hole was perforated in the gags of David and Harry so that the gavage tube could be inserted deep into the esophagus.

-Not the taste you're used to but if you have a bit of masochism in you this treatment may prove to be pleasing. In India, Yogi would beg for such an opportunity to clean up the slate and attain Nirvana. - Johnny informed them. - Steven will bring you up to date.-

They left after having reloaded the video, taking the full clip with them. Still, the question about the best mode to exhibit these images was not answered; the net would not be used, this much was decided, too risky.

They were half way through the tunnel when Johnny stopped and looked back.

-What if they were to get loose, I don't see how... but one never knows.-

-You're right, one of us should stay here for the duration of this contract. - Joked Deana.

As there were no volunteer the question lingered on. They had stopped and were thinking about this very remote possibility that one would get loose.

-I'll go back and inspect the arrangements once more-. Said Dudley emitting a heavy sigh.

And he doubled back to the cave. Upon inspection he could not see how any one could break away from these handcuffs. Hands and ankles were cuffed and no movement possible. Houdini couldn't break loose. He came back.

-Impossible to break loose ... unless they amputate their hands.... but I agree that impossible is an impossible word. Some risks I am willing to take and this is one. –

Nevertheless something would have to be done, not later than tomorrow. After evaluating several alternatives, it was decided that some sort of device would obliterate the cave as soon as the last of its dwellers would have passed away. What else could be done?

-Good idea, let's think a little more about this. Is there a way to trigger this explosion from a distance? – Johnny wondered.

What they were doing was morally and legally wrong, but nevertheless, they felt good about their action; pride was a better choice of word. Right and wrong, vices and virtues always dance together and often, to do well one has to bend a few laws and sometimes a few virtues. Capital punishment is a good example of right and wrong being associated to do ... good, if someone does not consider the somewhat high number of innocents being executed.

Society could have dealt with these people, but in following the legal prescription, the four O'Reilly children and their mother, as well as several other kids seen on the clips, would have been traumatized as much by the system as they had been by the abusers. Not forgetting the stigma of having been assaulted sexually: "she was raped would murmur in confidence these "holier than thou" with a non equivocal air of suspicion. "

Since fifty thousand years, no longer an animal and yet not quite civilized, man has often been perplexed about vice and virtue right and wrong. Soul and conscience are new adaptive attributes; some might say –values-. Somewhere during that period, our ancestors recognized that basic instincts were detrimental to their survival and that work had to be the counter part of pleasure. At the present stage of his evolution, man is still trying to cope with these same basic instincts: - Eros and Thanatos its counterpart-, proving Freud was mostly right. Civilization has turned out to be repressive and very much against our primal values.

For man's ancestors, there was no such thing as pedophilia, crime, right or wrong. The survivors were the ones with more testosterone, the most aggressive, the most efficient killers, robbers, cheaters and copulators. Later these primitive attributes, qualities then, were restrained. Today, these as well as most other pleasures are social and religious taboos serving the higher purpose of working in an organized society at the service of a few. Man likes and needs to be dominated....and accept the sublimation of his instincts. Evolution is marching on: reciprocity or interdependence the ultimate motor. The answer could be simpler: one day man recognized that violence was reversible. Since then the main social current has been to reduce this violence that keeps coming back.

Other than in the realm of technology and science, nothing much has changed over these years during which man has developed tools, arms, domesticated other animals and plants. Within the homo genus, a small minority is still allowed the birth right to be tyrannical and magnanimous, while keeping the multitude of their blood brothers enslaved. Science and technology have provided better means to survive and could one day make work obsolete, reversing the values by which man has lived; if it becomes the advantage of - organized domination -. Also science and technology have discovered better means to kill more efficiently, from a distance and thousands at a time. Genocides and extermination of entire species have become a specialty; is this return to barbarism or simply a non- repressive reality? Today, it is estimated that we are eradicating seventeen species every hour and that by the year two thousand and fifty, more than half of the thirty million species presently inhabiting the earth, will be extinct. But others will have filled some of the void.

Evolution is still very much in progress and will never stop. Although far from having achieved a civilized level; at least the objectives have been identified and could be within reach in a few thousand years, if we curb the population growth and put an end to the self destruction policy implemented forty thousand years ago by our Cro Magnon ancestors.

If evolution has produced geniuses like Einstein, Mozart, Michelangelo and so many more, it has also created monsters like Hitler, Stalin, Steven and... so many more. A step at a time is the proper way to win a race. Barcelo thought that their crusade would not solve the problem of child abuse but advance the cause a few inches.... And more than anything else grant him an honorable finale. He would never know the ratio of his compassion versus his narcissism. Does unadulterated altruism exists?

CHAPTER 25

"Prudence is fear on tip toes."

It was agreed that the establishment of a fully secure web site would be more difficult than Deana had initially presumed. Nothing fail safe, there was always the off chance that they would be discovered by some whiz kid in the justice department. Barcelo did not care as he had a stronger suicidal penchant at this time of his life; as always but more pronounced.

-I won't live another two years; this is my last and only worthwhile project. I don't mind dying for it; frankly I'd enjoy it. Better than a slow useless and futile departure in a hospital bed, punctured, intubated, massaged, resuscitated, defibrillated and generally put to death by torture in the name of medicine. –

-You've made your position clear and we have known this since the beginning of this affair, but being caught before the full completion of this job –Dudley called this a job- would not be of much value. We're trying to create a movement, start a trend, modify the popular thinking about pedophilia. Alerting the media will force sterner legislation. For the moment, the sentences are far from being a reflection of the harm done: three to four years in protective custody. These sentences are not served within the prison population as the abusers would be killed by the other inmates. Worse, in several countries, there is a history of police complicity to shield and protect the abusers. - Deana had continued to be the most dedicated.

-Well then, let's find a way to diffuse these clips and maybe make some money out of it so we can help the victims. Maybe a foundation which would be managed by a Television station. We give them exclusive rights and they set up a foundation to help the victims. – Johnny suggested.

-Good thinking, I like it. Edited copies of the clips would protect our identities. – Dudley agreed.

-The only danger would be that the Television Company would cheat and not create the foundation. I suppose that a prominent politician could negotiate the deal and be made the president of the board of this foundation, although I don't know who would be willing to be associated with such an unusual and not so legal project. - Put in Deana.

-The Television station would jump at this like bullfrogs on a tasty worm ... They would kill for an exclusive scoop like this. What can we demand of these people? That's an area we don't know anything about but, maybe… a fixed initial amount per clip with an increase indexed on the growth of the rating. I'll bet it would propel the rating to the ceiling. People would like this sort of crusade, even the rawness of the images would appeal to the viewers in general. – Said Johnny thinking aloud.

-People hate pedophiles, maybe because most of us have been pawed by these lecherous bastards at some point in our lives. The worse fear of a parent is to have his child abducted by some pervert. We all remember some of these horrible stories…. I was reading the other day that a South African man sodomised and killed twenty four pre- teen boys before he was apprehended. Unfortunately no one country has the exclusivity, the same atrocities are reported everywhere including our own country.-

Johnny was thinking again which was a good sign; he continued.

-This could work if we can find some credible person to represent us and negotiate the contract. These guys won't last more than fifteen days at the most, none will have Mithridate's staying power. True that there is a large pool of potential replacements; but let's capitalize on these.-

-I've been thinking about this all night and I know just the person. - Continued Johnny – I'll bet what's left of my failing health, that he'd enjoy this job as much as I do. He may even become the co-president of the board of directors of this foundation.-

-Are you thinking of Father Tim.?- Asked Dudley who had kept quiet, turning these ideas over slowly in his mind.

-You guessed it. He's looking for something to boost his self esteem. He has the impression that his life has been spent in the vain pursuit of a myth. Let's give him something tangible to grab and run with. –

-You realize that he would be holding our freedom in his hands. He'll be submitted to an intense and tough investigation. Will he hold together? Do you trust him enough for that? - Asked Deana.

-Only Tim can answer these questions. Let's have a meeting with the man. - Concluded Johnny.

Later on that day Deana followed the van with her own vehicle. It was time to ditch it. Johnny entered a side road and drove it into a ditch where it would be invisible from the road. A second and last inspection of the vehicle before he left a lighted cigar soaked with lighter fluid on the front seat: Increased temperature to the flash point, fire and destruction of the van.

-We have several minutes before it fires, don't go so fast. - Said Johnny.

CHAPTER 26

"Life has a meaning only if a worthwhile purpose is driving it."

Father Tim Donnelly was a good person but a mediocre priest. He had lost sight of the initial purpose assigned to priesthood. While attempting to find justification for his faith, he had strayed away from the initial motivation. The quick sand of uncertainty and doubt, exacerbated by the pursuit of knowledge, choked his faith.

He was old enough to have witnessed the pseudo remodeling his church had gone through in an effort to retain its former luster. Rituals like confession, communion, fish Fridays, interfaith-marriage, had been down played and softened but, never enough surgery to get rid of the ineptitude or, always too late. Fertility, abortion, birth control and more than anything else the unremitting discrimination against women in the church, were deep-seated points of contention for Tim.

While a legendary marketing success during the last two thousand years, the present public relation departments of most churches were incompetent or unable to make their voices heard by the fundamentalist and lethargic chief executives empirically assuming that people's behaviors did not evolve from one century to another. Always a century behind reality, as Tim would comment privately. In fact most religions were covertly following the Taoist philosophy where technological and intellectual advancements were discouraged. He had come to realize that religions were doomed, having committed the mortal marketing sin of not giving the customer what he wanted. Survival of all religions is directly related to socio – economic divergence: very much in control in third world countries, because of the catalytic action of - poverty and ignorance-; but loosing ground in affluent countries because of -affluence and knowledge-, the worse enemies of all churches.

Science and technology were attacking the credibility of dogmas and replacing them; scientists were becoming the new age priests. Religion without the supernatural is like wine without alcohol. Not much chance that this debacle would be contained any time soon as most popes had been , as was the present one, dinosaurs still living ten thousand years ago; - their saintly heads in their sanctimonious anal canals- , as Tim was telling his more liberated friends after a few libations too many.

Not much of a surprise that Tim was by-passed for promotions. His very inappropriate and improper frame of mind scared his bosses; could have been his Irish rebellious genes. Some of his colleagues, playing this political game with more -finesse- were on their way to greatness, one of them even envisaged as a future Cardinal, maybe a Pope. Tim was not sour, maybe relieved to have been left out of this race; still able to regret and, maybe correct his dumb decision of almost forty years ago.

As it was, Tim's life would continue to be a long succession of drab solitary moments. Religion, his business, under pretext of love but using scare tactics, had pretended that it could make the earth a better place. It certainly had failed. Tim could now see that the true objective of all religions throughout history had been political, serving ambition and propagating rather than alleviating injustice.

Only this dreadful desperation, coming out of the recent realization that he had screwed up his life, would greet every one of his future mornings and accompany him in restless slumber at night.

Scotch was a crutch, a savior that allowed him to forget about the career, the wife, the kids he could have had if, his intellectual qualities had been applied to the task of serving a worthy purpose, rather than to the service of a mythical figure, manipulated by a few to control the vast multitude. Scotch and books; the satisfaction of learning was fulfilling and allowed a compromise, an arrangement in the acceptance of his life as a useless drone preaching a salvation he didn't believe in and could no longer reason.

He had contained his libido except for a few instances when he had been literally raped by some kinky female parishioners aroused by the forbidden. Never had he been tempted to indulge in young boys or girls as was the case for far too many of his colleagues.

For the unprepared, erudition sparks awareness; the more you know, the more you realize the absurdity of inbred dogmas. Further increasing the depth of his disarray, knowledge was re-mapping Tim's brain and blotting out these unnecessary beliefs. Needing to justify and compare, he would surmise that his life had not been different than that of a farmer, plumber or doctor, realizing too late that he would have preferred living as a different entity. In the end, it is not uncommon that most cannot say that they have been happy with the way things turned out. Can one say honestly that he is contented with this life? As Freud said, - Happiness is no cultural value- . And it is debatable that Shakespeare was right when he proposed that: "Happiness is a thing that can be handed out by a person not having any of it."

At this late hour Tim was unhappy in his chosen vocation; would he be able to do something about this hard fact. He knew that the crux of the question lied in being in the right place at the right time: -if Cromwell was born again he, who had his king, decapitated and took his place, would not be but a simple merchant in London. - « Naître à propos. » The Right person, at right place, at right time and the guts to seize the chance by the hair.

Was there still time to change course, make a move? Only idiots and fanatics would stick to decisions they knew to be wrong. Only fanatics would support their rationality with untruths. Timothy had been a pragmatist with most of life's issues except what had been genetically imprinted in his genes like his fondness for good scotch whisky, and the Irish renowned penchant for rebellion and the supernatural. He had retained his natural fondness for good liquor and elegant living while the de-programmation of his Christianity had been in progress for several years and was now on a crash course. The result of his enlightenment was lurking ahead in ambush. He was petrified at the idea that he could dare rebel.

The damned phone had been ringing with the doggedness of an abscessed tooth. Coming out of his reverie, he was about to yield and answer when the answering machine took the relay. After his little speech telling whoever to leave a message and a number, he heard Barcelo's croaky voice.

-Pick up-, Said the voice, -I know you're there, probably sipping out of this gourd.-

Here we go again. He picked up.

-You caught me sinning. What can I do for you? On second thought, don't tell me anything. Where are you, I'll be over. I need some answers from you, the shit is starting to hit the proverbial fan.-

-I'll pick you up in ten minutes. I know it's late but it's important and should be of great interest to you. –

Was fate answering Tim's cry for a little animation, a little spice or the needed kick in the ass. ?

-I'll be waiting outside in ten minutes. - Tim hung up.

Ten minutes later Johnny's imposing old caddy was coming to a wonky halt in front of the presbytery. A shadow moved from the cover of one of the two patriarch maple trees guarding the church. Johnny and Tim shook hands without a word, each having the intuitive knowledge that this meeting would be the beginning of a significant undertaking. In tune with this new reality, sensing the importance of the moment, the old Cadillac began to regally roll at a slow pace towards Auburn.

-I'd like you to meet some friends of mine. We have a proposal to bounce off you. As you may have guessed it could have something to do with the disappearance of this Steven and of two others you don't yet know about: Harry Gorsky and David Smith. They were both involved with the O'Reilly family. - Johnny had the bad habit to look at whoever was sitting to his right while driving. Not for the faint of heart thought Tim who was pushing on a virtual brake.

-A coincidence surely... Maureen O'Reilly phoned me today and said that some Angel had mentioned my name, even... recommended me. I never figured you out for one of those winged assistants of god, but I deduced that you were the sword-carrying variety she was referring to. I'll see her tomorrow. - A pause. -Who are these friends of yours Johnny, are they the people you were looking for a few days ago? .... And who might have participated in the abduction of the step father? - He paused before going on.

-Don't answer just yet. It would be preferable that I understand the entire package before knowing some of the details. In a confused and compli-cated situation, too much knowledge is bad. I may choose to bail out and not go along with your proposal. - Pause again.

-Should I be questioned, which I certainly will be, let's remember that if lying is a fine art, even a science at which men of the cloth are masters, ignorance is still the best assurance that a secret will be kept.- – And please keep your eyes on the road, don't look at me.-

Johnny nodded and never said another word until they were in front of Dudley's house.

The door opened before they rang. Bare feet, in a low neck, one piece electric blue jumpsuit tied at the waist with a gold chain, Deana appeared in all her splendor and surprised even John. The incarnation of Satan thought Tim shaking her warm dry hand.

-Welcome to our home Father Tim, as Johnny calls you. - The deep throated voice was as sulfurous as in his wildest dream.

Her smile was a marvel of feminity and Johnny knew that she was doing it on purpose, openly flirting with a priest to test her charm against his faith.

-Here is a sight that will improve the quality of your dreams. – Joked Johnny.

Closer to reality than he thought and not that much of a joke as it turned out.

She flashed a still wider smile showing perfect teeth.

-Caught at my little game. Johnny is an old bird dog and nothing can be hidden from old bird dogs. Let's join my husband in the library. We've been editing some of the family clips. Tedious job but necessary.-

She preceded the two men knowing that her undulating back side was being stripped naked by a man of the cloth who would have to confess a sin by intent before saying mass tomorrow morning. How arousing.

Upon their entrance in the study, Dudley shut off the video. However not fast enough. Johnny had seen that he was editing the video clip depicting Smith with one of the O'Reilly kids. Part of a presentation for the television people; the kid's faces will be blurred out. The harsh treatment inflicted on the molesters had to be justified by loathsome and abominable acts of per-version. There were plenty of these to choose from.

Dudley stood from his seat to greet Tim, warmly shaking his hand as though he had met a long lost brother. Tim was impressed by the pervasive power and strength emanating from Dudley. He felt tiny in front of this man almost ten years his senior but still in top shape.

-I've heard so much about you father Tim that I feel I've known you forever. - Always the straight shooter, Dudley went to the heart of the subject. - By now you must have guessed that we're involved in making Lewiston a better and safer place for kids. But let's not get into the business portion of this meeting right now. –

Dudley paused and releasing Tim's hand, walked over to the far wall of the room which was taken up entirely by rows upon rows of different shaped and colored bottles artistically displayed on thick glass shelves. The exhibit was lit from the ceiling and behind, giving it a heavenly aura.

-Johnny told us that you were a connoisseur of fine scotch, I would be proud to show you my collection of some of the finest scotch ever distilled in Scotland. - Dudley said proudly side stepping behind the bar.

-Pure poesy, I've never seen so many bottles of good Scotch anywhere. Magnificent. - Said Tim who was looking at the display like a kid in a Toys R Us store.

Like soldiers, standing at attention while being passed in review, were several bottles of the finest products out of Scotland. Tim was reverently reciting the names: Macalan 12, 18 and 25 years, Knockdhu, 12 years, Dalmore 12 years, Tamdhu 10 years, Taliker 10 years, Islay mist 17years, Lagavulin 16 years, not even mentioning the Glen Morey, Glenmoragie, Glengoyle, Bunnahabian and others Tim had never heard of and could not pronounce properly.

Having completed his survey, Tim opted for a Macalan 12 year old Single Highland Malt. One of the best produced by the Scots; but then there are so many. While he was pouring the golden nectar, Dudley thought that he would show off some of his erudition.

From the corner of his eye he could see Deana looking up at the ceiling. She had heard this lecture several times and dreaded being in for yet another session. She hated Scotch. - Tastes like medicine. - She'd assert to spite Dudley-. While, as she dreaded, he was starting this lecture.

-We drink Scotch, wine or cognac but don't understand the cultures these products stem from. - Was Tim's answer and the cue for Dudley to get going.

-You must know that one of the very few favorable tidings missionaries brought to Scotland and Ireland was called Aqua Vitae. The name changed from Aqua Vitae to Uisge-Beatha then Usque Baugh and via other appellations like Ooska, Ooski and Usky became finally Whisky.

- All scotch to me. – Cut in Deana. - While Dudley paused to give Tim a very generous sample.

After adding just enough water, Tim carefully took a sip, thinking that religion had some good traits and would forever be known for its contribution to the world of fine booze. If he could substitute this elixir for the bad wine he was using for this rigmarole called mass, he might say two of them daily.

The subtle taste would linger on for a while creating another level of desire that he would have to satisfy; one more level, always more, never satiety. He sat down on one of the comfortable leather chair, complete relaxation taking over his body. Good Scotch, good wine and food always acted on his serotonin level and made him happy and serene.

Tim took another sip, the pleasure being already diluted by the insatiable search for improvement from which humans suffer; never fully satisfied always looking for betterment.

-I would very much like to hear the long and unadulterated version of your essay on Scotch. Let's do that at our leisure once we have discussed the real purpose of my being here. As Johnny would say let's get down to business. Curiosity is my strong suite. - Said Tim as Deana let out a low sigh of approbation.

-OK, we can relax and sample more of this good Scotch after we're done talking business. Let's start with some introduction. - Not used to long speeches he swallowed a few times before continuing.

-Johnny is responsible for having turned our lives around several years ago. He was more or less our guardian angel and helped both Deana and myself to get out of the rat hole we were born and programmed to die into. A few days ago, when he told us about the O'Reilly... - He searched for the proper appellation. - Job, we felt that we owed him and accepted to help.- He looked at his wife.

- Once we learned more about this situation, we knew it was something we would have done without our debt to Johnny. Deana was an abused kid and in a sense so was I. - Deana walked over to Dudley's seat and sat on the arm of the chair, exposing a perfect thigh for Tim to look at. – Johnny will continue.-

Without moving an inch, Johnny seemed to have grown. The little man was compensating his small size by a presence that would have been better used in a political career or out of a pulpit. He had been practicing his gift over several years and was good at it. First rule, establish a visual contact with the people you are addressing: he carefully riveted the attention of every one by looking into their "souls" as he was saying.

-We have an important decision to make, one that could involve you Tim.... as you've guessed.... Let's go back a week when you came to me and described a horrible situation involving an entire family enslaved by a sadistic pedophile, one that would not hesitate to kill or torture four kids. As far as you could guess, and we can now confirm that you were right, he was already selling them to other pedophiles.-

Johnny paused to cough and sipped some of the aqua vitae Dud had poured in his crystal goblet.

-You hesitated going to the police as this maniac seemed to have complete control over these kids: strangling the family cat, torturing and killing a rabbit and humiliating these children as only experienced psychopaths like him can. You were also afraid that if cornered he might cause an accidental fire and get rid of the evidence. – Another pause, another sip.

-I agreed with you and, thinking of my own five year old and, not having anything better to do until my blip disappears from the screen, I decided to get involved. Unfortunately I am now old and sick, and needed the help of some strong and trusted friends. Dudley and Deana have been associated with me during the better moments of my life. They agreed to look into this situation with me and here they are; involved up to their eye balls.-

A scratching noise in the adjacent room caused Johnny to stop and listen. Deana glanced at her watch, smiled, got up and opened the door to allow a large German shepherd to walk into the study as if he owned it.

-He usually comes in here at this time of night. He's harmless enough if we're here. Meet Mujik my jogging companion and the guardian of our modest home.-

Mujik wagged its tail and touched its nose to Deana's and Dudley's legs. He then zeroed in on Johnny, discarded him rapidly as a non entity, carefully assessed Tim, went back to Johnny and, after memorizing their odors, crashed his one hundred and twenty five pound mass of muscle on the carpeted floor, at the feet of his mistress. What a picture; Deana, in electric blue, and he, mostly black with a few ochre patches.

-As you know, - Johnny continued after a moment, - the O'Reilly family has regained its freedom. The police will not be interrogating and further traumatizing these kids, as the mother has decided to not lay charges against Steven.... What you don't know, but have guessed, is that we have possession of the pervert. He's now being submitted to what I've already described to you as "Mithridatisation". You'll remember the quarrel Mithridate the soldier had with his king and how he paid for his lack of judgment? -

Johnny paused a little as Tim had made a face at the sound of Mithridate, remembering the vivid description rendered by Plutarque and related by Johnny. He took a large sip and Johnny continued:

-There's more, I have to confess, and I stretch the word confession. Two of the five pedophiles you saw entering the house and abusing these kids are now in our power, being Mithridated with Steven. Their names are known to you and even though you will be as surprised as we were at one of them, we have absolute proof that they were involved, here, elsewhere and often.-

-You're wondering where this is leading. Frankly Tim, so am I. Planning a mission like this, is one thing, making it happen is a totally different ball game. I personally don't care what happens to me as you have probably figured out but, I fear the involvement of my friends could cause them to loose their freedom. Let it be known here that I would cover every one to the limit, and that we'll continue to be careful to the point of being paranoid. - And he added smiling. -Which I am naturally.-

-We're old enough to know what we're getting into and don't intend to be caught. - Snapped Deana. Her tone of voice alerted the dog who looked at her, then at Johnny as if he had been rude to his mistress. He yawned, baring enormous canines and went back to sleep.

-Don't be angry with me Deana..... Here is the plan- continued Johnny, - these three animals have been and will continue to be filmed throughout the entire .... - Looking for his word, he paused and played with the crystal goblet, - ... expiatory procedure, I suppose is the right word. Each day the previous day's film will be exchanged for a fresh one. The film will be edited into a fifteen minute clip, which will be given to a television station in exchange for the creation of a Foundation for the prevention of abuse to children. We feel that this will serve two purposes. One is that it will scare the shit out of would-be pedophiles and maybe save the lives of many children. Secondly, it will provide money for the foundation which will continue to perform its task long after this campaign is over and forgotten. - He stopped, tired.

-How do I fit? Do you want me to confess these bastards and open the gates of heaven to their soul? If there is a hell, it would be too mild for them. Unfortunately you may be providing the only punishment they'll get. – Interjected Tim.

-You fit in very naturally; we need you as a negotiator with the TV station, and as a co- director of the Foundation. The clips would be transmitted without your involvement. As far as we can see you would not and could not be accused of anything. Confirm this with one of your lawyer friends.-

Tim remained pensive for a moment, seeking advice from his crystal goblet.

-Are you sure that you're able to carry this project all the way?. Very special and unusual talents are required for this job and I don't know your friends other than as good law fearing citizens, even though great connoisseurs of Scotch. - Pointed out Tim as he was ostensibly taking a quick inventory of the very upper class bourgeois interior decoration.

Deana looked at Dudley who nodded and took the pole position.

-We're able to do whatever needs to be done-. Said Dudley. - Deana told you that we had been involved with Johnny from the beginning. At one point we had to help Johnny protect his interest against a New York Mafia family. Without going into detail, we had to take out four persons. We're qualified. - He smiled before continuing. –And we're off to a good start as you'll see.-Then he kept on. -Furthermore, Deana and I are action people and excitement has been scarce lately.... I guess we were becoming domesticated.-

Tim was thinking that he too had been domesticated for the last forty years. Like chance, opportunity is a fleeting shadow which has to be grabbed by its hair and subdued as soon as it comes within your reach. Would he grab it this time and could this lead to a reshuffling of the deck for him.

Maybe today was his special day, his meeting with the great organizer: Chance, fortune, luck, fate, whatever the name given, the master of our destiny. He drained the last drop of the excellent Macalan, looking at the empty glass as one would look at the corpse of a good friend or the last specimen of rare species.

Deana had been staring at Tim, trying to penetrate the intimacy of his mind. This man could screw them out of their liberty if he failed to keep his cool. He would be in the middle of very heavy traffic. Of his ability to dodge and evade the traps laid during the interrogations and scrutiny he would be subjected to, depended their freedom and the success of this venture. She thought he could have the right profile, but one never knows until the game is over. Whatever, the dices were rolling. She selected the 18 year old version of the same Macalan and refilled the empty glass.

Tim had played around the periphery of taking matters in his own hands so many times that he didn't have to spend hours weighing the pros and cons of this situation. Father Timothy Donnelly had made up his mind and yes, he would shake himself out of this bovine contentment, escape from this cocoon which had become a prison and either succeed or fail at something. As he had already failed, he could only improve his situation. Yes. And then louder than necessary as if he had reached some point of no return like when he had stopped smoking.

-Yes I'll do it... Who do I negotiate with? When, I suppose, is right now and how, is up to me? What am I selling and how am I supposed to have access to this material? I have so many questions that I think we need to sit down at a table and start taking notes.-

There was a general sigh of relief from the three who had been following closely, the interior battle Tim had been fighting. Damn hard to make a decision loaded with such a potential for trouble; hard for anyone, let alone for someone accustomed to follow a straight and narrow path.

The dog leading the way, they changed room and all sat around a thick oak dining table which would not have been out of context in a middle age castle. A very becoming setting as this project was in a class similar to those chevaleresque endeavors King Arthur, Sir Lancelot, Galahad and Queen Guinevere had been undertaking. The fire spitting dragons were no more dangerous than the establishment they were about to challenge. After a little more than an hour, a time table and a description of the tasks to be accomplished had been drawn up. Tim's notes read as follows:

Day 1: After consultation with lawyer, TD meets with the president of the Television news station BCD.

He shows the clip depicting the crimes committed and the sentence being carried out.

The cost to the station is a fixed amount of one hundred thousand dollars per clips and a quarter million dollars for each point increase in the rating, the base being an average of the last thirty days.

All monies to be deposited in a trust account pending the creation of a Foundation for abused kids, to be chaired by both TD and the president of the television company.

Subsequent clips will be delivered to the president on a daily basis.

If the parties agree, the first clip would be left with the President and shown on the evening news.

Day 1 and 2: Rigging the cave with explosives; feeding the inmates and collecting the other three O'Reilly abusers; this will take more than one day.

Final day: Destruction of the cave and of all traces of its occupants and visitors.

The details would have to be improvised as the action developed, but simplicity was always the key word. A letter of intent between the president and Tim could be signed immediately and the Foundation organized simultaneously with the delivery of the first clip.

The police would be trying to identify the perpetrators and Tim would be followed, questioned, his telephone line tapped.

-You realize they'll be after you like fleas on a dog. Are you prepared for that kind of continuous badgering? - Said Deana, still trying to make up her mind on the toughness of this priest.

-As I once admitted to Johnny, playing with facts is a game priests are good at. Dealing with the police will be the least of my concern. My biggest problem is the torture these bastards are enduring. This Mithridatisation is the worse kind of suffering I could imagine. Dante did not describe hell as being much worse. – Answered Tim, still flinching under Deana's gaze.

-There is something worse : Going to bed at night knowing that you'll be awaken in a few hours by a gin smelling, lecherous stepfather, or coming home from school to be stripped naked and raped repeatedly, knowing that you'll be going through the same routine the day after and... after. That's worse because there is no end in sight..... These perverts will die, unfortunately too soon, I wish I could do something about this. - Murmured Deana looking fixedly at a point on the wall.

Nobody said a word during one of the longest minute in Tim's life. Dudley walked over and gently touched his wife's shoulder. She shuddered and looked up at him, a tear finding its way on her cheeks.

-I'll be fine. Thanks darling. - She said as she turned her head and kissed his hand.

Tim could understand where these animals were faring better than their victims. He could not tackle Deana's need for vengeance and he would never again question the severity of the treatment. It was not his decision to make and Hell as described in the Bible was a little worse; on paper that is. Johnny broke the awkward silence that followed.

-Tonight is the last time we're meeting. Should there be a need to consult, I'll fake some ailments and be hospitalized. I can easily take more insulin which would trigger a diabetic coma. As you visit the hospital every day, you can check new admission...- Said Johnny following Tim's gaze in the direction of Deana, still reeling from her outburst.

That was it, the dices were rolling, and the locomotive had stirred the mile-long convoy, much heavier than its own weight. The huge steel wheels had budged imperceptibly on the rails. Inertia had lost to determination and there would be no stopping this force, which in the next few days would attain terrific momentum.

-Now, that we've taken care of this business, I'll have one for the road while you continue your lecture. - said Tim.

-Language I understand. - Said Dudley smiling and relieved. –We could continue with the Single Highland Malt Macalan and taste a bit of the twenty five years old. On the other hand why not open this bottle of Glenmorangie eighteen years old, a Single Malt I've been keeping for such an occasion. –

Taking one of the crystal goblets waiting for just that moment on the shelf, he carefully placed the glass on a tray while he opened this rare bottle. After sniffing the content he poured a generous measure.

-Taste it straight first, and then add a little water. – Suggested Dudley.

Tim did and agreed that this choice was the right one. During the next thirty minutes Dudley gave his very interesting lecture on Scotch. Deana sneaked out the garden door with Mujik the dog.

"Being Irish, Tim should have known that the paternity for the invention of Scotch was equally claimed by his country men. As it turned out the old saying that: "something good always comes out of something bad " had a role to play in the elaboration and the improvement of this famous liquor. The church and the state contributed to this task: the church by initiating the process and the State by compelling the distillers to go underground in several locations.

The tax men, because of their insatiable appetite for new products to impose a tax on, forced the Scots to go underground and to manufacture their national liquor in several areas, where local water, peat, oat or barley would be used. As good Scotch depends upon the quality of these ingredients, these circumstances contributed to create a very efficient research and development condition. In the end, as for the chaotic organization of the universe, a subtle variety of tastes, aromas, colors were developed. Natural evolution in the purest Darwinian tradition.

However before the refinement, the product evolved in the monasteries where the monks produced an alcohol called Aqua Vitae, precursor of the Scotch or Irish whisky. It was not long before the peasants learned to side track a portion of the oat and barley used for their bread to make whisky. Life was rough for the peasant and making alcohol served two purposes, his own enjoyment and increased revenues.

Of course enjoyment of any sort cannot be so blissful as to avoid taxation and very early, the cash strapped state recognizes the opportunity. As early as 1506, the Edinburg law limits the sale of Whisky to barbers who were the doctors and surgeons of the time. But as always, man found a way around laws and constraints. As Tao tê Ching said way before our era:

Man's technological achievements are a snare.

The more sharp weapons there are,

The more benighted will the world grow.

The more cunning craftsmen there are,

The more pernicious contrivances will be invented.

The more laws are promulgated,

The more thieves and bandits there will be.

More or less coerced to go underground by the arbitrary demands of the state, during the next two centuries, many distilleries sprang up all over Scotland. Whisky soon became the national drink of Scotland and Ireland. But as there was no organization as such, total chaos prevailed: the alcohol was often not aged sufficiently, the peasants drinking it often as it comes out of the distillers.

The Church or the Parliament is incapable of putting an end to this national trend. Chroniclers and reporters of this period were celebrating the qualities of this divine potion which, as one said, will be a cure to whatever you have and even prolong your life. In 1578 the writer Holinshed, wrote about Whisky:

« Taken with moderation Whisky slows aging and enhances youth, helps digestion, cures runny nose, chases away melancholia, lightens the heart, hardens the will, regenerates vigor, cures edema, dizziness, eye problems, zezayement, lipsing, and so many other ailments that it is god given when taken regularly. »

So, rather than continuing to butt heads with destiny, Charles the first created a fiscal tax and imposed a monopoly on production. Unfortunately this enlighten king is executed seven years later by Cromwell.

As always, the imposition of taxes promulgates the appearance of cheats and smugglers as surely as carrion will create maggots. A multitude of clandestine distilleries make their entries on the scene. As Robert Burns said: « Liberty and Whisky go hand in hand. ».

With the suppression of the Edinburg Parliament the industry goes almost completely underground. Only eight legitimate distilleries are declared at the end of the century but there were more than four hundred turning out thousand of liters of illegal Whisky daily.

Delation, -ratting-, is then used as a deterrent and rewards are offered by the state to the delators. The already resourceful and cunning Scots are quick in seeing an advantage in this amoral approach: they would denounce old and useless equipment, receive the reward which would finance the purchase of a brand new still.

The high point in this saga is when George the sixth visited Edinburg in 1822 and asked for a glass of Glenlivet which was illegally distilled.

Fine tuning was necessary and some order replaced the early chaos; several improvements in the fine art of distilling were implemented and minimum aging of three years becomes a law in the 1900 « Immature spirit act. ». In 1924 the marketing of Whisky is organized and the rest of the world learns about this elixir. The wars of 1914 and 1939 force an interruption in the production of Whisky but as soon as the cannons become quiet the distilleries begin turning Whisky. "

-There is so much more to tell. Later when this is done...we can sit and go deeper in the matter. We could explore the different tastes and aromas. This will require more time than we have tonight. – Said Dudley. Deana had come back at the end and was trying to hide a yawn.

Johnny was tired and Deana offered to drive Tim back to the presbytery. Johnny would stay with his friends a few more days. The project had done marvels and been a better cure than any of the new drugs; but the little man was tired and his body in dire need of various spare parts.

For a while longer Dudley and Barcelo continued planning the next days. Very busy days they would be: travel to Boston and New Jersey to collect the other three players, feeding the cave dwelling inmates and finally booby trapping the cave, something none of them was familiar with.

-More than a hundred years ago, this guy Marconi has been able to activate a relay from Saint John New Foundland to England. I'd feel stupid if we couldn't detonate a bomb from a distance. - Said Johnny.

Tired but exalted they went to bed around midnight.

—— CHAPTER 27 ——

"Civilization has never been an accomplished fact but only an aspiration that has always fallen short of its ambitious target."
A. Toynbee

Over the phone, the executive secretary had a voice like a file skittering down a rusty pipe. She obviously was a heavy smoker and kept coughing fatty liquid rattling coughs; emphysema was lurking in ambush if not already entrenched. It obviously was not a good day for Nora Douglas; her girl friend of the moment had packed her bags the previous night, pretending that the continuous wheezing and snoring was driving her crazy.

Tim explained the nature of his request as persuasively as thirty five years of priesthood had taught him.

-This is highly confidential and I cannot go into more details with a person other than the president. – He was repeating for the third time.

Tim had naively thought that his status as a clergyman would have opened most doors. Wrong, it had the adverse effect.

He was out of argument. Not a sound from Nora but he knew she was still listening because of the wheezing. She was outstanding at discouraging appointment seekers. Waiting silently, mechanically sucking on a cigarette and exhaling the smoke in Tim's ear as if doing it on purpose, she finally said in a pseudo oxfordian accent.

-As I already told you, Mister Levinsky will not be able to see you or anybody else for that matter. He is already seeing too many persons this morning. - Cough, cough, wheeze, wheeze...

And for the fourth time Tim repeated.

-I must insist, since I have an extremely important proposal for Mister Levinsky. You understand that sometimes, exceptions have to be considered and this is one. Good assistants can tell the difference.-

-Impossible before tomorrow and I'd need to know what it's about. - She said, enjoying the power trip.

Seeing that he would not get anywhere with logic and diplomacy, Tim changed tone and strategy.

-Of course, deciding assumes that the decider has a brain which, in your case is obviously not the case. - Tim said in a calm dry voice.

If he had been a good Christian, he would have had to confess the hatred he was developing for this bitch.

-Everybody claims to be an exception, as for the rest of your argument I have not heard it; please send a fax or e-mail with the nature of your request. I will then get in touch with you. – She was used to abuses and probably thrived on them.

-May you choke in your bile. - Mumbled Tim as he hung up.

But she was off the line by then and the more frustrated of the two was certainly Tim. She would be smiling now and regaining some of her lost composure. Nora had a bed mate replacement in mind; she would not be living alone longer than a day or two.

Reality for Tim was that his priesthood was not opening all the doors as he had expected. He should have said that he was a cardinal to go pass this Presbyterian warden shielding her Jewish President.

-You'll see to what extremes a modest but determined priest can reach. - And grabbing his brief case, he stepped out of the house, got into his car, almost breaking a window closing the door and was off to Boston without having had his second cup of coffee.

Not being pulled over for speeding was a miracle and he arrived in downtown Boston in less than two and a half hours. He was lucky enough to find a parking place and was soon standing in front of the Roman Catholic receptionist. She was impressed by the roman collar and immediately directed him to the corner offices when he said he had a meeting with the president.

Hidden behind large cannabis like plants in front of the office of the president, guarding it with her life was the desk of Nora Douglas: the Presbyterian dragon-lady and last line of defense. Without moving her egg-shaped half-bald head ensconced in sloping shoulders as if she had a sore neck, Nora darted two blood shot eyes upward and stared at Tim, surprised to have this priest standing in front of her.

-You may not remember me, we spoke this morning, I am Father Timothy Donnelly and whether you want it or not I will have a short meeting with your president. What I have to tell him is that urgent. I can't share this information with unauthorized and... incompetent personnel. - Tim's voice was tense and he was getting reddish under his white collar.

He had been right in his assessment: she was frustrated, a bitch and looked at him as if he was a parasite on the balls of a gorilla. Slowly, deliberately, she moved a bony right arm to grab her cigarette, took a puff while continuing her inspection of the alien standing in front of her. Then with a Machiavellian smile or rictus as Tim would later describe her smile, she said:

-Mister Levinsky is not in his office and he won't be until next week. You should not have traveled this great distance until I granted you an appointment. - And showing nicotine stained vampire incisive teeth; she emitted a cackle as if this little incident had made her day; probably had.

Tim was prepared for this answer and was getting ready to use the heavy artillery when providence manifested itself. The mahogany door to the left of Miss Douglas opened and a well dressed young lady graciously danced her way out of the office, saying goodbye and waiving to an invisible person. This had to be Lewinsky's office.

Some pretty good advice can be gathered from the Bible and he had read that to better surprise the enemy, first, fake submission and then move with the speed of light. So Tim bowed his head in feigned submission and started to turn around, as if to leave.

Miss Douglas, fearing that this incarnation of the devil would take advantage of the open door, had started to get up, ready to defend the privacy of her god using her decrepit body as a shield if needed.

When she saw that Tim had pivoted to leave, she aborted her movement to get up and, inelegantly dropped back on her comfortable chair which received the blow with a hissing sound.

Meanwhile, foxy Tim continued his rotation and completed a 360 degree, coming out of the spin, facing the now wide open door leading to Lewinsky's office. In a couple of quick steps he was inside the office and closed the mahogany door behind him.

Levinsky, still sitting behind a large oak desk, looked over his reading barnacles, surprised but not alarmed. People trust clergymen. Almost immediately the door swung open, pushed by the now out of control and puffing

Miss Douglas. Tim was already standing in front of the desk onto which he dropped the first clip. Paying no attention to the wheezing and now choking purple toad, and using his most impressive tone of voice, he lashed out, speaking articulately.

-This clip and ten more to follow will raise your rating considerably. You're the first on my list and will remain the only one if we can reach an agreement. Please take a few minutes and hear me out. I tried to make an appointment, but your very efficient Cerberus wants to make decisions, which could cost the company several millions of dollars in revenues. – He had accented heavily the two key words: rating and cost.

-I have called security; they should be here in a minute. This gentleman parading as a priest has forced his way without my consent. - Screeched out faithful Nora as if she was the victim of a rape attempt. Raped she would never be, thought Tim.

Looking at Tim, then at the clip and finally at his secretary, Levinsky said in a soft voice.

-If this priest thinks that what he has to show me is so important that he's willing to risk his life going through you to deliver his message, I'll listen to him. That will be all miss Douglas and send the security guards back to their crap game.-

Levinsky got up from his seat and extended a well manicured hand to Tim as a shocked Douglas was reluctantly backing out of the office muttering against Tim, humiliated and defeated but not out.

-Sit down please, I'm busy but I have all the time in the world to raise the station's rating, that's what I'm paid for. The name is Zigfridas Levinsky, the president of this company. - And he went back to his seat.

Tim remained standing :

-My name is Timothy Donnelly and I've been a bona fide priest for the last thirty five years. What I have to show and tell you is unusual : Two weeks ago I received the visit from an eight year old girl who told me that her step father was abusing her, as well as her two sisters and a brother. He was also selling them to other pedophiles. I was ready to go to the police but I hesitated because of the coercitive methods this bastard was using: strangulation of the family cat and torture of a rabbit to scare the kids as well as death threat against the mother. Last night I received this clip and a note. The note directed me to bring the clip to you. Apparently the step father and two of the clients have been kidnapped, judged and sentenced to a rather cruel death by some group I am not familiar with. This sentence is now being carried out and filmed continuously. The filming will continue until the very end which according to my unknown source should be in ten days or so. -

Without a word, Zigfridas pointed to a video monitor. In a few seconds Tim had the video turning and went back to his seat. It took only a few feet of the clip for Levinsky to jump out of his seat and move to a chair immediately in front of the screen.

The editing had been done by Deana and Dudley; amateurish but excellent. First it depicted the kids being assaulted by the step father and then by the five clients. Only the faces of the clients and of the step father could be seen, the children's faces had been smeared beyond recognition and rendered unrecognizable by even their mother.

In the background they could hear a female voice reading Plutarque's description of the torment soldier Mithridate had been submitted to. During the lecture, one could see the preparation of the scene, including the naked step father being immobilized in a contraption which would allow a full view of the body. The gavage scene was particularly colorful and for several minutes the yelling and raving of Steven filled the office.

-Yes, thought Levinsky, this will increase the rating if we're allowed to show it on the air.-

Tim interrupted his thoughts.

-This is the first one of a total of six sentences to be carried out. Two more of the pedophiles you saw on the clip have already been abducted and the other three will follow within the next two days. Needless to tell you that I have tried to convince my unknown contact to go to the police. Not a chance.-

-This is what they want. On a daily basis you'll receive a thirty minute edited tape or, if you prefer, you can do the editing yourself. A Foundation with the sole purpose of helping abused kids must be created. You and I will be co-presidents of this foundation which will be funded by the proceeds of the sale of the clips to the station. A hundred thousand dollars per clip and a quarter of a million per point increase in the ratings.-

Tim paused, looking at Levinsky who was rewinding the clip to view it one more time. Then on second thought he shut the video monitor off and looked at Tim.

-I am the father of two children, ages nine and eleven. Is it really possible that such atrocities find their ways in our society? It makes me sick. – He paused and then continued.

-I'll need to show this to the company lawyer, I'm not sure we can show this kind of material on the air. Do you mind? He'll come now.-

-No on the contrary, Tim answered, I have consulted with my lawyer and he doesn't think I am breaking any law if I provide a copy to the police. Which I will do when I leave here. The other clips will be forwarded to you personally.-

Speaking to a hidden intercom on his desk Levinsky said.

-Miss Douglas, cancel my appointments for the next hour and have someone bring coffee, juices and sandwiches. - Then he looked at Tim with a crooked smile.

-She's now choking with rage and she would spit in your juice if she knew which one you'd chose.... I hope she's not angry at me too.... I have to promote her out of here and get someone nicer-. He hit another button on the intercom and a voice answered.

-Al, please come in my office immediately we have an emergency.-

Within a minute the company lawyer was knocking at the door. A balding giant, thick glass, fiftyish with a pot belly the size of a two hundred pound pumpkin, Alfred Goldwater was surprisingly nimble on his feet for a man weighing more than three hundred pounds. Behind the thick glasses were smart, alert eyes, magnified by the glasses, scrutinizing Tim from head to toes. Satisfied he grabbed the extended hand and shook it warmly.

All of this had taken more than a full minute and not a word had been said. Tim was beginning to wonder if he was in the presence of a mute lawyer. That would have been a first.

-What's up Zyg, where's the fire?-

-Father Tim will give you a short résumé of a situation... imposed upon him, while I start playing this video clip. I'll want to know if we can air it on the news channel. Bear in mind that we will be receiving more of the same for maybe ten to fifteen days.-

Tim started his recitation but soon stopped as Al placed his index finger on his lips indicating that he wanted to concentrate fully on the clip before going into the details.

After several Jesus Christ and other obscenities, Al settled on a chair and carefully watched. When it went blank he got up and went to the bar and poured himself a large one from an expensive carafe. He didn't offer to share, thinking that they could do the same if they had the same need he had after seeing this video clip. He had seen a lot of similar videos in more than ten years with the company, but this one was by far the most sordid he had ever seen. Trying to find an analogy with other species, he came to the conclusion that man had climbed the rungs of evolution and multiplied ad infinitum both the good and the bad traits of the animal kingdom.

-Now I'm ready to hear your story Father.-

He settled down and closed his eyes as he drained his glass, taking in every word Tim was pronouncing. Once in a while he would open his eyes and scribble a note in a little black book.

When Tim was done, the big man got up and started a mile walk around the office while he was giving his professional opinion.

-This is rough stuff. However my opinion is that you can show it on the air as long as the police is given a copy of the clip. The children's faces are to be blotched out of recognition as was done here. As for the adults being filmed, they could sue the company if they are found not guilty. In this case, as I understand the situation, the question will not arise. - He went on.

-As you know this will appeal to both pedophiles and sadists. I doubt that it will deter any one from being a pedophile but delation will increase exponentially. There is no doubt that your ratings will explode. That being said, I hope that these sons of bitches will suffer as much as they deserve. Mithri...dati...sation is it? ... Proper handling. I have to remember the spelling-.

An interim agreement was drafted and signed by Tim and Levinsky. Al said that a Foundation would be created immediately and could start being operational within a month. These structures would not be immediately operational, in the mean time a trust account could be used to receive monies. Tim ended their meeting by saying.

-I'm leaving a copy of this clip and will deliver the original to the police as soon as I get back to Lewiston. A detective by the name of Paterson will undoubtedly be around to ask questions. He's been assigned to investigate the O'Reilly situation but is not getting any cooperation there. The mother is of the opinion that her children can recuperate from this experience only if helped by good professionals. She'll stay away from lawyers and cops.-

Zygfridas Levinsky, the president and Chief executive officer of one of the largest television news station, had signed a deal that would boost his rating and revenues to new heights. He felt good about exposing these pedo-philes to the public and hoped that it would deter some of them. If only one child was saved because of his action that would be enough. However Al was right, this would not deter any of these demented and sick animals from yield-ing to their sick impulsions; it would sharpen the public's eye and encourage delation. Same results in the end. Sometimes the end justifies the means.

-Mithridatisation, that's a complicated word but it will stick to the viewers' minds like these little yellowish maggots gnawing and feeding on the guts of the bastards. I hope we can have a blown up picture of a sequence where the balls of one of them is eaten. - He got up and stretched.

-Now let's get the board of directors' consent. - And sporting a wide smile he asked Miss Douglas to convoke a meeting of the board. -For this evening please and I want quorum.-

On his way out Tim could feel the burning eyes of Nora Douglas drilling a hole in the back of his head. He would have to bathe in holy water as soon as he got home to exorcise some of her curses. Walking by slowly he couldn't help pivoting and facing her before he was out of the danger zone. Displaying a paternal smile, he softly said.

-I hope you find a solution to your problem. You can't be that frustrated without a good reason.-

Tim spent the drive back structuring a long term rehabilitation program for abused children. How can they best be helped? Psychiatry could serve a useful purpose but Tim was ill at ease with this discipline; like the church, the psychiatrist penetrates the mind of his patients or victims as some call them; and like the church it can do more harm than good. Most psychiatrists he knew seemed more deranged than their patients. How can a simple human navigate in such troubled waters without being as disturbed as his patient?; the blind leading the blind. One of his friends was a physician and would have better intelligence on the subject.

When he reached exit 21 on the 495 he had organized a first draft in his mind. He would write it down in a proper format tonight and e- mail it to Al Goldwater.

As he opened the front door of the presbytery, the phone rang as if waiting for him. He recognized Barcelo's voice.

-Done he said; send unedited copies directly to Levinsky. - And then as an after thought, -Good luck and be careful. No more phone conversation please.-

CHAPTER 28

"Les jeux sont faits, rien ne va plus."

Johnny had another quarter and used it to phone Dudley.

-It went as we expected. Tim is back home. I'll be home in about thirty minutes. If you want to join me we can attend to the rest of the chores. I may start before you get there. So if I'm not....-

-Wait for us; don't go in that rat's hole alone. - Dudley hung up.

Johnny hadn't been inside his home since Gelda and Todd had found him agonizing like the sickly destitute he was. They had probably saved him from a lonely death as if there was any other kind. The doctor had said: -Another few hours and his number was up-.

Almost a month ago now; this incident had sidetracked his life from a pointless and futile dead end to this exhilarating and challenging reality.

He owed one to Gelda. What could he do to make it up to the mother of his last child? He could reason that she was not in a worse situation now than when he salvaged her from this gloomy scenario that she was desperately trying to escape from. Poor girl: from the frying pan to the fire; he had not improved the quality of her life and used her all he could. In retrospect he had not been a lot better than these very same predators he was now hunting. Maybe there was still time to do something for her. Todd was a more worthwhile cause. He would give the little guy a fair chance but didn't not yet see exactly how.

He opened the door with apprehension. The place was not any cleaner than it was a month ago, more dust had accumulated on the floor and the furniture. And what a smell; it took a minute to find the source of the foul odor permeating the place; he carefully placed the rotten potatoes in a heavy duty garbage bag before throwing it out back.

Like a stormy cloud, glum always loomed over him as soon as he entered this shack. In each square centimeter, the scars of his life, the hurts and sorrows were kept alive, energized by the drab settings, muted but condemning witnesses of his failure as a human. This is where he had spent most of his fifteen year relationship with the bottle; so many irresponsible and dumb actions coming to mind. During this fifteen year interval he had consigned his brains to a safe deposit box. Did he remember the combination; could he safely reopen the safe and retrieve his brain and spirit? And if he did would it function as a normal brain or would the neurons be dysfunctional?

Forty five years later, he was standing in this decrepit shack wondering how he had screwed up such a promising start. "The American dream come true", as Emilie was repeating in admiration. The marriage, the cottage, his own business; all this was not enough, he could not avoid chasing a bigger dream, elusive because it continuously changed shape and color, forever out of reach until it became disillusion and hallucination .

He had lived only a few years in this beautifully romantic -*Cottage on the Brook*- as Émilie had named it; she had made a wooden sign with the green letters carved in the pine wood. He closed his eyes and could see and hear the babbling and crystalline sound of the clear water of this vigorous creek as it raced to the sea. In retrospect he realized that this orderly portion of his life had been paradisiacal. Now, old and destitute, he belatedly could appreciate the calm happiness, the sound felicity of the few years he had lived with Emilie.

After Emilie, even if his wealth had increased exponentially with the Saint Augustine and all these other ventures he delved into, life had been downhill, quick and purposeless, booze and shallow women, like his life, frivolous and near sighted, chasing a never to be reached happiness.

-Fuck life and the living. - Muttered a sad Barcelo. But he knew that his instincts had been formed way back when he was a mere child.

Again, his chest was being squashed by anxiety. He knew the remedy: action. Mechanically, like a robot, he started picking up. Opening a drawer to place a teddy bear Todd had forgotten behind a sofa, he realized that he had not heard or talked to his son for almost a month. Gelda had not phoned or visited him when he was hospitalized; probably because he didn't have any money she could squeeze out of him. What a mess. It was better when he was too drunk to even think about respectability and responsibility and all the other ....ities. Only when Paterson told him about the bum checks Gelda was peddling around town did he understand why she dodged him.

Anger, frustration and narcissism had always been strong motors, driving his destiny over chaotic roads. Why was he doing this caper, why was he playing god, judging and sentencing these bastards hardly worse than he had been. Did he not have enough problems of his own? Wizened up by age he could face the truth about his motives: First reason, to enroll in this crusade and espouse such a cause was to forget his own failure and, the second, was that he wanted to die doing something honorable that his sons would remember him by. He would be a true narcissist to the end.

At least the O'Reilly kids would have a chance to live a full life; the foundation would look after them. In a way it was too bad his son Todd could not get some benefit out of this situation. But maybe there was a way, had to be... otherwise, with his destitute mother, Todd's future was as promising as Easter for a male spring lamb.

Feeling the walls still closing in, he had to get out. He wrote a note, telling Dudley that he was attending to the chores and to meet him there.

It took him less than five minutes to get to the cave entrance and about as much to move the truck tires hiding the entrance. Once upon a time, even though he never weighed more than one hundred and twenty five pounds, he could have moved these tires that were as heavy as he was, without breaking a sweat; today he was puffing and sweating profusely.

As soon as he had freed the entrance, the stench almost floored him. Something had to be done about this. There was an opening somewhere in the cave, way back where it became almost impassable. If uncluttered this well would allow the stale air to circulate out. The stink was so bad he could taste it. Holding his breath he had to backtrack and let the cave regurgitate out some of its putrid air.

-Poor bastards, the smell is bad enough without the other stuff. - He thought.

As always he had to reason that they deserved this severe punishment. -They have inflicted extreme suffering and now have to pay the penalty. - But it had been easier to intellectually arrive at this decision than it would be to enforce it to the end; he certainly wasn't taking any pleasure in it. Deana was the most dedicated and if not for her, the penalty would be extreme but quick or painless. Woman can hold a grudge longer than men and she had enough reasons to be vindictive.

-Hey, what am I doing, isn't this my plan, my idea? And furthermore a bullet in the back of the head will not sell to the TV station. -

Dreading to walk in alone even though he was sure that the patients were still restrained, he had decided to wait for Dud and Deana before going in, but after a while, impatient and thinking of the work load for the next forty eight hours he decided to surmount his fright.

Donning the smallest of the three blue protective garments, he picked up one of the heavy magna lite flashlights they had left at the entrance and quickly covered the distance inside the cement tunnel. Upon entering the cave he was blinded by the floodlight illuminating the scene. The only noise he could hear was the irregular breathing of the three Mithridates and the humming of the camera, this impersonal and inexorable witness. He shut it off.

The stench and the filth was unbearable, making breathing impossible. Steven, having been there the longest was the dirtiest, covered from his neck to his toes in urine and excrement. John could not see any maggots and was surprised that it took such a long time for them to appear on the scene, but getting closer to Steven he saw that they were under his dirty carcass, away from the light.

Appalled he backed up until he reached the wall. The other two were slowly catching up with Steven. The flies were busy dancing around in the flood light, hovering over the bodies like vultures. The skunk carrion they had brought over the previous day was serving the intended purpose of populating the cave with flies and maggots as well as not improving the fragrance.

Thinking of his friends at the Department of Environmental Protection, he could not help but laugh thinking about what they could charge him with. He was sour about the DEP and blamed them for his misfortune. However, deep down, he knew that he, alone was the only one responsible for his collapse. Finding an emissary goat had always been a way out; victimization is a more palatable aspect of failure.

He removed three pre- filled gavage bags from the carton. As he was to start forcing this slop down Steven's throat, they all woke up from their stupor and started to moan and emit muffled scream. Working his tongue around the duct tape, Gorski had pushed enough of the gag to be able to mumble and Johnny could make up the words.

-Not my fault, I was abused, can't help myself now. I tried and tried but always gave in. Tried and tried ...... Thought of killing myself but couldn't. Then it became easier....-

That he had been abused when he was a child was consistent with what the psychiatrists were theorizing: more than sixty percent of the abused became abusers themselves; a vicious circle of causes and effects; like life. Steven was babbling meaningless sounds, unable to talk because of the gavage tube inserted in his stomach. They were all loosing their minds, Johnny thought, as he would, if placed in the same situation.

He was about done when Dudley walked in.

-You should have waited for us Johnny. In your condition it's unreasonable to move these truck tires. Anyway thanks, we'll be out of here faster. Not my favorite place.-

Johnny continued, helped by Deana. In a few moments, it was done. How many more feedings? This part was taxing.

There was this unfinished business of collecting the entire O'Reilly clips. Smith had some stacked some place. Johnny removed his gag.

-We need to know what you've done with the clips involving the O'Reilly kids.-

Smith focused his eyes on Johnny's face and was quick to cooperate. Johnny noticed that his beard was growing fast; maybe the stench and excrement were good for the growth of hair.

-I rented a storage vault. The address is on the key, in the pocket of my pants.

-That was easy thought Johnny. Too easy. He may be tired of fighting. He didn't even insult us or implore....-

-Did you bring the bomb kit? - Asked Johnny to Dudley.

-Yup and it shouldn't be long before we have an impregnable and self destruct fortress; from within and without. –

They exchanged the previous day film and replaced it with a new one. In a little more than fifteen minutes they had rigged a bomb which would blow the cave and set fire to the entire tire dump. The cocktail of phosphorus, nitrate and fuel would be ignited by a spark. The extreme temperature created by the phosphorus would reduce the bodies to ashes. The fire would sprout

out of the entrance tunnel and also out of the ventilation well, enflaming the scrap tires; burning during several days before any one could come into what would be left of the cave. Probably nothing left of anything or anyone as the blast would have imploded the walls and laid everything to rest for the eternity. This catastrophe will be activated from a distance of about one thousand feet or triggered by an intruder walking in or out of the cave.

-I don't think we'll be back here before thirty six hours. Let's give them all more water. - Deana said having a second thought.

She didn't want any of her boarders to die of dehydration. She had made up her mind and was going to see this project to the very end.

Going back in, she turned the camera off and gave everyone an extra ration of water. Don Smith, the younger and stronger of the three had been very cooperative, even when asked to help for the O'Reilly clips. Like Johnny, Deana had been intrigued but brushed it off as an indication of despair and pragmatism. Nevertheless, to be on the safe side, she went over to inspect his riggings. She bent down to have a closer look at his arms.

His left arm came out like the head of a snake.

-Dud, she yelled, come quick.-

Smith had been able to cut off his left thumb. His hand, much smaller without the thumb, had wiggled out of the handcuff. Realizing that Deana was on to him he had grabbed her and was trying to bring her down to the ground. With a complete set of fingers Smith would have succeeded in disarming Deana.

Dudley didn't have to do anything as Deana had her .45 out in a flash and blew Smith's left elbow at near point blank range. He let out an inhuman sound, more of rage than pain. Deana had her foot on the now useless left arm. She stared knowingly at her associates as if to say I told you.

-Right-. Said Johnny who understood the mute message.

-Lesson number one, let's always check the bindings. Lesson number two, let's never walk in here alone. - Johnny thought of what might have occurred if he had started with Smith. He could have been killed by the very strong Smith, with or without his left thumb. Paranoia had failed him.

-What do we do with him he'll be dead of massive infection in less than a day and a half. - Asked Deana.

-Only if the infection can travel to the rest of his body so, let's do what the pirates did, cauterize the wound and place a tourniquet above the elbow. –

-Cauterize the wound? How in hell do you want to do that? - Dudley asked. -I won't do it - said Johnny-, because I'm gutless when it comes to these "hands on" operations but there's a blow torch that I brought as part of the emergency equipment. It's in the back. –

He found the blow torch, lit it and handed it to Dud who, after looking at the blue hissing flame handed it over to Deana. She gave him an once-over look that women of the world throw their weaker counter parts and she started moving towards Smith. Barcelo was still wondering whether she had enough hatred in her to go ahead with the gruesome treatment when she quickly knelt down and cauterized the gash created by the amputation of the left thumb as well as the gun wound to the left elbow. Smith's expiation became very loud, then he lost consciousness having almost levitated out of his bonds. The stench of burning flesh mixed with the already putrid odor was of such potency that it could have been successfully used in bio chemical warfare.

-Let's get out of here before I suffocate. – Said Dudley.

Deana calmly switched the camera back on, and after having inspected all the other bindings, walked out of the cave. By then, Smith had regained consciousness and was trying to say something unkind to Deana.

-Whatever you're threatening me with, you'll find that an adult is more difficult to impress than a ten year old girl. In the mean time keep dreaming, it will pass the time away. Dreaming is all you have left because you'll never again touch yours or anyone else's penis or vagina. – Were Deana' s parting words.

She ran out, realizing that it would be more and more difficult. Another feature film would be haunting her nightmares for the next fifty years. This new vision would have to take a number and join the queue.

CHAPTER 29

"Whoever tangles with monsters must take care not to become a monster."
Nietzsche

Information gathered from the three captives allowed a reconstruction of the puzzle. The identification of the other three pedophiles was easy to complete. The Better Business Bureau, and other credit information agencies, provided full addresses, telephone numbers, as well as credit rating. All three were outstanding citizens, wealthy, law abiding, non-descript except for the fact that they were part of the privileged few of the world.

James Rupert, age 55, inherited several thousand acres of woodland in the state of Maine. He lives in Dedham, Mass. Is unmarried; works from his home and from an office in Boston. Holds a pilot license and has built a private landing strip on his property.

Madeleine Whortington, age 61, owner of a modeling agency, never married; lives in a high rise condominium building, 2772 Dorchester ave., Boston, with her old and disabled father. Place of business, a few minutes away from her condo. The father is exceptionally wealthy.

Cyrus Alpasha, age 64, retired art dealer, lives in Ridgewood, NJ. Was never married, nothing unusual to report; old money, and lots of it.

-They seem to have it all, yet they're looking for this little extra thrill. - Mumbled Dudley when he read the files.

-We can start with the furthest and collect the others on the way back...- Suggested Johnny.

That made sense. If they left immediately they could be in New York around seven o'clock and in New Jersey approximately one hour later.

Johnny had rented one of these very comfortable motor homes. Travelling without interruption would allow them to best utilize their time. The motor home was also large enough to hide the drugged bodies of their captives.

Piggy backing the Chevrolet Corsica belonging to Deana they would have unobtrusive transportation while in the danger zone. They would be gone only twelve hours at the most and Tim would feed the dog once and take him out in the yard for his number one or the other.

Going south, Johnny would pay all expenses with his credit card, leaving a wide trail. On the way back, cash would be used. If all went according to plan the schedule would look like this:

Ridgewood, New Jersey. Alpasha would be picked up in less than ten hours or around twenty three hundred hours; Rupert, in Dedham Mass., around six in the morning and finally Madeleine Whortington, in Boston, close to nine as she was walking to work from her condo. Johnny had made a reservation in one of the trailer park in Fort Lee NJ. They would check in early and leave around 2 o'clock in the morning. On the spot, the Corsica would be used to make the collection and then hitched back to the motor home.

-With a little luck we'll be back tomorrow by twelve o'clock, in good time to feed our cave dwellers... – Deana observed.

Barcelo left Lewiston alone, driving the impressive Motor Home as if he had done this all his life. Deana and Dudley preceded him in the Corsica and waited in the first rest area after Portland. There the Corsica was hitched to the Motor Home, Deana and Dudley travelling incognito from then on while studying a detailed map of the areas they would visit during the next twenty four hours.

These Motor Homes are really what they publicize: home on wheels, with a kitchen, a living room and a bedroom with a small but suitable bath room. The bedroom featured a large bed that the three invited guests would be monopolizing on the way back.

Deana was taking a nap when they reached the camping site in Fort Lee New Jersey at six twenty five. After checking in they ate some of the food they had brought with them so that they would not be seen in any of the restaurants. Their first target was only a few miles away.

CHAPTER 30

"Tout dégénère entre les mains de l'homme."
JJ Rousseau

Ridgewood NJ. Cyrus Alpasha, art dealer, horse lover and pedophile.

At fifty three, Cyrus Alpasha was a wealthy, semi retired art dealer. From birth to retirement, his business and passion had been buying antique furniture and paintings, specializing in early American artists. Parallel to his bread and butter business, he had acquired for his very private and personal viewing, a collection of child pornographic paintings and photographs. Although difficult to assess with a reasonable degree of scientific rigor, he could boast of possessing one of the most valuable collection of pornographic pedophilic paintings and drawings in the world. He would sometimes allow other connoisseurs to admire his treasure. Several millions of dollars had been offered from other aficionados. He had always and would always refuse to sell.

-I don't need more money and this is more satisfying to me than anything money could bring.-

Cyrus had never married as women were of no interest to him. As a matter of fact he had never been intimate with a woman. Sometimes, when social functions demanded it, he would hire a hostess, never taking advantage of the complete package.

His childhood had been spent mostly in English boarding schools. As early as eight years old he had been sent to a boarding school of excellent reputation. His parents were of the opinion that a rigid upbringing in the best of English traditions would be appropriate for their only son if he was to take over the family business. He would come home twice a year, once for the Christmas Holidays, and again in June. Come September, he would again cross the Atlantic. His mother would visit with him once or twice and his father would write every month, always on the first Monday. The summer vacations would be spent doing various chores related to the family business. No other activities but that of learning the fine art of purchasing or selling antique furniture or paintings by early American artists.

Most often students surpass the teachers. He soon became one of the best in the profession. Upon becoming a rich orphan after the car accident that took the lives of both his parents, he had no trouble taking over the business and upgrading it to the highest levels. His English accent and old school mannerism were a distinctive asset.

During his youth, spent in two prominent English boarding schools, Cyrus had attained fairly good academic results, a good seat in the saddle and become as good a cricket player as can be expected from an "American chap". After the first few months Cyrus had blended into the boarding school life. As is often reported, in these "males only" institutions, like prisons, boarding schools or monasteries, toying with homosexuality is an outlet some choose. Like many of his colleagues, pre-teen Cyrus had been promiscuous with older students, filling in the role of the female, in the amorous pursuits of these sexually frustrated adolescents. When he, in turn became an adolescent, he continued the practice of homosexuality with younger students and soon became a bona fide pedophile proselyte with a touch of sadism added. While most of his boarding school acquaintances would revert back to the standard heterosexuality, Cyrus' sexual inclination was set and he continued in adulthood, stepping up his level of refinement to new frontiers. Like Oedipus, esthetes are always looking for the ultimate in all things.

His association with Smith had started more than five years ago when Smith arrived unannounced, asking to see his private collection of painting and photographs. Always suspicious of strangers, he had denied having anything to show him other than the early American paintings which were hanging in the show room. Smith had taken with him a portfolio of infantile pornographic photographs. He showed Cyrus his collection and they soon became associates. During the next several years, Cyrus bought several of Smith's photographs.

Smith was using his daughter as his principal model. One day he introduced the live model to Cyrus. Who went wild and paid ten thousand dollars to Smith to be left alone with her one night. It would be his first sexual association with a female, although a juvenile. The girl was twelve, and even though used to special sex, took a long time to recover from this one night stand.

As his daughter was growing older, Smith had to use outsiders and he finally was caught red handed, when one parent realized that if the photographer demanded to be left alone with the subject "in order to obtain the ultimate photograph ", the real purpose was to shoot pornographic pictures. A suspicious mother walked surreptitiously into the studio and was horrified at seeing her nine year old daughter naked and posing in what her lawyer later described to the police as: suggestive, indecent, lewd, seductive and sexual postures. She had snatched her daughter under one arm, clothing under the other and ran to her car yelling rape all the way to the police station. The police arrested Smith and seized several child pornographic pictures. He was sent away for four years.

Cyrus enjoyed travelling. He would take several trips to countries where child prostitution was tolerated. Brasilia, India, Sri Lanka were his favorite destinations. He had to be careful at home and relied on the likes of Smith and Steven to provide special situations. Being wealthy, money never presented a problem and was a strong incentive for Smith and Steven as well as other pimps.

Truly an aesthete, Cyrus Alpasha lived in a museum like environment. The walls of all rooms in his ancient manor were covered with paintings, the finest carpets covered the floors, and the most exquisite furniture was elegantly disposed in the spacious rooms. In the garage, were three vintage cars: a 1952 Ferrari, a 1956 Jaguar and a rare De Lorean. Music was a constant companion in the house, part of the background; like the paintings and the silk Chinese carpets. A Bose complex sound system continuously diffused the best of classical music.

If women were of no interest, he loved animals and particularly horses, a reminder of his days in these exclusive boarding schools. For an amoral monster like Cyrus, who would not think twice about abusing and maiming the bodies, the souls and minds of his young victims, this almost paternal fondness for horses would seem conflicting. Of course a psychiatrist would have pegged it to some theory or created one.

He had always owned a few horses that he would ride regularly; until one Sunday afternoon when he was thrown. – Don't ride again ever. - Had ordered his doctor.

Thoroughbreds and Arabians were his favorite but he had owned several warm blood horses which he would purchase in Holland, France or Germany. In his small but luxurious stable, he was keeping "Laika", an Akal Teke mare and her foal out of Candid Regent, a grand son of Northern dancer. He had purchased Laika on one of his trip to Ukraine; the former eastern countries were economically poor and it had been easy for him to satisfy his sexual fantasies as well as his love for good horses. Akal Teke was a breed of horse created long ago and renowned for its endurance and stamina.

Is it not in what is now Ukraine, that the horse specie became domesticated about six thousand years ago? The pastoral people living in the steppes east of the Dnieper owed their expansion to the horse. It was because of the horse that the Huns could dominate the world for the next five thousands years. The value of the horse as a war machine, ended when the Polish cavalry was defeated by the motorized divisions of Hitler in September 1939. However during the previous five thousand years, the horse was a military machine and allowed Attila and his Huns to defeat the Romans; Genghis Khan to rule over Russia and China; Cortes and Pissarro to subdue the Incas and the Aztecs, and so on.

Cyrus had once asked his psychiatrist.

-Why is it that being around horses brings me serenity? Often when I feel devastated by the awareness of the freak I have become, cleaning the stalls and brushing the coat of Laika, brings back some serenity to my fucked-up mind.-

He had a very distinctive English upper class way to pronounce "fucked-up"; it would always make the psychiatrist's wife smirk when he would mimic the accent for her amusement.

A young stable hand came three hours every day to manicure the grounds and exercise Laika while the foal would canter around trying to distract her.

Cyrus was bored; life was trouble free and luxurious but, dreary. He had everything but lacked the essential: peace of mind and tranquility. His sexual pulsions had always taken his brain over and he could not see the day when his hormone driven body would give him respite. At one point he had even considered castration but his psychiatrist did not believe that his pedophilia would be cured by surgery. Chemical castration could bring relief, but he would have to take the medication; maybe one day, but not for the time being. He had good intentions but lacked the will power to implement any decisions. "Isn't our reason slave to our passions? " His psy would confirm that his volition was not under his control. Whose then? Would he ask?

Travelling to exotic places where he could satisfy his hunger for young flesh was sometimes more trouble than the pleasure he would derive; these kids were too docile, his sadistic side was not sated. He had contemplated buying a sexual slave, maybe two and keep them in house; too risky, furthermore the kids would grow up and become a nuisance. He would then have to get rid of them. How do you get rid of a fourteen year old human; the slave owners must have had the same problem after 1861 when the slaves were freed.

── CHAPTER 31 ──

"Man is the saddest of all spirits because he has a body and the saddest of all animals because he has a spirit."
Verine

Alpasha's manor or domain was a two story, ancient red brick house built more than seventy five years ago. Nestled in the middle of a fenced-in four acre lot, the tiled shingle roof could be seen from the road, the property concentrically sloping like a crater. Magnificent old trees hid most of the mansion. The neighbors were as affluent and their houses as superbly camouflaged.

About two hundred feet from the main building, a small brick stable, of the same vintage as the main property, was also partially hidden in the trees. From the road, Deana could see at least two horses in the paddock: a mare with its foal. They had not anticipated this; but it could be a plus.

-Let's see if we can get Alpasha to come to the stable. If that doesn't work we can always walk to the house as tourist with car trouble.-

Parking the Corsica a mile down the road, Deana and Dudley walked down the road as two lovers out for a stroll. Johnny stayed in the car awaiting Dudley's call.

Sneaking into the paddock from the road and getting the beautiful mare to come over to them was a cinch. Deana had pocketed a few pieces of sugar should Johnny's blood sugar fall; she became a good friend of the animals in just a few lumps. The mare was as domesticated and tame as a house kitten. Taking hold of the halter Deana nonchalantly walked the mare to the stable, the foal romping around.

The sun had set around nine o'clock and the moon was timidly taking over the space. In this bluish half-light, it was difficult to discern Deana's shadow merging in with the larger outline of the mare. At this time of the evening the mosquitoes become a pest; the mare was eager to sleep inside the stable and followed docilely. A small voltage yellow bulb was lighting the inside of the stable; two boxes, one larger than the other, presumably to accommodate the mare and the colt. Leading the mare she walked in this larger one followed by the colt; she slid the door closed.

Now they had to get Alpasha's attention. Deana started banging on the door with a shovel, as if the mare had difficulty to redress after rolling on her back to scratch. This, she remembered was a frequent cause of accident and feared by horse lovers. After five minutes she was ready to give up when a light came on at the rear of the manor. A man of around the right age to be Cyrus Alpasha approached the stable at a very slow jog.

-Here he comes. - Said Dudley.

She stopped beating the door with the shovel and walked inside the box so Alpasha would not see her before he entered the box. Dudley locked the door after her.

-Hey what's this noise all about, did you lose your foal. And who in hell let you in. Luke must have sneaked back this evening. - Out of breath and worried, Alpasha was checking the stable.

Suspicious, from the outside he looked in the box; after a moment which seemed an eternity to Deana, he started to slide the heavy door. Crouching under the feeding trough, Deana remained concealed, her dark clothing hardly discernable from the wall.

He walked in, closing the door after him so the colt would not escape. The mare went to him, friendly. Satisfied he patted the animal on the romp and turn to walk out.

When he was half way to the door, Deana made her move just as Dudley was closing in from the other empty stall. Alpasha saw the large shadow and turned around to retreat into the stall where he ran into Deana. Shoving her .45 into Mister Alpasha's plexus, she raised her knee and hit him hard in the groin.

Dudley was right behind and opened the plastic bag in which was concealed the gauze saturated with chloroform. He held it over the struggling man's mouth and nose. Alpasha was soon out and fell on the floor half way into the box. Dudley shone the light on his poupon face and was satisfied that they had the right person. He dragged him out of the stall and closed the door.

-Phone Johnny, it's the right guy. - Deana looked and nodded.

There was a road way leading to the stable and Johnny materialized in less than a minute. Now gagged, tied and unconscious, Alpasha was stuffed in the trunk of the car and away they went.

It took less than thirty minutes to get back to Fort Lee and the camping site. There they transferred their prize, rolled it in a blanket and placed him perpendicularly at the top of the bed.

Number one, two to go. At two o'clock as planned, they left the camping ground after asking directions to get to the 95 south. Most probably a retired cop, the gate keeper had some friendly advice to dispense.

-If someone rear-ends you in a deserted area don't stop floor it. We've had several incidences where hoodlums would smash a car and, when the passenger got out they would rob him and sometimes rough up the poor man.-

What a surprise these little brats would have; but not much chance of this thought Johnny, and he was on his way, knowing that the old cop would remember his face until the end of time.

If Cyrus Alpasha was living alone as they had established, his disappearance would not be noticed before morning when the maid would come in; maybe even later, as Deana had given enough hay to the horses to last them until noon.

-Let's hope the other two are as easy and we'll be home before noon. - Said Deana yawning. She was soon asleep on the living room sofa while Johnny drove the motor-home back to the highway, direction New York.

Driving around New York City at twelve thirty in the morning is a piece of cake and almost worth the exercise. Johnny couldn't help but reminisce when they had traveled to New York to settle the disagreement with the Rossini family. That arrangement had lasted more than ten years and would still be flourishing if the Maine Department of Environmental Protection had not messed it up. He felt jilted by the department. They had allowed several entrepreneurs like him to organize their lives around the collection and storage of scrap tires; then the DEP had suddenly realized that it could be dangerous. Johnny agreed that some precautions could have been taken but who was he to know that lightning could light a bonfire that would burn and pollute for several days. The real reason for the government's intervention was that most if not all the dump sites owners were evading income tax; whatever the reason, that game was over.

Johnny rested while Dudley drove for two hours. He quickly showered, shaved and changed his clothing for a blue cover all; he then became the navigator for Dudley. They would be an hour early and agreed to park the motorhome in a shopping center, unhitch the Corsica and grab a hearty breakfast.

-Wake up sleeping beauty. We're ready to hit the road after you check our patient.-

Deana woke up in the midst of a recurrent nightmare. She was reliving her struggle in the prison shower: crouching behind the fat bitch stretched out on her back under the shower. Deana was holding the monster's sparse hair while tilting the head backward so that the spray from the shower would fill her gaping, toothless mouth. Throughout she repeatedly slammed her knuckles on the Adam's apple of the powerful bull-dagger. The girl's massive arms could not protect the fragile throat as Deana had pinned one of them with her thigh and kept hitting the same spot under the chin until she felt the cartilage becoming granular. At the same time, and this was a new twist to the nightmare, she was choking on a stench similar to that of the Ali Baba cave in Bowdoin.

Barely nineteen when jailed for shoplifting; the judge thought that justice would be better served if she'd spend three months in jail for this petty thievery: a bottle of channel no 5, a Revlon lipstick and a deodorant.

-We hope that these three months will prepare you for a normal and honest life. - The magistrate pronounced while ogling the great body of his victim. He knew better; as Nietzsche wrote. – *Those who associate with monsters become monsters*. - Since when could living with hard core criminals redress a fragile mind; but the prison system needed to be kept full.

The fat lesbian had made her move attacking from behind, wrapping two enormous arms around Deana's waist, wrapping most of the slight body with her blubber; not unlike a phagocyte digesting a virus or an anaconda choking a goat.

The previous day Deana had witnessed the tactic when a tenderfoot had been attacked and raped by the fat butch and her friends. Day and night, they would continue to torture the poor girl until she became sick enough to be noticed by the guard and removed. Alone, young and pretty Deana did not have to be told that she was next.

Being in jail was more or less a sinecure for the likes of Thelma Brookland. She would be in a preferred environment to satisfy her perversity while not lacking any of the comfort she was used to: sex, cigarettes, drugs and booze. Like a school yard bully, she would harass the weaker inmates and take whatever was available.

Terrified by what she had witnessed but drawing courage out of her despair, Deana had worked out a plan. Having developed a strategy allowed her to sleep that night; she fell into a dreamless sleep while going over the moves one last time. She was ready for Thelma or for any one trying to enslave her; no way would she become a sexual victim again.

Out of the corner of her eye, she detected a movement outside the shower stall. Rather than facing the in coming two hundred and fifty pounds Thelma, flapping veined udders a blue ribbon-winning Holstein would have been proud of, Deana feigned a carefree attitude continuing to apply more soap on her waist. And seeming to cooperate she turned her back to Thelma and advanced to the back of the stall, right under the shower nozzle.

She had reached the far wall when she felt the huge arms coming around to take hold of her soapy and slippery waist. Taking support with her extended arms on the terrazzo wall while bending her knees slightly, Deana tensed her entire body and exploded like a bow, snapping her head backward to the full extent her neck would allow.

If the hurt on her own head was any indication, fat Thelma would be dazed if the point of impact had been her chin or nose. Butted unexpectedly on the chin the fat bitch's knees buckled and she slowly crashed to the floor unable to hold on to Deana's slippery waist.

Deana`s game plan was simple. Nowhere to run to, this fight had to go the limit. She quickly turned around and kneeled behind the collapsed naked mountain of goat cheese and pinned one of the arms between her thighs. Inserting her index and auricular finger in the large nostrils, she tilted the head backward under the full jet of the shower. She then started hitting the now exposed wind pipe with her fist. It took more than three minutes for all movements to stop. Thelma was dead.

What had started as a routine jail rape of a smaller pretty inmate by a larger and stronger bull-dagger would end up as another unsolved homicide. Like yesterday, the other inmates, naked and dripping, watched but did not interfere. On the contrary, today, one of Thelma's friends tried to intervene but was tripped and held under the shower nozzle for a while. The gallery calmly applauded when the immense maggot went limp and defecated on the wet floor. She was dead and would not harass anyone anymore.

As usual, the prison guards were paid to stay away until the rape was consummated. On schedule, casually walking in ten minutes later, they discovered a very dead Thelma. There was not a thing they could do, no one would tell and they could hardly believe that Deana had performed this impossible task alone.

She stirred and looked around finding her bearing. After drying the perspiration from her forehead and neck, Deana opened a black leather bag, out of which she took a syringe and a vial containing a yellowish liquid. After puncturing the rubber seal of the vial with the needle attached to the syringe, she pulled the plunger back and aspirated most of the content into the syringe. Two steps away, a large lump on the bed, Alpasha was waking up, moving and mumbling. She found a nice vein on the man's right arm and injected him with the full content.

—— CHAPTER 32 ——

"Vice and virtue are products like vitriol and sugar."
H Taine

One little piggy went to the market and found......James Rupert.

For his immediate neighbors and business partners, James Rupert was a good looking, distinguished and proper gentleman. Trim, well dressed and wealthy, he would be attractive to most women but had always shied away from females. It dated back to when he was fifteen years old. An older cousin was visiting for the summer and had intentions uncharacteristic of a Baptist young lady.

She had been trying to snare James for more than a week when she finally succeeded in being at the right place at the right time. James had been curious about sex, but like most young boys, skittish about paying more than lip service to the subject. His cousin Catherine was a good looking, vigorous young girl, barely two years older than he; this age when not yet a full grown woman and no longer a girl; spending the summer in this prim and proper fundamentalist setting bored her profoundly. Nothing better to do during most of the day than to nourish her fantasies; isn't sexual exploration a constant preoccupation for adolescents and always a good way to fight boredom?

And it happened as expected: One hazy Monday afternoon, they pushed opened the large rotting wooden door of the old barn. Their promenades around the property had been taking them closer and closer to this gloomy relic of ancient time; for different reason, the exploration of this refuge had been the unspoken objective of both since the first day.

-What a nice old barn, do you think it would be ok to go inside? - She had candidly proposed. But until now, James had always avoided taking this last step of pushing the door opened.

Easy to open but It was difficult to close the large partly unhinged door. The effort left them perspiring and breathing hard; or was it the anticipation. Once inside the old barn, the daylight could hardly penetrate through the cracks in the walls and roof; a soft half light, speared on the south side by a multitude of laser-like sun rays, hitting the ground at a forty five degree angle. For a moment, possessed by the spirit of this weird environment, they remained silent, listening for unusual sounds, searching for creatures in ambush behind an old cart. A cat scuttled out through a broken board. She touched his arm for comfort.

Ankle deep in hay, Catherine made a few steps, looking at the high ceiling, intercepting with her hands the golden energy piercing the thin roof. A few swallows were silently flying in and out catering to their fledglings. She stood immobile a long moment; then she span around and pressed her body against his. He could feel the imprint of her budding nipples burning a hole in his puny chest. Her hands were around his back while his hung loosely, pinned on his hips; James' mind was frozen in neutral. Slightly taller Catherine raised her hands, cupped his head and kissed him on the mouth. Not one of those innocent first kisses where the lips barely touch, where the lips remain dry, no, it was meant to be a passionate kind, her tongue trying to invade his tightly closed lips. Grabbing his hand, she dragged him to the loft where hay from last year would provide a proper setting and maybe a comfortable cushion for what she had in mind. First sexual experience for James only.

She pushed James down on his knees and, standing up over him, proceeded to strip completely. In a minute she had removed dress, shirt, undergarment, panties and even shoes. As naked as the day she was born, she was slowly pivoting to expose her complete body to stunned and open mouthed James. Catherine was a bit plump but nevertheless exquisitely round, budding in the right places with a downy spot at the junction of her thighs.

James was awe struck and didn't have a clue as to where to begin but was nevertheless feeling very funny all over. He had read about the subject but was about to find out that some experience cannot be acquired from books. She bent down and rubbing her hard nipples over his hair started to help him remove his shirt, then his shoes, then his pants and finally pulled down on his boxer short exposing his ....penis.

She then did something that screwed poor James' life forever; a pivotal moment for our Romeo. Catherine's experience had been with older boys who were quickly aroused showing an erected and pulsing penis as proof. Looking at James' tiny, un-erected, flaccid penis, she giggled. The giggle increased to an uncontrollable laugh. James, ashamed and not understanding why he was not visibly aroused by this naked body started to cry. He then got mad and grabbed Catherine by the neck. He would have choked her to death if, for some unknown atavistic reasons, his penis had not started to react and become as hard as in the morning when he had a full bladder.

By then Catherine feared for her life and submitted to James awkward copulative technique, helping him find his way. When finished taking his pleasure he rolled back and still holding her wrist, told her.

-I'll kill you if you ever tell anyone about this.-

She had been unusually aroused by the brutality and had, for the first time, experienced what she later identified as an orgasm. Young James had a need to be brutal and would only get an erection if she cried. Catherine was discovering that her real sexuality involved masochism while James was developing a latent sadism; a perfect couple. During the following days, she would masturbate him and herself endlessly, while he was pulling her hair or pinching her buttock. Soon they decided to improve their scope of activity by inviting a ten year old neighbor to accompany them into the now infamous barn.

A neat looking kid, well mannered and properly educated, Ted, tried to run away when Catherine began her strip tease. James forced him to watch. They then removed his clothing and while James was holding him, she masturbated the now not so unhappy ten year old boy while she placed James penis in her mouth. He immediately had an orgasm and before she was finished with the boy he had had another one. He had found his way.

Over the next two weeks they relentlessly pursued their research, all three performing various functions on each of the partners interchanging roles as often as they would think of it. When with tears in her eyes Catherine had to go back home, James and Teddy continued to meet in the barn. James found it even more pleasant just the two of them.

In September, going back to boarding school, he was devastated but pragmatically obeyed the rules. Teddy and his family moved to California. James had identified his sexual preferences: forcing young boys to have sex with him was what he would spend the rest of his life pursuing.

The sadism imprinted in his neurons and now organized as a strong and essential behavioral pattern needed to be tamed. After a while he found that real and total submission, not the feigned variety he knew Catherine was often pretending, became necessary for him to achieve fulfillment of his sexual fantasies. That scared him as it was in contradiction with everything taught him since birth by a strictly no non sense puritanical setting.

He tried to change his way of thinking, attempted to have normal sex with female partners but had to submit to the evidence: he was a bona fide pedophile as well as a sadist. That would never change. So be it and he submitted to this tyranny without further questioning his destiny.

Several years after this famous summer, he had graduated to real sadism, enjoying situations like the one he had experienced at the O'Reilly family. It wasn't the first time Steven had provided fresh partners and new experiences for him and others. It was costing a lot but what is money for. Knowing that these kids would be completely fucked up for life made him feel like superman. He had abused all three kids and spanked the six year old. He had viewed the clip featuring his prowesses so often that he had had to repair the broken tape twice. He would phone Steven soon to have another session. Maybe he could take one of the kids homes with him for a week.

When hard up he would drive in the vicinity of one of the youth centers in the Boston area. Often he would be lucky enough to pick up a desperate kid in need of a fix. After shaving every hair of their bodies he would submit them to whatever he had dreamed of and concocted. He sometimes would keep them drugged, tied and gagged for two three days. He would then release them and give them a large enough amount of money to purchase their silence. Whatever the money promised they would not come back for a second helping of the same.

James Rupert's compulsion had led to the ultimate in sadism: torture and death. He had been dreaming of this ultimate thrill for several years and was getting desperate to execute his plan. Disposing of the body was the most difficult part but he had devised a way which he thought to be foolproof.

After three days spent in abusing one of his victims, he had finally decided to test his theory. He subdued the thirteen year old boy, stuffed him in a weighted nylon sleeping bag and loaded the package in his Cessna. A pilot since he was 18, he had a private landing strip adjacent to his property.

Flying over one of the lakes in the middle of the family two thousand acre woodland holding, he had dropped the bag in the deepest part. Weighted with fifty pounds of nails the body would never be recovered. He was now ready to do it again and the intended victim was the eleven year old Don O'Reilly.

Steven had agreed to sell Don, like a pound of flesh or a spring lamb, for one hundred and fifty thousand dollars. The amount was of little importance to James Rupert. To Steven it was a way to increase his power over the rest of the family as well as assuring his financial security. He would blackmail James Rupert.

CHAPTER 33

"When a fool seems reasonable it is time to place him in a straight jacket."
E A Poe

The gang of three, as they would jokingly call themselves, came off highway 95 at the Dedham exit without any precise plan. So far improvisation had worked well. Going north on this highway for approximately two miles they reached a large shopping mall where they parked the motor home and enjoyed a substantial breakfast.

The open ended strategy they had decided upon was again as simple and hopefully would be as successful as the preceding ones. No frills, no complication, find the simplest, most discreet and efficient way to get in and out. What can be less noticeable during the summer months than a gardening crew walking on a lawn early in the morning? Dudley and Deana, disguised and dressed as gardeners would start trimming James Rupert's cedar hedge; close enough to the front door so Rupert would hear them and come out. It was obvious that Rupert had already had his own people performing this task. He would come out screaming.

The bacon and eggs hit the spot and after the second cup of coffee they were wide awake. Not much conversation, looking forward to a happy conclusion. Contrary to the usual weak coffee served in North America, this one had character and realigned eye balls in front of the holes pierced in the skull for that purpose.

-We'll need ten minutes to get to the house and the same to close the deal. Let's go, but before that let's check the cellular phones to make sure they work in this area. - Deana said.

Johnny was driving the Corsica with Dudley in front. They soon arrived in front of a sumptuous property featuring two huge stone pillars guarding a cobble stone driveway leading to the house. Grabbing shears and rakes they had brought for that purpose, Dud and Deana got out of the Corsica and walked down a path separated from the driveway by a stone fence.

Johnny drove on for another fifteen hundred feet, turned the car around and opened the hood as if having mechanical trouble. He angrily kicked the front tire and started futzing under the hood as if he knew what he was doing.

Dudley and Deana nonchalantly reached the old and stately stone house. The mansion was a master piece of early eighteenth century English architecture, girdled by edges and flowers. It could have been displayed in any issue of house and garden magazine. Everywhere, little ponds scattered over to break the monotony, different trees, beds of magnificent flowers punctuating the emerald green of the grounds, was the matrix enclosing this gem of a house. Some two hundred feet behind the house was a hangar, opening onto a private air strip; a white Cessna was parked along side the hangar.

No dogs, at least not of the alert variety. Not a sound from the neighbors, sleeping soundly at five o'clock in the morning. Only the paper boy could be intruding, but he had already been there; Deana was happy to see the morning paper under a rose bush, six feet to the left of the main door.

They started doing what gardeners do, clipping away, making as much noise as was credible. It was not long before their strategy produced the expected results. A shade had been moved, and then the front door opened on a portly man, the right age to be James Rupert, obviously naked under a crimson bath robe. He was furious to have been awakened and even more infuriated to see his beloved hedge being hacked at by amateurs.

-What the hell are you guys doing? You're in the wrong place, get away from here before I call the police. –

His voice was strained; anger filled but kept low, as if not to arouse the neighbors. Dudley looked surprised, even offended.

-I'm sure this is the right place. We were dropped here by Ted of « CLEAR CUT Inc ». He just left us here to go to another contract. Let me phone him on his cell phone. – Dudley replied as he started moving closer to the front door.

While Dudley was speaking, Rupert was looking for his newspaper. He saw it in the usual place, and walked over bare foot in the flower bed to retrieve it. Deana, who had purposely been working in this flower bed, moved between the door and Rupert, as Dudley was continuing his approach. He repeated:

-This is a misunderstanding and if we can use the phone we'll be leaving. Sorry about waking you up. - As he was speaking, he grabbed both shoulders and spun the man around like a weather vane.

He then placed a hand on Rupert's mouth while the other was finding two large testicles that he squashed as hard as he could. That got Rupert's undivided attention and Dudley began pushing him towards the half opened front door.

From one of her ample pockets, Deana retrieved a plastic bag, out of which she pulled chiffon soaked with chloroform. Without impeding the progression towards the door, she placed it over Rupert's nose. The pressure on his testicles had already paralyzed the man and the chloroform put an end to the intolerable pain. Dudley charged him on his shoulders and crossed the threshold.

While unloading the limp body on a couch, Dudley continued talking as if he was finishing the conversation started outside.

-We'll be just a moment and we'll leave as soon as we can reach our employer on the phone.-

Deana had closed the door after surveying the immediate environment. Not a soul in sight. She quickly took out her formidable silenced .45 and inspected the first floor of the house as Dudley continued his masquerade of phoning his employer.

-Hey Ted, you left us at the wrong address. Come back and pick us up. This guy wants to call the cops.-

He hung up, gagged and tied the unconscious Rupert before going up the spiral staircase to inspect the second story. As he reached the last step of the solid oak stairway, he heard a toilet being flushed. He was waiting in ambush when a bald headed adolescent walked out, stark naked.

-What's your name kid? - Asked Dudley as he pushed him hard against the wall, imprisoning both arms in his big hands.

-Hey what's going on, you're hurting me, leave me alone. - Half screamed the kid.

-Shut up and answer my question.-

-I don't know anything about his business. The dope was his, not mine. Don't bring me in, my parents would die if they knew that I ...- He didn't continue. Avoiding Dudley's eyes.

Dudley knew what the poor kid was about to say. Once hooked, they'll do anything for this fucking dope and bastards like Rupert knew where to look for sexual partners; sexual victims being a better word.

-Are you the only one in here?-

-Yes we're alone. He's a fucking pervert and it's about time you guys caught up with him. - Then as a second thought, he continued.

-He bragged about having killed one kid. Said he had dropped his body in a lake. At first I thought he wanted to scare me more than I already was, but he gave so many details that I believed him. Details like stuffing the still live boy in a weighted sleeping bag, then transporting him in his plane, listening to the poor bastard yelling and then dropping him..... Nut, a fucking nut, that's what he is. Thank god you're here. – Said the kid, who thought the police was raiding the house.

-We won't harm you. Don't try to see us or to remember anything about us. I'll tie your hands and feet. Gag you and put a tape over your eyes. Then I'll put you to sleep. – Said Dudley.

Realizing that he wasn't dealing with the police, the adolescent started to wiggle fearing that he would be harmed by another pervert. Last night had provided him with enough depravity for a lifetime. When tied to the four posts of the bed, at the mercy of this bastard, he had been convinced that he would also be travelling inside a sleeping bag weighted with fifty pounds of nails, to a resting place at the bottom of a lake. Never again, not even for a million would he be picked up by one of these nut cases.

Gently Dudley pushed the kid in a bedroom where, by the look and smell of it, he had spent the night. Nylon ropes were still attached to the bed posts. He laid him on the bed, tied and gagged him. He was about to leave when he turned back and covered him with a blanket; Deana would put him out until noon. Once asleep the bonds would be loosened so that he could get away.

-We're done here. - Dudley told Johnny on the cell phone.

He walked down the stairs and helped Deana stuff Rupert in a large orange plastic bag of the sort used to carry twigs and leaves. She had found several of these in the kitchen and lining three together she had developed a perfect body bag. She punched a few holes near the top so that Rupert would be able to breathe. Unfortunately the plastic could not take the weight and it began splitting. Looking around in one of the closets she found a brand new nylon sleeping bag; that would do. She opened it wide, wrapped Rupert's body into it and zipped it up, leaving an opening for air. It would be counter productive to carry a corpse back to Bowdoin.

As Dudley was opening the front door Johnny was pulling in the drive way and backing the Corsica as close as possible to the front door. It's amazing how much volume a car trunk will hold if the parcel is soft and malleable.

The operation had taken less than thirty minutes from the time Johnny had dropped them to the time they departed. They were getting to be good at this.

-Where did you find the sleeping bag? - And then not waiting for a response. – Maybe this kid was telling the truth after all. I'll know soon enough. - Mumbled Dudley.

-What are you talking about? Anyway, he'll fit on the floor between the bed and the wall in the motor home. This will leave enough space for the lady. - Said Deana. And she exhaled deeply letting out a low pitched victory cheer.

-This one may have been a real artist. - Said Dudley. – Let's go, so much wickedness is scary -

—— CHAPTER 34 ——

"The true egoist will accept that others are happy if he is the cause of their happiness."
Jules Renard

Madeleine Worthington, Victim and predator.

If in general life is misery, one should at least not feel targeted by fate; chance governs our lives as it does the rest of the universe. Chance is the architect: Darwin proposed this hypothesis to support his theory: - *Organisms are in a constant flux of aleatory mutations*-; only those mutations improving survival probabilities as demonstrated by the surviving mutant, become part of the genetic package.

Why are they passed on to the next generations? While these modifications happened strictly by accident, not because of a perceived benefit to the animal or the plant, - often the contrary occurs-they will become part of the hereditary package only if survival of the organisms is enhanced or at least not impaired. Should it be a deleterious change, the organism carrying the mutant gene, will be less able to fend for itself and die before it can reproduce. For instance we rarely see two headed calves surviving to procreate, they usually die before having had a chance to reproduce, the modification being a handicap to their survival.

Until economic stability was achieved, handicapped children did not survive. Today, these individuals survive in most countries, those able to procreate pass on the genes which have effected their mutations, further adding to the 70 000 billion possible combinations that intervene in sexual reproduction. The question posed here : are deviant mutations such as those found in pedophiles, mass murderers, sexual abusers, part of the human genome or induced by the environment of the subject or simply, as said Freud, an unrepressed search for pleasure.

Pit bulls, may be programmed to be gentle or malicious even though they have been selectively bred to carry and propagate an aggressive trait in their genes; or can they? Won't they be more prone to bouts of ferocity than for example a Labrador who is bred for his gentleness and docility? Is it the same with humans? While we have made unprecedented strides in improving our knowledge of the human genome we certainly are still far from being able to rearrange the wiring of the mind once it is organized with billions of neuronal communications. It seems that the primary program always lurks from its hideaway and takes over. And there is the epigenetic conundrum to further complicate this biological maze.

Chance was good to Madeleine Worthington: she was born in a wealthy family, the first and only child of Adolph and Myriam Worthington. Chance was dreadful to Madeleine Worthington: her mother died when she was only three. The father never remarried.

Having inherited a more than substantial fortune, Adolph spent his entire life managing his assets and increased the size of his wealth to heights that would have given dizzy spell and scared his father and grand father. He was a good manager and today, at age 83, even though bedridden, he still administers his sizable estate with all the sagacity of a Warren Buffet; as a matter of fact he has always followed the lead of Mister Buffet and held a substantial number of shares in Berkshire Hathaway.

While an expert in money matters he was a monstrous, execrable and despicable father. Like most powerful men, Adolph had an insatiable craving to phagocyte and possess. Debased by his demands, his wife had been driven to suicide; once the sole parent to Madeleine, his instinct soon drove him to have inappropriate relations with her.

As soon as she became conscious of the wickedness of this relationship Madeleine tried to break away from this domineering father; but always, either his mental dominance over her, or the fear of being disinherited, had defeated her good intentions. He was as carefully managing his daughter's mind and behavior, as he was managing his investments: prohibiting steady relationships with young men or anyone for that matter, and always demanding that she be attentive to his needs. At the same time he would lavish her with expensive gifts. Devoid of self respect Madeleine could not find enough resources to prevent this programming of her brain and the wrecking of her life.

It became a way of life and a " pis aller" for Madeleine. Not knowing anything else, having grown into this situation from age three, it was easier to suffer through it than to evade from it. In time, the glue became so sticky that she was not able to extract herself from the trap and she continued living with her father, submitting to this inappropriate relationship during more than 50 years.

Money buys most material things and Madeleine had no material needs unfulfilled. Her modeling business was thriving; she was driving the best cars, had access to all that money buys, but she would have to cater to her father until he died. Unfortunately the old man was holding on to life, not in a hurry to go to hell.

-Madeleine come here a moment. - He would yell at her, and she would trot to his bedside forever the submissive little girl.

From age thirteen, she had gradually sublimated devotion and adoration into hate and contempt. To assuage her own situation she had taken relief in abusing young boys. Almost defensively, when only fourteen, she had abused the son of a cousin she was caring for after school; he was the first. Her "shrink" had interpreted this as a revenge on her father through younger males; humans tend to equalize the level of miseries from the top down never the reverse. She would have liked to practice her villainies on larger males but was not up to it yet.

She had a cat: Myriam, named after her mother. Myriam was all of fifteen years old. Madeleine would have died for that cat. Her father, knowing her affection for the animal was always threatening to "get rid of her", pretending:

-I'm allergic to cats and she'll have to go one of these days.-

Adolph was not aware that he was playing Russian roulette when using this approach to control Madeleine. She would not hesitate to kill her father if he really threatened the life of Myriam the cat. The animal represented Madeleine's only link to reality. Cats are not immortal and Madeleine had mourned the natural death of several of her feline companions. Always there would be a ritualistic burial in one of the animal cemeteries, with appropriately engraved tombstone. Always a new cat would be purchased, this kitten identical to the predecessors and perpetuating the name Myriam. A sample of the current Myriam's DNA had been taken and frozen; a clone would be made of Myriam when she died. Money can satisfy most whims.

In the final analysis, as pointed out by her psychiatrist, the value of the inheritance, the threats on the cat, the lavish gifts he would give her, as well as other subtleties, kept Madeleine dancing to the tunes the incestuous monster would play.

Five years ago, Madeleine had met Steven through one of their mutual friends in the Modeling industry and had since been a steady customer of his. Always the same routine, Steven would procure a young boy that she would brow beat, humiliate, spank, dress as a girl to finally arrive at the climax of her program.

She always wondered if there would be a need to continue these perverse habits when her father went in hell where he belonged. Probably not, she thought. For the present, her perversity gave her the sense that she was getting some sort of revenge. Doctor Murenby, her " shrink" said it provided her with a personality of her own; being able to control another human being alleviated her own servitude to Adolph Worthington; a sort of revitalization of her lost self respect.

Wondering if she would have been a normal person if raised in a proper environment, the shrink had answered that:

-You would undoubtedly have been a normal person had it not been for your early and unremitting unusual experience. You would have married and would have had kids of your own instead of cats.-

She sometimes deplored not having had a family and used to cry at night even as late as in her thirties. But then her father would slip by her side and her sorrow would metamorphose into hatred and repugnance.

Doctor Murenby had surmised that hatred and total submission was playing in her father's hand. That's what Adolph needed to be aroused. Forcing her into submission while perceiving her tremendous hate and repulsion, was the pleasure he derived from his incestuous relationship.

-Nothing is out of reach for the powerful, nothing too good or too bad. Like for the "super being" Nietzsche created, new rules could be made and old ones adapted to accommodate the super man he was: Adolph Worthington, super rich and powerful, superman because he cheats and gets away with it.-

And he continued.

-He made you his daughter and his property, his slave, as a replacement for Myriam his wife. She who deserted him by committing suicide without his permission.-

His wife Myriam was such an obedient and submissive creature, his creature; then one day he came home and she was no more, having chosen to die rather than to continue being a victim and a prey.

-In a sense you're paying the price for your mother's escape from hell. - Diagnosed doctor Murenby.

-Oh Mother, - Madeleine would sometimes pray, - I understand your decision, but why did you not take me with you. That would have been a true act of motherly love.-

—— CHAPTER 35 ——

"We should all pardon our enemies; but not before they hang."
H. Heine

-The last one. Let's hope that it goes as smoothly as for the others. We've been either lucky or very good. If you weren't with me Deana, I'd think that you were making a Guinness record class cuckold out of me.- Muttered Dudley, saying aloud what the others were thinking.

-You know I wouldn't do a thing like that. - Replied Deana with a sweet smile.

Amazing how she could be so angelic most of the time; they both knew better. He could still vividly see her cauterizing the hand and the elbow of that devilish Smith. Angels can be cold.

It was decided that Johnny would remain in the Motor Home and rest while Dudley and Deana would visit with Madeleine Worthington. Driving in and around Boston is hectic anytime but requires nerves of steel during morning rush hour. They left the Motor Home around seven and figured they would be in front of 2772 Dorchester Ave. in less than an hour. It took a little more than seventy minutes which didn't disturb their plans, as Deana always planned with a twenty five percent margin in her favor.

The street was following Fort Point Channel and the Condominiums were extravagantly plush with the security one would expect. It was out of the question to casually walk in as they had been able to so far. The abduction would have to be carried out on the side walk. Madeleine was known to walk the four hundred meters to work every morning.

They parked the car midway between the condo and her place of business. Miss Worthington usually arrived at work between eight and nine, and from eight, Dudley was walking up and down the side walk. The circulation was light on this street and the sidewalk was near empty except for a few joggers, trotting alongside the channel; but they would be too busy sweating and breathing hard to notice anything unusual. Joggers are seldom attentive to the scenery, focusing on the task at hand and trying to avoid stepping in dogs' droppings.

A few cars had been coming out of the underground garage but as far as he could determine, Madeleine was not in any of them.

-Ah , there she is.-

Too far to see her face but it had to be her; late fifties, a slim and elegant silhouette. He had seen her in various stages of undress but he remembered her face perfectly, drooping lower lip, cold hard eyes and a prominent nose. As she approached, he tapped on the roof of the car although that was unnecessary; Deana had recognized her in the rear view mirror.

About a few hundred feet down the street, two joggers were puffing their way towards them, trying to talk as they ran. They would be by the Corsica before Madeleine reached it. No one else using the side walks within several hundred feet and the few cars driving by were all speeding, late for work.

Dudley opened the hood of the car and seemed intent on fixing something, only his massive rear end protruding from under the hood. Deana had come out of the car and was telling him off while also bending inside the open hood.

-So big yet so stupid. It's your car, you should be able to fix it. I'll be late as usual. Why can't you earn enough to buy a good car not a play toy.-

The car door was opened and partly blocking the side walks. As Madeleine Worthington walked by, Deana jerked out from under the hood and bumped the lady. She dropped her crocodile bag. Deana apologized while moving to box Madeleine between her, the car and Dudley:

-So sorry I didn't see you coming. This big oaf is so clumsy.-

-Never mind I'm not hurt but be careful next time.- Spat out the arrogant Miss Worthington as she bent down to retrieve her bag from the dirty sidewalk.

Using Deana as a shield, Dudley who had emerged from under the hood, placed one knee on the ground as if to help Madeleine recover her bag. Grabbing Worthington's right forearm with his left hand, he exploded a short right jab to her chin , just as he had done so often when confronted with aggressive drunk customers at The Saint Augustine. The big fist travelling only a few inches but at great speed, the movement originating from the knees and hips found its mark. Madeleine didn't see the blow coming and never knew what hit her.

Standing close behind, Deana supported her under the arm pits, keeping her upright. They swiftly pushed the limp body over to the back door which was still open and, after wedging Miss Worthington onto the floor, between the front and back seat, Deana threw the expensive crocodile bag in after her. A blanket which had been lying on the seat just for that purpose was spread over the inert mass. As Dudley was closing the hood, Deana got in the back seat and they were off. It had taken less than a minute from the time Madeleine Worthington had been bumped.

As they were driving away unhurriedly, Deana looked around and was satisfied that they had not been seen. Reaching for her little black bag she retrieved a fully loaded syringe removed the protector cap and lifting only a corner of the blanket injected Madeleine Worthington with enough anesthetic agent to keep her sedated for the next four hours. Then she crawled to the front seat with the expensive Gucci bag and relaxed a while before talking.

-You know I'm glad it's over, but I don't remember being so keyed up. Maybe the last time was when I broke my step father's knees after removing his testicles. I can still hear the bones breaking. The son of a bitch. That's why I want to see this through. You understand don't you?- She sounded almost apologetic.

-I know darling, I know. – Said Dudley soothingly.

He was concentrating on his driving and did not want to get involved in a complicated conversation with his wife. He knew just how it was, she had been dreaming about it enough since they had been together that he knew every stinking detail of her ordeals.

Deana had started her search of Worthington's handbag and was happy to confirm that the sleeping witch on the floor was Madeleine Worthington who would be late for work this morning and forever after.

It took considerably less time to drive back to the Motor Home as they were not bucking the traffic. When they arrived, Johnny was as they had left him, mounting guard, sitting in the driver's seat. He seemed relieved to see them back so soon. Not yet ten o'clock and they were ready to head back to Lewiston.

-What took you so long, are you getting sloppy? –He managed to say while trying to see under the blanket.

-This parking lot is still vacant and we could move the merchandise now or a little further down the road where there will be absolutely no one. –

The shopping center was slowly coming to life for another day of business; too many people who could remember seeing something unusual; maybe a video surveillance for the parking lot.

-Let's drive a while Johnny, Deana and I will lead the way, follow us until we stop. - Suggested Dudley.

Ten minutes later they made the transfer and hitched the Corsica back to the Motor Home. They restored the original plate on the little car and, except for three gagged and drugged clandestine passengers, were very legit.

CHAPTER 36

"Gorski's home."

-Harry I'm home-

Shouted Anne Gorski as she was closing the front door. She had been delayed half a day coming home and surprised that her phone calls were not answered.

-Harry, where are you? I'm home. - She repeated.

Climbing the stairs to the second floor, she abruptly paused on the first step noticing the bare floor in the living room. Her Chinese carpets were no longer in place. She hurried upstairs fearing that a thief had broken into the house, stolen the carpets and who knows what else.

In front of Harry's office, she could see that the door had been forced open and closed again. His office was his castle, his private garden; Harry would spend more time in this little room than any where else in the house. The door was always locked and never could she enter, he'd do the cleaning himself.

-I'm writing a book.-Was his answer to her questions.

-Oh, she would say, how marvelous. Let me read it, maybe I can help.-

-Not until it's finished. It's more difficult than I thought.-

Always the same dialogue always the same desire for privacy as if he was hiding something. He would not even tell her what the book was about.

She knocked on the battered door and waited, listening, no answer, no noise.

-Are you OK Harry? - No answer. –Answer me damn you.-

She now feared the worse; the carpets missing, the door broken, the car in the garage, his clothing still on the bed and Harry had not answered her several telephone calls. He had to be in his office.

Anne was a slight woman. The door sustained her efforts to open it. It would take a larger person than herself to break it open. The massive oak door, equipped with a special lock was meant to prevent all entries, particularly hers. Whoever had broken it open had slammed the door back and the lock had snapped shut.

She ran down the stairs, in search of something heavy, not ready to phone 911; he could have been taking a walk in the neighborhood park which would explain the car in the garage. No she thought, Harry never left the house on foot and why would the carpets be removed, the door of his office broken? But she could not find any traces of forced entry anywhere else in the house.

Out of breath and hyper ventilating, she forced herself to sit down, to breathe slowly and deeply: ten respirations per minute each held five seconds. The perspiration, dripping from her fore head was increasing the nervousness. Last year she had taken a course on how to relax and stay cool when confronted with difficult situations. She had been successful in regaining her composure several times during the last months: her menopause was playing havoc with her mind. After only a few minutes of deep, slow, belly breathing, it worked once more. Signing up for this course had been the best investment she had ever made. Like pushing a button, composure was back. She slowly went to the fridge and filled a glass with ice cubes and water, drank it and felt the coldness of the water flooding her distressed brain.

Ten minutes more; she would wait ten minutes more. Then she would ask Tom, her long time neighbor and friend to use a crow bar and break open the door. Let's not phone 911 unless you know you have an emergency, the warning said.

Ten minutes went by, Harry had not returned. She walked over next door. Tom was home.

-I don't like breaking doors open but if this is what you want me to do I'll do it.-

Tom was a large man and the door, already battered by Dudley, yielded after the second try with a ten pound hammer she had found in the garage. A quick inspection reassured her that her husband was not lying on the floor. A second look on the desk divulged Harry's secret: a few pictures were still there. Tom who was behind her saw them as well and prudently retreated out of the office.

How does one react when suddenly realizing that her husband of more than thirty years is a fucking pervert pedophile? Standing off balance in front of this desk, lined with these horrible pictures, some of them depicting her husband in action produced a feeling of such emptiness deep within her soul, that Anne stopped breathing. Time stopped, as it would during a nuclear explosion, she had lost her ability to move, to breath, to think, just standing there, frozen like Lot's wife had been when fleeing Sodom and Gomorra. Mercilessly she fainted. Tom carried her to the next bedroom. He then dialed 911.

He had several minutes alone and he went back into Harry's office. Anne was weeping, almost inaudibly, a soft hopeless sound. He returned to the bedroom and sat on the side of the bed just holding her hand, not saying a word. His mind could not come up with anything constructive or reassuring; Tom was a practical man.

-Should we not close that door for now, you may want to think over your next move.-

Nothing much to think about; the evidence undeniable; the man in the pictures was Harry: front and side ways; he was sodomizing this young boy; there were more pictures of the same with other kids. The photos had all been enlarged and the horrendous details were perfectly represented. But yes, better wait until she could confront her sick husband.

-You're a good friend Tom, thanks... You're right, I'll wait until I can talk this over... with some one before going to the police.-

What a mess. What a way to end one's life. The magnitude of this situation crushed her, destroyed her instincts. Her fibrillating mind could not make sense of the information it processed. All her senses were alerted; adrenaline was flooding her arteries and the effort demanded by her body to cope with this overload was draining every last gram of energy, leaving her ragged.

When the police came, she refused to be transported to the hospital.

I feel a lot better now; I'll see my family doctor this afternoon. -

She had reported the theft of her expansive carpets and the cops looked around for evidence; found none, not even forced entry to the house. After writing down the description of the carpets they left.

In the afternoon Anne saw a friend of the family who was a lawyer. After looking at the photos and at one of the video Ken concluded:

You have to either burn this ...garbage or give it to the police. You won't have to testify against your husband but you may want to prepare your divorce..., unless you want to continue sharing the same roof with this sick person. Think about your children... -

The children; indeed the children; she was not there yet. Anne remained silent for a long moment and finally said :

You're right, I don't want to continue living with a pedophile. This god-damned picture I saw on his desk will haunt me until I die. I may never have sex again.–

And tears inundated her eyes and streaked her make up. Sex was not an important part of her life but the companionship she had enjoyed with Harry had been tranquil. Her Titanic was sinking. Could she find a life boat or better... sink with it. What about the children how would she tell them. Had Harry been improper with them? So many questions, no answers.

It was late afternoon before the police lieutenant Paterson took the deposition and collected the pornographic material. Why so many cases of infantile pornography all of a sudden. He couldn't help establishing a parallel with the O'Reilly family. He asked Anne before leaving.

-Do you know if your husband knew a family by the name of O'Reilly living here in Lewiston.-

Anne thought for a moment but could not remember having ever heard Harry mention that name.

Back to the precinct, Paterson phoned Mrs. O'Reilly and said that he wanted to have a chat with her the next day.

-As you wish Lieutenant but I've decided not to pursue this matter any further. Steven has left us, so much the better and I'll leave well enough alone. If he ever comes back I'll file a complaint. – And she was thinking:- after I've killed the son of a sow.-

-I respect your decision but would like to talk to you just the same.-

-Fine, I'll see you, but the children won't talk to anyone.... I know you understand. - And she hung up.

Paterson understood and agreed with her decision. Too often he had seen the system backfire and deliver a final blow to the victims. In the best cases, the victims were further traumatized and stigmatized as defective human beings, forever soiled by their misfortunes. As if these poor abused kids needed to be brow beaten by foxy and devious lawyers who would go to any length to free their guilty clients. Paterson was of the opinion that some defense lawyers were often as bad as their clients.

CHAPTER 37

"Thinking is the cheapest of all pleasures."
Spinoza

Deana had good cause to wonder about man as a species. A person cannot be hurt as much as she had been without either becoming complacent and pragmatic or an angry survivor looking for answers and retribution. More a rebel than a gullible sponge, a brick at a time, Deana had built a model which almost satiated her need to better understand certain traits of humanity.

With anxiety and panic as constant escorts, that she had been a poor student was not a surprise; how can a ten year old kid be an alert student when she dreads coming home. She often wondered how many other kids were facing similar situations; ashamed she never mentioned her situation to friends.

Looking for deep rooted answers, she had been astonished to learn that, not some magic wand, but evolution had been the artisan, the crafts-man of all species, including man. No one had bothered telling her about this: God was credited with the creation of all things. God was behind this mess she thought; but he had let things follow their natural course as he had decided; was she told.

That chance had been and was still the architect of the universe and humanity, took a while longer to grasp. What was the role of this divine inter-vention she had been brainwashed with? Why the ethical difference between man and the other earthly creatures? Was consciousness "god given" or a product of evolution, or a by-product of the ability to think; or all of the above.

She accepted more readily that cultural traits were a product of the environment and of social requirements in the context of law and order. The analogy between training her dog and educating a child was easy to grasp.

Religions had conveniently used man's need to believe in miracles; extirpating the truth, buried under layers upon layers of opportunistic deceits, had been a long drawn-out exploit in itself. Bit by bit, after more than twenty years of effort, she was proud to have reasoned this enigma on her own; at least to her satisfaction.

Her readings on primatology taught her that among others, our immediate cousins the chimpanzees, both the larger -pan troglodytes- and the smaller variety the -pan paniscus- or the bonobo, are avid patrons of sexual pleasures. She also learned with some stupefaction that we share more than 98% of our genes with the chimpanzees; so much that someone has called the modern man: -the third Chimpanzee- and written a book on the subject. This close relationship could account for the animal nature of some of the sexual tendencies homo sapiens still carried forward as well as other predatory and survivor' s behavior. Were these exceptions or the hidden portion of the iceberg making up the structure of our culture? But then cultures were never static, continuously modified and remodeled to fit the environment; shaping it and being determined by it.

Deana was not sure that aberrations such as pedophilia came out of consciousness, the result of this continuous search for pleasure enhancement Homo sapiens is known for; or was it simply because consciousness caused man to invent good and bad, true and false, useful and harmful. And yet we are related to all creatures sharing our earth; and so far as we know, animals, whether our close or distant cousins, are unable to experience neither of these emotions. The animal world has no rules other than those imprinted in their genes: food and sex, these rules or call them instincts, oversee reproduction in a survival-of-the-fittest context. Deana was proud to have figured out this part of man's history.

She was aware that a few tribes were still practicing the Cro-Magnon way of life; their number rapidly fading to zero as evolution does not tolerate gross differences among the same species. They, like the bonobo's are on a constant search for food or pleasure, have no reserve whatsoever as to the mode of sexuality they practice: hetero, homo, pedo, communistic or whatever else they think of, libidinal imagination or sexual instinct being the only motor, as reported in Papouasie New Guinea.

Deana had come to formulate the theory that morality was a people gadget invented by religions to rule over the masses. In the animal world or in primitive tribal population, remorse is not triggered by the practice of one mode of sexuality or another; guilt is strictly a cultural trait, a rule of law dictated by traditions.

For that same reason, animals are eternal, as they do not foresee their deaths and conversely - bad- or –good- does not exist. Sexuality without man made morality becomes a natural impulse and a need to be satisfied like eating and defecating; sexuality can be a social nose-rubbing, like shaking hands for the modern man.

Her lectures had brought her to think that when there were surplus food and security; man would live out his fantasies. Wealth allowed a constant search for pleasure and the right to take libidinous license. These reflections had been obsessing Deana for a long time. She had been receiving first hand tutoring on the most perverted and warped behaviors encountered in the Western hemisphere; the last few days had rekindled her interest in the matter.

It was a surprise for Deana that a woman like Madeleine Worthington, having otherwise the world by the tail, could be so wicked and devious. Right or wrong we tend to think that the male of the species is more susceptible to such extremes. She had seen what females could do in prison, but the prison environment is conducive to the extraction and distillation of the ultimate wickedness and depravity out of its population, male or female.

-In a chance meeting with a female psychiatrist last week, I was told that more than 85% of the population is or has been subjected to some kind of sexual abuse by either members of the immediate family or friends. The degree will vary from improper touching to repetitive rapes. I thought that I was an exception but it appears that others have suffered a similar or worse fate. This psychiatrist also said that because there were so many of us exposed to this behavior, that it had always been a sub culture, you know .... taken for granted. She mentioned names of famous people who had incestuous relationships, for example the pharaohs and some great writers. – Said Deana breaking the silence. Dudley had been daydreaming and was startled.

-I knew that, most kids at school had been pawed or molested by someone. Some of the teachers would also be grabbing at whoever was strolling by. – Added Dudley.

-Have you ever heard of a woman pedophile? - She continued.

No... I don't think I ever have, always men, which does not mean there aren't any..., maybe more discreet. - Was his answer after mulling the question over.

-I have to satisfy my curiosity. I'll talk to this woman Worthington. – Deana said readjusting her shoulder holster.

The imposing Motor Home stopped in front of the gate of the former BRE Inc. Standing proud, the gigantic maple tree, a magnificent piece of work with its rugged stocky trunk supporting branches as thick as most trees seemed to greet them once more. The hunting platform, from which Dudley had stalked Weinstein and his body guard had rotten away but Dudley still remembered precisely where it had been, as well as every second of this first -job-.

They had worked a routine which assured a maximum of security to get in and out of the cave, but it was always with apprehension that they removed the huge truck tires masking and obstructing the access. And then, that overpowering, putrid stench hit them like a Tsunami.

The protective clothing had been placed a few feet from the entrance. They would change and then proceed carefully to the cave. After a while the odor seemed to become less abrasive, sweeter.

This time, three trips had to be made from the Motor Home to the entrance of the cave. One by one they dragged the now awakened bodies.

-You're probably wondering which one of your victims' relatives or friends has caught up with you. Nothing like that, we're a private party; we're here to judge you and put an end to your little games. - Dudley stated as he lined them along side the west wall.

Wiggling and trying to break out of their bonds the gagged individuals could not utter a sound, only the eyes moving and telling a story of panic and desperate fear were an indication of their state of mind. In the cave, the stench alone was indicative of the predicament they were in; the end of the road: Shoal, Hell, l'enfer; whatever the name given to Satan's kingdom, where justice was ultimately rendered, this was it. They were caught and it could only go from bad to much worse.

They had always believed they could cheat with impunity; that nothing could happen to them, that they could usurp the rights of their victims, rape them, torture them, humiliate them, and use them as sexual slaves without danger. They now realized that they were caught.

This cave was far from having the looks of a court of law; more the "Lex talionis, an eye for an eye" situation. Not the civilized law, not a court of justice where their rights would have been protected at the risk of flouting the rights of the victims.

They could see that their kidnappers were like them: ruthless with a touch of sadism; maybe more than a touch. Their secured cocoon fostering evil had been shattered, disintegrated; suddenly, these actions, which to them had gradually become natural, because of the impunity they had had so far, were exposed as they truly were: shameful, weird and cruel.

-The O'Reilly kids. Lewiston, last week. Means anything to you? – Eye movements indicated to Johnny that they were on the same page.

-Your host Steven is over there. - And he pointed with his hand. –He's in the process of expiating his crimes against the O'Reilly kids.-

Johnny had pointed to the middle of the room where Steven, Smith and Gorski were spread out like a star fish missing three tentacles. Soon the count would be right.

Muffled sounds and grunts, not unlike the dissonant sounds emitted by hogs being fed, were echoing on the low vault of the cave. The crudeness of the flood lights burning the scene was blinding. The three sinners' eye lids were half opened, squinting, trying to see beyond this luminous partition. Thousands of flies, bred in the gut of the decaying carrion skunk were avidly accomplishing their destiny of eating and reproducing on the three humans. Proteins are proteins no matter the source. Johnny had researched and found that under the proper conditions it takes less than twenty four hours for an egg to hatch and a voracious maggot to emerge from that egg. Maggots' appetite is insatiable.

-To make a long and complex story short,- said Deana addressing the new comers in a low and well modulated voice, -we have seen the video clips depicting your little games with the O'Reilly family. We have tracked you down and brought you to this cave. You'll be judged, sentenced and executed if found guilty. –

-We're going to let you take the stand, one by one and we'll hear what you have to say. But before we'll show you the video clips of your sexual prowess's with children. After careful verification of your identities, sentences will be passed and you'll be… "Mithridated" if found guilty. -

As Deana was ending her speech, the first clip was being projected. James Rupert's face could be seen on the screen. It was frozen long enough for all to match it with the Rupert they had abducted. After this first projection Rupert's gag was removed and Johnny asked:

-James Rupert, is this your image we have just seen on the screen?-

Completely conscious, adrenaline is a remarkable substance, arrogant Rupert spat in Johnny's direction and didn't answer.

Deana answered for him.

-Not a doubt in my mind that he's the same person. He's as guilty as Charles Manson. We sentence you to be Mithridated. At least you can appreciate the swiftness of the legal procedure.

From where he was sitting, Rupert could see Steven and the other two. Was he to suffer the same fate .....? Total incredulity sat in. - I'm dreaming..., this is not real.- His last memory was the Boston Herald newspaper in the flower bed and this large gorilla cutting his hedge; then, blank, nothing until now. Where was he, how could anyone treat him in this fashion. Where were the police, for which he paid taxes; his rights violated, his person tied up in a sleeping bag like..... Could it be that the relatives of this boy had found him out...? Then, his natural arrogance took over and he started to swear, threaten and give orders; as if it could save him.

-Your last victim, this boy you played with last night, told me that you had stuffed one of your victim in a weighted nylon sleeping bag and dropped him, still living, from your plane in the middle of a deep lake. Is this true? - Asked Dudley.

This last detail was news for Deana and Johnny. They looked at Dudley and then at Rupert.

-We'll need an answer. The parents of this kid need to know that their son is not coming back. You'll tell us his name and exactly where you dropped him. - Continued Dudley.

-Fuck you, I don't have to tell you anything. ... release me and I'll tell... he's still alive.... - Replied Rupert, quick to seize the opportunity.

That was a new twist. Dudley had not figured that this bastard could have kept the kid alive. Chances were that he had not. Thinking about his next move for a minute, Dudley then walked over the table where the famous pair of blacksmith tongs was laying. He picked it up and walked slowly back to James Rupert.

-You're lying to save your ass... I don't believe the kid is still alive, but you'll tell me the truth. I won't enjoy doing this but I'll skin you alive until you tell us exactly where you ditched that body. I believe this kid was telling the truth and that you dropped your victim from your plane. The nylon sleeping bags found in your house are proof enough for me. Why in hell do you have to go to that limit to .....? – And to punctuate his sentence, he pinched a large chunk of fatty tissue from Rupert's bare thigh.

It took but a few minutes and less than a square foot of this rough peeling to obtain a complete confession. The name of the lake was Cheesuncook Lake, north of Greenville Maine, in the middle of the family woodland holding. The name of the adolescent was Pietro Di Angeli. While James Rupert was singing his little heart out, the video was rolling away. The Boston area police would be able to fish the body out if they watched the News on TV.

The only thing I regret- had said Rupert before Dudley gagged him , - Is that I didn't have the time to conclude my deal with Steven and send Don O'Reilly to join Pietro.- Then looking at Steven:

-You son of a bitch, always the greedy vulture, by copying the clips you sold us out. If I ever get out of this mess there's a sleeping bag for you. -

Rupert had realized that Steven had made copies of the video clips. This was contrary to the agreement. That and only that, was the cause of their trouble. Otherwise they would have been enjoying life and its little pleasures until their natural deaths. James Rupert was pissed and ratted on Steven. It took a minute for the three avengers to understand the full horror of what Rupert was saying. Steven was to sell the O'Reilly boy to be tortured and killed.

-Let's make certain Steven lives as long as possible. Give him penicillin preventively if this is what it takes. Farmers keep their chicks and calves from being sick by doing just that. - Was Dudley's idea.

Dudley was getting angry and for the first time, had a tangible reason to feel good about their project. Until now he had not been certain that it would serve a purpose to keep the perverts alive. This last piece of information gave the entire project a new dimension. Don O'Reilly's life had been saved. If they needed justification for their actions, this was it and on tape for the world to see. Deana took out the emergency kit they had brought and accompanied by a loud staccato scream, smeared the skinned area on Rupert's thigh with iodine. She then applied a bandage to the wound and taped it.

After what he had witnessed, Cyrus Alpasha was less arrogant and tried to negotiate a monetary redemption. He offered a million dollars for his life and would have gone to several more.

-I never killed anyone and never intended to. I like kids, that' s the way I am and there is nothing I can do about it. I tried and tried.... Nothing works. You can't treat me the same.... -

-We're not doing this for the money, we'd refuse five million. Your expiation will be shown on the Television news channel and a foundation helping abused kids will benefit from the proceeds. - Dudley told him before he retaped his mouth.

-You're last Madeleine Worthington, and frankly I was wondering why a woman .... These crimes are usually the prerogative of men. Tell me why you seem to enjoy so much hurting and humiliating young males- Said Deana.

Madeleine had been watching in horror while Rupert was questioned. She would not bet much on her chance to survive. Twisting her mind during the interview of the other two, she could not come up with anything to save her ass. Had it not been for the horrible torture they would endure during the next several days, she would have been serene about her fate. Life had been a bitch and dying was not a problem....

-You have no rights to kidnap us and you're not going to get away with this.- Worthington started to reply as soon as her gag was removed. Deana cut her off.

-I'm giving you a chance to end it quicker or get out of this situation. I believe that you've been abused and more or less re-programmed to be what you are today. I may be wrong but someone in your family is the abuser. –

A ray of sunshine; feminine solidarity could do something for her. After hesitating a moment she nodded. Deana looked at Dudley who understood. He picked Madeleine Worthington up as if she was a potato bag and moved her to the back of the cave where she could tell her story. While she pleaded for her life, Rupert and Alpasha would become the missing tentacles of the star fish arrangement.

Finding a chair, Dudley tied her in it and went back to help Johnny.

-Drink this, it should clear your head and bring you back to the world of the living. - Said Deana as she offered a bottle of Four Roses.

Madeleine drank gluttonously straight from the bottle and almost choked. Deana had removed her hand cuffs and placed them on her delicate ankles. Madeleine Worthington rubbed some blood back into her wrists while she was collecting her thoughts. The alcohol had helped chase away this immense panic which was so overwhelming that she could hardly talk let alone think.

-You have five minutes, I'm listening. - Said Deana.

-It goes back a long time...- Started Madeleine and she told her story.

Deana was happy to have followed her nose. Madeleine's story was worse than hers. At least, she had been able to deal with it; only bad dreams remaining.

-You can't probably see why I have this need to get back at males of any ages to compensate for the humiliation I have been and, am still today, submitted to by my father. I doubt that you'll ever be able to help me as I have seen your faces and could identify all of you. Maybe you'll kill me quickly. That would be better than going back to my former life. -

-True, you could identify us, but maybe there's a way out of this for you. We're not senseless killers and are doing this to help some of the kids enslaved by guys like Steven and Rupert. I need to talk to my friends. I'll be back in a minute. Don't try anything as it would seal your fate.-

Johnny and Dudley had finished force feeding the five guys and were more than ready to leave the area.

-Oh Oh said Dudley, I have a feeling that we're not going to Mithridate Miss Worthington. –

Here is the story and the plan. -Said Deana.

Not bothering to be discreet in front of the other five guests, they weren't going anywhere, she told the story and her plan.

-Frankly I wasn't looking forward to putting a woman through this ordeal, no matter how wicked she might be. So be it but I hope that you know what you're doing. Our immediate future is in your hands darling. - Dudley advised. Johnny nodded.

Deana went back to Madeleine Worthington.

-Here is what I propose; the decision to live is yours. You'll come out of this alive under the condition that you donate a cool five million dollars to the foundation, and give me the list of all your providers. I'll accompany you to your home tomorrow where you'll cause your father to have a fatal heart attack or die of whatever method will be deemed safe for you. I have an idea on the subject. You'll be filmed while in the act of murdering your father.

You'll also remember that we have you performing on video. In the mean time you'll be untied but never away from my eyes. I have killed twice before and maimed and emasculated the stepfather who had abused me. With my bare hands, I took out the lesbian who thought she could rape me at will while in jail. Also... I have this toy, - and her right hand came out flashing a five inch stiletto, - and I'm a dead-shot with this forty five.-

As she was finishing her sentence her right hand had dropped the knife back on the table and moved to the shoulder holster.

-You see the white stone on the far wall.-

At twenty feet, Madeleine could see a small button like white stone encrusted in the wall of the cave.

-I'll hit it three times in less than two seconds. –

And she did, to the astonishment of Johnny and Dudley who came charging with their weapons drawn.

-Do you agree? –Said Deana replacing the three spent shells.

Visibly impressed, Worthington replied.

-Yes I do. Even if I had another option, I'd go along with this program. The key word is "kill my father". You have no idea..... The office... I'll need to phone the office. We don't want to alarm any one. – And then she continued.

So close to a terrible agony and death; like a condemned man pardoned at the last minute, her mind was overflowing with adrenaline and disbelief. Her thoughts had never been clearer; she could take in the situation with an acuteness she had never yet experienced.

-Some of these clips will show my face. I'll be recognized. –

-We'll remove the clips where your face is showing or blur it out. – Replied Deana.

-When do we do the part about my father, that's what I've been wanting to do for the last fifty years. You wouldn't believe the number of times I prepared and planned for just what you propose. Never had the nerve to go ahead with my plans. You were much stronger than I.-

-I had to or my kid sister would have also been a victim.... For your father's demise, tomorrow morning is when.... You'll need to get someone to take care of him tonight.- Deana said while looking for the empty shells on the floor.

On the way out Madeleine Worthington began shaking and sobbing like someone who has seen hell and lived to tell. She stopped and looked at each of the five naked men shrouded in a clear plastic suit, writhing and thrashing under the intense light, spread out like a grotesque star fish. Looking at Steven, already disfigured, his skin covered with a crusty ochre plaster among which maggots were having a feast, she realized that Hell, if it existed, could not be worse than what she was seeing.

The video camera had resumed its function of coldly chronicling every second of this story. When the star fish stopped tramping about and grunting the humming of the camera and the buzzing of the flies could be heard. The smell and the horror of it all overpowered Madeleine, she fainted. Dudley carried her to the Motor Home where she would spend the night with Deana in attendance. In the morning the two girls would drive to Boston.

Good, thought Dudley, and to top it, five million to the foundation. Works for me.

CHAPTER 38

"Revenge only, can stifle hate."

Drinking a large scotch as a chaser to a strong soporific Madeleine Worthington slept like a lamb. A shower and a copious breakfast resurrected her from hell and a deep slumber. They left at five in the morning and would hit Boston a little after eight. The modeling agency had been advised that the boss was sick and would be away for a few days. A nurse had spent the night with Adolph Worthington. On the way to Boston, Deana continued her probing of Madeleine's long term intentions.

-I've been seeing a psychiatrist for such a long time that I don' t remember when I started…. What I know is that two of them died on me…… I didn't kill them they died of old age. Other than finding some justifications for my actions, not much help from any of them. The last few days have come closer to solving this problem than any other actions taken in the past. Once the cause has disappeared, my problem and all its consequences, direct and indirect will go away. I never had the guts.-

Madeleine was stretched out as much as allowed by the diminutive habitat of the Targa. Eyes closed, she had been talking to her new shrink. In a few hours Deana had been able to unravel her life-long problem and find a solution. The means employed had been … drastic but… hell… they worked. Pussy footing around the issues is never a solution.

-Could be- said Deana, -but remember that old habits die hard.-

Madeleine nodded, obviously not listening. After a moment she came out with the question that had been haunting her since she had awakened that morning.

-I still don't know how we'll …snuff him out? -

Deana was negotiating a curve which could not be managed at the speed she had been travelling. She enjoyed the rapture very high speed provided. Hearing the question she could not keep from smiling.

-The Maya way,- said Deana. -Painless, safe and efficient. –

Madeleine opened her eyes and looked at Deana, thinking that this was a joke she had to laugh at. It was not a joke.

-You have an unusual culture when it comes to putting people to death: Mithridate the soldier and now the Mayas...- Remarked Madeleine with what could have been a faint attempt at smiling.

Smiling was good; she had not smiled in a while. The old bastard was an artist when it came to think of new ways to.... do things, why not cater to his artistic taste, she thought. The road was straight and Deana could devote her almost total attention to the Maya story she had read some years ago. And she gave a short lecture to Madeleine.

-Why reinvent the wheel. History is full of helpful methods to end life. In the Maya culture, as in all cultures, flirting with death was a way for young men to seduce girls who believed that the genitor of their children should be irresponsibly brave ..... Getting utterly drunk was and I suppose still is, one such way. But there is only so much that can be ingurgitated before the body defends against it and vomits the excess. In order to by-pass these natural defenses, the Mayas would insert a tube up their anus and pour the alcohol directly into the colon. It would immediately be assimilated in the blood, bypassing the liver and its defense system for alcohol. As a result, more alcohol gets to the brain. If in sufficient quantities, the alcohol will anaesthetize the central nervous system and breathing will cease.... I brought enema tubing and a bag to be filled with alcohol in lieu of the usual laxative solution. –

-You're devilish..... I thought I was the sadist. -Said Madeleine. -I like it.-

Satisfied, she closed her eyes and fell asleep. The ordeal she had gone through had siphoned all energy from her body; Deana couldn't help but to feel sorry for the woman. For more than fifty years her mind had been manipulated and her body abused by this animal, her father. It would take a long time for happiness to come back, if ever. Some compromise could set in and make life palatable if not marvelous.

Both were dressed like jet setters. The chic tailleur Madeleine was wearing on the day of her abduction had been cleaned and ironed. Deana was wearing an Armani outfit. Driving her 911 Targa, she fitted right into the Worthington social level.

The doorman gallantly opened the door for them and said that he would park the car. Going up the three steps leading to the elevator, Madeleine stopped in front of a full length mirror. For the first time she could see some determination in her eyes. For the first time she was looking forward to punching the number eleven. What had been a daily return to her golden prison was now a triumphant entry that would open a door to freedom. Using more force than necessary she punched 11 once more. Quietly with only a slight hissing sound the elevator brought them to the eleventh floor.

Rather than using her keys, Madeleine rang the bell. Like a majority of North Americans, Martha was plump heading rapidly toward obesity. After recognizing Madeleine through the peep hole she opened the door.

-Thanks for bailing me out Martha. - Said Madeleine. – How is my father this morning?-

-As usual, crabby but healthy. He asked for a drink already and I gave him a Cognac. He was more civilized after drinking and I had to give him several of the same last night until he finally slumbered off into sleep or coma.... He kept asking for you. –

-I know how he is. –

She paid her fees adding a generous tip. The nurse left without saying goodbye to the old man; she hated him but the money was good.

At that moment, Adolph, thinking that his daughter was alone in the house, was requesting her presence at his side. The cognac was fanning the ardor of his passion. Even at his old age the toad was horny.

Blushing, Madeleine looked at Deana and walked to a bedroom from which the voice had emanated. The immensity of the room surprised Deana; on the walls several paintings from known artists; an erotic Picasso painting was presiding. Three large sculptures were disposed randomly and old antique furniture graciously placed here and there. In a corner, partly hidden by an herbaceous wall and a small pond where fish of all colors could be seen swimming, electronic equipment, of the kind found in the offices of the larger stock brokers, were buzzing away, keeping an eye on the world of finance.

-Father, I'd like you to meet a friend of mine, she's here to help me... get rid of the cause of my problem. I guess you know who... that cause would be.-

Deana walked to the bed where the old man was sitting, flashed a radiant smile at him saying.

-Look at me Adolph Worthington; I'll be the last person you'll ever see. Your next appointment has been long overdue and Lucifer doesn't like waiting.-The old man was surprised to see Deana and flabbergasted by the speech.

He had not anticipated that his daughter would dare bring a stranger into his room. Deana could not help from comparing this image with a painting of Voltaire when he was about eighty, a few weeks before his death: the most remarkable feature was an aquiline nose, longer because of the skeletal and scraggy face; the eyes were set by a dark yellowish leather beaten skin, burning with a strange flame, dark but yet luminous as if feverish or already burning in hell; the emaciated neck could have been broken by a strong wind; the scalp was shiny but for a few strands of hair; the lips were thin, to the point of disappearing into the mouth, which was toothless, the denture resting on the table next to the bed; here and there, old age brown spots completed this picture.

-What is this all about? Madeleine, have you been telling our little secret to strangers. You know that I'll disinherit you if you have. - Threatened the tyrant.

-To do that you'd need more time than you have. You don't have any more time dear father. You've used mother and then me for more than fifty years. Being disinherited would be a small price to pay.-

Alert, Madeleine grabbed the cellular phone the old man was trying to reach and also yanked at a medic alarm hanging from a gold chain around his neck.

Deana had been observing this drama and still needed to be reassured that the old guy was guilty as accused. As she was pondering this question, Adolph Worthington's right hand shot out from under the blanket and grabbed Madeleine's breast trying to hurt her. At the same time his left hand was yielding a five inch letter opener. Before Deana had time to step in and remove it he had had time to plunge it once into the tender flesh of Madeleine's side.

-I won't die alone you selfish bitch. You'll come with me. – He was yelling at the top of his lungs.

Madeleine wasn't hurt badly the blade having skidded on one of the floating ribs.

-Whatever you do, don't hurt him; his death has to look as natural as possible. – Shouted Deana as Madeleine was about to strike back. She nodded and pulled back.

While the old geezer was now hissing like a snake, Madeleine went into the bathroom and came back with a towel which she used to compress her wound.

-If you're up to this let's do it before he alerts the entire building. –

Deana jumped on the bed placing her legs on both arms already pinned under the thick cover. Adolph could not move and amidst funny gargling noises she started to pour Cognac into the old gentleman's mouth; a little at a time letting him swallow small gulps.

-He must have sleeping pills? – Said Deana.

Madeleine found the bottle of seco barbital and pinching his nostrils shut, dropped two in the toothless mouth when he came up for air. It took an eternity and a quarter of the cognac for Adolph to stop writhing and jerking.

Deana then jumped off the bed, removed the blankets, turned him over, lowered the pajama and inserted the enema tubing up his anus. The connecting bag had been filled with the rest of the cognac.

-You're up Madeleine.- And Madeleine eagerly applied pressure to the cognac filled enema bag. Slowly at first then faster, the cognac ran into the colon of her father.

Deana could see that Madeleine was enthusiastic; looking squarely at the emaciated carcass of the old bastard as she was squeezing the enema bag. During that time Deana had brought out the video camera and shot a two minute sequence of Madeleine attending to her father's last breaths. Ten minutes later, the sleeping pills and a half liter of cognac up his anal canal produced the expected results. Adolph Worthington was pronounced dead.

Replacing everything as it was, but leaving the sleeping pills near the bed as well as another bottle of Remy Martin, of which they had flushed half down the toilet, they were on their way with a sigh of relief.

-I'll never sleep here again. Too many ...- and she searched for the right word, not finding one that could appropriately describe what she felt. –You know what I mean.-

The doorman had brought the Porsche to the front and was holding the door for Madeleine. Next stop was the bank where Madeleine gave orders to wire transfer five million dollars to the newly opened foundation account. The bank manager did not even blink at the request.

-Your credit is as good as your father's. How is Mister Worthington? - Asked the manager.

-He's having the time of his life; never been better. - Replied the heiress.

Later that day Madeleine came home and reported the death of her father. The police had to treat this death as suspicious and asked for an autopsy. The coroner ruled that the old man had died of an overdose of cognac and sleeping pills. Out of deference for the family he did not characterize the death as suicide but as accidental.

Madeleine inherited upward of four hundred million dollars in cash, bonds, shares and various other assets. The paintings, sculptures and a stamp collection were not included as she pretended they belonged to her. The estimated value of these artifacts was more than one hundred million. Thanks to her father, Deana and Warren Buffett, Madeleine Worthington was now one of the richest women in the USA.

A few months later, she phoned Deana to tell her that a bank account had been opened under her name in the Cayman Islands. A deposit of two million had been wired to open the account.

-I am learning to live. This is largely because of your intuition. If you're around the Boston area, or ever need anything, please come on over. I'd enjoy that more than you think. -

CHAPTER 39

"Injustice begets injustice; violence breeds violence."

Maureen O'Reilly had asked Father Tim Donnelly to be present during the next "Paterson house call". -Why not- thought Tim; although well aware of the danger he was courting with. He used this pretext to arrive early as he needed some private time with the O'Reilly family.

Tim was convinced that nothing good for the kids would come out of further involvement with the police or the court. Not only would it not lead to the conviction or the arrest of the criminals because nobody would find them where they were, but it would really interfere with the reinsertion of the children into the normal world.

He could not tell the lieutenant that Steven was already serving time and paying dearly for his crimes; but he could tell him that a special television program would be shown that same evening for the first time and then every day thereafter, three times per day , for as long as possible. But then, the lieutenant would already know about this.

Tim's lawyer had given the first video clip to the police that very morning. Paterson had probably not seen it yet but would soon have the confirmation that Tim was more involved than appeared. The television station had identified him as the courier and some explanation would have to be given to the lieutenant. The official version of the truth was that Tim was the unwilling pawn, involved solely because the O'Reilly family was part of his flock.

Little Jody was on guard duty behind the window and opened the door before he could ring. She grabbed his hand and without saying a word led him to the living room where her mother was waiting. The room was impregnated with a deep sorrow; he felt awkward subdued by the pain.

-How have you all been? Is life starting to get back on stream? – Asked Tim feeling that the question was dumber than dumb.

-It will be a while. - Murmured the mother.

She didn't say another word for ages it seemed. Then she cleared her throat; crying a lot leaves the throat raw. Without further hesitation Maureen zeroed to the heart of the subject. This priest was not visiting to enquire about their health. A problem had to be solved.

– Glad you're here early. We have to put a stop to any investigation by the authorities. It would be a catastrophe for my children. And what for, nothing good would come of it.-

-We all agree. – Answered Tim using the imperial we. -However we'll have to cooperate with the police and answer all the questions without lying. - Then looking at the children he continued. -You don't have to remember everything and you don't have to volunteer any information. I wanted to have a chat with you so that we understood the rules. – Said Tim.

For a long moment, he looked at each of the children. Don the older boy was almost an adolescent. He would have the hardest time to forget enough of this tragedy to live a normal life. He would need help from a competent psychiatrist, not one of those loonies listening to frustrated old ladies or manicured precious gentlemen in search of a reason to live. A real good shrink, if such an animal existed, could help a lot. This is where the foundation would help to find competent and honest physicians. But Tim knew from experience that time, this exceptional healer would slowly ease this horrible episode out of their lives. They would never forget this monster but would carry on with their lives. In a few years Steven would be a bad dream, then his face might disappear from their memory bank, maybe not.

Miriam and Gail, ten and nine, had a better chance of emerging from this nightmare without too much scarring. They would be more resilient. Women have been abused for thousands of years. The evolution has probably provided women with a special program to survive the worst of abuses. Women, like camels have been trained to endure pain, high endorphin level most likely.

Little Jody would be fine if left alone by the media and able to take refuge in anonymity. For all of them including the mother, knowing that they were avenged was a giant step in the long journey back to sanity. But the long term sequels were real. It is difficult to survive any encounter with a monster without becoming one; let's hope that none of the kids would develop into a pervert animal.

Of much more immediate concern to Tim was the television coverage of the execution of the sentence. Not concerned that the O' Reilly family would be recognized as they had been carefully erased from the clips. His fear was that the criminals would be identified and that their own families would be ostracized by the population. All of a sudden these innocents would be perceived as bearing a contagious disease and placed in quarantine.

This entire venture was nothing but a fragile castle of cards at the mercy of one question: "Could the O'Reilly kids hold their tongue? Would they tell this hot news -in confidence- to some of their friends, who of course would diffuse it...? " How to deal with this was on Tim's agenda this morning. He stood up and started pacing in the living room.

-ABC will be showing video clips of the people who abused you. These criminals – he was always looking for the proper word-, are exhibited being punished for the sins they have committed against you and other kids. – He perceived fear in Don's face. – Don't worry, no one will recognize any of you; your faces have been ...erased out of the film. Only you, not even the police will know that you were the victims. ..... - He let his words sink into their brain. –But, you may want to tell one of your friends..., just one, your best friend. It is so difficult to keep a secret. –

He had been staring almost accusingly at Miriam.

-Miriam, who is your very best friend. – She answered that Catherine had always been her friend.

-Have you told her about Steven? – She answered that she had not; she was ashamed.

-Will you be tempted to tell her about Steven when it's on the TV and every one in your school talks about it?.- She hesitated a moment. – No she said, I won't-. But Tim knew that there was a real danger.

Maureen had been following this dialogue and could see where Tim was going.

-I see where you're going, Father Donnelly. I'll work on this and we'll all learn how to keep a secret; no one will tell. - Then after a silence. - I have decided that the children will not be interviewed or interrogated by any one. As a matter of fact, they will not be present when Lieutenant Paterson shows up in a few minutes. I'll answer for them as it is my right. -

She had consulted a lawyer. Her mind was set, dead set.

-You made the right decision. - Said Tim. – One last piece of advice, don't look at the news channel, the torment being inflicted on these people is ugly. -

As Maureen didn't answer he added to break the silence.

-I'll take that coffee now. – Maureen got up. Then stopped, looking at him with her large blue eyes.

-I'll watch it once, alone. I'll need to see them suffer. Only this will erase these pictures of my children being abused. –

Don had been sitting quietly on the edge of the sofa. He stirred.

-Me too mom, I'll want to see how they pay for ....I would have liked so much to kill them...I planned it several times...-

Don felt that as the only male left in the house he should have given his life to save his sisters.

-It may not be a bad therapy to see it once.... It will change your hate into pity. Hate can only hurt you more. You should seek the advice of a good shrink. I may know one. - Answered Tim. He did not know one but would start looking.

He would have liked to push on but Paterson's car was pulling up in the driveway.

-Remember that no one knows that you're in these clips. They may want to trick you, saying they have been told or can recognize you. It will be lies. Don't be caught by their little games and keep your mouth shut; don't even discuss this among yourselves. –

Lieutenant Paterson was surprised to see Tim sitting in the living room sipping a cup of coffee. He was clearly annoyed as was betrayed by a persistent sarcastic half smile. Quickly he recomposed his usual poker face knowing already that there was more to come.

When Maureen advised him that the kids would not be a part of this interview or of any others; he looked up at the ceiling, then at Tim but said he understood.

-It's the duty of a mother to protect her children. On the other hand it's my professional duty to prevent people like Steven from hurting other children. You know that the law demands that you report any unlawful actions. It's really a legal obligation.–

-My legal obligations will have to take second seat to my maternal instinct. I have made up my mind after receiving legal advice. I'm prepared to go to jail if necessary but the children will be left out of this case.- Maureen had raised her voice significantly.

Knowing better, Paterson did not reply. He was beaten and would not mess with this or any other mother; but the season was open on this priest. He turned to Tim.

-If you are wondering, the answer is yes. I've been given a copy of the video clip your lawyer remitted to us this morning. I presume that one of the criminals being shown is Vanaas also known as the Steven in question?-

-I'm not certain. I'm only the messenger in this affair. – Replied Tim keeping a prudent distance from any of the facts.

-I'd like to have a chat with you, we need to know more about what is happening. Maybe there's nothing more for the police to do. – The lieutenant added, fishing.

-Let's meet right now if you have the time.- Continued Tim always anxious to get any unsavory commitment over with as rapidly as possible.

-Fine I'll follow you to the presbytery. – Then looking at Maureen he continued. –You remember the bottle of gin I took two days ago? – She nodded. –It had Steven's finger prints on it all right and it allowed us to identify him ... by his real name. Steven is really Hans Vanass, from Monticello, Arkansas. He has been arrested several times in Arkansas, Florida and Washington, always for indecent exposures and child abuses. He served some time, was released and continued his life of depravity and degeneracy until he vanished, after having been found not guilty in a case involving a family such as yours. The widowed mother of three children had laid charges against him saying that he had abused her children over a period of three months. Then, out of a blue sky, she retracted and said that the kids had lied. But the kids had been examined by doctors who found that they had effectively been raped and abused repetitively. There was nothing the District Attorney could do. The charges were dropped.-

The silence that followed Paterson's declaration was heavy and lasted. Maureen was congratulating herself for not involving the law. Tim and maybe also Paterson, were starting to see the soundness of Barcelo's approach to self justice.

Realizing the danger her family had been exposed to during these last months, Maureen could feel her scalp tightening and her face turning the brightest red; all her senses were alerted as if the danger was still present.

She would be so careful from now on. Never again would a man be allowed to live with her family. She vented her hostility at Paterson.

-How can freaks like that be able to fool the system for so long without being neutralized? Isn't there a way to determine if and when a known pedophile is cured? Don't we know that these people never get better, and that their desires, their cravings will always overpower and suppress their will to reform. There is no hope of remission for these animals. - ..... As no one was answering she continued, -We have been the witnesses of horrible crimes committed by these bastards and yet their rights are protected over those of the community. ...Like allowing a hungry wolf to shepherd lambs.-

She could have kept on for hours on that subject. Often in the past she had been horrified when learning of these crapulous crimes. Now that it was her family, she could only applaud at the alternative offered by these angels; this Vanass or Steven as she knew him, would not be back to haunt them, trying to scare them into keeping silence and retract.

-I hear you Maureen. We're not cold blooded robots. Frustration is a constant companion and always we have to weigh the pros and cons of allowing criminals to walk free against the possibility of misjudging innocents. - Lowering his eyes to the floor he continued. – In a way if these pedophiles are guilty and it appears, and this Hans Vanass certainly is, your way of dealing with them might be absolutely suitable. The justice system is getting so complicated in its search for perfection, that it leaves the door wide open for those who can afford the best of lawyers.- He was now looking squarely at Tim, letting him know that he was not duped.

-Detective Paterson, you're doing your job as best you can but I have to repeat that I'm just a pawn in this scenario. However, if I had to get involved, I would be tempted to ....assist in the administration of this quick and radical justice.- Even though he knew that silence would have been golden, Tim needed to reply if only to express solidarity with Maureen O'Reilly.

Paterson gave Tim a tired and pragmatic smile. The rest of the conversation was courteous and didn't amount to anything. Bottom line was that the mother would protect her brood from further trauma. No medical examination, no interrogation, no formal deposition and complete anonymity. She would not obey a court order. And she made it even clearer:

-If the media has knowledge that my family was involved, I'll sue the city and the whole world. My lawyer told me that he would do it on a percentage basis and enroll the assistance of the very best of his colleagues.-

These were the last words pronounced by Maureen before Paterson left. He couldn't get anything more from her and was at peace with this. He followed Tim. Maybe the good father could be squeezed a little and confirm what he already knew. In a sense he was relieved that he would not have to further expose these already battered and wounded kids. What for anyway; the Vanaas person was being taken care of and serving a social purpose for the first time in his wicked life.

His conversation with Tim did not yield much more than what he knew already. Tim was as vague as a bishop turned politician and repeated several times that he had been the messenger in this affair. His position as the parish priest made him a logical choice to assist the O'Reilly family.

-I have agreed to help because I feel strongly that these pedophiles have to be stopped. In a sense I'm happy to be of help. As you'll see when you look at the clip my lawyer remitted to the District Attorney this morning, these people are sadistic murderers of the worse kind.- He continued:

-Freud was interested by the subject and said that "Perversions are not merely detestable but also something monstrous and terrifying as if they exerted a seductive influence. The perversions seem to give a –promesse de bonheur- greater than that of normal sexuality." -

Paterson was impressed by the Freudian quotation. That the priest had studied Freud did not surprise him. Part of the priest-job was to understand the intimate nature of man. What he knew about perversion was acquired in the field, not by books. He and Freud had arrived at the same conclusion: perversions were detestable, terrifying and monstrous; and many supposedly normal humans were depraved and pervert; he knew several.

Drilling his hardest inquisitive stare into Donnelly's cranium, he saw that brow beating an old priest would be tough. It became obvious that Donnelly was convinced of doing the right thing; the priest was on a mission.

-I saw the clip before coming over and I have to agree with you, these people are satanical: they hurt for the pleasure of hurting, they like to see others suffer, yell, beg, cry…. I vomited my breakfast.-

-I've heard confessions from a wide variety of sick bastards but these beat my reality. Are there more running loose? - Asked Tim.

-Unfortunately there are, and among persons we least suspect. Very difficult to build strong cases against them, there seems to always be a doubt. Frightening their victims into retracting their allegations is difficult to prevent. These people play with different rules. The lawyers are experts at discrediting and smearing the young victims, to the point where often the victim appears to be the seducer-aggressor. Lawyers can be so good at deforming the truth. I can't say that I blame Maureen O'Reilly.... Guess what I'd do in her shoes. – Said Paterson, as he was leaving.

CHAPTER 40

"God created the earth but asked the devil to manage."

Wednesday night, six o'clock. After another day's work in hard working America, people are relaxing before dinner. Such a place is Gurner Maine, the home of Robert and Julie Milner, a family of five plus Babe the Labrador. In a moment they will sit at the table, eat, listen to the kids' story and look forward to when the little brats will be in bed.

-Come and get it. – Said Julie still wearing the white nursing costume daughter Emily likes so much.

-Give me one more minute honey, I'd like to see the coverage of this.... astonishing news. It won't last but a few minutes....Hey, you should come over...- Answered Robert.

Curious, she comes into the den where the TV set occupies the better part of a wall. With weighted words, the newscaster was warning about:

-*Very disturbing images of nudity and violence. This is the first of a series of clips we'll show you every day for the next several days. If an image is worth a million words, I'll let this first clip take you to the bottom of hell where these children are being tortured and sexually abused by these creatures ... These kids could be yours.-*

A fiftyish woman commentator came on the screen and repeated once more that parents should use discretion in allowing children to watch. She continued while the images were depicting horror in its purest form.

-Is there a worse crime than child abuse, pedophilia, compounded by sadism and enslavement of the victims? As a reporter in the Vietnam War, I thought I had seen the worse in humanity. Well...what I saw a few hours ago is far worse than anything I have ever witnessed. ...The scenes you'll see tonight are a day old and will continue to be projected until the abusers are in hell where they belong. Yesterday morning, the station was contacted by a priest who had been coerced into acting as courier between the TV Station and a group of citizens. These citizens had fallen upon a terrible situation where a family was sexually enslaved by the new stepfather. This posse felt obligated to act; and not trusting the justice system, has taken over as judge and jury. – And she continued.

-As you'll see in a minute, this monster is beyond what any sane person could imagine. There is no doubt in our mind that this posse, which we could compare to the avenging angels of the Bible, has saved these kids' lives, by kidnapping the stepfather. The ... unusual sentence is giving this animal a taste of his own medicine. –She kept on as the pictures were being shown.

-Why not let the law take care of this problem? The answer given was that the laws are too often protecting the abusers at the expense of the victims. For exorbitant fees, there are lawyers who can and will select then manipulate juries. Criminals who can afford theses lawyers are almost certain of impunity; the witnesses and the victims, brow beaten or confused by their expertise in this type of cross examination.

-We are not promoting self justice but reporting facts. This station cannot help but think that justice, as it is administered today, seems to be -more for the haves than for the have nots- for the rich and influential than for the poor and destitute. When children are concerned we, as responsible parents and human beings, think that it is our duty to ...participate in ridding the world of the scum's who abuse it....And we do: in projecting these images, and also, in sponsoring a Not for Profit Foundation, to help the victims of pedophilia. -

As the commentator faded out of the screen, she was replaced by the distorted face of a man, in the process of doing what pedophiles are in the habit of doing to their victims. While the action was unclear and fuzzy, it remained very explicit and unequivocal. The victim was unrecognizable, even the voice had been disguised so his moaning could not be identified.

The commentator returned on screen and continued her commentary: the bondage of these four children had been going on for more than a month, she said. She also explained how the family cat and a rabbit had been tortured and killed by the pedophile in order to impress upon the kids that they should submit without telling. As she was saying this, some pictures of the cat and the rabbit being tortured were shown.

-Unknown to us or to the police, this group of citizens has abducted the pedophiles you have just seen. They have carefully identified the criminals from the video clips taken from the home of the victims; then they have judged and sentenced these mad dogs. This harsh sentence is actually being executed and consists in a torment which was popular some 2500 years ago. -

And she then described in some details the torture Mithridate the soldier had endured. Johnny had to admit that she was almost as good as he was in relating the Mithridate anecdote.

The following images showed three humans naked under clear plastic sweat suits, wallowing in their own excrements. The yelling and crying heard by the viewers would not be easy to forget and would occupy their dreams. It lasted but a few seconds.

Then the commentator came back on screen, appealing to any one, kids or adults, to look around and try to flush out pedophiles.

-*Any children who have been improperly treated are urged to tell their parents or guardians.* - She took a sip of water from a glass the viewers could not see.

-The station hesitated before agreeing to air this material. But in the end, the chance that it could save even one child from being submitted to sexual enslavement was deemed sufficient motive to run with it. But we caution every one: this is a very serious offense with horrible consequences for persons falsely accused. Please act with prudence when accusing someone. However, if unsure, give the child the benefit of the doubt. Let the police investigate and be the judge of the validity of the accusation.-

-Jesus Christ, said Robert, I know one of them, it's Harry Gorski. I can't believe what I just saw. –

-I know him too and I also know another one, can't remember his name though. – Added Julie.

They remained speechless for a long moment thinking that it could have been their children, who at the very moment were going through the usual pre meal jamboree. Nothing like the noise made by three healthy kids to cause reality to snap back into its proper gear; without further comments, Robert shut the TV off and sat at the table.

-Shayne, could you say graces. - Said Julie to her ten year old.

She didn't really believe in religion but went through the motion. Robert was a devout Christian and the kids could make up their own minds at some future date.

Alone in her living room, doctoring a second martini, Anne Gorski was reflecting on life in general and her future in particular. It was unusual for Anne to have a drink other than on Saturday night. Tonight like the previous night she had found comfort in alcohol. -Why not if it could help me survive. - She thought.

She had mechanically flicked the Television on but was more focused on her own drama than on the world events. That is until she saw the naked body and the distorted face of her husband in the process of practicing onanism on a young boy. She forced herself to listen to the commentator. When the news clip was over she went to the telephone and yanked out the wall connection. She then went over to the bar and made a third and stiffer martini which she half drank before sitting back down.

-At least I know where the son of a bitch is and.... that he won't show up ever again.-

She raised her glass to a portrait of Harry on the wall and drained it. Looking at it she said in a low emotionally charged voice:

-I hope these maggots crawl inside your ass hole and give you the thrill of your life.-

She then got up, took the portrait down and threw it in the fire place. In less than an hour she had burned everything that could bring back the memory of her life long companion. Only the outline of the portrait remained on the wall as a mute witness to her sorrow. « Fantastic» had the last word but she had to scrub the entire wall to remove the last traces of Harry.

The energy spent did her the world of good and around ten thirty, tired and quite drunk, having continued to sip martinis while scrubbing the walls, she went to bed and slept until six the next morning. She then plugged the phone back in the wall and dialed her son's number. Hopefully he would not have seen the TV coverage. She was not that lucky; he had.

Isabel Smith was also watching the six o'clock news. – That's why he's not coming back home. He won't ever be coming back this time. Good riddance. - She was delighted; God had listened to her prayers. Having been on the receiving end of her husband's perversity, what she saw didn't surprise her in the least. For the last two years since he had been released from jail, she had been afraid for her life. Her daughter was past salvation, her mind had snapped long ago and she had become a compliant partner. Several times, Isabel had made the decision to talk, to go to the police; like her several attempts to stop smoking she had always put it off.

Facing neighbors and friends would be difficult but easier than living with the animal that was her husband. She still had bruises from the last beating. Probably too late to save some part of her daughter's future which was now as dark as her father's soul. –My fault. I should have been brave enough to protect her-

-He's done screwing up others' lives. I'll pray every day of my life for these angels. Too bad they don't make this a steady job, I know other wicked bastards in need of salvation. – And she laughed out loud at the thought of Don being eaten alive by maggots.

The ABC switch board lit up like a Christmas tree. The five extra receptionists hired in anticipation of this tidal wave, weren't able to cope with half the calls. Typically a minority of callers wanted this communiqué off the air while most of the others were congratulating the station for its courage. Some were even offering to donate money to the Foundation. It was a success and the rating started an even more than expected rise. At this rate the station would owe a fortune to the Foundation.

Not only was ABC's switch board jammed up but police switchboards throughout the listening area had to cope with an avalanche of phone calls, some from victims, others from friends or neighbors of victims finding the courage to act. A few of these calls would be defamatory but others were real life dramas that the police would deal with, at their pace: with medical examinations, psychiatrists attempting to determine if the victims had been abused or were lying, and then lawyers, court rooms and media. Several bona fide cases would be flushed, some of the victims humiliated and discouraged, others vindicated. Unfortunately there would also be victims of false accusations; and those would be wronged for the rest of their lives; guilty until proven innocent.

The newspapers were quick to join the party. On the following morning, one editorialist wrote:

« *A twenty three year old girl, hospitalized for cervical cancer, was raped on her hospital bed by her two brothers and her father; it was a continuation of something that started nineteen years ago. From age four she had been used and abused by her father who allowed his two younger sons to join in.*

Pedophilia, child molesting, wife beating and abuses of all kinds, flourish in all social strata. Rich or poor children are exposed. The abusers can be either a frustrated weaklings, in search of compensation and cheap pleasures; or powerful people believing that everything is permitted to the rich and mighty. They can be parents, strangers or professionals exploiting their children and clients. From teachers to baby sitters, from fathers to mothers, from confessors to policemen, this virus can strike any one and ruin the life of the victim. Sometimes, to preserve their anonymity the abusers will kill. Sometimes to satisfy a sadistic pulsion the abuser will torture his victim to death. The worst scenario is when the child is enslaved and used for several years as is this case in point.

How do we, as a society deal with this depravity that concerns a lot more people than we dare admit? Psychiatrists contend that perversion is a form of rebellion against the established order. Most perversions will never materialize, confined within the fantastic imagination but some cross over into the reality. These perverts had often been abused themselves. If only to put an end to this infernal cycle, serious efforts should be deployed by our government to eradicate this crime and protect future generations. »

Then, to paint the problem on a world wide scale, statistics were shown, the poorest countries way ahead; life has a lesser value in countries where poverty rules. A foot note advised that: (This picture does not include sweat shops and down right slavery, still rampant in several countries.)

India: more than one million child prostitutes
Brasilia: more than 500 000
Thailand: more than 100 000
Philippine: more than 100 000
Sri Lanka, the USA, Canada, UK, France, Belgium etc

CHAPTER 41

ABC had been broadcasting its special news program twice a day for the last four days. The ratings were climbing to vertiginous heights. The board of directors, initially split, some questioning the correctness and the ethics of this news story, was now overwhelmingly heralding Zygfridas Levinsky as the director of the century. Money speaks louder than some moral or ethical question and removes all doubts. Furthermore, as Levinsky had explained, supported by Tom:

-These crimes have never received the attention they should, unless the abused child is from a wealthy family; which is seldom the case; they abuse their own kids but keep it quiet. A good example is this good looking, Caucasian, harp playing fourteen year old who was abducted from her expensive bedroom. For more than a month the media plays this to the hilt; in another part of the country, an African American of the same age, impoverished, not playing any instrument, is abducted; local TV treats the event as a fender benders or a bar fight.

- Same human beings, same sex, same age, wrong color and poor as hell ..... I'm Jewish, my people have been deported, gassed, tortured and frankly, a rebellious fiber has been twitching from within my body for several years... trying to be a player in this arena. I will no longer repress this urge to stand up and do what has to be done in the name of humanity.... You know, assist a person in danger. . .... (Long silence during which he looked at each of the board members: three were Jewish, two Christians of some sort, and the rest atheist or agnostic. All were erudite and well aware of the political and religious game; most had a hidden agenda.)

-I know that you will back me up and stay for the fight. ... Because we'll have one and a good one..., what with do-gooders... politicians, ... and the churches, ... The pedophile fraternity of the world,... these freaks who thrive on the edge of good and bad, will try to prevent us from rattling their cages, ... from disturbing their quietude with all weapons at hand.-

As was to be expected, the station had received threats and criticisms: from politicians, churches, private citizens and various law enforcement bodies. The law was not favorable to having posses abducting, and judging, sentencing and executing criminals. Nevertheless, overall, the public was mesmerized by the spectacle, looking deep into its societal conscience to justify this action. From time immemorial crowds have been ardent followers of cruel demonstrations.

Tom, the company's chief legal officer was digging in, preparing for an attack from the Justice department. Not a surprise, this had been foreseen and a two million dollars provisional budget submitted to the board. They had finally agreed that while it would cost several millions to defend against the Justice department, the company should, if necessary go all the way to the Supreme Court. The cost involved would amount to little compared to the publicity and public relation fall-outs.

In a country where even the sexuality of the president is openly questioned and becomes a subject of discussion for kindergarten toddlers, news of this importance could not be kept from the viewers. Older Americans have been thought the meaning of the word fellation thanks to a certain Monica; only fair that light should be shed on the much more heinous crime of child abuse.

An independent survey, sponsored by ABC, had established that the vast majority of the people were in favor of the station's initiative. However and not surprisingly, the cruelty of the sentence was judged excessive by some.

The survey involved two thousand five hundred and three persons, out of a significant geographical, social, ethnographic, age and religion cross section of the population... The questions and answers were as follows. :

1. Have you been the object of sexual abuse during your youth? 45% yes, 14% no, 41% no opinion.

2. Is the law dealing adequately with child abuse?73% no, 14% yes, 13% no opinion.

3. Are you in favor of the initiative shown by this citizens'committee? 61% yes, 25% no, 14% no opinion.

4. is the sentence severe enough, too severe? 45% severe enough, 55% too severe.

5. Do you know child abusers in your neighborhood? 47% yes, 53% no.

6. Do you know wife abusers in your neighborhood? 67% yes, 33% no.

7. Do you think this action will have positive effects? 78% yes, 12% no, 10% no opinion.

8. In your opinion what should be done to child abusers? 74% prison, 26% Medical treatment.

9. Do you think the ABC station is right in airing this?78% yes, 22% no.

10. Do you think lives will be saved because of this TV coverage? 88% yes, 12% no.

11. In your opinion can pedophiles be cured? 72% yes, 10% no, 18% no opinion.

This survey was conducted before Rupert's confession to torturing and killing the Di Angelo boy. The planned, livestock like purchase of a young boy, further convinced the viewers that these "avenging angels" were rendering a civic service, helping and assisting persons whose lives were threatened and in mortal danger. Without a doubt they had saved the life of the Lewiston child. The TV commentator had been very explicit in demonstrating that the Di Angelo boy had been tortured several days before being enshrouded alive in a weighted nylon sleeping bag and dropped in a lake from a plane. The same fate would have been that of this second kid.

-We should soon be able to confirm that the police divers have recovered the Di Angelo body. –

The social intelligence was on alert and would start demanding better protection against such incurable and habitual criminals. One caller on a live TV program had made an accurate assessment of the situation:

-All a question of money, there's more profit for the city if its police force hands out speeding tickets by the shovel full than for solving lurid crimes. -

The follow up survey confirmed the ire of the population by a significant increase of the yes votes. Lex talionis –an eye for an eye- still has its place with most of the denizens of the world. Like racism, xenophobia and genocide, lex talionis will keep on presiding over our actions for several centuries.

As for public flogging in Afghanistan, stoning and amputation in Iran, hanging in Baghdad, kids dying of hunger in Africa , the Khmers Rouge killing bourgeois with shovels, this TV coverage was nothing but a spectacle for the mass to enjoy and the TV station to cash in. Like Frederick Nietzsche said: "of *all animals, man is the cruelest. He's never happier than when watching a tragedy, a bull fight or a crucifixion. "*

In retrospect, the ABC show was not worse than the direct reporting on the Gulf war for instance, or the spectacle of a cape water buffalo being devoured live by a pride of lions, the bovine having been darted with a tranquilizer and handicapped by the image chasers, so the pride of lions and the camera man would be comfortably at ease to perform their respective job.

Our collective conscience clears up if the ugliest details are left untold. Give them wine, bread and a good show Nero had said. Only the fairest of the Christian maidens would be served to his lions while the Romans were gulping cheap wine, as beer and hot dogs at a WWA wrestling match.

People loved the twice daily show; for a few hours, they could forget the real issues in their lives: when feeling sorry for one self, comparison to others 'misery is the best cure. Nothing has changed much since forty thousand years, when our Cro Magnon ancestors cannibalized some of their Neanderthal cousins.

On the fifth day Johnny reported to Deana and Dudley that even though they had administered massive doses of penicillin, Steven's body had released his evil soul to the devil during the night. For the last two days, Johnny had insisted that he alone was to attend to the cave people.

-I left the body in its proper place with the others. The little creatures will complete their assignment whether the body is alive or not. In two days only the bare bones will remain. ... If we're looking for images with a punch, this is it. We could have several more days of TV coverage, whether the bodies are breathing or not. I'll feel better when they're all dead. -

And then he added.

-I don't think they're suffering any longer. They seem to be unconscious, not feeling anything any more.-

The now famous TV commentator had been up to the new challenge, having long since, prepared for the inevitable eulogy:

-One of the child molester died last night. He was only forty years old and, statistically would have lived another thirty some years. During these thirty years, if left unchallenged, he could have ruined more than one hundred and fifty young lives, most likely killing most of them after devilish tortures. Like the AID virus, some of these kids would have been contaminated and programmed, perpetuating the pedophilic virus in future generations. Who knows how many kids have already been affected and, had he been allowed to pursue his only life objective, how many more would have been destroyed. Last week we learned that he had agreed to sell an eleven year old boy. The asking price was one hundred and fifty thousand dollars. We also learned that this Lewiston kid was to be sexually abused, tortured and, finally killed by his ....-new owner-...... After this new fact, those of us, I for one, who still had some reservations about the harsh sentences, are reconsidering our initial position.-

While it is difficult to have precise statistics, experts on the subject think that a pedophile will wreck the lives of five to six kids per year, maybe more if he is in a position of authority : a teacher or a kinder garden educator or a priest for instance. Some of these kids, maybe the luckiest, will be slain by their abductor. The others will carry their shame and relive this nightmare throughout their lives. Some of them will become pedophiles. We are told that pedophilia is a disease of the mind which is contained with extreme difficulty. One can surmise that those contaminated should be either cured, if possible or if not, removed permanently to protect our children. –

The commentator, a mother and a grand mother had laid it on rather thick. Premature execution as a cure was a bit strong and she was asked to stick to the approved text, not to adlib in the future.

The nation's news papers were not singing in unison:

-...predators have no rights.... God cures all and these abusers should be given a second chance...... pedophiles always relapse and should be put away for life.... Surgical emasculation for all pedophiles.... chemical emasculation for all pedophiles...-

One of the most prominent papers produced an exhaustive study whereby it was established that pedophiles relapsed almost one hundred percent, even if emasculated, chemically or surgically.... Nothing to do with hormones, all in the mind....lobotomize all pedophiles? Some others thought that less cruelty would have achieved the same results; others thought that it was barbaric but justified. The international magazines like Paris Match, Der Spiegel and Ho La, were delighted to show these gory pictures with their own comments and statistics. Paris Match had been digging into child abuse and never missed a chance to shed light on the most lurid cases. All agreed that it was time to act. The French and Belgian papers were using this story to rattle the cages of their own complacent governments.

The remaining four molesters, penicillin helping, were cooperating by staying alive. They had achieved a level of notoriety similar to that attained by the Boston strangler or Jack the Ripper. In London where everything is a reason to bet, odd were five to one that Smith would be the last to die.

The mayors of Lewiston and Auburn were putting extreme pressure on their police forces. The fact that two of their constituents were displayed as scum bags for the whole world to see, was embarrassing. They felt the shame of this event as they would have been proud if one of their constituents had won an Olympic medal.

Even though lacking his usual drive and motivation, Lieutenant Paterson was doing his professional best. He had questioned Smith's and Gorski's wives and once the identities of the other Mithridated criminals had been established, he had traveled to New Jersey and Boston. There he had tried to establish a link, glue some pieces together, build a case, and draw some vague profile of these angels. Nada.

Going back to the O'Reilly family had not yielded results other than to get his ass singed by a court order. He knew that it all stemmed from there. If he could interrogate these kids on a one to one basis he would identify the members of this brigade. After a while it became an obsession for him to know; what he would do with the information was something else, he had the uncomfortable inkling that he would, for the first time in his career bury the evidence remembering vividly the poor girl who had been abused for twenty long years, by her still at large father...

On three occasions he had questioned Father Donnelly only to crash into the same stone wall. Tim was the messenger, as he kept repeating. He had even retrenched behind his Roman collar. Out of spite Paterson had obtained permission to bug Tim's telephone; but the judge had refused to let him bug the O'Reilly's phone.

-If, as you believe, they are the ones implicated in this sordid affair, they have suffered enough. Leave them alone. – Said the judge.

The judge had often been powerless to sentence some of the pedophiles that he intuitively knew were guilty. Now, as a father and a grandfather, he wasn't unhappy that something was being done to punish these often untouchable molesters. Well versed on the subject; he had had the task of studying similar morbid, grotesquely disfigured pictures presented as evidence and he remembered some of the testimonies. One is never immunized against these atrocities; he had been kept awake at night and would no doubt continue to have nightmares. Like Satan himself, the pedophiles were out there, in ambush, lurking and waiting for the right moment to grab their victims. The TV commentator had said:

-Has any one of you ever imagined being captured by one of these freaks? Helpless, hands and feet cuffed, raped, humiliated, and submitted to inhuman torments for days before finally being discarded during one final agony. -

After a pause for more effect she ended :

-Their hunting grounds are school yards, school rooms, presbyteries, offices, homes, always on the look out for the right moment. Worse still, are those pawing their grand children, children, nieces or nephews and even worse those who kidnap a kid from the street and getting rid of the evidence after they had their perverted amusement. What these Angels are doing is not all that wrong if it can save one child... and, we now know it did. –

CHAPTER 42

"Death is the only tutor to the incorrigible."

On day eight, Johnny could not safely go to the cave. His instinct told him that Paterson had a tail on him. That the prisoners didn't eat wasn't much of a problem. It would hasten their death and become an act of mercy, but the fact that the TV station did not receive the daily clip was a problem. The avid and faithful viewers were appreciating the destructive action of the numerous maggots on Steven's carcass. As Johnny had forecasted, only the bare bones were left on his arms and legs. Most of the skin and flesh of his face, chest and neck had been recycled by the maggots, the rats and some other creatures he had not yet identified, leaving only the hair and a chain holding a gold locket. The empty eye sockets were Dantesque.

He could not take a chance on Tim's phone not being bugged and had to revert to plan B: back to the hospital for a few hours, time enough to confess his sins to his favorite priest.

He drove and parked his car a few blocks from the hospital, took a double shot of insulin and walked into the emergency room near fainting.

-You've been imprudent again Mister Barcelo. - Said the nurse in à tone she would use to scold one of her brood. She continued. - You'll be going into a coma soon. - And with this final statement she called the doctor. They took care of the problem and resurrected Johnny one more time.

-You're too weak to walk out, we'll have to keep you overnight. - Ordered the doctor as he went his way.

-I'd like to see a priest. - Johnny asked the nurse who was fluffing his pillow.

Eleven o'clock in the morning, Johnny knew that Tim should be around. Thirty minutes later Tim came in his room carrying the infamous brief case.

-Mister Barcelo in person? What's wrong with you this time Johnny. Nothing serious I hope.-

-Naw, I'll be ok. - Said Johnny while scribbling on a pad.

Tim bending over his shoulder could read: -I am being followed by the cops. Cannot feed the boarders nor retrieve the clips today. Please contact Deana or Dudley.-

-Would you like to tell me about your sins or would you rather have communion this fine morning-. Said Tim as he retrieved the piece of paper and stuffed it in his pocket.

-I'll have communion if you please. - He felt he had to play the game so communion it was; first time since his mother had died.

Tim did not stay very long, pretending that several patients needed his services. He got to a public phone and dialed Dudley's number. Deana answered.

-Tim here, I haven't received the parcel you were to send. It might not have been posted …. If so I'll pick it up. –

-Dudley probably didn't mail it as he was supposed to. Come over I'll have it ready- Deana had picked up the hint. He was there an hour later.

-What's up father Tim. - Said Deana perspiring from having spent the last hour training. Dressed in the shortest of shorts and very tight wet cotton T Shirt, she was even more desirable than the last time he had seen her.

-You'll be responsible for my damnation Deana. I am but a normal human and the sight of ….well, you know…. is overwhelming. – Damned that Pope who imposed celibacy.

-I'm sorry about your conscience. I feel that priest must be tested once in a while. Anyway, I don't see why something so natural should be so holy and untouchable… – Answered Deana smiling candidly.

Tim could feel this twitching sensation and had to think about something ugly to make it go away. Barceló's ugly face did the trick.

- I'm not here to ogle your delightful curves. Johnny is back in the hospital…. No, no, nothing neither serious nor real. He's being followed by the cops and won't be able to feed the animals as he said. He's worried more about retrieving the clip than feeding the inmates though. Anything you can do?-

-Sure I'll go. Time to take a shower. I'll take care of the chores for the next three days. Hopefully these critters won't live as long as the good soldier

Mithridate. That would make it eleven days in this Club Med. - Answered Deana as she wrapped a towel around her neck.

She is so desirable, so feminine, and yet so cold thought Tim. Women had been forced to be good at enduring pain for such a long time; they could bear so much more than the males of the specie. It would be logical that the pain they could inflict should be directly related to their tolerance factor. That increased his arousal. Tim was intelligent and had used his mind to enjoy a private imagined life over the years: his fantasies were sometimes as vivid as the real thing.

-I'll leave before I make an even bigger ass of myself.-

He went back to the hospital only to be told that Johnny had signed himself out again. Some things never change.

When he dialed the ABC's number Levinsky was free. There were papers to sign and decisions to make. He also wanted to talk about the sale of rights to foreign television companies and magazines. Germany's Der Spiegel, France's Paris Match and Spain's OH La , had asked for exclusive contracts last week and were already showing pictures in anticipation of an agreement. Big bucks were mentioned; why not. As in wars, money was the name of the game and the bigger the audiences the faster will the objectives be attained.

-We're overwhelmed by demands from all over the world. - Said Zygfridas on the phone, - Since we may be issued a court order to stop the broadcast in our own country, we should carefully look at these alternatives. The pirates are showing some of the pictures any way... picking them up from television. You can do anything now without paying for it.-

His Jewish genes could not help but rebel at being robbed. He continued.

-There seems to be a powerful lobby applying pressure on the attorney general. Could it be acting on behalf of the pedophile fraternity...? I wonder. Stranger things have happened.-

-Remember this sordid affair of the pedophile Dutronc in Belgium. This man kidnapped two girls and hid them in a dungeon he had built in the basement of his house. They were raped and abused for several days, then starved to death in a nine square meter pitch dark cell. This network had links at the highest level. When I have doubts about what we're doing, I ask your friend Nora to bring me the Pedophile archives. My conscience quickly clears of any doubts. -

-I know what you mean- Tim replied, - my memory is overloaded with pages upon pages of unsavory confidences; some people need to brag about their misdeeds. Confession was a bottomless pit where unimaginable atrocities mixed with jansenistic avowals where buried until the next time. Fortunately we no longer have to condone these abominations. I could be in Boston in a few hours. I'll let you buy dinner in a good restaurant. – After a moment he added. –I'd like to see how we could be of assistance to the spouses and parents of abusers. They're left with the humiliation and the ostracism after the criminals are put away; it's a deterrent to delations by closed relatives.? Think about it. - And he hung up.

CHAPTER 43

"J' ai fait ce rêve stupide que l' honneur fut un jour à la portée de tout le monde."
Georges Bernanos

"I have made this stupid dream: that honor was within the reach of every one."

Paterson was far from being a meat head. Having spent more than forty years dealing with the bottom layers of humanity, where vices thrive like maggots in muck-heap, creates a bank of knowledge in behavioral science. Over the last million years, using his superior brain, man has developed imaginative ways to be evil. Eddy Paterson had acquired what he would jokingly classify as a Ph.D. in low life psychology, or Ph.D. in LLP. For instance, he had been quick to pick up on the fact that Barcelo had been on the look out for shadows and that he had taken evasive actions; Barcelo was good but it confirmed his suspicions that he was not unrelated to this Avenging Angel caper.

While Eddy Paterson was becoming sympathetic to the cause these Angels were fighting, his sympathy would not interfere with his determination and commitment to get to the bottom of this affair and find out who the players were. As he once said to a junior colleague.

-After a few years you'll see that this job becomes routine. Like plowing a field, you till rows after rows until the ground is broken into tiny lumps, without emotion or stress, mechanically like a robot.-

He was good at his job and took pride in getting at the truth no matter how deep it was buried. Like a hound dog, he would relentlessly track his prey, finding the small signs that unveil the mystery. He would wash away layers upon layers of filth to get to the bottom, where the infection hid.

His intuition and street smarts made him politically inept and he had reached his professional ceiling as Lieutenant. He would retire a lieutenant and that was fine with his aspirations; but he took pride in being one of the best detective there was.

Following his nose, he let his intuition take him to the Hospital where two possible players had spent some time together. Asking questions to the staff did not yield much until he went up to the fifth floor and questioned Jennifer King, the psychiatric nurse who had been assigned to Barcelo during the first few days of his hospital stay. Barcelo had been categorized as an odd ball and the hospital did not fancy suicide under its roof.

-Now that you mention the name, I remember that Mister Barcelo and Father Donnelly spent quite a bit of time together. That Barcelo was in need of counseling is not surprising considering the life he led. – Stated Nurse King. Then she went on to say. -Almost immediately following their last meeting, yesterday morning, Barcelo signed himself out of the hospital for the second time. As if in a hurry to do something very important. He wasn't really well enough to be discharged either time. –

-Is Father Donnelly in the habit of chitchatting with the patients? – Had asked Paterson.

-No, Father Tim usually seems blasé and gets in and out of the rooms without much more than the usual –How do you do and god bless you-. Jennifer answered.

Of all the patients in the hospital, Johnny had been one of the very few to attract the good father's attention. They had met three times. Once would have been in the line of duty. A second time could be construed as a follow up to the first time, but a third time was enough to justify a red flag. Father Tim Donnelly had not been associating with any one since the occurrence of the O'Reilly drama. He was present in the O Reilly's home and was chosen as the negotiator with the TV company. Coupled with Barcelo's evasive action when tailed, prompted Paterson to ask for a phone tapping exemption. The judge had given permission to bug Barcelo's phone but it was disconnected for non payment. He could use the excuse of the bad checks to question him although he had the conviction that Barcelo's young wife was the culprit. She had been identified cashing these checks while Barcelo was half dead in the hospital.

When he had exposed his theory during the daily de briefing, the chief of police did not believe that a bum like Barcelo could be involved in such a grandiose project. Eddy did not agree.

-Remember that he was an unusual entrepreneur before he hit the bottle. Built the largest scrap tire dump in the eastern USA and created the Saint Augustine, a plush and profitable private Club. There are rumors that he defended both these businesses from the New York mob. My opinion is that he can move a lot of dirt if he puts his now sober mind to the task. – Snapped Paterson, pissed off at his superior for not considering his opinion.

Paterson had done his home work as usual and the chief finally agreed that it could be a lead. They did not have anything else to chew on.

-OK go ahead. Not much meat...but it seems to be all we've got.-

Immediately, on the very first day, it became obvious that Barcelo had sniffed his shadow. That Barcelo had been looking for shadows and had found them out was, for the lieutenant, a strong indirect proof that he was involved.

-I checked with the admitting nurse of the emergency room and he was really sick. Almost comatose she said. They wanted to keep him for the night but after seeing this priest he checked himself out again. – Officer Coopers reported to Paterson confirming what Paterson already knew.

-What is the name of the priest he saw? - Paterson asked as if he didn't already know the answer to his question.

Coopers went back to his notebook and replied that it was a Father Donnelly. After a moment of reflection, Paterson said :

-Forget about Barcelo, he's on to you. Follow the priest instead. He's involved.... - And as if to himself: -Who do I find the first time I come to the O Reilly's, who is the co-president of this Foundation, who has negotiated the financial contract with the Television Station, who is always two steps away from Barcelo and vice versa, but more than anything else, who is the confident of kids in trouble...Tell me Coopers, who would you see if you were in trouble and couldn't talk to your parents.?-

This is why Father Tim was given an escort going to Boston. Not being as paranoid as Barcelo he never detected it and went to his perfectly legal meeting with Zygfridas Levinsky.

Tim enjoyed good food and the meal offered by Zyg was top. Pier Nine is the place to eat fish in Boston. While indulging in oysters and lobsters, sipping a great wine, they had agreed to go ahead and sell rights to three of the larger Magazines in Germany, France and Spain. Three hours later Tim drove home, followed by a now very tired and hungry Coopers.

The following morning at the de briefing meeting, Coopers had this to report:

-He had a dinner meeting at Pier Nine with Zygfridas Levinsky. The dinner lasted three hours during which they each ate a dozen oysters, a large boiled lobster and drank a bottle of Sancerre, coffee and cognac. Then he came back. - Coopers reported to the brass.

After a silence during which the salivary glands initiated their digestive process at the evocation of this repast, the mayor looked at the chief raising his shoulders in discouragement.

-We have a more immediate worry, which is good news for a change. I've been advised that tomorrow, the Attorney general will issue a court order to stop this broadcast. This sorry incident will then cease to be mediatized. –

The mayor was simple. Little did he know that the TV station would fight tooth and nail for its right and that the Supreme Court would eventually have to decide; not some political lobbyists, pursuing a very private agendas. Democracy is not all that bad when used efficiently, by the right persons, for the right purpose... if sufficient funds are available.

-In the mean time how are we supposed to cope with all these phone calls we're receiving about children being molested. We've not been able to cope with most of them even though several seem real and would warrant full investigations. We just don't have enough staff. - Lamented the chief.

-Do what you can with what you have. We will not hire more cops nor change priorities. It will blow over. - Said the mayor; dumb to the limit of belief thought the chief.

Often, in the heat of a debate, words are spoken that come back to haunt you the rest of your life. The majority of those present looked uncomfortable with this answer. Paterson, more than the others, seemed ill at ease almost ashamed. He was a police officer, a father and grand father; this answer was unprofessional, heartless and downright stupid. Some of the current priorities could be moved to allow the new emergencies to be assessed properly.

A young journalist for the Lewiston News was waiting outside the meeting room. As usual the spokesperson for the city briefed him officially:

-We're on the trail of the kidnappers and expect to have concrete news for the media any time soon. – To which the reporter retorted.

-I understand that you're receiving a large number of calls related to pedophilia and child abuse. Is the city able to cope with the increased volume?

-Our actual police force is well able to cope with these calls. - Replied the assistant mayor as he walked away.

The reporter was busy taking notes when Paterson touched his elbow and motioned with his head to follow him outside. Once outside the building he looked across the street at Denny's. In a minute they were sitting in the restaurant grabbing a sandwich.

-The truth is that the mayor is not going to do much to investigate these calls our receptionists keep receiving as a result of this –Pedophile brigade-. None of these are related to finding the criminals in the news but are either complaints or delations. New cases. As always some will be real while others will be the creations of quacks. We have also been told that the Attorney general will issue a court order tomorrow; he wants the broadcast to end. Political pressure it would appear. - Recited Paterson looking at the entrance afraid to be caught having a sandwich with the enemy. He continued.

-This is unofficial and my name is not to be mentioned. I'll cut off your balls if there is as much as a hint that I have told you any of this.- Said Paterson.

- The bastards..., who are they protecting anyway. Don't worry Eddy, I won't mention your name, I know better. Thanks, I owe you one. - Answered the journalist already asking for the bill.

- Wasn't your sandwich good? – Asked the waitress.

- It was but I have a paper to write. - Answered Baker.

Theo Baker was still young enough to be naive and could not agree with the mayor's position. He was unhappy and felt that the kids in distress were also being abused by the city fathers. It was clear that Eddy Paterson was intellectually against this position. Theo did what journalists do when they are unhappy about something. He wrote about it.

The following morning, the Lewiston News had a complete coverage of the meeting, the position of the city in both the official and officious decisions taken. He also quoted the mayor's officious point of view on the subject.

« CHILD MOLESTING BRUSHED OFF BY MAYOR. BECAUSE OF BUDGET CONSTRAINTS. CURRENT DELATIONS OF CHILD ABUSE NOT INVESTIGATED. ATTORNEY GENERAL TO STOP BROADCAST OF PEDOPHILE BRIGADE. "Mayor feels that calm will come back after the Attorney General's injunction and that: "no money should be spent to investigate these phone calls"»

The news paper editor went on to tell about current budget constraints not allowing careful assessment of all the complaints. Up in arm about the attorney general's injunction to the TV news channel to stop broadcasting this unique story, the journal offered to act as mediator and advisor; proposing to help the delators in obtaining immediate response and justice, going as far as ratting to the Federal Bureau of Investigation if the city could not respond fast enough. Telephone numbers and Web addresses of the journal and the FBI were given as well as those of the city.

-Who are we protecting? - asked the irate journalist. – Are we a country not caring for our children? –Are we allowing pedophiles to once more hide behind our legal system? - Aren't the children our most precious resource?-

The journalist had introduced a doubt into the equation, a doubt that no one cared to be associated with. The bottom line was as it had always been: people are the voters, politicians the *votees* and no matter the ability of some of the *votees* to manipulate the former, in the end, the democratically correct truth always surfaces over the lies.

Every morning Melinda, the mayor's wife would get up before the rest of the family and enjoy a quiet moment before starting her day. Sipping a cup of coffee while she glanced at the headlines had become her favorite moment of the day; worth getting up for. However, that morning, when reading her copy of the journal, Melinda became agitated and stormed into the bathroom adjoining the bedroom where his lordship was shaving his mayoral chin.

-You must be tired of being the mayor of this city. - She told him throwing the paper into his face.

Wiping his face, cursing his wife's pre menstrual syndrome, Gerald Dooley glanced at the headlines and then stopped shaving to focus on the article. After reading the headlines and half of the editorial he raised his eyes and said.

-Who's the fucking rat? - It's got to be one of the younger officer present at the meeting. I'll never know.-

That was not the right answer. Melinda took a deep breath.

-Never mind who the rat is. The administration is the rat in this case. You my fine friend are the elected rat..... What are you going to do about this? If I understand correctly, you've been receiving phone calls about children being molested by pedophiles and you, the mayor, the protector of these kids, are recommending.... no, wrong word....., you're ordering inaction because of budget constraint. Is it because these kids don't vote. You politicians are fucking disgusting. .....I disagreed earlier with the brutality of this coverage but now, I see that it is necessary to shake the world out of the historical complacency about child molestation. – She was using the exact words used by the editor. She slammed the door leaving mayor Dooley with his thoughts.

Dooley didn't have his cup of coffee at home that morning. Arriving at the office fifteen minutes earlier than usual, he found the staff already reading and commenting on the newspaper headlines. His phone message box was full with eleven messages. Reading through the list he pulled one by the police chief and another one by Stella Firestone, the congress woman, a fine republican.

-Don't even try to find out who the rat is. Just get more people on these delations. - Was his revised recommendation to the chief of police.

The chief had read the editorial from the Daily News and had reassigned available police officers to follow-up on these calls. Paterson was the coordinator of this task force.

-Don't worry, I'll sit on this like a crocodile mother hatching her eggs. – Answered the chief. He was much happier with this new more politically and humanly correct approach.

The congress woman was another story.

-I suppose you have read this morning edition of the Lewiston News . Is what I read the truth? - She was using his wife's earlier verbiage almost verbatim.

-Of course not. - Lied the mayor. – As usual, the reporters have been manufacturing news. We have made these calls our priorities. Each and every one of them will be properly investigated.-

-Of course, priorities as of this morning I'd bet a hundred to one. Keep me abreast, the Attorney General is also mentioned in this editorial... An editorial with which, I want you to know, I am in complete agreement.–

She took a sip of her coffee and pulled on a cigarette before continuing.

-This could become a major political issue and I don't need that. – Then on a second thought she continued. - Neither do you. As a matter of fact I wonder why, we, as a society, needed to be jolted out of our shorts by some Vigilante group?- Is it because some among us may be pedophiles as the editor suggested; or because our heads are so deep into our political ass holes that we can't extract them out.?- She hung up.

When the city's Business manager came into the mayor's office a little after nine thirty, he found him looking out the window, smoking his fifteenth cigarette, as noted by a quick inventory of the full ashtray on the desk; a personal best.

-I need a drink but it's a little early. These fucking journalists will drive us batty.-

Ray had a sly smile and said in a baritone voice well suited to sing Handel's Messiah that he would come back later. He had decided to run for mayor in the next election and this situation was not against his best political interests.

The rest of the day was spent answering phone calls and reading various versions published by other news papers throughout the country. The news had been picked up around the world. ABC TV news took advantage of this unexpected support and editorialized on the subject, immediately preceding the daily "*Mithridatisation clip*".

The VP of Legal affairs for the ABC CY phoned his lawyers in New York and told them to stop billing hours on this affair.

-The Attorney General will now stop his action against us. I'll bet the order will come from God, so stop working on this. You hear me, no more billing as of now. - Being a lawyer he knew that billing was what law firms did best.

CHAPTER 44

"No one looks more like an innocent than a culprit above suspicion."

On the sixth day, the world was fully aware that even in America, this heaven of democracy, children were at risk of being abused by pedophiles. Not exceptionally, the journalists were taking situations out of contexts, hinting, suggesting with half truths that the villains were influencing the government. A pure coincidence, a computer operated pedophile sex scandal unmasked by the FBI brought more heat to the subject.

Had they been identified, this –*Vigilante Brigade*- would have been offered juicy contracts by some of the largest magazines and TV stations in the world. In most countries, newspapers had picked up on the Lewiston Daily News and confirmed that they also cared about the well being of children. Even in countries where kids are an economic resource being used as cheap labor and peddled to perverted tourists as sexual objects, newspapers were ganging up on Americans. Of course it was not worse in the USA than anywhere else in the world, on the contrary, probably a lot better, but today the American flag was sitting in the accused box and being flogged by Lilliputians. The top dog is never allowed a mistake; the alternative is to have its rear end bitten by the pack.

ABC's rating curve was climbing beyond the chart. Their competitors were having a fit. The first official coverage by the foreign magazines would be available on most news stands in two days. Most had already printed pictures and written articles before signing multi million dollars agreements with ABC. They had printed twice as many copies as usual, even more than they had printed for the last controversial USA election report; it was expected they would be sold out by the end of the first day.

The attorney general had initiated action to stop the coverage before the "Lewiston editorial" and before the congress woman Firestone got on the case. Now caught in the middle of a swan dive which would land flat and look more like a swan song, he could not easily back off.

Just as he was reflecting on this dilemma, his secretary came in solemnly pointing to the telephone, making a sign that it was HIM. He picked up, listened a good minute and answered.

-I know Mister President.... - The President cut him off and continued.

-Do you think you have a leg to stand on with this, legally speaking I mean... because, politically we both know where it's going. - Commented the President.

-We were absolutely sure... but now... I am beginning to have second thought. It's not as clear-cut as initially projected by my staff. The station will retain the best law firm and has so far done what the law required. –The Attorney general replied, bracing himself for a blast.

After a moment of heavy silence, the President came back with a flat.

-Keep me current and remember that in the USA we don't fuck around with the freedom of the press.-

He then terminated the communication, unhappy about the decision the attorney general had taken on his own. Freedom of the press had to be respected at all costs, and furthermore the President was not a pedophile, his sexual inclination well known and perfectly natural if a little tumultuous and on the liberal side.

At about the same time the bailiff walked pass Nora Osborne and delivered the injunction to the president of the ABC Television company. All the clips were seized. But copies had already been shipped outside the country; future clips would not be received by the station unless the injunction was lifted.

This injunction was oil on the fire. The news commentator's opening statement on the eighth day was that the Attorney general had imposed an interruption of the coverage.

-ABC is appealing this decision on the basis that it interferes with the freedom of the press. Our lawyers are hopeful that the Attorney General will respect the right of the people to know the truth. We cannot predict when this debate will be resolved but you'll be kept current daily. -

One way or the other, the station would benefit as people would take side and watch the political game being played. The villain in this case was clearly the attorney general. She continued her lecture.

-The freedom of the press and the right of the American people to know could be violated by this injunction from the attorney general. Lobbyists not pleased with this coverage, shouldn't be able to influence our government. In the mean time the Station had sold the rights to this coverage to foreign magazines and foreign television stations. - And she went on with their names. Ending her comments she could not refrain from repeating that she found it astonishing that: - the protection of children would take a back seat to political consideration.-

The Attorney General was made to look like a righteous child molester and the appointed protector of this confraternity. While the feasibility of this injunction had been assessed carefully by his staff, the President had coined the assessment: - near sighted and politically dumb. - In its legal jargon, the injunction included phrases such as: – *Unlawful and barbarous action being heralded on national TV. Torture being shown directly on TV. Possible copy cat encouragement. Adverse social reaction suffered by the relatives of the kidnapped victims. Pornographic material being shown on national TV. Etc...*

When analyzed by brilliant and Cartesian young legal minds, within the confines of a sterile boardroom, these reasons seemed sufficient to issue the injunction; they probably were. However, after seven days of intensive media coverage, during which a strong collective endorsement of the ABC's audacious initiative had been developing, this injunction was considered unfounded. All other considerations, however warranted, were perceived as being accessory and siding, even aiding the abusers.

The Attorney General had his legal ass kicked by the Boss and, in turn reprimanded his staff, reproaching them that he had not been properly advised. Looking for an emissary goat he was quick to see that the lobbyists responsible for stirring the pot and indirectly accountable for his blunder should be carefully investigated. Could they be pedophiles as well as political morons?

-I want a complete and, I stress the word complete, file on the lobbyists who initiated this catastrophe. Get it done by the FBI but don't stop there, dig wherever you have to. I want to know everything, from their favorite color to their sexual preferences. - He had adamantly ordered his special assistant Adam Simpson.

-I'll get back to you tomorrow with at least a portion of the report. - Simpson answered overjoyed with the mission.

CHAPTER 45

"When man kills a tiger, it's called "sport"; when the tiger kills a man, it' s called "ferocity". This is all the distinction there is between justice and crime."
GB Shaw

The following afternoon, Adam Simpson, a good looking young lawyer, thirty-ish, elegant dresser, intelligent, ambitious and well born, opened a drawer and took out a file earmarked:

« Lobbyists report from Adam Simpson / Injunction ABC News Channel / Lewiston Daily News »

He started writing a report which would go directly to the desk of his boss, the Attorney General Robert Morrison.

"PERSONAL AND CONFIDENTIAL

standout box start

To :The office of the Attorney General

From :Adam Simpson, Special Assistant

Subject:ABC TV injunction / Lobbyists

end standout box

The following information has been obtained from the usual sources.

William Schacter,

Date of birth, 2 June 1937

Address: 2734 Lincoln Ave, Swanton, VT

Married, divorced, three male children ages 31, 34, 35."

Then he paused, looking at an antique frame, occupying the center place on the wall opposite his desk. In the middle of a parchment, in bold dark letters, were written two words:

"Scripta manent".

His father had given him the frame for his twenty first birthday. Since he did not know the difference between Latin and Chinese, Adam had looked it up and found that it meant: "Writings leave a permanent trace".

He remained pensive for a few moments; this affair had the potential to turn into a political nightmare. The less in writing the better it would be, if and when the shit hit the fan. After mulling over his decision while pacing the floor he picked up the phone and dialed 12. The Attorney General himself came on line.

-Sir, this is Adam, I have a partial investigative report on the two lobbyists involved in the ABC injunction. I started writing a report but now think that I should talk to you first. You can then decide if you want this in writing.-

-Come on over. – Said the man and he hung up.

A moment later Adam was knocking on the Attorney General's door, carrying a thick file under his right arm.

The door was opened by the man himself who stepped aside to let his young colleague come through.

-What is it that you don't want frozen for posterity. - Asked the now curious Attorney General.

Rearranging and buttoning his coat after having dropped the file on a table, Adam sat down and started what would be the beginning of a witch hunt. Some of the subjects turned out to be bona fide witches of the broom flying and satanic variety.

-The two lobbyists in question in this affair are William Schacter and Reegan Mc Kinney. Both these men have had successful careers in the business world and after early retirements at age fifty five decided to use their experiences to help others achieve their goals when government agencies became involved.-

He continued :

-So far nothing unusual. Their past is virginal and, on first look the present is also A1... However, a quick survey of Schacter's spending habits indicated that he is a frequent traveler to Thailand. Ten round trips this year raises a red flag if we are investigating a pseudo pedophile link to lobbying activity. Does he have close relatives, a special research interest there or why has he travelled at great expense to Bangkok ten times over the last twelve months and eleven the previous twelve months. All these trips are short trips from four to six days.-

At this stage the Attorney general, who had been reading another file, became attentive, opening a legal note book and grabbing his golden Mont Blanc. He was about to take notes which was most unusual; Adam felt his scalp tighten and his face redden with excitement as he spelled the names of the two lobbyists and repeated their ages and addresses for his boss; then he continued.

-Schacter 's wife split twenty five years ago. She raised the three boys who, at that time were six, nine and ten. We were able to trace the woman and the kids. They are living on the west coast. A special investigator visited the former Mrs. Schacter and after dancing around the reason for her divorce twenty five years ago she finally admitted that it was necessary for the children's safety. She refused to go into more details.-

Adam stopped and glanced over his notes; more to let the first two pages sink in than to make sure he had not forgotten anything.

-Mrs. Hildebrand, that's her maiden name, never remarried, telling the investigator that once was enough. She raised her children and with the financial help from her former husband and her own parents, was able to provide a university education for all three. They're all psychiatrists, very successful, with offices on the west coast. That's the extent of the information our man could extract out of Mrs. Hildebrand-Schacter, so he located the sons and found that all three were specializing in psychiatric care for abused victims. That's where he stopped, waiting for more specific orders.-

-What about the other person, this Mc Kinney. - Asked the Attorney General.

-We couldn't find anything on him that would raise a flag one way or the other. Still married to the same wife, two kids, three grand children and obviously not the Alpha member in his association with Schacter. But we're still digging. Regarding Schacter, we have asked the CIA to investigate in Thailand. Maybe the authorities there have something on our man.-

The Attorney general fixed his gaze on a favorite ceiling spot, directly above one of the two chairs in front of his stylish desk. He would always fix on that same spot when coping with a complicated issue. Those unaware of his habit would soon become ill at ease. In fact, this was a tactic for disassociating himself with the emotional world allowing him to make cold decisions. In these moments he would turn into a ruthless psychopath.

He was turning in his mind the obvious question: Why would a sixty some year old man travel to Thailand twenty one times during the last twenty two months. A quick mental calculation which he would ask someone from his staff to confirm indicated that Schacter had spent upward of one hundred thousand dollars in non deductible expenses or had it been claimed as lobbying expenses? Maybe it was bona fide lobbying expenses; did he have a contract with a Thai firm...?

-You made the right decision. Your father was a smart fellow. Keep digging... discreetly if you please and report to me as often as you receive new information, any... new information. Also tap their telephones and contact Schacter as soon as possible; a friendly unofficial visit. See how he reacts when you mention our surprise at the number of trips to Thailand; ask him the name of the Thai company he's dealing with. And don't forget to get a complete Internal Revenue report on both these persons and their lobbying company. -

CHAPTER 46

"Lies, like oil float, on top of the truth."
Henry Sienkiewicz

At sixty one William Schacter, was a chubby giant. He had been forced into early retirement from an executive job with one of the airline companies when his employer merged. After travelling for a month he had decided that fifty five was too young to retire from the business world. He created a consulting company specializing in lobbying.

During his travels, he had had occasions to meet other business men with the same fondness for teens. He was a specialist in the matter as well as a long term customer; he invested some of his severance pay in a child pornographic business. Where else than in Thailand, a country he had visited several times before and where tolerance of the sex tourism was attracting pedophiles from the world over.

William Schacter had been a pedophile for as long as he could remember. He had stayed away from his own children for several years and came to think that he was cured. Unfortunately, one day that he had been drinking, his wife being away, he had walked into the bedroom of his oldest son. Thereafter all three of his sons had had to submit to his passion for children. Fortunately his wife became aware of his behavior and divorced him. In a way he was relieved and agreed to pay a generous alimony. Protecting her children's privacy, his wife remained close-mouthed about the cause of their divorce: gross incompatibility the paper work read.

The kids were seen by the very best psychiatrists and able to recover some normality in their lives. Brilliant students they became prominent psychiatrists for abused children. One way to cope with a problem is to understand it completely. Personal experience is unbeatable when it comes to psychiatry and they had intimate knowledge and experience in this area.

All three of Schacter's sons were homosexual; could it have been a defective gene received from the father? Whatever the cause, they accepted their sexuality without further attempting to fight what they knew to be a natural inclination. Their mother was heavy hearted; she would have liked to be a grandmother. As it was, she would not have to worry about her grand children being abused.

In Thailand, Shacter's partners were two women: Lucia and Mia Cheng. When Mia was eight years old, she had been sold by her family to be used as a child prostitute where Mia was the manager. Then at seventeen she became too old to be of any value; for two years she worked as a room maid in the brothel where she had spent her youth; protected by Lucia, most probably her cousin, she soon became a hostess. At seventeen she had already a huge experience of this particular milieu.

She had recognized that voyeurism was almost as important for some of her clients as hands-on. Adolpho, a Portuguese photograph of great disrepute had been secretly shooting hot sequences involving unaware customers. She teamed up with the photograph and filming some of the better moments her customers were experiencing began a little business on the side, selling the clips to German, French, Dutch or any customers who would pay the exorbitant prices she would exact for her art work. A good clip would fetch one hundred dollars US, a fortune in Thailand, and pocket change in Germany or the USA.

William Schacter had been a long time customer of most of the child brothels in Thailand. He had met Lucia and Mia several years ago. When she offered porno clips to Bill, he recognized the opportunity and made Mia an offer. She accepted immediately: Bill was to put up twenty thousand dollars to rent a studio, purchase the best of equipment, and sell the films world wide through a WEB site. Mia would manage the business and provide new material on a regular basis. This venture had been going on for five years and explained the frequent trips Bill made to Thailand, coming back via Zurich where he banked his share of the profit.

The authorities were kept at bay by whatever means deemed necessary. Lucia, Mia's mentor and long time protector, had been in this business for several decades and knew most of the law enforcers. For a few baths, they closed their eyes on sexual businesses of any kind including child prostitution and enslavement. The reputation Lucia had built was reaching out into most of the affluent countries of the world. The money this trio was sharing was substantial as well as tax free.

But can you stay out of the radar screen for long when travelling frequently to Bangkok? The American embassy was quickly aware of the frequent trips Bill was making to this country and had been inquisitive. When a demand for information came from the CIA it did not take very long for a reply to be forwarded by fax.

-William Schacter is a frequent visitor to this country and seems to have a business association with a Mia Cheng, owner of a movie studio in Bangkok. The information we were able to gather on his partner is that she was and still is an employee at one of the country's most successful child brothel. The authorities say that their business is legitimate and that the company (Web Production inc.) is paying its due to the government. While actively participating in the operation of the business, M. Schacter is not one of the principal of the company which belongs to Mia Cheng and her cousin Lucia.-

Upon receiving this report, special assistant Simpson phoned his contact at the Internal Revenue Services. After a few hours, he received an answer to his query.

« - William Schacter residing at 326 Rosewood Ave, Milton Mass., did not declare revenues from a foreign source. He has revenues from a pension and from his USA lobbying company. His total revenues last year amounted to one hundred and three thousand dollars. He has paid income tax on fifty eight thousand dollars. »

Special Assistant Simpson mulled this over for a minute before picking up the telephone and phoning the Washington office number of the Schacter and McKinley Consulting company. After identifying himself and the purpose of his call he asked for an appointment to meet with M. Schacter regarding their lobbyist activities in the ABC affair.

-Yes, of course I'll see you, but I don't see why you need to see me, - said Schacter. We have done what we're paid for and while I realize that this is becoming a hot issue.... – then after a few seconds of silence he said that he would be pleased to meet with the Special Assistant to the Attorney General whenever it suited him.

The morning after, at ten o'clock sharp, Adam Simpson walked in William Shacter's office where a petite agile older secretary offered him a cup of coffee while he waited.

-Mr. Schacter is on the phone and will be with you in a minute or two.-

From where he was sitting Adam could hear an emotionally charged conversation; charged with anger and frustration deduced Adam. When Schacter came out of his office, his face was still flushed but otherwise in control. Extending his hand:

-I still don't know how I can be of service but you're welcome. -

Adam was in the habit of carrying hidden recording equipment. Taking notes was inefficient in recording tones of voices and details like breathing, pauses and these little hints that one only picks up upon listening a second or even a third time to a conversation. He activated the device and walked into the office; Schacter closed the door after having ordered his secretary to not disturb them.

The office was spacious and elegantly furnished with old American furniture. On the walls three very nice early American paintings added a touch of patriotism, no doubt very well for the business of lobbying. The desk, behind which William Schacter presided, was the nicest piece in the room. At least one hundred and fifty years old, it must have been owned by one of the former presidents, thought Adam. He looked around but could not find any souvenirs imported from these frequent trips to Thailand. Obviously this page in Schechter's life was meant to remain private and secret.

He chose the only modern piece of furniture to sit down and opened his brief case. With slow elaborate movements he retrieved a yellow legal notepad from the brief case. He would not need it as the taped conversation would be more reliable than his notes but it looked more professional.

-Mister Schacter, let me come right to the heart of the subject. I have been asked to see you by the Attorney General who has issued an injunction to ABC TV, partly as a result of your ... influence on several of the members of the senate. After yesterday's article in the Lewiston Daily News, we've been swamped with demands to rescind the injunction. It became of interest for us to know the identity of your client in this affair.-

-My client is a company which would like to remain anonymous. Legally I don't have to answer your question unless you have a court order. - Schacter replied.

Schechter's voice was modulated and careful. Listening to the tape would be enlightening.

-Of course you don't have to answer and if we think the importance warrants it we will get a court order. As you know some of the newspapers have hinted that the lobbying company might have been working on behalf of a group protecting the interests of pedophiles and the distributors of juvenile pornographic material. We don't think this is true but we nevertheless have to be absolutely certain. –

He waited a moment thinking that Schacter would come out with the name. He did not, so Adam continued with his trump card.

-This client of yours wouldn't be located in Thailand by any chance. ?-

Ascending gradually from his neck to his face, a magnificent crimson red flushed the now disturbed Schacter; not unlike an angry or scare octopus thought Adam. Sudden increase in blood pressure triggered by his hidden motives to travel so often to Thailand, thought Simpson. Schacter took a sip out of a glass on his desk, trying to dissipate the embarrassment of his arterial blood flowing so close to the exterior of his face. Thailand was his secret and he had not realized that frequent travelling to a foreign country would become suspicious.

-I have a special interest in Thailand. I am somewhat an amateur social behaviorist. - He managed to say avoiding Simpson's eyes.

-Social behaviorist- repeated Simpson pausing the necessary thirty seconds for the effect to sink in.

He was tempted to tell him that they knew of his interest and had themselves developed a special occupational curiosity about his hobby. He paused another long moment, scribbling meaningless words on his yellow legal pad. The flush on Schacter's face was still manifest as the special assistant continued his line of indirect questioning which worked so well with intelligent persons.

-Our embassy in Thailand has been aware of your frequent visits to this country. As you know the government is trying to insure the safety of all travelling Americans. - Having trouble keeping a straight face at this shameless lie.

Adam Simpson was a true blood "all American boy" and perversion was as abominable for him as Communism had been for McCarthy or Hitler. He now was certain that Schacter was a fucking pedophile. He had been vindicated in his suspicion of Schacter's sexual habits and could not help but despise him.

Simpson picked up his brief case and slowly replaced his yellow legal pad without further looking at Schacter's still crimson skin texture. Flashing a wide smile in the general direction of Schacter, he stood.

-It has been nice talking to you Mister Schacter although I don't have answers to our questions. – And then on the way out. -We at least know that you won't cooperate without a court orders.-

He was already turning the door knob when Schacter regained enough of his composure to be able to use his voice.

- Please, please, sit down. There is no reason for me to not cooperate with the Attorney General's office. I'll tell you what you want to know.-

And he told Adam that his client was a rival Television Station. The name of the game was competition and a reaction to a substantial fall in rating and revenues. The company was trying to put an end to the hemorrhage.

He opened a drawer and produced a contract with the Company in question. Adam looked at it briefly and then asked.

-Is this one of your steady clients or a new one. –

-A new one. We figured they had tried several other consulting companies before coming to us. My partner wanted to pass but the money was good and I knew that I could be successful. - Replied Schacter.

Adam sank back into the quick sand like chair and had taken his note pad out of his brief case once more.

-You knew that you could be successful.... - He repeated before continuing. - Thank you very much for your cooperation. Needless to say that this information will remain confidential.-

He left after having reluctantly shaken the flaccid hand extended to him by a now panicking Schacter. Schacter was caught; his Thailand business would not remain a secret very long; what with his Thai lawyer blackmailing him. Running might be the best way out; the IRS would tag him for several millions of dollars in back taxes and criminal charges, prison maybe..... Jesus Christ almighty, where are you now that I need you.

CHAPTER 47

"Poverty breeds crime."

Thailand is a country of 514 000 square kilometers with a population of 55 millions, speaking Thai and practicing Buddhism. The population is 99 percent Chinese. At the beginning of the eighth century, chased by the Mongols, the Thais had emigrated from the Yunnan province, in south China.

From Charybde to Sylla; for the next centuries they were subordinated to the Khmers before breaking away from their yoke during the thirteenth century. The name of the country was then Siam. The Siamese fought with all their neighbors: the Khmers, the Birmans their hereditary enemies, and the French who were in Vietnam. In 1935 the king abdicated and the country is now a constitutional monarchy.

The population is rural for the greater part and lives essentially in the plain of Menam. As is usually the case for ex colonies, the natural resources like latex and tin are controlled by foreign companies, the raw material being exported to be turned into marketable goods. This is where the real money is made, which is particularly true if the raw material is sold for next to nothing by the parent company breaking even in order not to pay taxes.

The rural population can hardly make ends meet. As in the India of the thirteenth century, Buddhist philosophy coupled with a hot and humid climate, took the fight out of these populations. They accept, almost welcome their Karmic fate as a way to end the recurrent life cycles and the endless reincarnations by achieving Nirvana. While we are still toying with the idea of euthanasia they treat life as a living hell and culturally welcome death.

Under these conditions and with this frame of mind, it is not unusual for poor farmers to sell one or more of their daughters. The little money they obtain will help support the rest of the family for a while. Better this than having the children abducted by recruiters, who roam the country side in search of fresh recruits.

Mia's parents were poor farmers living from hand to mouth some twenty kilometers from the village of Pattawa. Pattawa is to sex what Las Vegas is to gambling; a commodity enhanced by the fertility of the poor's. As an advance for Mia's future income the parents received a few thousand bahts from a recruiter.

-She'll be better off with us, eat well and be happy. – Promised the recruiter, a toothless man with a patch over his left eye.

Mia was eight and immediately put to work in a brothel specializing in pedophilia. Like most eight year olds, Mia had no idea what it meant to be a prostitute. Even though she was culturally prepared to be obedient, Mia was not prepared to be raped by an old Birman trader as an introduction into the working girls' paradise. This lecherous old pig had paid a lot because Mia was a virgin; who is not a virgin at eight? The initial investment the brothel had made was recuperated ten fold right then.

When most girls are still playing with dolls, Mia set up to survive in this raw universe. The older girls in the brothel were relying on their faith and citing learned and tried paraboles to give a sense to their lives. This complicity between religions, philosophies and day to day realities, gradually convinced Mia that she was expiating for terrible sins committed in a past life that she could not remember.

At least this was a justification; better than being raped repeatedly unjustly, and she soon stoically accepted her fate as a form of penance, realizing that crying and being unhappy would not bring relief to her misfortune; on the contrary, it would enhance the pleasure of some of her clients. Soon she became a good technician and fulfilled her duties as a provider of sex to pedophiles of all ethnic backgrounds: laughing, crying, being angry and rude, whatever the client needed to soil the bed linen with a few sickly spermatozoids.

Mia had been hungry all her life and eating enough to satisfy this constant craving for proteins rendered sexual slavery almost acceptable. In a few years she had become a beautiful young girl, lucky enough to remain free of disease or permanent injury. While she didn't have a formal academic education she was always looking for bits and pieces of information on any and all subjects; often from her more gentler patrons.

Most of her co-workers were lifeless, following the Buddhist philosophy and capitulating; surrendering to the libidinous whims of their customers and chewing as many Ayaba pills as their meager allowances would allow them to buy. Mia would send all the money to her family. She never took drugs or alcohol.

Inevitably, the day came when a client refused her; -too old- he had said. Mia was now a young lady. The fatidic day had come and she was now an adolescent, no longer of any value as sexual merchandise for pedophiles. Often those retired teens were thrown in the street; because of Lucia, Mia was lucky and became a room maid in the brothel. This place had been her home for the last ten years. She was now paid for being a maid and was grateful for the few baths paid to her at the end of the week. (One dollars is equal to five Th bahts) How defenseless would she have been on the outside, an easy prey for the cold-blooded pimps roving the streets of Bangkok always looking for new slaves; disposable merchandise, throw away humans. She would not have survived more than a couple of years: worked to death, dying on the side walk.

As sexual workers were often from the same geographical area, it was not surprising that Lucia, the matriarch of the brothel was also from Patawa. This fragile bond created a long lasting relationship, the only one either ever had; Lucia took Mia under her wings. The biological instinct of motherhood is powerful; Lucia never had children of her own. Like a seed dropped randomly in a desert, Mia fitted perfectly and took root in the tough old heart. In two years Mia had made her teacher and protector proud; she was ready to become a hostess and maybe grow out of this sordid business.

-Put on your blue dress. We're going to see a movie. - Lucia ordered one rainy afternoon.

Mia had never been to a movie theater. After the interminable India-made tear jerker, Lucia took her to a restaurant. During the meal, the old survivor told her protégée that she knew a movie producer who had been making films in the brothel. This had been the real purpose of the outing.

-He owes me a favor and I'd like you to meet him.-

They met Adolfo, a Portuguese amateur photographer and film maker, who, in repayment of a favor owed Lucia, educated Mia in the fine art of shooting amateur video clips. A good student, she soon could covertly shoot action scenes at her place of work.

Adolfo would buy these films from Lucia and make a handsome profit reselling them. But...Adolpho was a gambler and when he had to run away from Thailand, his life being threatened for non payment of gambling debts, Lucia continued to run the business. After a year she turned it over to Mia.

-I'm old. I want to rest and prepare for my death. The business is now yours. In return I want you to take care of me for the few years I have left.-

Lucia must have been all of seventy five but looked ninety; having smoked from age ten, her skin had the texture and the color of a rusty metal roof. Mia agreed and then became the owner of a small movie producing business.

Selling the clips to rich foreigners was not as easy as she had thought. One day, showing one of her latest production to Schacter, a former admirer and client when she was a child, she was made an offer. After talking it over with Lucia she accepted.

Schacter invested enough capital into the business to buy state of the art equipment and rent a studio. He also set up an efficient marketing network on the Internet. Soon the new –WEB Production- company was a successful venture. Lucia, getting fat and happy, was proud to have been the creator of this success and enjoyed the advantages brought by prosperity: new house, new furniture, servants, a chauffeur driven limousine, unlimited Ayaba, cognac, expensive cigarettes and Cuban cigars: nothing that would further her enlightenment or search for Nirvana but allowed her to sample paradise. At seventy five Lucia was having serious doubts about reincarnation, Nirvana and other metaphysical considerations; even more skeptical when her best earthly interest would be at risk. After all, if reincarnation was to cleanse the soul and prepare for eternal nothingness, why not edge your bets and enjoy a few good moments while still breathing.

-I have already repaid every sins I could have possibly made during my previous lives.-

The relationship between the two women was one of admiration and devotion. Lucia had been the only person having a gram of humanity for Mia. Both were from the "hmong tribe", coming from the same poor village and both had suffered through several years of sexual slavery. They had created a mother daughter bond. Furthermore and as important, Lucia was the best business advisor concerning governmental affairs and business transactions in Thailand. Over the last sixty five years spent in the business of procuring pleasure, Lucia had developed contacts at all levels of society. Key politicians, policemen, business men, local and international crime king pins, were in her debt for something or other. Nothing was written but she had a terrific memory.

Schacter and his new partners had created a Thai company with ramification in Switzerland; as he wanted to remain a silent partner, his shares were held by a Thai lawyer. The studio was a show place, a legal facade where some bona fide movies were shot, sometimes at a loss. The real bread and butter business was the child pornographic web site. Like an alcoholic working in a bar, Schacter could make money out of his vice; this business brought Schacter a high degree of libidinal satisfaction. On a one to a hundred rating, his job satisfaction was ninety nine; the fragility of his legal status and his subordination to his Thai lawyer being the only hiccups.

When Adam Simpson, the Attorney General's special assistant walked into his office, Schacter was ending a tumultuous conversation with his Bangkok lawyer. A large amount of money had not been deposited in his Swiss bank account. It was not the first time that the lawyer had used some of the funds to cover his gambling debts. While royally paid for his services, the young lawyer could see that the kid porno business was a gold mine. Lucia had warned Shacter to be more careful of lawyers. Greed, once more, would turn out to be the grain of sand in the gear of this otherwise smoothly running machine.

-I'll be travelling to Bangkok next week. In the mean time I'll expect this money to be in my account at the Swiss Bank in Zurich. I know that you've been using these funds to cover some of your gambling losses. Either you stop this...... unauthorized borrowing or you'll be out of a job. – Snapped the angry William Schacter.

-It would be imprudent to switch law firms.... - And coming out with his ace in the hole he continued -Did you know that you are under investigation? One of the secretaries at the embassy told me that questions were asked about you. Think about it carefully before you do anything.... stupid. - The lawyer had replied before crashing the phone so hard that his secretary walked into the office to see what the problem was.

He had never been so openly rude and obviously threatening. Hanging up with a deliberately slow and gentle gesture, William Schacter realized that he would have to deal with this time bomb. The legal approach was out, the lawyer would rat and use blackmail as currency; Lucia; as always Lucia would be helpful and of sound advise. This old girl was invaluable. She had a way to make problems disappear; sometimes the cost had been high like when a known businessman had discovered that his secret gambols with kids had been filmed and were sold worldwide on the net. An unfortunate mistake Mia had made and would not repeat. She still giggled when reminded of the incident.

CHAPTER 48

"Et qui pardonne au crime en devient le complice."
Voltaire

"Those who absolve crimes become accessories."

The coverage of the "Mithridatisation" had been interrupted for less than forty eight hours. Under pressure, the Attorney general had rescinded the injunction. The powerful photo magazines Match, Der Spiegel and Oh La had taken over the reporting and the diffusion was almost world wide. Some of the very Catholic countries had opted to ban the magazines; not surprisingly, most of the Islamic countries under Sharia law allowed marriage with pubescent girls of nine with older men, these girls condemned to illiteracy and at the mercy of their master.

The revenues accumulating in the Foundation's bank account would last several years. If properly invested the capital could, like for the Nobel foundation, be almost eternal. Tim and Zygfridas had agreed on some remarkable by-laws: one was that all victims of abuses could benefit from this Foundation, including battered wives, their children and close relatives of the abusers. These close relatives are often subordinated when the abuser is the bread winner. Not only would they be deprived of their daily bread and butter but would also be ostracized by their community. If people are quick to blame an entire country for the crimes of some of its member, Germany being a good example, holding all members of a family responsible for the crimes of the father or a brother is a reality. The family becomes guilty by association.

Tim convinced Zygfridas, that a little compassion and support for these secondary victims would remove the apprehension of the "after delation" period. How often had he seen a mother closing her eyes and pragmatically allowing her husband to have inappropriate relations with her daughter because he was the bread winner; or because he would beat the life out of her if she dared speak.

-Only by helping financially and morally those depending on the abusers for their bread and butter, can we give them a real choice. - Said Tim to his partners.

-This will not be easy to implement but I see where this clause should be advertised. I wonder how it can be done without falling into the trap of paying a bounty for delation, like the IRS. - Reflected Al.

-A bounty..., why not pay a fucking bounty if it brings the bastards to justice. - Had answered Tim, surprised at the coarse language he had used. Goldwater applauded.

In Washington, it became clear that the emissary goat had been found. The Attorney General needed one and Simpson could easily convince him that William Schacter was it. He was a recognized pedophile, having abused his own children, as well as several other children in Thailand, the USA and else where, owner of a company whose business orientation was the production and diffusion of child pornographic material on the internet. To top the sundae with a cherry, Schacter was also a candidate for an in depth investigation on the part of the IRS. This investigation would not cost anything but on the contrary, would be a good investment in man power and resources.

-You won't be able to prove anything in the USA. The proof is in Thailand where our man never thought we'd have tentacles. He forgets that we have been present in Thailand since 1941. It warrants a trip; please leave as soon as you can. You've done very well so far.-

It was unusual for the Attorney general to be laudatory. He felt relieved now that the pressure was lifted off his shoulders. The President had not phoned him today. He had downgraded this affair as a low priority incident.

-I'll be on my way to Bangkok in a few hours. I hope that I won't have to travel with Schacter. It would be embarrassing for both of us to be on the same plane. - Replied Simpson who had already reserved a seat on a flight to Paris from where he would continue to Bangkok.

-Excellent initiative. We may want to see if we can keep Schacter here until this thing is thoroughly investigated. – And then as a second thought. – Only if we have good legal cause. Are we there yet? -

Simpson replied.

-Too soon yet sir. There is always the off-chance that we're barking up the wrong tree or that we won't be able to prove the allegations. - He was of the opinion that smart ass lawyers could have painted Hitler as a philanthropist.

That same evening Simpson was on a flight to Paris Charles De Gaulle airport where he would embark on a Thai Airline flight to Bangkok. The flight to Paris was uneventful and he had a few hours to kill before leaving for Bangkok. Lingering in the first class lounge where he had been upgraded by his travel agent, Adam was only half amazed at the number of men who might qualify as pedophiles; some of these same persons may identify him as a potential pervert.

Thailand was a known pedophile haven and heaven. Tourists were not all pedophiles but some of them would be. Simpson wasn't long in guessing that most of these persons were going to Thailand indirectly, coming to Paris before purchasing their tickets for Bangkok. It was an oversight on the part of Schacter who would still be incognito if he had transited via Toronto or Paris.

-Flight 003 to Bangkok is now boarding from gate seven. - Said the flawless voice of the airport public system.

Twelve hours later he was landing in Bangkok after having ingested more expensive food than ever in his entire life. Farm land Wisconsin alimentary regimen is strictly beef, pork and potatoes. Caviar, foie gras, lobsters, champagne and cognac are as scarce as papal poop.

Between drinks and meals, Simpson got deeply interested in a book Kathleen, his soon to be wife, had offered him before he left: "The Third Chimpanzee" by Jared Diamond. A most interesting book, an eye opener, she had said.

-Some of your behavior became much more acceptable when I realized that you share more than 98% of your genes with the Chimpanzees. - She had commented half jokingly.

His religious, more or less creationist background was challenged by the idea. He could not help but smile at how his grandfather would have reacted to this suggestion. Where was God's magic wand in this scenario.

After take off he opened the book, at first out of curiosity, not convinced that he would read these seven hundred pages; then he found that it was written by a respected anthropologist and easy enough to read; by the time he had reached page twenty he was hooked.

He agreed with the diagnosis Diamond had posed: becoming a smart animal, man, this third chimpanzee has been using his knowhow to defeat his own purpose and destroy his universe. Will he change hat in time to become a protector of his planet rather than its most efficient destructor?

-Pretty damn frightening that by the year 2050 there will be twelve billion of us. - He had spoken out loud. His neighbor a taciturn Saudi looked at him as if he had been shown a girly picture.

Frightening to think that every hours there are seventeen species disappearing from the earth; at this rate, half of the thirty millions species now existing on earth will have disappeared by year 2050.

-Unbelievable that we could be so destructive without a purpose. – He had again disturbed his neighbor.

Frightening that if there were invaders from outer space, they probably would not be more generous and pacific than we have been with neighbors and new comers. The Homo Neanderthals for instance, a half brother that we have cannibalized and annihilated. Frightening that the president of the most powerful country of the world had rejected the Kyoto agreement on the protection of the environment, arguing that he did not have sufficient scientific data to justify putting the brakes on pollution, while in the same breath, with scientific data supporting that the project was unfeasible, he would launch the craziest and costliest star war project. And the greed displayed by large corporations; cheating and bluffing until they are caught after a dissatisfied employee rats on them or when the shit hits the fan and create a major financial catastrophe.

But who knows, maybe the President is wise to prepare a defense against some of the dictators sharing our world; after all, terrorism is now also used by the poor of the world after having been the prerogative of the mighty for so long: Nicaragua, Latin America, South Africa, the Caribbean Islands, Haiti and so many more, brow beaten by the rich and powerful countries. Nevertheless, thought Simpson, it would be smart to play along with Kyoto; like the life after death enigma edging one's bet is never stupid.

After an hour of reflection on this subject, while sipping champagne, Adam was on the verge of reviewing all previous conceptions and dogmas imposed upon him from birth. Dawning on him like a storm on a hot and muggy July afternoon was the doubt that religion may not be the solution but a large part of the problem. These magnificent rebels: Buddha, Jesus,

Abraham, Pythagore, Confucius and Zoroastre had the same purpose when they got conned into improving on the religions of their time: reduce the number of gods, make earth a better place for all including women and the poor's.

-Fine while it lasted, too bad their disciples screwed up by twisting things around. - Muttered Adam.

This time the Saudi person got up and looked at Adam as if he was a lunatic. He wobbled over to the stewardess and mumbled something before sitting down again. Adam laughed and had to admit that his behavior could seem bizarre.

–*Fuck him*- he mumbled again. -I beg your pardon. - Said the Prince. – Who thought he had heard –*Fuck you*.-

-Sorry about this, I must have been dreaming. - Said Adam, biting his tongue to keep from laughing.

He could see where religions had failed repetitively almost on purpose. For more than ten thousand years, their heralded purpose had been to make all men equal and better; the contrary has occurred. More wars with better armament, more efficient genocides, increasing inequality, more injustices and intolerances and more enslavement of the multitude by a few.

And he looked at his neighbor accusingly. Saudi Arabia where intolerance, injustice and enslavement were made into laws: women did not vote, did not drive, and had limited access to education. Saudi Arabia is a country where the king and his family milk the natural resources dishing out just enough crumbs to their people, so they will not rebel. These petro dollars are invested in the USA and Europe rather than developing the economy of their country, in fear that education and emancipation of their countrymen would lead to the abolition of this nonsensical monarchy.

Whenever half the population is fifteen years old or less and unemployment rampant, a storm is brewing; so what better parade than to blame this situation upon a common enemy. Hate then becomes the unifying common denominator. He was on the verge of engaging his neighbor in a philosophical discussion when the hostess materialized.

-Could I refill your glass sir? - Asked the very polite and elegant stewardess. She had been watching and felt that a little more would put Adam to sleep and avert a rowdy discussion.

He could smell the jasmine fragrance and her breath was charged with what he believed to be the closest thing to pheromones. His interior voice was saying. - Enough of that grape juice Adam Simpson, special assistant- while another voice was muttering.

-I should not but please do. Thank you.-

Her eyes were as profound as his soul of the moment. Like oceans, souls can be shallow or abysmal. When wandering too deeply, the mind can be trapped by depth sickness and never resurface. Once before he had experienced a state of mind so crystalline that he could see beyond the purpose of life. He remembered having mulled over the thought that: –*Man comes from nothing and goes nowhere.* - He got up and went to the bath room; pissing always brings one back to reality.

Adam had not advised the American embassy that he was coming to visit. He did not want any official knowledge of his trip until he was on his way back to the USA.

-We'll be landing shortly at Don Muong international airport, please attach your seat belt. - Said the hostess.

Looking out the window he could see the Menan River and the numerous canals quartering Bangkok. Just before landing he marveled at the sight of a luxurious golf course.

Tired of being pent up he hurried out of the plane as soon as the doors opened. His luggage was one of the first to spin around the carousel and he could clear customs before the rest of the passengers. An hour later he was registering at the hotel Oriental. From the airport, the cab driver had tried in vain to divert him to another –*much better hotel*-, but Adam had not accepted the offer; as a result he got a light speed ride and little conversation from the now sulking driver.

He slept four hours, used the gym for an hour and drank two liters of water to re hydrate his parched body. After a scalding shower he was in the lobby asking for a detailed map of the city. Adam made it a point to always know where he geographically was.

Before leaving the USA he had telephoned Shacter's lawyer, a certain Muong Taksin. He gave the address to the cab driver and ten minutes later was talking to the receptionist. The office was plush and of a style used by foreigners. The furniture could have been purchased in New York except for two large pictures depicting two elephants shielded with elaborate shining ornaments. Their defenses had been truncated and the tips covered with silver sheaths.

Muong Taksin, fortyish, thirty pounds overweight, was a model of obsequiousness. His receding hair line had uncovered a nasty looking mole which could have been a cancerous growth. Taksin was gloating, already tasting the blood that he guessed his client Schacter would be loosing in this battle against the US government. He would be around to pick up loose pieces and take his place in this WEB Company, maybe take full control over the Swiss Bank account. Later he would grab all of the company from these two sluts as he called them. Two fragile women were no match for a smart lawyer.

-The purpose of my visit is informal. I repeat that I am not officially representing my government or the office of the Attorney General.... Mister Taksin. We have reasons to believe that one of our fellow American is involved in a company producing child pornographic movies and distributing them on the Internet. - He paused a while to let this sink in but more so he could study the face of this colleague from another country.

Eyes shifting, Taksin was playing with a letter opener carved out of ivory. Adam continued.

-It is not a secret that you have incorporated this company and also, that you are acting on Shacter's behalf for good reason. Before going to the extent that the law will allow, we always make certain that we are acting judiciously.... – Adam stopped again inviting questions. Nothing only an increase in the fidgeting with the dagger letter opener. Adam continued.

-I have two questions... I remind you that you are under no obligation to answer. The first: Is William Schacter, indirectly through your office, a principal in WEB Co; and the second one: Is this company producing child pornographic movies. ?-

Having said his piece Adam sat down, his concealed device had been recording since he had entered this office.

-The answer to the first question is yes. I am acting on his behalf. I feel free to answer your questions if Mister Schacter is operating outside the laws of his country of residence. As for the second question, and as far as I know, WEB Co is a legal entity producing short documentary films, commercial advertising spots and at least once, tried to produce a film for the screen. .... No child pornographic material. - Replied Taksin. He was not about to destroy the object of his cupidity.

-Is this company paying income taxes in Thailand? - Asked Adam.

-Yes, my office is filing every year since the incorporation of WEB Co, four years ago. Let me show you last year's copy.-

He opened a drawer out of which he pulled a bulky folder. After glancing through it for a moment he took out a sheet and handed it to Adam.

-This is the résumé for this year. As you will see the company has paid three million Thai Bahts to the government. I believe this to be close to seven hundreds thousand dollars.-

Adam glanced though the sheet and could see that total revenues were ninety two million Th Bahts. He could see where several hundred of thousands of dollars had been pocketed by Schacter over the last four years. He could also see that this lawyer was the kind he would stay away from. The son of a bitch was flushing his client to steal his business. What happened to *honor among thieves*?

-Do you think I could have a copy of this entire file? -

Taksin seemed to consider the question with seriousness. After humming for a while he agreed and told Adam that it would be delivered at his hotel in the morning. He then decided to go all the way and try to scare Schacter's partners with this god sent Assistant to the Attorney General of the most powerful country in the world. This might come in handy when he made his attempt to appropriate the company from the two broads.

-Would you like to meet Mister Schacter's associates? –Adam was still reading the résumé and did not answer, Muong continued. – As you probably know, William Schacter will be arriving in Bangkok in the evening. He stopped over in Zurich on the way.-

-We have no jurisdiction over Thai residents and I don't want to meet them. Thank you very much.-

And then as an after thought.

-I suppose William Schacter is dealing with one of these Swiss private banks. ?-

-No he's using Swiss Bank. - The reply was swift. Judas Muong had answered with a sigh of satisfaction. Wasn't he a good citizen.

Walking out of Taksin's office after a last look in the deep décolleté of the teen age secretary, Adam felt in need of a bath; this Taksin was as bad as Schacter, more a pathological case than a criminal. Three thirty, the interview had taken less than twenty minutes.

So easy to obtain the information he needed to nail Schacter to the IRS post; this lawyer had an agenda of his own, not hidden whatsoever. He was taking over WEB Company and would continue the sale of kid pornographic material. What a scum bag.

—— CHAPTER 49 ——

"The subtle art of deciding consists often in being cruel at the right time."

William Schacter was a realist and knew that his future was seriously compromised in the USA. His last conversation with his lawyer had left no question unanswered. He had thought Muong to be a friend, a confident and had given him full power including access to the Swiss bank account.

One of the reasons for the detour via Zurich was to open a new account in another bank where the money would be safe from this thief. A private bank and a numbered account would be better than a large bank.

It was the tenth time he would travel via Zurich since the beginning of this venture. He met his account manager and explained what he wanted done immediately. Fraulein Heidegger was efficient and had always served him well. He wondered if the magnum of Champagne and the kilo of caviar he had proffered every Christmas was the reason for this excellent service. Probably not.

-We are transferring all but twenty five thousand Francs from your account into a new one. This second account will then be closed and the money paid out in cash. – She looked on the screen of her computer and looked up at Schacter. – You know that you will be walking around with more than two million US Dollars.?- He knew.

After less than half an hour he had the money neatly packed in his brief case. It was a short walk to the *Gruber et Fils Private Bank*. He was expected and received the red carpet treatment. A numbered account was opened and the more than two million US Dollars safely tucked away for rainy days. The entire procedure had taken less than three hours. It left him with the feeling that he had avoided the worse. The first part of a safety net had been created.

On the way to the Airport he phoned Mia and asked to be picked up the following morning. She always met him. William had his own permanent apartment in the spacious mansion occupied by the two women and their household servants. This magnificent mansion was a show place and keeping the grounds alone, cost a small fortune. Mia's imagination was incapable of conceiving such magnificence. Always looking for bargains, Lucia had been opportunistic and bought the place for half its value when the owners had been found dead of a mysterious disease.

-If Lucia is well I'll need to talk with both of you as soon as possible.-

The problem of the lawyer had to be dealt with. The expected money transfer had not hit the Swiss Bank and never would; not much of a loss, only fifty five thousand dollars but the intention was evident. Muong would sell him to the feds and would try to grab the business from the two women. Good luck ass hole he was singing in his mind as he fell asleep in the first class seat.

-No drinks, no food if you please. - He was always reasonable, knowing that jet lag was controlled easily by being abstentious during the flight.

As always, the old but luxurious Bentley was parked a little distance away from the terminal. The driver had dropped Mia in front of the International Arrival. She would phone him when ready to be picked up. Carlo was a young man from the same village and his parents known to Mia's family. She could trust him. Later, maybe, she would have a child from him, although she would not marry ever; using him as a stud only, like animals do.

The flight from Zurich arrived on time. Soon Mia could see the passengers creeping out of the passport control section. Most looked as if they were coming out of surgery. William was by far the worse of them: truly the portrait of an exiled American never going home again. Perspiring profusely, his eyes were shifting, his lips trembling and his hands folding and unfolding behind his back as if he was trying to hide something. The pressure and the stress were getting to him. The not so sharp custom officers were alerted by his nervousness and started searching his valise; nothing there.

-Do you have anything else to declare? Asked the older of the two officials.

-Nothing except this belt. – Mumbled the panicking Schacter. While he knew that he had no call to be afraid, his mind was acting up as if he was confronted by a terrible danger.

-Please take it out and give it to us. - Said the officer suspecting that this customer must have something to hide in order to be so disturbed.

Schacter did and the custom agents opened the money belt. They were surprised, expecting to find drugs or other illegal substances in this belt. Money was not an illegal product, on the contrary. They started to count the cash. When they had reached one hundred thousand they looked at each other and replaced everything in the belt, not bothering to count the rest. They looked at this mountain of a man who was scared beyond logic and waved him by. Schacter was paralyzed and could not move holding his money belt in his hands.

-Are you sick sir? - Said one of the two. -If not you can go.-

By then Mia who had been witness to this scene had come down to the arrival level and managed to work her way to Schacter; she grabbed his arm and pulled. The mountain moved. With the other arm she reached over and secured the money belt on her shoulder; by the weight of it she knew it contained a lot. A porter who had also assisted to the sorry scene was following the odd couple. There was more money in this belt than he and his five brothers would earn in their life time. He could snatch the belt from the girl and run for it.

If Mia had always marveled at the way Schacter looked coming out of the plane, now was not a good example. Surprised by his behavior and deadly pallor, she also asked if he was sick.

-No, I'm not sick. A little worried. I'll be fine now that I am here. ... We have a major problem. Let's get away from here, I'll tell you and Lucia what we're facing. –

Not letting go of Shacter's arm she phoned Carlo who pulled in a few minutes later. He got out and placed the baggage in the trunk of the Bentley. The porter was by now only a few meters away looking around to plan his escape.

Carlo opened the door to let his passengers in and turned as the porter was making his move, snatching the belt away from Mia as he was pushing her in the car. Not fast enough though. Back in Patawa and also in Bangkok, Carlo had been an almost professional football player. With lightening speed he had caught up with the porter. Grabbing him by the shoulders he turned him around, backed up a bit and jumping as if to hit a football in mid air, connected with the thief's chin. The guy crumpled without a sound while Carlo recovered the money belt. Unperturbed, he closed the rear door after giving the belt back to Mia. Schacter had not even seen the incident having already taken his place in the car. Just a blink, her eyes connected with Carlo's; she felt an exquisite sensation, took a deep breath and handed the damned belt over to Schacter.

-When would you like to see Lucia? - Mia asked Schacter.

There was a small atroupement on the side walk, the porter was coming back to life, as poor as before except for a hell of a headache and maybe a broken jaw.

-As soon as possible. Now if she's available. What I have to tell you both is urgent. We'll need to act quickly.-

Mia looked at him, served him a cognac from the well stocked bar and remained quiet for the rest of the hour long trip to the house. The cognac brought back some color to Shacter's cheeks and his mind could function better by the time he got to the house. Ten thousand miles away from this clear and present danger was reassuring; he had recuperated his faculty to think and plan.

Carlo took Shacter's baggage to the apartment permanently assigned to him. Shackler quickly undressed and slipped under the shower; when Mia knocked on the door he was coming out, an revitalized man. Still naked he opened and let Mia in. She had seen him in various states of naked-ness when he was in better shape and she, much younger. Bare-ass nude, Schacter was even more voluminous than wearing clothes. This accumulation of milky blubber surmounted by a small head resembled a picture of a queen ant that Mia had been appalled by: at least fifty times the size of the worker ants serving this small headed sovereign.

-Lucia will be delighted to see you as soon as you're ready. I must say that you look a lot better now.-

-I'd like you to be present at this meeting. It concerns you as well. - William said trying to dry his back side.

Mia stepped in and took the towel away from him. She was in a hurry to get this over with, her curiosity piqued.

They went into the elegantly furnished living room where Lucia was in the process of arranging flowers in what looked like a real Ming vase. She turned without interrupting her important task and said.

-One half of every one of our friends is a potential traitor. A French man said those words three hundred years ago. He was so right.-

Lucia was never surprised by life's vicissitudes; ups and downs like days and nights, like low and high tides. She did not know exactly what the cause of Shacter's obvious panic was, but was betting a hundred to one that Taksin was involved; she had foreseen this for a while. Silently she finished arranging the flowers and from a distance looked at her work of art, satisfied that it was almost perfect.

A young girl smartly dressed in a black skirt and a white chemisier came in with a silver tray set with a porcelain tea pot of exquisite design and assorted cups. Korean porcelain thought Schacter. The apprentice maid laboriously deposited the tray on a table. Lucia would serve tea as was the custom. Looking at the girl exiting awkwardly Lucia smiled almost maternally.

-The others are teaching her. She's from Pattawa like the others, family is important. As it is the misery of Patawa has glued its people in a large family. – She said to Schacter as if he cared. Stressed as he was, he did not give the girl a second look. Libido takes a second seat to panic.

When the tea was served and every body sitting comfortably, William got up and started pacing. He needed to pace in order to prevent the top of his head from lifting off like a Cape Canaveral space ship.

-I know that you are a woman of little words so I'll cut the preambles...... The Attorney general of the USA is on my back. My lawyer Muong Taksin is a traitor and a crook. You had warned me. .... I have proof that he has stolen money from me and I fear that he'll sell me to the Government. The Internal Revenue Services will want to know how much money I have in Switzerland and the FBI will want to look into the business of children pornography on the Internet. -

Lucia had also stood and was rearranging a leaf or a petal out of place in her flowery master piece.

-What do you want us to do.?-

-I thought about it and came to the only possible conclusion. I'll sell you my shares. The only thing I'll want will be monthly payments and a place to stay in Thailand as well as a Thai passport. I think you can arrange this easily after... Muong is out of the way.-

-How much. - Asked the old woman.

-Thirty six months at twenty thousand dollars per month. I'll be available as an advisor and will not work with anybody else. I am ready to retire from business.-

Lucia looked at Mia and after some sort of telepathic communication, gave her answer.

-We accept your offer. The first installment will be deposited in your room this afternoon. Now.... what about Muong.....? – With his index finger Schacter drew a line under his chin. Lucia understood the message.

-It will cost you ten thousand dollars to take care of Muong. - Lucia had been compiling a dossier on Muong Taksin. She had foreseen this day .... Not much remained unknown about the life of this gambler, crook, Ayaba user and chaser of pre-teen girls. She even knew about his love of vintage cars.

Schacter nodded. Strapped around his waist, he had two thousand one hundred dollar bills, two hundred thousand dollars in cash for miscellaneous and emergency expenses. To get rid of this Muong Taksin, five times as much as what Lucia had demanded would have been cheap.

-It should be done quickly. He'll sing his little heart out and try to move in with you.- Pointed out Schacter.

-I think it could be done tomorrow morning when he goes to work.... I'll need your passport for the visa.... As for a place to live your apartment is yours for as long as you want. The price you are demanding for your shares is ten times less than the real value. ... Is that all? If so I'll have to use the car this afternoon. - Agilely she moved towards Schacter and extended her had to seal the deal. Without another word she left.

On the way out she told the young girl in training to be careful, as the tray and the tea pot were worth a fortune and that she would take it out of her pay for life if she broke anything.

Over all, this new deal was the very best that could have happened to Mia and Lucia. Schacter was becoming a danger for WEB Co; only a question of time before he would attract big trouble.

Relieved, Schacter went to his room and fell asleep immediately. He knew from experience that his problems would be half way solved by ten o'clock tomorrow morning and completely by five of the same day. Travelling back to the USA was out for a while if not for ever. Could he be extradited? With a good lawyer he might be able to work up a pardon in due time; but why, did he not have all he wanted here in Bangkok: freedom, money and the rest.

—— CHAPTER 50 ——

"There are times when everything works; don't worry it doesn't last."

The outside temperature being near forty degree centigrade, relative humidity in the ninety percent range, the air conditioning system was working overtime in the old Bentley. Lucia had phoned one of her old friends, the largest distributor of Ayaba in Thailand. Ayaba, this amphetamine made by the Birman's and consumed by almost twenty percent of the Thai population was to the Thais what beer is to the Irish and coca cola to the North American kids. Priced at one TH Baht, -*about twenty cents US*-, it was affordable by the general public. Ayaba costs a few pennies to manufacture and at this low selling price still yielded a very handsome profit. Approximately one billion of these pills are sold in Thailand yearly: US dollars revenues of two hundred millions dollars.

-I'm on my way to see you. - She had said without mentioning her name. After a pause the answer came back.

-Always a pleasure to see you Lucia. - He had not heard her voice in a while.

When the Bentley stopped in front of a decrepit, windowless and seemingly abandoned warehouse, a young man stepped out from under the shade of the only tree on the street and opened the door. She could see a bulge under his over laundered shirt and had no question as to what it was. Another young man was standing on the roof over the only door, with what looked like an AK 47 hanging from a shoulder strap.

-Follow me please, you're expected. - The voice was rough but the tone polite.

Out of deference for the old visitor, he maintained an overly slow pace, opened a side door and let Lucia step in while he returned to his post. This warehouse was the nerve center of the Ayaba distribution network in Bangkok. There were several millions Th Bahts worth of Ayaba in inventory as well as the cash revenues from the previous day. Surrounding the warehouse and out of sights were several armed young men. No one could penetrate the one hundred meter perimeter without being challenged.

Another young man sporting the same accouterment as the other two, displaying a huge automatic pistol hanging from his belt, led Lucia to a smaller door opening on a large windowless room. After getting used to the dim lighting, Lucia was able to make up a large wooden desk, monopolizing a quarter of the space. Not a piece of paper, not an ashtray, not a pencil on this piece of furniture; its Teak surface shining like copper, reflecting the image of the obese personage sitting behind it.

Almost disappearing under the mass of blubber, a straight wooden chair, completely out of style with the sumptuous desk was squeaking its protest every time the large man twitched. Out of deference to his visitor, he managed to stand up, which was amazing considering the mass of loose and unnecessary flesh his head was attached to. Lucia looked at him and smiled.

-You're looking good Lucia, too bad I already have four wives. - And he grabbed her tiny almost mummified hands with one of his fingers.

Lucia smiled, remembering Tom Yu when he was a skinny and starving hustler. Her smile was warm, almost maternal. After sitting Lucia on a plush sofa, Tom went back behind his desk, dragged his wooden chair a few meters from Lucia and carefully, almost a balancing act, sat down, taking great care to have his back at a ninety degree angle. That was difficult considering the immensity of his belly pulled over his knees by gravity.

-My back is not improving but this straight chair helps a lot. What can I do for you Lucia.-

Several years ago, Lucia had helped him start his business when she had lent Tom YU enough money to pay for his first order of Ayaba. She had previously introduced him to the Birman manufacturers who were steady customers of the brothel. Tom had paid the money back but, as he kept saying, still owed Lucia his life. Lucia had catapulted Tom into a position of power where he could be of service. Not surprisingly, Tom was also from Patawa and most probably a cousin; like stray cats on an island, it seemed that everybody was related to everybody in Patawa.

Lucia opened her purse and pulled out a Romeo y Julietta numero Quattro which she lit with her Cartier gold lighter. When finished with the ritual of holding the flame under the tip of the cigar she inhaled deeply, thinking of the long arduous road she had covered during the last sixty five years.

-Do you know Muong Taksin, the lawyer?

Tom was aware of just about everything of interest going on in Bangkok. Information was the key to being successful in his business and he had several –ears- as he called them, listening to the gossips of the city.

-Yes, I've heard of him. - Then after a moment. - Not very honest. A gambler who does not always pay his debt.-

-That's the one. We would like to see him dead. An accident maybe. – Lucia was straightforward and did not beat around the bush.

-When would you like this unfortunate... accident to happen?-

-Tomorrow or sooner. I have fifty thousand Th Bahts in this bag.- She pulled a brown paper bag from her Viton purse and placed it on Tom's knees.

Tom took the bag, opened it and closed it again before giving it back to Lucia.

-No need to pay for this service.-

-This is a business deal and the money is not from me, so I want you to take it. - Tom took the bag and threw it on his desk.

-As you wish. It will be done tomorrow morning, before ten o'clock. - Was his answer after studying the note Lucia had handed over with the paper bag.

The note contained the address, time Taksin left his home and the license number of his car, a 1995 blue Alfa Romeo Disco Volante.

After asking about Tom's wives and kids, two of which were working with him, Lucia eased herself up from the sofa and left. She was escorted back to the door where one of Tom's son led her back to the Bentley.

-Believe it or not young man, your father was once as slim as you. - Twenty five years ago, this eldest of Tom's son could have been his twin brother.

Back in the cool comfort of her limousine, she phoned once more. Thirty minutes later she was sitting in the office of a high ranking technocrat. The man smiling warmly at her was in his fifties, trim and impeccably dressed; obviously the most important person in this building.

- What can I do for you little mother?-

She gave him the passport.

-This man needs a three year visa. He's writing a book on Thailand.-

After glancing at this passport for a few seconds, he nodded and said.

-No problem I'll have this ready tomorrow. I can have it delivered to your address. –

She pulled out another bag from her Vitton purse and slid it across the desk.

-For your people, as I know that you won't take anything from me.-

He got up, kissed her on both cheeks and without a word marched her to the door.

-Come to the house one day. I'd like you to meet my wife.-

Yanusi was the son of a cousin also from Patawa. More than fifty years ago, coming out of the jungle, this poor creature had died soon after her arrival in Bangkok. Lucia was twenty five at the time and took care of her son. The kid had a superior intellect. Pursuing a dream that she would never reach, she sent Yanusi to the very best private schools. He received a university education, then Harvard and Yale, nothing less. A good student, Yanusi had completed a Ph.D. in economy and coming back to Thailand had been working for the government, quickly reaching the highest echelons in the administration. Lucia was very pleased about his success and considered him a son.

-I'd like very much to meet your wife but what should I answer when she ask me what I have done all my life? - She replied with a sad smile.

-You have done well and a lot of good. To me, you have been a savior. My wife is understanding and would see the good in you. I'm proud of you.-

-I'll think about this. Maybe, yes maybe....... I'd like that. - And she left wiping a tear from her left eye, her right eye never cried.

As there was nothing much more for Adam Simpson to do in Thailand, he relaxed the rest of the day waiting for the documents promised by Muong Taksin. The airline company confirmed his reservation for the following morning. He would have liked to visit a while but he did not dare, his boss would disapprove.

The well oiled machine of the USA administration would follow its course. Once in motion, like a large ship, nothing could stop it. It had been too easy. Upon returning home, William Schacter would experience the full embrace of the long arm of the law: red carpet treatment, room and board for a long while and, a melt down of his illegally acquired money. The legal tentacles would not release their hold any time soon. Adam preened himself for having done his job with brio. The Attorney General would be pleased with his work and annotate his personal file. Maybe an early promotion; and he could propose to Kathleen.

CHAPTER 51

"Civilization is founded on the suppression of instincts."
Freud

Seven o'clock; as every morning Muong Taksin went directly from his bed to the shower. His ritual was simple, first two minutes scalding hot water then ice cold and he would repeat the procedure several times. During the entire procedure he would sing: light tenor when the water was cold and as deep a baritone as he could when it was hot. His state of mind was reflected by the choice of the tune: if it was Bizet's Butterfly, he was in a sour mood and his wife would be cautious, if it was Mozart's Les Noces de Figaro, his mood was on the sunny side. The morning of the fifth of July, Figaro was being presented with such enthusiasm that his devoted and submissive wife was afraid the neighbors would be alarmed and call the police.

-I have an early meeting this morning. Only coffee.-

He finished tying his scarlet-red bowtie while she was pouring a thick as tar, ink black coffee in his favorite mug. The strong coffee washing down a couple of Ayaba would get him going and erase the sluggishness he felt as a result of too much Teacher's last night. Celebrating his victory over the pedophile Yanki required most of the bottle.

-I'll be back earlier this afternoon and we'll go out for dinner tonight. We have something to celebrate.-

She looked at him almost in disbelief. He had not taken her out to dinner since they were married four years ago. Working too hard, as he was saying, lying through his gold capped tooth. She knew her husband was addicted to gambling and was afraid that this weakness would be his down fall. That he played around with his teen age secretary was of no importance to her as she was finding her husband repugnant.

His sapphire blue 1995 Alfa Romeo was parked in front of the dainty cottage he had bought with the overflow from Shacter's business. Every night, he would cover his little jewel with a plastic tarpaulin so the birds would not tarnish the exquisite polish of the enamel. In the morning, upon removing the tarpaulin, he would inspect the vehicle looking for the slightest blemish.

Before dawn, that morning, a burly man had already lifted the rear of the tarpaulin to read the license number; then he had walked back to an old pick up truck and lit a cigarette after offering one to his companion. They drove to the end of the street and waited.

The daily commute to Muong's office lasted approximately forty minutes; sixty kilometers of pure enjoyment. Handling his precious automobile had become an oasis of total relaxation for Muong, a diversion from his constant money problems. Listening to his favorite opera, he would experience an almost sensuous pleasure: switching lanes, passing slower vehicles, braking, accelerating, demanding from the racy little car, bursts of speed that it seemed to enjoy as much as the driver. For almost two hours every day Muong was a grand prix pilot.

That morning, completely taken by his impersonation of Schumacher listening to Carl Off's Carmina Burana, he never saw the dusty pick up until it bumped the rear fender of his precious Alfa. Just a little scratch by the sound of it; however, the careless driver would end up paying for a complete paint job as had been the case last year. He was a lawyer, his business was to go after and obtain the very maximum.

He pulled alongside the road. There was not much traffic along this secondary road; the dilapidated bluish and rusty pick up pulled up behind him. Out came the driver, a burly man of about thirty, dressed in bleached blue jeans, a soiled gray shirt, loosely hanging over his belt. From the passenger side, uncoiled a very tall and lanky twenty some individual, more the clean cut type, still holding on to his rolled up news paper.

Muong was already evaluating the extent of the damages when the driver of the pick up craned his neck to look at the very small scratch on the left rear fender. The paint was removed on ten centimeters but the metal was not dented.

-Nothing serious. I can't even see it. - Said the driver with an amiable grin.

-Wrong you are my friend; this will require a complete paint job. This is an expensive car, a collector's automobile and I can't tolerate the smallest scratch. - Replied the lawyer with a condescending grin.

As the rangy young man bent down to also inspect the scratch, he came up close to Muong, shoving a hard object in his rib cage. The newspaper was hiding the object but Muong was certain that it was the small end of a gun.

-We'll sit in your car and fill in the insurance paper.- Said the young man in a cool calm voice, pressing harder on Muong's ribs.

-Hey, don't get excited, I was joking about the paint job, as a matter of fact .... Let's forget about the incident. - Mumbled Muong, beginning to realize that he had been snared like a neophyte. Under the protective cover of his profession he could always change his mind later.

The driver grabbed his arm, hurting him with an usually strong grip while Lucky Luke continued to drag him inside the Alfa, entering the vehicle on the driver's side and sliding over to the passenger seat. The stocky driver opened the back door and sat down after grabbing Muong's hair with a strong no nonsense hand.

-What's going on, I told you to forget about it.- Yelled Muong feeling the panic surge in his groin.

Not listening, the tall fellow opened his newspaper and showed the revolver.

-Keep quiet, it won't be long and it won't hurt. - His voice had a soothing effect.

At the same time, he pulled open an envelope that he was also hiding inside the folded news paper and produced a syringe into which there was a clear fluid. Still holding on to Muong's scalp, the driver of the pickup pulled the head to one side so the neck was exposed. Deftly, Lucky Luke exchanged the gun for the syringe, purged the air out and, finding the jugular on the first try, injected the full content. At the same time, several Ayaba amphetamine pills were forced down Muong's throat. To force him to swallow the pills, a small gourd filled with water was forced into Muong's mouth while his nose was held closed. He coughed but swallowed, so scared that he could hardly move.

Without a word, the two assassins held him loosely. Muong could feel his heart racing, his head becoming lighter and his thoughts diffuse. As his heart rate was getting closer to three hundred, Muong felt dizzy rapidly sinking into a state of well being; then lost consciousness while realizing that he had under estimated Schacter. They released their hold and looking around were satisfied that no one had witnessed the execution of Muong Taksin.

Lucky Luke opened a little tube and with the tip of his index finger, applied a touch of make up on the small pin hole entry mark of the 25 gauge needle. Inspecting his handy work, he was satisfied and replaced the empty syringe in the envelope. No one would be aware that Muong had been injected seventy five Milli Equivalence of potassium chloride.

When in excess, potassium chloride causes the heart to fibrillate by disorganizing and messing up the signals governing the heart pulsation rate. Muong had died of cardiac fibrillation which could be attributed to the amphetamine pills the coroner would find in his stomach and blood or, to a preexisting although not diagnosed heart condition.

Later that morning the police stopped to investigate the stalled vehicle. From the patrol car they had seen the inclined head of the driver; he could have been sleeping or sick. He was dead and already stiffening. A suspicious death but the coroner would not find excessive amount of Potassium Chloride as the dying cells release intra cellular potassium into the extra cellular space. Heart attack, one more: Ayaba and overwork.

Around the same time a special courier delivered William Shacter's passport to Lucia; there was a tourist visa attached to it. The visa allowed him to stay in Thailand for the next three years with the possibility to renew automatically if necessary.

Earlier that morning, William Schacter had phoned Muong's office to arrange a meeting sometimes that day. He was scheduled to see Muong at eleven o'clock. When he arrived at the office for his meeting, the secretary advised him that Muong was not in yet. She seemed disturbed. He was relieved.

-Wait a while he shall not be long. It's unusual for him not to be in the office by eight o'clock. I phoned his wife and she told me he had left early this morning. Must have had a meeting I was not aware of.-

Schacter knew that Muong's secret meeting was with the angel of death. He sat down and felt the stress slowly draining out of his body, like the puss exuding from a lanced abscess. For the first time in a week he was relaxed. Waiting thirty minutes, he told the secretary that he would phone back in the afternoon.

Adios Muong Taksin may the devil forever play with your soul as you have played with my money.

CHAPTER 52

"Every action finds its cause in the satisfaction of the person accomplishing it."

Lieutenant Paterson had been ordered to stop his investigation. The mysterious disappearances of Gorski, Hans Vanass alias Steven and of Smith had been elucidated; from video tapes on the television coverage, Paterson had been able to identify five of the six major players in this drama. The woman remained an enigma. She had been there at the beginning and then no more. As with the children, her face had been blotted out of the initial clip. Three of the five pedophiles were from the Lewiston - Auburn area.

Some of the nation's newspapers had named Lewiston, the New England paradise for pedophiles. The good news was that the area would be safer without these three.

Paterson was not unhappy that this incident had attracted attention to child molesting of all vintages and descriptions. Like most kids, as a child and teenager he had been exposed to lecherous and libidinous adults. Several of his friends had also been pawed or molested. They would sometimes comment on these incidents among themselves but would rarely dare tell their parents; vindication was not worth the trouble of going through the investigations. Only the worse cases, those resulting in injuries or pregnancies, or involving kidnapping, were processed by the system. The others were minimized by the establishment, the kids often given hell for ratting on their attackers and accused of exaggeration or misrepresentation. Even today the number of non family related kidnapping in the USA is a frightening five to six thousand a year; where are these kids, what do they become or worse how do they die?

Our society is the product of a complex cultural evolution; a melting pot into which each new ingredient changes the composition of the finished product, which is therefore never finished. Paterson thought that today was probably better than four hundred years ago. He had been shocked when reading a declaration by Saint Thomas of Aquinas on incest, expressing the opinion that - *incest between sisters and brothers should be prohibited because it could increase the complexity of the already difficult and emotion charged family life-*.

-I would expect a stronger message on the part of this church endorsed philosopher.-

His wife agreed with him that the practice must have been widespread for such a non committal statement to be made by a father of the Church. His wife was a college graduate and well read. Not the least of her quality was that she adhered fervently to the feminist movement. Her pet theory was that rape was construed as something natural, pooh poohed by most politicians, religious fathers and not the least by the fathers of psychiatry Freud and Jung. "A man's world, still linked to our uncivilized beastly ancestors". Man's arrogance is reaching new heights when he believes that being raped is every young girls'unavowed longing.

One would expect a stronger more directive declaration from one of the few philosophers the Christian church has ever approved of or from the father of psychology. This feeble statement, coupled with other writings on the subject is an indication that incest and rape were ignored before the twentieth century.

Going a step further one can establish a parallel between incestuous relationships and that of some spiritual fathers who turned out to be pedophile priests.

-What is difficult to cope with is the complicity of the church. Moving pedophiles from one parish to another, leaving behind a string of abused children does not seem to be charitable or in the spirit of the religion, whichever denomination. .... This *hush hush* backwoods approach is a continuation of the tolerance society was exhibiting three hundred years ago. ... Imposed celibacy is not the solution, might even be one of the causes.-

-Eddy, Eddy, stop twisting your detective mind about this. You'll only be excommunicated if you continue with this line of thinking. - Replied his wife.

Kids and women, the weak and fragile links of our society have always been man's prey for the purpose of satisfying his sexual instincts. Until now, society has tolerated that women are mistreated and battered by their husbands, boy friends, fathers, brothers. Under the cover of thousand year old writings, most religions are perpetuating this injustice by treating their women as objects, relegating them to the function of reproduction, while the rest of the world looks the other way. The Koran stipulates that: « *the woman should be kept in the bedroom where she belongs.* » The Roman Catholic Church is not faring any better, excluding them from all and any offices other than as man's servants and conveying the message that : "she should be available for her husband whenever he has the desire." Paterson also knew of some sects, where girls rarely reach puberty with their hymen intact, lecherous old men responsible for their desecration.

During his career, Paterson had seen the worst but could not help dreaming about a particularly sad and horrible affair: About five years ago he answered a call from the director of the Lewiston general hospital. He went over and the director told him this terrible story.

-One of our patients, a twenty one year old girl is dying of ovarian cancer. She's young to be dying of this particular cancer but this is not why I called you. The evening nurse left a note on her report of last night saying that the father of this patient had been caught in bed having intercourse with his dying daughter. At the time she thought that he was the husband. Then, interrogating the afternoon nurse we learned that a younger man, had also been seen copulating with the patient that same afternoon. It turned out that this young man was the patient's brother.-

He continued after a pause.

-This morning I questioned the patient. ... To make a long story short, she admitted that she had been forced to have sex with male members of her family since she was four, maybe before. First her father abused her, then the two brothers and their friends. –

Paterson had taken out his note book and had started writing. He stopped.

-Since four... and she's now twenty one, seventeen years.?-

The director nodded and averted his eyes, ashamed to have to describe such abjection.

-Let's go see her..-

This was the beginning of an investigation that uncovered one of the worst cases of abuse he had seen.

When she was four the mother had jumped ship, leaving behind two sons and a four year old daughter. The father, a thirty three year old man, had then systematically abused his daughter and trained his adolescent sons to do the same. The poor kid was conditioned to perform for the men of the family, and later for any one who might have a few dollars. The neighbors looked the other way as did the youth protection agency, the grandparents and the rest of these good people, not wanting to « get involved ». Even now that she was sick and dying, these animals continued to rape her.

Paterson thought he would be sick. It had taken Karine some time to start talking but once she was promised police protection, Paterson could not shut her up. For more than an hour she gave details and names, while Paterson filled pages and pages of his little note book. At the end, crying but delivered of this awful burden she asked for a priest.

-I know that I am dying. I don't want to go to hell. They have fucked me since I was a kid. That was a sin. Now I want to die in peace. -

-You won't go anywhere but in heaven if there's one. You've already been in hell .- Replied Paterson, wondering where God had been during these seventeen years; looking the other way like the rest of the people.?

It took another hour for a young constable to be assigned as guard to Karine's room. Paterson waited for the constable to arrive, holding the poor girl's hand.

-Nobody gets in to see her unless you're present. - said Paterson to the constable.

-Not even family members? – said the constable.

-No and you are to arrest the father and the two brothers if they show up, I'll get the warrants. - replied Paterson.

Paterson had spent more than three hours with Karine and as he was leaving her room, a fifty some year old man was trying to get past the constable. He doubled back.

-Are you this girl's father? –asked Paterson.

-None of your fucking business whose father I am. Why can't I visit my daughter? - Replied Nelligan.

-You just answered my question. I'm placing you under arrest for the crimes of incest and rape against your daughter. – Paterson replied as he signaled to the constable to cuff him.

The young constable was not long in getting the message. Placing his enormous hands on Nelligan's shoulders, he spun him around and neatly cuffed him, while Paterson was reading the prisoner his rights. He did not want the bum to sneak out on a technicality.

The two brothers, ages twenty six and twenty eight, were apprehended in their home a few hours later. Two uncles, one cousin and two neighbors were also arrested.

Unfortunately the girl died a few weeks later, before the case could be presented in front of a judge. In the absence of the key witness the state dropped the charges. Paterson had considered being the avenging angel in this affair but could not run the risk of jeopardizing his career and family life for the pleasure of being the executioner of these rats. Now, after five years, he had lost track of them. They moved out of the State as soon as released. The only pain they had suffered for this horrible crime was several beatings administered by other inmates during their incarceration. Someone had leaked the ugly truth to the milieu.

As it was now, Paterson did not doubt that they were abusing somebody else in another part of the country.

-I wish I knew where these bastards are. I would toss them to this -brigade-. Muttered Paterson.

If you mull an enigma long enough the truth finds its way to the surface. When all clues were analyzed, it became clear to Paterson that the priest Tim Donnelly, Barcelo and yet unknown others were members of this –brigade-. Given enough time he would find out; he always did. Strangely he felt more and more comfortable with the notion of not bringing them to justice.

If the Mithridatisation was taking place in the Lewiston area he was fairly sure he knew where to start looking. Posting Barcelo's whereabouts on a map he had come to the conclusion that the cave in question was somewhere around the tire dump in West Bowdoin. He could not see where else it could be. If he, Paterson, was the instigator of this caper, that's where he would hide.

When interrogated, Barcelo had been frank and honest. He had not hidden the fact that he hated pedophiles and kid abusers, and would not hesitate to deal « *properly* » with these five depraved individuals if he was the ring master. But he had made a point when he had said:

-Look at me Paterson, do I look the part. Can I kidnap five adults, bring them to a cave and torture them to death? I wish I was.-

Paterson had to agree. Alone, Johnny Barcelo could not pull off this job and organize such a grandiose spectacle. But as the entrepreneur he had been and still was, once one always one, he could have pulled the strings. And furthermore thought Paterson, Barcelo has nothing to lose; his life is finished, his drug addicted present wife is not worth living for but, deduced Paterson, his five year old son could be a reason for Johnny to live for.

-You're not getting any younger. What is the name of your son? Do you have any plans for him? - Had he asked Johnny.

Barcelo had not answered the question but Paterson, always looking for telltale signs, had detected slight moisture in his eyes.

-The past is the past. I wish Todd had not been born; life will be difficult for him. His mother is a tramp and I'll die soon. - Sadly replied Barcelo. By then the tear had formed.

Paterson had investigated all of Barceló's friends. Not digging deep enough in his past, he had missed Deana and Dudley. They had been out of Barcelo's life for such a long time and lived in such a different world. All his other more recent acquaintances were insensitive bums, incapable of getting up in the morning, let alone be a part of this altruistic mission for which real guts were needed.

He had tried to convince Maureen O'Reilly to cooperate with the police, - for the greater good of humanity- he had said. To no avail, she maintained that humanity was better served by the –angels- as she called them, and that her children did not need the ordeal the law would impose on them.

-What could you do that these people are not doing. I feel satisfied that anyone abused by these five criminals have been vindicated. Better than they would have been by the system. You're a nice person Mister Paterson and frankly I like you, but, if you bother me or my kids again I'll file suit. –

That was it and the judge had warned him to stay away. So be it.

After his conversation with Paterson, Johnny knew that it was just a matter of a few days before they were caught. Paterson was a hard nose hound dog, would never quit searching for as long as he was breathing. Tim Donnelly was safe enough but his friends Deana and Dudley were at risk.

-I can't risk their freedom. I have to end it. - Decided Johnny.

So he began the final preparation for his swan song, his everlasting retirement. He was not yet fixed on the decor he would select for this finale, but it would be grandiose, something to remember. A sly smile cracked his thin lips.

Almost ten days since the beginning of the TV coverage. Smith, Gorski, Alpasha and Rupert were still alive. The awareness that pedophilia was a problem to be dealt with rather than buried, was being recognized as a political opportunity. Congress woman Firestone had been making waves; asking for laws that would increase the severity of the sentences for these kid abusers, as well as a life time follow-up after their release from prison.

-Let's implant a chip up their asses. Let's always be on their tails. - She was saying in private. –Otherwise there will be no respite.-

-If I am a mother of a five year old toddler, I'll want to know if the nice man living next door is a pedophile waiting for a chance to paw or kidnap my child. I'll want my rights to be protected even if it means violating some of the abuser's. - And she would continue.

-These people are sick and incurable. They should be under forced medical surveillance on a continuous basis. Not just prison, but a life time control of their every moves. Do we allow mad dogs to roam the streets? Yet they're less dangerous. - She said, answering a question on a talk show. The public agreed.

The results expected had been surpassed by parsecs; it was time to exit and put a glorious end to this show before the public should change its flighty mind. Public opinion is as shifty and as mighty as the wind and has the ability to shift direction without warning; like the Pitaraq, an Icelandic wind, which will blow a soft breeze from the south for a while then come back from the north at velocities of more than two hundred kilometers per hour.

The Foundation would be taking up the baton. It had been decided that it would provide the best of treatments to the victims and their families and also to the families of the abusers.

-We're receiving substantial amounts of money from the public. The revenues from the Station alone will be in the area of ten million dollars. Overall the Foundation will possess a capital in excess of twelve millions dollars. - Announced Alfred Goldwater at the last Foundation meeting.

-I'm very pleased with how this affair has turned out. – Replied Tim, now employed full time in his capacity of co-president.

So pleased and so taken that he had asked for a leave of absence from his bishop invoking failing health, which was not a lie as he was becoming dizzy and sick of duping his reason. But he was not about to become an apostate; why rock the boat, and his present man of the cloth status served his purpose.

A key question remained unanswered for Johnny Barcelo. Now was the time to be creative.

-How do I sign off? Easy to address the question of suicide when you're sick and depressed. Very different when you can see pleasure in living. I have never felt so good. My life has a purpose and I take pleasure in getting up in the morning. - He had confessed to Dudley.

His subconscious was slowly elaborating a plan to sneak away discreetly while remaining available for other –jobs-. Now that he had regained a considerable portion of his self esteem and health, he was tempted to stay a while longer. Serene, he had come to realize that there was nothing so energizing and soothing as being able to pick and choose your time of departure; ending it before an unpleasant and grueling agony sets in. Without the suffering and the degradation of a long agony, death was not so bad; only a question of accepting the cold fact that life ends.

Would this change of plan jeopardize the safety of his friends? A signature and a closure had to be provided in order to put a stop to further investigation. Who else but he could be identified as the perpetrator and vanish with the explosion. But did he have to die? With enough financial resources, he could disappear, assume another identity and maybe continue his action. Like Jesus Christ he thought.

Johnny had this not so crazy notion that: when Jesus Christ was removed from the cross at three o'clock Friday afternoon, Jerusalem time in the year 33, after only six hours of exposure on the cross, he was still alive and in reasonably good shape. Johnny had made a thorough due diligence and could support his theory by the fact that Jesus' great uncle, Joseph of Arimathie, member of the Sanhedrin but nevertheless a disciple of Jesus, had claimed the corpse on this Friday night; Pontius Pilate giving the authorization.

Was it not this same Pilate who, a few years later, was fired from his job for accepting bribes? Could he have accepted a bribe from Joseph to allow Jesus to live? Nobody will know for certain as the interest of the church are better served if Jesus died on the cross and resurrected; but another unanswered question amidst so many others.

Barcelo was vehement that he could support his claim further by the well documented fact that the victims of crucifixion, could last a minimum of thirty six hours before exhaling their last breath. Not unusual for death by asphyxia to relieve these poor bastards after as many as three to four days. The merchant Arimathie was Jesus' great uncle, on his mother's side and had spent several years with Jesus.

-Yes- Johnny would reason, - I agree that he was lanced by the centurion but the wound could have been superficial for another small bribe. These people were not against a quick profit.-

This is how Barcelo had surmised that Jesus had lived several years after his –resurrection-. Not being dead made it convenient to make appearances here and there and then to vanish via a fake –ascension- like so many other prophets had done before: Moses, Enoch, Ely and Esau to name but a few.

-I don't know if he vanished completely out of the Christian sky or if he remained in the background; anonymously managing his not so educated apostles. They certainly were not cut out for the mission dumped on their shoulders. How else can we explain their sudden vigor after the ascension of their leader? Maybe Jesus could have continued his operation a few hundred kilometers from Jerusalem, under a different name or simply blend out of the public picture and live comfortably with the help of his rich uncle .- And he would continue with a smile. – Why not with the beautiful Mary Magdalene, a rich and beautiful sex kitten.-

This explanation made more sense to Johnny than the death, the resurrection and the ascension. This model was an alternative he was developing. Simple, it could work without jeopardizing the freedom of his friends. He would have to crawl up the ventilation chimney and see where it landed, and if he could squeeze through the tunnel. Then he would need a car, money and a new identification. That was possible but he would talk it over with his friends.

——— CHAPTER 53 ———

"I have spent my life resisting the urge to end it."
Franz Kafka

On the eleventh day, Smith died. The self amputation of his thumb, the wound on his arm and the unorthodox cauterization had taken their toll: generalized infection that massive doses of horse penicillin could not curb. The body was left in place; the others were no longer conscious, reduced to a sporadic meaningless babbling. For the last few days, without Deana's knowledge, Johnny had been mixing a large quantity of alcohol in their daily food intake. They had paid enough of their debts.

Early that morning he had sneaked over to the church and had left a note for Tim; the note asked for a meeting that evening. Dudley's place would be convenient if it was considered safe. As most of the police pressure had been redirected towards investigating real and more actual crimes, neither Tim nor Johnny thought they were being followed. Johnny who had a nose for detecting shadows had not sensed any for the last four days.

At eight o'clock, parking his car three streets away, Johnny sneaked into Dudley's residence through a back entrance. It opened into a beautifully set garden. He had never been in this part of the house and was surprised at the elaborate organization of Deana's Zen garden. For a long moment he remained standing in awe. Huge six foot high black boulders were disposed here and there in the garden. Most of the surface was covered with white sand, raked to perfection, not a ripple showing. A board walk meandered around the stones and two wood benches invited meditation. Two islands of vegetation and a pond, into which he could see the ripples made on the water surface by several gold fish swimming about, completed this scene out of a Buddhist monastery.

Lost in the admiration of this corner of paradise, he was brought back to reality by the sensation that he was being stared at. Slowly turning his head, he saw a somber mass some fifteen feet behind him. The dog..., he had forgotten about Mujik the dog. A low menacing growl was ascending from the animal's throat, like the first shivers of an earth quake. His territory was violated; not allowed unless one of the masters was present.

Remembering his name would help but Johnny could not think of the damned name. Alfred, No. Harry? Mujik? Yes that was it, Mujik.

-Mujik, please don't hurt a poor little old man. - Pleaded Johnny.

Nothing doing, the dog was not moving either way. In the mean time he had bared two impressive canine teeth. Head low, ears pointing, eyes fixing the prey, tail immobile and tense, growling but not barking: all business. Johnny felt bare ass naked, this dog would kill him in less than ten seconds; and it would hurt.

-Deana where are you. Help. - He managed to utter more to himself.

As if answering his silent call for help, the patio door opened and Deana stepped out. Without moving his large head, eyes still fixed on its prey, the dog stopped growling, waiting for further orders.

-You're a foolish young man Johnny. Mujik doesn't like anyone coming in the garden. A red light comes on if the back door is opened and by chance I was close enough to see it. –

Then looking at the animal, she motioned with her hand. He came to her, tail wagging as if saying: - See I'm a good guard dog-. Johnny agreed with this mute statement.

-Go in while I circle the block with the dog. Want to see if you were followed. –

And she went out through the same door in the fence, the dog following at her heel.

Johnny went in the house and could hear voices in the library. Following the sounds he found Tim and Dudley already looting Dudley's scotch reserve.

-You look a lot better than you did when we started this contract. - Said Dudley not surprised to see him come in from the kitchen.

Johnny had recuperated to almost perfect health during the last twelve days. He felt good. While he was still as indigent, Barcelo was in a better physical shape than he had been for the last twenty years. Not smoking, hardly drinking, exception being Dudley's scotch, eating almost properly and sleeping well had done the trick. He even had gained a few precious pounds.

-I feel fine. In fact, that's the reason I called this meeting. – Said Johnny, sitting down.

Dudley was pouring some Glenlivet 12 years. Just what Johnny needed after the dog incident.

Deana was coming back from the garden. The dog came to Johnny and sniffed him professionally, as if he wanted to remember not to scare him the next time he came through the garden entrance. Johnny even ventured to pat him on the head.

-He'll know you from now on. You look good for a guy who was dying two weeks ago. - Repeated Deana.

-It feels better coming from you than from these two. Thanks Deana, thanks to you all, I feel good, too good to blow myself up with the last three of our guests. - He continued - I'd like to vanish without vanishing. Like Jesus Christ. You know, seemed to die but lives under a different name for a while longer, continuing to do a job.-

They all looked at him for a moment. Then Tim coughed and asked.

-What do you mean like Jesus? He died on the cross, end of story.-

-I think otherwise. I think he faked his death with the help of his rich uncle who bribed Pontius Pilate and the centurion on duty. Faking his ascension to live happily after was the easy part. He had accomplished his mission, the structure was in place and he could exit or take a secondary role in the organization providing the moral guidance these dimwitted apostles needed. Two thousand years ago it would have been easy to travel one hundred kilometers and live under an assumed name; no TV, no identification, no pictures, no finger printing ....-

Deana smiled at this tall tale. Why not and who cares thought Dudley.

-Interesting assumption, I'll have to think about it for a while, not impossible as several historians go as far as questioning the very existence of Jesus. Could explain several miracles. -Answered Tim.

-I see what you mean- Said Deana. -You want to live elsewhere under an assumed name and...... maybe continue this war against pedophilia?-

-That's it. But for this I need money, and a new identity. I have planned the disappearing act and there won't be any trace of me except what we want the cops to find. - Replied Johnny.

He let this sink into the cortex of his three friends while he sipped some Glenlivet. Great stuff indeed.

-Would we continue to be involved? - Asked Dudley.

-Only if you wanted to and if it was safe. I don't see why the TV coverage would not continue to be offered. Remains to be seen and evaluated further when new situations occur.-

-I can see how you can sneak out of the cave before it explodes, but how would you acquire another identity? - Asked Deana.

He then explained carefully during the next ten minutes how he would be filmed and go on television announcing the end of the Mithridatisation as well as the destruction of the cave and of himself. Then, the cave would really be blown to oblivion, enough phosphorus inside the cave to render all bodies untraceable. At temperatures reaching two thousand degrees nothing remains. A few minutes prior to the blast he would have crawled out of the ventilation shaft he had explored the day before. From there he would use the two way radio to trigger the blast.

-My death, resurrection and ascension. – He quipped jokingly before continuing.

-I'll need two hundred thousand dollars hidden in a car, registered to the name of my brother Claudio. The car should be inside the old Bowdoin Anglican cemetery. This is where the ventilation shaft ends, well camouflaged in a thicket growing on the east side. I'll then drive to Montreal and fly to Portugal with my brother Claudio's passport. I'll stay in my home country for a month or so, long enough to have a new passport made under the name Claudio Barcelo, he was born in Portugal and won't live another six months. This will be my new name and I'll get in touch with you after a few months. –

-When do you want to do this? I could take care of the vehicle by tomorrow morning. With a slight modification to your plan: I'll buy a three year old four by four and you can leave it at the airport. I'll declare it stolen in a few days. Just make sure your prints are not found. - Said Dudley.

-OK for the car, less risk. I'll be ready by tomorrow or the day after. Time is of the essence. Every passing day increases the odds of being identified. I stole my brother's passport last week and he won't know it's gone before he dies. He's not planning to leave town, emphysema complicated by lung cancer are killing him. – Said Johnny.

-The money will not be so easy. Two hundred big ones ...- said Tim.

-I don't need the entire amount now, half for the present and the rest when I am in Portugal. I'll give you instructions later. –Replied Johnny.

-I can live with this said Dudley as long as the foundation can cover the amount. -

-What about the explosion. - asked Deana. –How can we have this live if everything is blown to hell?

-I'll make a final clip in the cave and remove the film which will be remitted to the TV Station like the others. The station will have it the following day. I'll have flown out of Montreal to Lisbon the previous evening. – And he continued. -I have set the bomb with a two way radio that can be activated from the cemetery. I wouldn't want to miss the fire works. The video equipment will be re-positioned on the hill overseeing the dump so that the blast can be recorded. You can recover it and send it to the station if you think it's safe. -

-Always the artist.... ok with me. What about you Tim do you have any ethical problem with that? - Asked Deana.

-Less than if he had killed himself. I feel at ease with this. We have contributed to improve the lot of several kids and save the life of at least one. Continuing is a must although I don't fancy Mithridatisation as a deterrent. Something else a little less repugnant should be considered.-

They all nodded, even Deana; she had had her fill.

-Last thing..., my son Todd. –

-I think I can find a good home for him. His mother is unfit as you said and it should not be too difficult to convince her to do the logical thing for him. I'll follow up and make sure he's taken good care of. - Said Tim.

-Later on I'll want to see him and do whatever I can. - Said Johnny. This was the only sad part to this caper.

After toasting with a Macalan 25 years, they parted as they had come, Johnny through the garden gate with the dog at his heels but friendly this time.

CHAPTER 54

"The road to excesses leads to sagacity."

For a week, Johnny had been sleeping like a log and it was past nine thirty when he woke up. His head was clear and after drinking a cup of instant coffee he went over the scenario of this final act; the next few days would be exciting to say the least. Always this elation when it came to bouncing back out of a mess.

Assuming that the vehicle and the money will be at the expected place that very evening, he was prepared to stage the finale either that night or early the next morning. The last clip in the cave would immortalize Johnny Barcelo as the primary player. He would even say a few words; short but to the point. Then he would explain that, being sick and old, he was committing suicide with the last three criminals having no intention of spending his last hours in front of judges being harassed by lawyers.

He would then crawl out of the ventilating shaft, install the filming equipment, activate the mechanism and detonate the bomb. Wearing a disguise, he would then travel to Montreal. Reservation was already made under the name of his brother Claudio, whose passport he would be using. Even he could not tell the difference between his picture and his brother's. The last clip would be delivered to the TV station, without taking the precaution to remove his fingerprints; should work.

But there was Paterson: who had developed an agenda of his own concerning the Pedophile Brigade as he called them among other chosen words; he had decided to take matters into his own hands. Having two days off he followed Barcelo; his spare time was his to do as he pleased. He had to know... this caper was quickly becoming an obsession.

Convinced that the proof was somewhere around the Bowdoin tire dump, he had been snooping around the dump site since four o'clock that same morning. Wearing sophisticated camouflage garment, well hidden in the ticket, east of Barcelo's mobile home, he was patiently waiting for the man to emerge. Cursing Barcelo for sleeping so late it was 10.05 when he saw the front door open and Barcelo come out sipping a cup of coffee.

As if taking a stroll he started walking in the south-western direction. Paterson gave him five minutes and followed. Five minutes was just enough time for Johnny to remove the truck tires hiding the entrance of the cave and put them back as he would not be coming out via the same route. The ventilation shaft would take him to the cemetery, the car, the money and freedom.

By the time Paterson reached the limit of the property, Barcelo had disappeared. Looking around, even climbing on a heap of scrap tires, he could not find him and wondered where the elusive bastard had disappeared. Tracking was impossible as there were too many tracks of all kinds, including deer tracks.

He decided to go back to his look out and wait for Johnny to reappear. More than two hours later he realized that the little goblin was not coming back. Paterson could not know that his target was squeezing out of the cave through the shaft, pushing the video equipment and the last clip in front of him.

By then it was past twelve o'clock. Out of spite he began walking towards the old cemetery where he was surprised to see a pick up truck concealed behind old Mac Vicar's tomb, the largest in the cemetery. It would have been impossible to see the vehicle from the road. Puzzled, he was assessing this new situation when he saw a slight movement behind a thicket bordering the cemetery. Surprise was replaced by incredulity when the movement materialized into the form of Barcelo. Paterson had his binoculars and studied the silhouette of this ghost for a while before coming to the conclusion that: yes it was the stroll himself, but that he was not violating any laws, wandering in the cemetery. He hid and watched.

Before the arrival of Paterson, Barcelo had had time to crawl out of the ventilation shaft and position the video equipment so that the explosion that would end this event would be filmed from the outside. He had in his pocket the little two way radio where the flashing red button was asking to be pushed. This would detonate the fuses which in turn would ignite the gasoline soaked nitrate, hydrochloric acid, sulfur, peracetic acid and phosphorus mixture. There was approximately one hundred pound of nitrate, ten gallons of gasoline plus five gallons of the other ingredients. He felt that more was better than not enough.

Not changing the rules of the game, continuing to be paranoid and meticulous, the *mighty goblin* walks to the road, where after inspection of the area he backtracks to the hidden vehicle. There, thinking that he is alone he checks the content of the glove compartment where he finds the keys, an envelope containing one thousand crisp hundred dollar bills and the registration under the name of Dudley. Satisfied that he can end this caper right now he quickly disguises himself and prepares to blow the cave and leave.

Johnny had marched less than twenty feet from where Paterson was concealed: his camouflage blending into the scenery as foliage, color and shade of this beautiful fall day. When Barcelo moved behind the tomb Eddy Paterson broke cover and advanced carefully to keep his target in sight. During these last hectic minutes, his target had been busy preparing the video equipment to give his master piece a final touch of bravura; focused on his work he had not noticed Paterson sneaking up on him. Not unlike the voice of god addressing Moses on the Sinai mountain top, Paterson's words broke the silence.

-If I had not witnessed your talent as a make up artist, I wouldn't have recognized you.- Said Paterson, not a little pleased with his performance as a Sioux.

Barcelo's heart stops beating; then picks up a thousand a minute. The little man jumps out of his breeches and turns around as if bitten by a snake.

-You scared me out of my fucking wits. - Gasped Barcelo holding on to his chest-. Quick he realizes that he is wearing a wig. – I'm going to a Halloween party that's why I'm wearing this disguise. - Barcelo naively explains while his brain is figuring out a possible next move.

Two options: overpowering the policeman was out of the question. He could not out run Paterson either; so the only option left, other than giving himself up, was to blow the cave up immediately and be caught doing it. That final gesture would erase all traces of his friends in the cave. But he would spend the rest of his life in jail, not in Portugal. Not good. Paterson would figure everything out and find the ventilation shaft, then the last of the patients. One option is no option he thought. He had decided to run back in the ventilation shaft and blow himself up with the cave; Paterson would be kept at bay. He was pale, almost fainting:

-You've caught me red handed, with the smoking gun burning my hands. -Said a now resigned goblin while clutching the little black radio transmitter.

Paterson sees his movement and backs away a few feet; raising his hands in a gesture of peace.

-Wait, don't do anything… yet. – Said Paterson who guessed what the little man was about to do. – Sit down, let's talk. - He sat down on the tomb-stone base. Johnny backed away a little but remained standing. - For a few days I've known that the author of this show was you but could not prove anything. Still can't prove anything…. I'm not even supposed to be here, I'm on vacation. – Barcelo was catching his breath back.

Paterson removes his head gear, not wanting to scare Barcelo into blowing up this scrap tire heap. He remembers these words "Nothing to lose transforms a person into a formidable opponent". Barcelo had amply proven to be suicidal. He continued.

-I was certain that you were keeping these sick bastards in your dump but couldn't find where. In the mean time I've come up with a decision that might surprise you…. I won't apprehend you or whoever else is doing this with you. - He stopped to see the effect of his words on Barcelo. - I'll leave here in a minute but in return I want a favor.-

Coming back from a near catastrophic ending Barcelo cannot believe what he is hearing. He needs to rest and crouches, still holding on tightly to the transmitter. A miracle was in the process of happening. He catches a little more wind and speaks.

-What can I do that would keep me a free man? - Then his mind steps into his brain and murmurs that "If it's too good to be true…" -Is this a trick. Better not be - Answered Johnny waving the black box in the direction of Paterson.

Still sitting on the Mac Vicar tombstone, more relaxed and lighting a cigarette.

-Not a trick, just a bit of discouragement at not being able to protect the victims of those psychopaths. I've been at this game forever. – He pulled hard on his cigarette, the first since four thirty this morning. - Let me tell you what has changed my ethic: About five years ago I was called by the director of the

Lewiston general hospital ... - And he told Karine's tragic life story and the unhappy ending where the criminals wiggled through the mesh of the system.

Johnny has found a nearby tombstone and seems to unwind.

-I've been trying to follow their tracks and finally found them last week. As I feared, they are still at it. I want you to take care of this situation as you have taken care of the O'Reilly's. There is not a thing I can do, even though I know they're abusing pre-teen girls and boys living with them. If you agree I'll give you the address and leave you to finish your job here, whatever it is that you intend to do. I suppose that this is what you're in the process of doing and... has something to do with this two way radio you're holding so tightly. You're not listening to the Hit Parade are you? – Paterson was holding on to an envelope held tightly in his left hand.

Cautiously, but wanting to believe what he was hearing, Barcelo reached out and grabbed the envelope from Paterson; his index finger on the little red button, just in case. At his age, he was not about to start trusting the police.

-Done deal, I'll do it gladly but don't play tricks, I'm about to blow this dump up to the sky. You don't want to be around. –

-I haven't been here, haven't seen you or... that truck. Wait an hour before you light up the sky of this peaceful village. - And then as if remembering something.

– If I have other possible assignments, I'll let the good father know about them. – He had to let it be known that he was aware of the details of this caper; well of most of them.

He turns and walks in the direction of the road. Once there he half turns, waives and says:

-Good Luck and congratulations. You've done well and I'm proud to have known you. -

True to his word, written in bold block letter, the envelope contains Nelligan's new address as well as other nasty details of his new life. Johnny feels the tension vanish from his shoulders. Looking long and hard at Paterson, he lets go a sigh of relief and waives back at the old cop.

-I can't believe it, we could even be friends. - Mutters Barcelo. He looked at his watch, two thirty.

At three he activated the timer and started the Cherokee, drove a mile and stopped. At three fifteen he heard the deep and loud rumbling explosion.

He stayed another minute just enough to see the first black smoke bellowing over the BRE CO scrap tire dumb site.

Portugal would be a good place to rest for a few months.

THE END

CPSIA information can be obtained at www.ICGtesting.com
Printed in the USA
LVOW080817070613

337365LV00001B/7/P